Karen,

Find your Spark!

Finding
MR. WRONG

USA TODAY BESTSELLING AUTHOR
A.M. MADDEN
JOANNE SCHWEHM

A.M. Madden

Joanne Schwehm
xoxo

Table of Contents

CHAPTER 1

Brae

THEY HAD ALL BEGUN TO look alike. I swore I'd seen this man before. It had to be his boring navy suit or the questions he asked. Even the small conference room with its plain white walls and cheesy inspirational quotes looked familiar. My eyes landed on the plant in the corner that had seen better days. The poor thing looked limp and neglected . . . much like how I felt.

"We'll be in touch." Firm handshake, fake smile, and I was out the door. I'd heard that line more times over the past month than I had in my entire twenty-seven years—sixteen times, to be exact. Living in the city that never slept, you'd think I'd be able to find a job, but no.

I'd been a marketing sales representative for a large cable company for the past five years. My goals were always met, and I'd even won a few sales awards. But now I couldn't sell myself if my life depended on it.

Here's a tip: never date your boss. Stefan Wilson might be one of the hottest men I'd ever met, but because I caught him pounding his secretary, I was now pounding the pavement. He wasn't the love of my life, but we were in a committed relationship. *Asshole.*

Hoofing it to the subway after my last interview, I checked my emails, hoping for a stroke of luck that one of these jobs panned out. The only email sitting unread in my inbox was from an online cable affiliate who was once my client. I could sell the shit out of her network. Shelly and I had become fast friends and out of all my clients, I missed her the most.

> Brae,
>
> I know you're going through a lot right now, but I have the perfect thing for you! It's a social experiment sponsored by Flame Relationship Services. You'll spend six weeks on a tropical island with a bachelor of your choosing. The event is next week, and lucky for you, the female contestant had a death in the family, so she can no longer participate. And lucky for me, you're my friend who has the free time to help me out.
>
> What could be so bad? Bachelor of your choosing, six weeks in paradise while being wined and dined, and a cash prize.
>
> Win/win, especially for you.
>
> So, are you in?
>
> Little minor detail, I need a response today.
>
> Chat soon!
>
> Shelly

After a roll of my eyes, I clicked the link and scanned the rules. What caught my attention was the prize. Half a million dollars? Holy shit! As I continued to scan the fine print, my heart raced in my chest. I could do this. Images of me stranded with a stranger flashed through my head. This had to be the craziest thing I'd ever considered. If I thought too long about it, my good sense would have me tossing my phone in my purse without a second thought, but maybe, just maybe, this was the answer to my prayers. Yes, why not? I had the time. Without further negative thoughts, and with just a few more keystrokes, I replied to Shelly, telling her I wanted in. Her confirmation and instructions came quick in an email, along with the attached contract. I skimmed it, electronically signed, and sent it back a few minutes later. It was a done deal.

♡♡♡

I gripped the lapels of my coat with my fists, pulling them together over my chest in an attempt to keep the cold air off my skin. Tonight, I was meeting my girls at José Ponchos for happy hour. All I wanted was to sit my ass down and maybe forget what I just signed up for as a cocktail warmed my insides.

José Ponchos was packed with business people and the typical Friday night bar goers. It was so easy to decipher between those looking to wind down and those wanting to go down. Some women looked refined, while others looked like they were on the prowl, and it was only 5:30 p.m. for God's sake.

Vanessa, Desiree, and Cassie, my best friends, were sitting in a booth off to the side. Cassie waved to me, ensuring I spotted them, and with each step toward their table, my feet screamed at me to take my stilettos off, but they'd need to pipe down for a bit.

"Hi!" I said as I slid into the booth, and they all looked at me as if I had grown two heads. Apparently, my voice was too chipper. "What are we drinking?"

"Margaritas are on the menu for tonight." Vanessa smiled. "I ordered a pitcher for us." She grabbed the glass container and poured some for me.

In one large gulp, I finished half of it. My face screwed up as my eyes squeezed so tight I thought my eyelashes would stick together. Wow, that was tart. I blinked as a small shiver coursed through me and turned my attention back to the girls.

Cassie reached across the table and patted my hand. "No luck with the job hunt?"

"Who knows?" My shoulders slumped from the sheer exhaustion I felt over the process. "You know how it goes. They say they'll call, but I'm sure as soon as I walk out of the office, my résumé lands in the recycle bin."

"Sweetie, you'll find something." Desiree smiled. "It'll just take a bit more time."

I shrugged one shoulder, and said, "We'll see."

Chatter from the other patrons filled the air. It wasn't so loud that we couldn't hear each other, but as the bar filled, the volume increased.

The way Vanessa eyed me had me asking, "What?" I glanced down at my professional outfit, wondering if she thought it was prudish.

"You look weird. Like the cat that just ate the canary. Plus, your hair is a bit disheveled." I brought my hand to the top of my head to smooth down whatever errant strands there were. "Did you just have a quickie in the ladies' room or something? What's that on your face?" My hand flew to my cheek. "Wait, is that . . . dried spunk?"

"Eeewww," Desiree and Cassie gasped, and then looked at me with curiosity.

"Oh my God," I said with disgust. "It most certainly is not. I've been running around all day in the freezing cold. I'm sure it's dried snot." *I couldn't muster up the energy or desire for a quickie right now,* I thought with a shake of my head. "Crap, I hope this wasn't on my face during the last interview." I grabbed a napkin and wiped my cheek. My hand snatched my iPhone out of my pocket before I took off my coat.

Taking another sip of my drink, I tapped the screen of my phone, bringing it to life. I clicked on the link Shelly had sent me. "Look." I handed the phone to Cassie, and Vanessa, who was sitting next to her, looked at it as well.

"A social dating experiment?" Cassie gawked at me as if I were crazy, while Vanessa's lips grew into a rueful smile.

"Brilliant. This is genius! You have to do this." Vanessa flapped her hands as if she were fanning herself.

Desiree grabbed the phone away from Cassie and studied the site. "Do you realize what this says? You need to stay on a tropical island with a man for six weeks." She continued perusing the screen with wide eyes. "The upside is he can't be a sociopath since they did a short background check."

"He could also be a hot piece of ass!" Vanessa exclaimed. "Plus, what does she have to lose? She'd get money, a vacation, and a man out of the deal. Sounds like the trifecta to me."

I snatched my phone back in defiance. "The money and vacation are fine, but I don't want a man. No way. After what I just went through, the last thing I want or need is another dick with a dick. Plus, I get to pick the guy. There will be three to choose from, so I'll just pick the one who sounds like he can't commit." Stealing

Shelly's words, I said with a shrug, "It'll be a win/win."

"You're crazy." Cassie shook her head. "What if they all want to commit?"

"No she isn't, and she could just pick the one who sounds the hottest," Vanessa countered. "Be sure to ask if he has a big cock. You know, just in case. Just because you're stuck with the guy doesn't mean you can't have fun with him. Besides, who would want to go away with someone who has a little pecker?"

"She can't ask anything personal. Did you read all the rules, Brae?" Desiree interjected, her lawyer mode in full effect.

"Most of them. It's fine. I need the money. My savings will only keep the banks off my back for so long, and I've worn out more pairs of shoes hoofing it to interviews. Winning this money could solve my problems. It would be such a weight lifted off me. Plus, six weeks isn't that long."

I chose to ride the Vanessa vibe because Cassie and Desiree were making me second-guess everything. I needed to be one hundred percent confident going into this. Plus, I'd already signed and Shelly gave me the spot. From what I understood many applied, but once the original contestant backed out she didn't have time to find a replacement on such short notice.

Vanessa's eyes cut to the right, and I followed her line of sight to see a man at the bar ogling her. "I'll be back. You're doing the right thing, Brae. I can feel it. We'll be supporting you. Right, girls?" Her eyes flitted between us as she slipped out of the booth. Everyone nodded and Vanessa was off to talk to the handsome stranger.

"When is it?" Cassie asked before sipping her drink.

"Two weeks from tomorrow. That'll give me enough

time to go shopping, pay my bills, and come up with my questions for Mr. Wrong."

Desiree laughed. "You're really going to go through with this?"

"Damn straight I am. By the time the six weeks are over, I'll have a killer tan, half a million dollars, and no man." My confidence soared the more I convinced myself this was a great plan.

"What are you going to do if you fall for him?" Cassie cocked a brow. "It could happen."

"It won't happen. I'm swearing off men for a while. Trust me, I know what I'm doing." Just the thought of liking the man I'd be spending time with sent a chill down my spine. No way. I would stick to my plan.

We all looked toward the bar as Vanessa tossed her head back and flipped her hair over her shoulder, laughing at whatever the man she was talking to had said. Yeah, she wasn't leaving anytime soon.

"Well, ladies, I'm exhausted." I grabbed my coat, slid out of the booth, and kissed them both on the cheeks. "I'll talk to you later." I looked at Desiree, who still had a concerned "mom" look on her face. "It'll be great, Des. Just wait and see. Would you like to come over tomorrow and go over the fine print with me?"

"I'll call you and let you know what time I'll be at your place."

I smiled at her, knowing that was what she needed. She was the caretaker, the sensible one of the bunch. "Great, I'll have wine chilling."

With another quick wave to Vanessa, I hailed a cab and made my way home.

By the time Des showed up, I had already enjoyed three glasses of wine. She was adamant about going over the details of the dating contract, but I just wanted the money and would do almost anything to get it.

"I see you're going to be taking this seriously." Des shook her head and poured herself a glass of Merlot.

"Des, it's a no-brainer. I'm doing this to satisfy your OCD." We sat on my sofa while Des reached for the iPad. Sliding her reading glasses on, she began scanning the screen. "You look super smart in those." A hiccup escaped me, followed by a giggle.

Des rolled her eyes. "Number one." Her tone was serious, so I did my best to sober up and pay attention. "All of your questions must be geared toward romance, relationships, or dating."

"So, I can't ask how many inches he is?" I asked with a snort.

"No, you can't." Des did not look amused.

"Girth?"

"Did Vanessa put you up to this?" she huffed. "Can you please focus?"

I put my hand up in surrender. "Okay, what else."

"You both must stay on the island for a full six weeks or forty-two days. If you hook-up with someone else on the island, or leave for even an hour, and they find out, the experiment is over and no one gets a dime."

"How would they know? Are there cameras?"

Des scrolled through the contract. "No. It says there will be unannounced visits from people affiliated with Ignite Your Spark. You both must be present."

"What if I need to pee and I'm not there?"

"Will it take you an hour to pee?" She raised a brow

in a silent scold. "Again, let's concentrate, shall we?"

"Whatever, I'll hold it."

"There will be planned activities for both of you that you must engage in."

"Like what? Chess tournaments? Scrabble? I'd kick ass in Scrabble."

Des took my glass of wine and set it on the table. "I'm cutting you off." She shook her head.

I let out a sigh. "What activities?"

"Romantic dinners, island excursions, couple massages."

"Oooh! I hope my masseuse is hot!" I raised my brows, and she frowned.

"That would be breaking rule number one—lusting after a man other than the one you're with."

"I'll make sure I get the fat old woman."

Her eyes scanned the page, and then she said, "Hmmm. Challenges." When she didn't get a response, she repeated, "Did you hear me? Challenges. You will both have to complete team building challenges."

"I'm a team player." I went to grab for my wine glass, but she slapped my hand away. "What else?"

"Your location won't be disclosed to anyone other than the producers of the show, except for one person of your choosing to be your emergency contact."

"Awww, will you be my person?" I batted my lashes at her.

"Yes, who else would you choose? Vanessa?"

"Yay, you're my lobster!"

"Brae." Her serious tone worried me a bit. "Did you read the last line?"

I looked at my iPad as Desiree moved her fingers over the screen to magnify the text. Then she read out loud, "Couple will be married on the forty-second day. Family and friends will be welcome to attend."

"I'm sorry, what?" This time when I went to grab my wine, she let me.

"Married, Brae. You need to marry this guy. You were wrong. You don't get to walk away with a killer tan, half a million dollars, and no man. The man is part of the deal."

"How did I miss that? Let me see that again." I snatched the tablet from her hands, and sure as shit, that's what it said. "You're a lawyer, can you handle my divorce?"

"Yeah . . . in a year. Plus, you need to make four public appearances together promoting your loving union." Desiree's eyes were filled with concern. "Brae, this man is a stranger. It's bad enough you'll be sharing a room, but a life? You may get the money up front, but it says if you aren't married for the full year, you have to give it back. You're depending on this stranger to be your knight in shining armor. Even if it's temporary, do you want your first and, hopefully, only marriage to be with a guy you'd know for a month and a half at that point? One who's so desperate, he turned to a dating service?"

She was right. I jumped to my feet and began to pace, my hands on my hips and gaze penetrating my carpet. It wasn't like I could get a loan. I was unemployed, for God's sake. There was no way my parents could find out about this. At that thought, my stomach rolled. "My mother is going to flip out. She has so much on her mind as it is. If I call her in two months and tell her I'm getting married, she's going to have a stroke! Not to mention my father! Holy shit! What have I gotten myself into?" I cried, throwing my hands out at my sides.

My heart was beating so hard, I was ready for it to burst out of my ribcage, and my skin became clammy as I continued my fevered steps, the anxiety feeling like a living force inside me. Nausea washed over me and I ran to the bathroom, getting there just in time.

"Sweetie, are you okay?" Desiree pulled my hair back and handed me a cool washcloth.

"You'll be there for me, right? Will you handle things for me?" I wiped my mouth and stood. The more I thought about what I signed on for, the more bile churned in the pit of my stomach.

"Of course I will. We all will be. I'm sure even Vanessa will think this is insane, but you signed the contract. It says here if you break it without just cause, you could be sued." I bet the original contestant was happy she had a death in the family. I was beginning to think she lied.

Back in my living room, we assumed our places on the couch. "Like I said before, I'll just pick the man who sounds like he wouldn't be good at having a committed relationship." I nodded, reassuring myself of my words. "When we get to the island, we'll make a pact to separate after we leave. Easy-peasy." At this point, I was convinced my decision was brilliant, until I saw Desiree's face.

She looked up, with sympathy etched in the lines of her forehead. "Sweetie, it says you need to live as husband and wife for a year. Living in separate places is not the norm for married couples."

"Oh. Fuck." *I was screwed.*

Chapter 2

Jude

THE SETTING WAS STRAIGHT OUT of one of those horrid awards shows Americans went gaga over. Velvet ropes corralled the hordes of crazed overdressed New York socialites hoping to get in. Two intimidating men whose physiques looked more like refrigerators than humans stood guard at the door. What the hell was happening, and why the fuck was I here?

Kyle.

Dammit. The fucker said it was a work function he needed to attend, and once he made an appearance, we could take off. I'd bet my last dollar this wasn't a work thing at all. Knowing my friend, that chick he was banging was going to be here tonight and he lied to get me here.

I strutted up to the two kitchen appliances with eyes and gave my name. One quirked a brow at my accent. It happened every time. People assumed I was a Swedish model without a brain in my head, and most of the time I let them assume.

I waited, feigning boredom as they scanned their

clipboard. Without a word, one of the ogre twins moved the velvet rope, granting me access.

With each person allowed entry, the crowd became more irate, and my passing through was no exception. Here these poor saps were dying to get in, and I wanted no part of this night. At least Luca would be coming as well. Lucky for Kyle, Luca often stopped me from beating the crap out of him.

When the three of us attended Yale University, Kyle's antics would often get us into all sorts of trouble. Most of the time with chicks; once with the disciplinary committee. Each time, it was Luca who convinced me to let him live another day. What happened when a Swede, an Italian, and a Canadian walked into a frat house? Chaos.

Thrust together because we were foreigners, no one could have predicted the friendship that culminated between us. Even though Luca and I spoke impeccable English when we arrived at Yale, we often depended on Kyle to talk our way out of situations—which proved to be a mistake on many occasions.

Once inside, I forced my eyes to focus in the dimly lit room. It was massive, loud, and jammed with people. My phone buzzed in my pocket. When I fished it out, a text from Kyle announced they were sitting at the bar.

The first thing I said when I reached them was, "I want a Belvedere with a twist . . . on you." He dragged me here. The least he could do was buy me the most expensive drink I could order.

Kyle smirked. "Fine."

He repeated my drink choice, telling the bartender to add it to his tab.

Only after I took a long sip did I speak. "You. Owe.

Me. Big." Another smirk meant he knew it. "Seriously, what the fuck are we doing here? And be honest. I don't buy your crap that this has to do with work."

His eyes cut to Luca before landing back on my scowl. "It is work. Just drink your ridiculously expensive vodka and relax. Where else do you have to be?"

He had a point. After a long, stressful week, I needed to relax a bit. I wouldn't admit that out loud, though. It would serve me well to have him thinking he owed me one.

I scanned the scene. Round cocktail tables and club chairs all pointing toward a curtained stage filled the dance floor and my initial thought was Karaoke. I despised Karaoke.

"What's happening here tonight?"

Kyle glanced over his shoulder at the stage. "Some trivia thing."

This didn't look like a trivia crowd. This crowd was here for very specific reasons. The girls were dressed to the nines and the guys may as well have had stylists for the occasion. My untucked white button-down and dark denim jeans would have to suffice.

Photographers lined the perimeter, snapping pictures of the guests, and a camera crew was setting up at the back of the room facing the stage.

The closer I looked, the more I realized the female to male ratio was a bit skewed. "Why are there so many dudes here?"

"Ask him." With a palm up, Luca deflected to Kyle, sporting his typical Italian *what the fuck do I know* tilt of the head.

"You have thirty seconds to start talking," I said without humor, lifting my vodka while my gaze remained steady on Kyle's face.

Just as I opened my mouth to start my countdown, a spotlight lit a perfect circle against the black velvet curtain stretching across the stage. Applause drowned out the music and a man and woman emerged, smiling wide while waving to the crowd.

The man wore a tuxedo and looked like he could be the host for Wheel of Fortune, and his booming announcer voice supported that theory. His partner was a busty blonde who squeezed herself into a red sequined gown two sizes too small.

"Hello, ladies and gentlemen! I'm Chip, and this here is my lovely wife, Barbi."

Chip? Barbi? More like Dipstick and Busty.

"Welcome to *Ignite Your Spark,* sponsored by Flame Relationship Services. We believe true love sometimes needs more than that initial spark. It's not just about striking the match, it's also about stoking the flames. Via Ignite Your Spark, we bring two people together who are a perfect fit on paper. Once that spark catches, we provide all the necessary tools to keep the embers of romance from flickering out before they can become a blazing fire."

The busty blonde smiled wide at what her co-host had just said. I heard the words, but they weren't registering in my brain. All I kept thinking was, again, *why the fuck are we here?*

"Chip and I founded *Ignite Your Spark* ten years ago, and are proud to say we are responsible for over three hundred marriages to date. After our own romance sparked to life . . ." While she continued to ramble on about how they met and came to be, I turned back around on my bar stool and drained my Belvedere.

"So, tonight," Busty continued, "we are proud to announce one of our best social experiments of all time. We stand behind our theory that love often needs help to flourish, but what would happen if you didn't see the person you are emotionally connecting with? What if all you have is that emotional connection to work from? Tonight, our female contestant will blindly interview three males selected at random from our twenty finalists. Once her questions have been answered, she will then choose one to escape to paradise with for forty-two days. If they find love, they will be rewarded financially, and by the most divine gift the universe can offer—finding their soulmate and eternal flame."

Dipstick nodded at his wife like a big toothy bobble head. "Our female Spark is currently backstage waiting to meet her Mr. Right. We had an overwhelming response from over ten thousand applicants vying for the opportunity to find their Mrs. Right. We will now announce who the three lucky Sparks are." He pulled out a notecard and grinned at the crowd. "Spark number one. Will Chad Heathrow please come on up?" The spotlight swung to the crowd, searching and landing on a Ken doll wearing a navy blazer and khaki slacks. I had enough nieces to know Ken dolls were dickless. He high-fived his friends before jogging up to the stage.

"When are we leaving?" I whisper-shouted to Luca, and got shushed by the woman beside me.

Kyle leaned closer, and answered, "Just relax. Order another drink, eh?"

With each word out of my friends' mouths, and Kyle adamant that we stay, I came to the conclusion that Kyle must have signed himself up for this ridiculousness. What an idiot. "Did you sign yourself up for this shit?" I asked Kyle. "Does this have to do with that chick you're banging?" He waved a dismissive hand, and I leaned closer, saying, "I'm outta here."

"You can't!" Kyle gripped my arm in panic. "I, um . . . you need to be here."

"Why?" The hosts began chatting with the Ken doll, and all the pieces seemed to snap into place. The way Luca and Kyle ignored me, I knew . . ."What the fuck did you do?" My voice increased in volume as the noise in the room lulled. Glares from surrounding tables did little to deter me. Kyle's eyes grew wide as Luca laughed his ass off. "Are you fucking kidding me? You signed *me* up for this?" I looked to Luca, who was now facing the opposite direction, his shoulder shaking in a way that meant he was still laughing. "Hey," I said with a snap of my fingers, "did you know about this?"

"Maybe," Luca said on a shrug.

"Motherfuckers!"

"Relax, you won't be picked." Kyle leaned closer when more people around us glared in our direction. "Your odds are one in twenty."

"And if I am?"

A chick turned around and pointed a finger at us. "Shhh!"

"Oh, well, then, it'll be fun to watch you squirm for a few minutes. Remember a couple months ago when you hooked me up on that blind date for my birthday? Let's see, what was her name? Randi? Randi with an i." Luca and I both started laughing. "Yeah, real funny. Especially when she excused herself from the table and I ended up using the urinal next to her. I mean, him." Luca bent over, grabbing his stomach. "Assholes."

"You were just jealous your date's dick was bigger than yours," I said on a chuckle.

"Fuck you. Now, I hope you do get picked." He smacked me on the back. "Payback, my brother. And if you get picked, so what? I could be doing you a favor. You get to be on a tropical island with a hot chick, or at least I've been told she's not a chick with a dick."

"You've seen her?"

"Well, no. But the original female was hot. When she backed out, I'm sure they picked an even hotter one."

"Backed out? What if she's a cougar looking for my blood?"

Luca laughed, and mumbled, "Well, that would be fantastico," while smacking his knee at his own little joke.

"Shut up."

Kyle glanced at him and fought to hide his grin. "We could hope."

"Cocksucker!"

"Relax. She's not a cougar, although that would be awesome. The age bracket is between twenty-five and thirty-five. These are just details. The point is, it would be a nice getaway with a gorgeous stranger for six weeks. Compared to what you did to me, this is a fucking gift. Think of all the sex. How hot is that?" He lifted his beer and winked. "You're welcome."

"I can have sex whenever I want, and I don't have to leave Manhattan." I dragged a hand through my hair to keep it from gripping his neck. "Have you lost your ever-fucking-mind?" I asked, incredulous. "Who the fuck is going to run my company for six weeks? What I did was hilarious. What you did is a felony. You forged my name!"

"Oh please. I perfected your signature years ago. It's your word against mine in a court of law." He pointed to Luca. "He knows nothing, so don't think he's a witness.

And as far as your business, you have an international army. The finance world wouldn't even miss you."

The crowd went wild when the Ken doll waved before taking his seat on stage.

"Okay, we're looking for Spark number two. Will George Kroft please come on up?"

I sighed in relief at the sound of a name other than mine. The same deal with dude number two occurred. He stood on the stage blushing through his introduction. His round face, protruding ears, and neck were all as red as a tomato. The man stood no taller than five-feet, and his beer belly deserved its own introduction.

Luca let out a short, loud laugh. "Oh boy, do I hope you get picked."

Just as he said that, I heard, "Spark number three. Can Jude Soren please join us?"

All three of our jaws dropped as the spotlight searched the crowd for their last victim. Kyle stood and clapped my back, bringing attention to whom they were waiting for. The beam of light swung to where we were sitting, landing on me.

"I guess I lost my bet," Kyle shouted above the crowd. "What are the chances?"

"Yes, Kyle owes me a hundred," Luca bragged.

"You fucking bet on this?" I scrubbed both hands through my hair and was surprised none came out at the roots. "What. If. She. Picks. Me?"

Luca leaned forward and raised his drink. "Just be your charming self, I'm sure she'll want nothing to do with you."

I was going to kill him—them. First him, then the other one. Dismember their bodies piece by piece. I began cursing everyone and everything in my native tongue, the Swedish words flying out like bullets.

"Dude! I have no idea what you're saying."

I leaned in, getting right into his face. "I never signed anything," I said through gritted teeth.

Kyle snickered, "Oh yes you did. And if you don't get up there, you'll get sued."

"I'll get sued? You mean, *you'll* get sued."

"Potato, potahto." He whipped out a folded packet of papers and thrust them in my hand. "I swear, I combed through it. You're good."

Before I could strangle him, the host brought the crowd's attention straight to me with a wave of his hand. "Jude, come on up!" This chaos unfolded like a slow-motion picture. The spotlight captured the entire chain of events, with me yelling at Kyle and threatening his life.

And all this occurred while the host insisted, "Hello, we're waiting. Do you already have a case of cold feet? The wedding isn't for forty-two days."

"Wedding?" I bared my teeth to Kyle like a Doberman about to attack. "I'm going to fucking kill you."

"There's a prenup clause that states you each take away what you brought in. She can't get your money—unless you want her to, that is."

Did he just say prenup? "I'm not doing this!" I threw my hands up, no longer giving a shit who heard me.

"Too late! Go!" He pushed me forward and I almost passed out as I walked through the crowd, up the stage, and beside the two hosts. I think I answered questions; I couldn't be sure. Every set of eyes focused on me—the men leering and women hooting and hollering like I was a male stripper.

Busty eye-fucked me while placing a red clawed hand on my arm, and said in a breathy voice, "Are you ready to turn your spark into a raging flame?" Channeling a porn star, she added, "Jude."

What the fuck was happening?

I searched the bar to where my asshole friends sat watching. Kyle and Luca were cracking up at my expense. A question forced my focus away from them and I fumbled through my answer. When I looked back, they were gone.

The only thought running through my head was, *once this is over, I am going to jail for murder.*

The two other victims sat in director's chairs beside a large white screen that split the stage in half. A single chair on the other side of the divider waited for its occupant. The three of us wouldn't be able to see her, nor could she see us, but the crowd had an open view of the entire stage.

Busty took my hand in hers, led me to my seat, and snatched the now damp and wilted papers from my grip.

Dipstick asked for the audience's attention as he read through the rules one by one. I listened to bits and pieces, but words like *true love, soulmates, marriage, happily ever after,* and *forty-two days* were the only ones I heard in a long monotonous drawl.

"Okay, Sparks. Here we go. The only responses allowed must answer the question you are asked. At the end, you will each have the chance to ask one question of your own. It cannot pertain to any personal information, physical appearance, occupation, religion, politics, or finances. Please answer all questions honestly, and be sure to be your own charming selves."

A loud guffaw echoed from the crowd, and when I

looked up, I saw Luca losing his shit while sitting beside Kyle at one of the round tables centered in front. Kyle kept reprimanding him, which seemed to fuel Luca's hysterics.

Fuckers.

Chapter 3

Brae

"STAY STILL, FOR CHRIST'S SAKE!" Cassie scolded. Every part of my body trembled. My nerves controlled each of my shaky movements. "Your lips look like Angelina Jolie's on steroids."

Vanessa spit into a tissue and swiped at my lips. "I'll fix it."

"Oh my God! Did you just use your spit on my lips?" My nose wrinkled in disgust.

"Shhh, you're making it worse." Vanessa continued dabbing away, and when I spun to look in the mirror, I was horrified at the woman staring back at me. Heat shot through me and I began to sweat, my skin turning clammy.

"My face is all red. It looks like I contracted a disease. Why am I so splotchy?" Holy shit. Was I breaking out into hives? Pointing at my chest, I said, "Are these hives?" I was going to have a panic attack.

Shelly appeared, smiling, "Ten minutes."

"Crap." In a flurry, Vanessa powdered my cheeks,

Cassie blotted my lips, and Desiree leaned against the wall, tsking.

"Breathe, sweetie. It'll be fine." Shelly placed her hand on my shoulder. "Drink this."

She handed me a glass of wine, which I downed in one smooth gulp. I introduced Shelly to my girls. Vanessa asked, "So, how hot are the guys, have you seen them?"

We all looked at Shelly, waiting for her reply. "I have, and I can't tell you. Don't worry about anything. You'll be just fine. They'll love you." Fine? I felt anything but fine. She told my friends she had seats reserved for them at her table and left us alone once again.

Keep your eye on the prize. Keep your eye on the prize, played over and over in my head. Once my girls were done fussing over me, I looked myself over one more time and let out a small sigh of relief. The wine settled my nerves and now that everyone had stopped touching me, my blotchy skin returned to its natural pink hue.

"Brae," Cassie's soft tone settled me a bit, "you've got this. Just be yourself and you'll make the right decision. Who knows, maybe you'll find your spark."

I patted my friend's hand because she meant well. "You keep forgetting I'm not looking for a spark. I'll pick the worst choice possible, and before you know it, Des will be handling my divorce a year from now." She nodded at my words, but by the look in her eye, I could tell my friend didn't agree with my assessment.

Shelly popped her head back in through the door. "We need to get to our table. Brae, good luck. They should be calling you out in a few minutes. Do you have your questions?"

I held up the blue note cards in my trembling hands. "Yes, I'm all set."

Before I knew it, I was escorted to the stage. Applause and whistles bellowed on the other side of the curtain. I heard a male announcer reviewing the rules I had studied as if there'd be a test on them. After he finished, the crowd silenced. That was the minute I knew things for me were going to change.

A booming voice came over the speaker. "Please help me welcome our female Spark!"

I stood stock still, frozen in place. After a deep breath, I smoothed the fabric of my black sheath dress and stepped on to the stage, praying I wouldn't fall flat on my face. My legs shook with each step I took as I walked to my seat. An opaque white fabric wall separated me from the men. Even with the spotlight, I couldn't see shadows or outlines of what could be on the other side.

This was it. The ultimate blind date. I should have demanded more wine.

The emcee asked if I was ready and all I could do was nod before he told me to take it away. More applause resounded, mimicking my heartbeat. I waved to the audience, placed my notecards on my lap, and gave the best smile I could.

"Hi, Sparks." I sounded ridiculous. "Let's start, shall we?"

I cleared my throat. "Spark number one, how would you describe your perfect first date?"

"That's easy," Spark number one said on a masculine chuckle. "First of all, it's a pleasure to meet you . . . kind of." I thanked him before he continued. "We would go to her favorite restaurant, then to a movie. Of course, I'd bring flowers and would want to get to know her."

A very faint, but very audible groan came from behind the curtain. A seductive female voice said, "Now, now," causing a few chuckles from the crowd.

"Thank you, Spark number one, that sounds lovely." *If that were what I was looking for.* I adjusted myself in my seat. "Spark number two, same question. Describe your perfect date."

"I'd ask you to come to my house so I could introduce you to my mother." The audience laughed, but I wasn't sure he was kidding. His nasal tone sounded serious. "Then I'd take you to meet my best friend, who owns the best comic book store in all of Manhattan."

"Thank you. Sounds interesting." *And there's no way in hell I'd do that.*

"Spark number three. Same question."

"Maybe take her to my favorite restaurant," a sexy European accent responded. I couldn't pinpoint whether it was French, or maybe German. "Then back to my place to fuck," he continued. I almost dropped the cards from my hands, and every male in the room cheered.

His arrogance was practiced. This guy was trying to make up for something he lacked. "So, no flowers?"

"I don't need to bring gifts, you'd have me. But if you'd like something, I could bring a blindfold and cuffs."

The crowd gasped. I searched for my friends, and when my eyes caught sight of Vanessa, she was licking her lips while giving me a thumbs up.

"That sounds like it would be fun for you."

"Trust me, you'd enjoy it."

"Okay, moving on. Spark number one, if I asked the last girl you were with to tell me one thing about you, what would she say? Just one."

Spark number one answered, "That I'm thoughtful."

Awww . . . he sounds sweet, which earned him another strike.

"Spark number two, same question."

"That I'm smart." Hmmm, boring.

"And number three?" Couldn't wait to hear that one.

"That I have a big cock." Of course he'd say that.

All the men in the crowd guffawed and the women applauded. *Why the hell were they clapping?*

"Number one, what was the last gift you gave a woman?"

"A dozen roses." His response caused an internal eye roll.

"Number two?"

"That's easy. A photo album. It was my mom's birthday last week and I made her a scrapbook." I cleared my throat to camouflage my chuckle.

"I'm almost afraid to ask, but number three? Same question."

"The best orgasm of her life." I had no control over my thighs clenching together at his words.

With each of his responses, the females in the crowd clapped harder, my friend Vanessa leading the enthusiasm. I could only imagine what he was doing behind the screen to elicit such a positive response for his crass answers.

I waited for the noise to settle before I ignored him to continue. "Next question. Number one. Did you play sports in high school?"

"I was the quarterback of the Varsity football team."

A foreign voice mumbled, "Of course you were," and laughter erupted at his rudeness.

"Number two?"

"I was captain of the debate team."

"Is that a sport?" I asked with sarcasm.

"Yes, it could be physically challenging." The crowd laughed, but they seemed to be laughing at him rather than with him.

"Number three? Did you play a sport?"

"Nope. I couldn't find a jockstrap big enough."

My spontaneous laugh erupted before I could stop it. "Let's move along, and remember, number three, keep your description to yourself."

"Yes, ma'am," he quipped.

"Starting with Spark number one, then two, and three following behind, what is your favorite meal?"

Number one: "Lobster, champagne, and chocolate covered strawberries for dessert." That was now strike number four.

Number two: "Corn dogs. I'm not into anything fancy."

I giggled. "I've never had a corn dog."

"Food on a stick is my favorite. They're quite delicious."

Ignoring his confirmation, I asked, "Number three?"

"A can of Reddi Wip and pie." This man's voice and his responses set in motion Kegel exercises I hadn't done in years.

"Dare I ask what flavor?"

"Does it matter?"

I groaned out loud. "Moving on . . . again. I only have two more questions for you. Do you men play any instruments?"

Number one said, "Guitar." *Hmmm, sexy.* Number two said, "No." Number three said, with pride, "Clitoris."

The place went nuts with laughter, clapping, and a few comments such as, "I can't believe he said that," and, "I bet he's good at it too," filtered up to where I sat on the stage. The emcee stepped in to quiet down the crowd.

"Ladies and gentlemen, please. Okay, Female Spark, continue, if you would."

"Thank you, Chip." I paused a moment, debating on giving him another chance. Wondering what he'd say prompted me to ask, "Number three, care to change your answer?"

A few seconds of silence passed before he said, "Meh, I'm good." What a prick.

"Okay, last question. How would you propose?"

Number one said, "A candlelit dinner followed by a carriage ride through Central Park. Number two proudly replied, "Hide her ring in a Cracker Jack box and take her to a Star Trek convention. I'd lead her to Dr. Spock, and with him looking on, I'd ask her to dig through the sweet treats to find the prize. Then, I'd drop to one knee and ask her to be my Klingon for life."

"Holy fuck. Dude, are you for real? You going to have your mom there too?" Number three chimed in with that sexy accent of his.

Number two replied, "Oh yeah, mom would be there. She's a huge Captain Kirk fan."

"Okay, thanks, guys," I said before a fight broke out behind the screen. "I appreciate your responses."

"Sweetheart, you forgot someone." That voice had my thighs pressing together again.

"Fine, Spark number three, how would you propose?"

"We'd fly to Vegas, you'd get my name tattooed on your ring finger, because I don't do jewelry, and then Elvis would marry us."

"I didn't ask about a wedding. I asked about a proposal."

"You wouldn't have a choice, sweetheart. For me, it's one in the same."

Holy shit. "So, I assume you'd have my name tattooed on your finger as well?"

"No, definitely not."

"Why? You don't do tattoos?"

"I have seven of them." With that, the crowd once again erupted in laughter and chatter. This guy was a real piece of work, and he just made my decision a no-brainer.

Jude

I SAT CONFIDENT, THINKING THERE was no way this chick was going to pick me. The two tools next to me were deep in thought, preparing their one and only question. Meanwhile, my arm was slung over the back of the chair as I relaxed into the fabric, counting the minutes until this circus was over.

Number one looked like he just stepped out of the pages of a fashion magazine and number two was a complete dork.

The emcee stepped on stage. "Gentleman, you get one question to ask our female Spark. Remember, the same rules apply. You can not ask about looks, where she lives, or what she does for a living."

Tool number one asked, "Do you believe in love at

first sight?"

There was hesitation, but then her sexy voice said, "Yes, I do believe it could happen."

Of course she does. I glanced out and met Luca's eyes. He mouthed, "Super hot." I didn't care if she was the next Heidi Klum, there was no way I wanted her picking me.

Tool number two came up with a stellar question. "What are your thoughts about living with your in-laws until we can save enough to buy our own home?"

Shit. This guy didn't stand a chance, which now made mine fifty-fifty with Prince GQ. Part of me wanted to pay him off just so he'd shut the fuck up.

She didn't even hesitate to say she wouldn't move in with his parents. No doubt this dude lived in the basement and got his rocks off to Captain America instead of Wonder Woman.

Here we go. I pondered my question with careful consideration and almost changed it considering the other ones, but I went with it anyway. If for nothing else, I was curious. "What are your thoughts on putting out on the first date?"

Her raspy voice exclaimed, "Not happening. I'm not that type of woman."

"You say that now. Maybe you should reserve that answer until we meet." I stifled a chuckle and looked up, seeing Kyle and Luca cracking up.

The emcee and his wife stepped center stage. "Wasn't that fun?" The audience responded in-kind, and he grinned while nodding. "I have a feeling there's a spark about to ignite. Are you all ready to hear who our female Spark has chosen?"

Get the fuck on with it, I thought as everyone in the place clapped and cheered in excitement, including the idiots to my right.

"Okay, Miss Spark, who do you choose to continue this journey with?"

Everyone stopped breathing, including me, waiting for her response. She cleared her throat before saying, "First, I'd like to thank the three gentlemen for coming tonight, and to all those who applied to compete. After serious consideration, I feel my chances of finding love would be best with . . ."

A long dramatic pause stretched for what seemed like hours, and my palms began to sweat waiting to hear her choice.

"Spaaarrrrk nummmbbbberrrr ttthhhrrreeee," filtered through the speakers, causing a hushed lull in the room.

Wait, what did she say? She said three. She fucking said THREE!

If her response had hands, one would be squeezing my heart while the other squeezed my balls. Chaos ensued in the club and my opponents sat stunned beside me with their mouths hanging open as I began to plot Kyle's death.

Chapter 4

Brae

BASED ON THE REACTION OF the crowd, I picked the right one . . . which was wrong for me. They may as well have been cheering for a rock star with the way they carried on. Well, the women at least. The men all looked shocked for some reason.

The photographers in the room captured every moment, including my panicked demeanor.

When the hosts came to stand beside me, my heart pounded from nerves. They each hugged me while uttering words of encouragement. Meanwhile, I couldn't calm myself down. If I thought the mini panic attack I had backstage was bad, that was nothing compared to what I felt now. My knees wobbled, my skin felt clammy, and I was pretty sure I would throw up if I opened my mouth to speak.

"Ladies and gentlemen, we'd like to introduce you to our female Spark, Miss Brae Daniels!" I offered a wave and a closed mouth smile, on account of the bile in my throat still making it dangerous for me to speak.

"Spark number one, please come meet Brae. Brae, this

is Chad Heathrow."

A handsome man emerged from behind the screen. His sandy brown hair was neatly styled, his preppy outfit was impeccable, and his disappointed smile was genuine.

This is good, Brae. You didn't want him. He could be someone you could've fallen for, my conscience argued.

He gave me an affectionate hug before walking off the stage without so much as a backward glance.

"Spark number two is George Kroft."

The men in the crowd began chanting, "George! George! George!" When he emerged with a huge grin, his short arms were raised high like an Olympic athlete.

George looked just as I imagined . . . to a T. I stood several inches taller than him, forcing his gaze up when he said, "Awww, dammit. Mom would have loved you," while appraising me from head to toe.

He shook my hand, his clammier than mine, and waved to the audience before heading backstage.

"Okay, everyone. Here is the moment we have all been waiting for. Brae, it's our pleasure to introduce you to your Spark, Mr. Jude Soren!"

Jude. His name was Jude? Shit.

I wasn't sure what the delay was, but after a few long moments, he still hadn't come around the divider. When the females jumped to their feet in a standing ovation, my eyes cut to Vanessa, who was betraying me by pumping her fist in the air while hooting. This man clearly made a fan of my friend. Cassie and Des both looked like they felt sorry for me.

And then . . . he appeared.

Fuck. Fuck . . . fuck . . . fuck! What did I do?

A tall, lean, sexy as sin man emerged wearing a white

button-down shirt and dark denim jeans that fit him like a glove. Chestnut brown hair with hints of golden highlights had that just fucked look going on. At least a day's worth of scruff covered his sculpted square jaw, spreading upward to also frame the most perfect set of male lips I'd ever seen. He stalked toward me, a livid look on his face. If at all possible, that made him even hotter. No levity, no smile, just a pair of gorgeous eyes piercing a scorching hole right through my body.

I was screwed—completely and utterly screwed.

The host beamed, either choosing to ignore the fact that we were shooting daggers at each other, or he simply didn't care.

"Brae and Jude, please mark the beginning of this epic romance with a kiss."

That one command seemed to fuel his fire. He walked straight up to me, forcing me to take a step back. Stopping him with firm hands on his chest—his rock solid chest—I tilted up on my toes and pecked his lips.

"Yeah, that won't do," he rumbled in that intriguing accent. Grabbing my ass with two hands, he pulled me hard into his body and crushed his lips against mine. At contact, my hands were now sandwiched between us. His tongue burrowed its way into my mouth without warning. If it could speak, it would say, "*I'm here, deal with it.*"

His grip on my ass tightened as his other hand traveled up my back, under my hair, and around my neck. My knees buckled, and he must have felt my weight giving in because he moved a thigh between mine to hold me up. I was now straddling his leg while making out with this complete stranger who was all man. From his rock hard pecs beneath my touch, to the way he commanded my body to submit, to the scent of his cologne, all managed to cause me to forget where we were.

The screams and shouts of the crowd should have snapped me back to reality, yet I couldn't guarantee I'd stop him if he were to lay me down and fuck me right here on the stage. The more his tongue caressed mine, the more my brain refused to function. Simple motor skills like breathing, or even pushing him away, failed me, and it didn't look like my brain was going to reboot any time soon.

As I said, I was completely and utterly screwed.

Once he allowed me to come up for air, his lips twisted into a cocky smirk. It was the type you wanted to slap, and the kind that made your panties damp. Nose to nose, I could now see the true color of his eyes were greenish-brown rimmed in gray. And they were the sexiest pair I'd ever seen.

The hosts ushered us to a smaller room behind the stage, and Jude grabbed my hand, pulling me along like a puppy on a leash. Shelly, two guys I'd never seen before, and—thank God—my friends were in attendance. A tray of filled champagne flutes sat on a small table. As everyone entered the room, they each took one in passing. I purposely did not, not needing anything to muddle my already muddled thoughts.

Vanessa charged toward me, pulling me away from Jude's grip without apology. "Holy shit. I can't believe you picked him," she tried to whisper, but failed when he chuckled at her. I took it upon myself to add more distance between him and us.

Cassie and Desiree joined us, quick to tell me how gorgeous Jude was. "Even though he's an absolute prick," Des added so only we could hear.

"Who cares? Every female in the room was turned on

by his answers."

"Which was why she should have picked number two," Des quipped.

"And then what? Spend a year with a complete dork watching Star Trek with his mother, who would never in a million years grant me a divorce? I figured if I had to do this, based on every female's reaction, including Vanessa's, why not spend the time with someone who was apparently easy on the eyes? Yes, he's a complete asshole, but it's only a year. I can handle him."

"Famous last words," Des mumbled.

Undeterred, Vanessa continued. "I agree with Brae. He's hot as fuck. I've never, and I mean never, seen such perfection in a man. I'd volunteer to be his spunk funnel any day!"

"Shut it!" I said as Cassie gasped and Desiree's mouth dropped in shock. I looked over my shoulder in panic to see Jude talking to the two unknowns, shaking his head at whatever they were saying. Thank God, he didn't hear her.

Vanessa shook her head. "My friends are prudes." We rolled our eyes. Annoyed, she jammed her manicured finger into my boob for emphasis. "Seriously, he is one fine hunk of man, and you need to climb him like a tree."

It was official. Even though I was going to paradise, it would be hell. I was being punished by the universe, and the severity of this retribution could only mean I was a serial killer in a former life.

Shelly waved Jude and me over, looking proud as punch. "Well, since you two have seemed to hit it off, here are your airline tickets. There's also a copy of the rules and guidelines once you get on the island."

Jude had yet to speak, but his intense staring

continued. "Can we have everyone's attention?" Shelly shouted, and Jude took my hand again, gripping it tighter than before.

The host glanced our way and raised his glass with a smile. "Please help me toast our happy new couple." I watched in a daze as the room lifted their flutes, Jude included. With everyone's glass in the air, Chip then said, "Congratulations to Jude and Brae. May the love you find blaze on forever." The nausea that inflicted me since I signed up for this charade returned full force at the mention of forever.

One by one, those in the room took their obligatory sips. Jude did as well while looking down at me. My eyes focused on his Adam's apple bobbing from his swallow, and my mouth went dry. Without invite, he placed his flute against my lips and tilted. I had no other choice but to drink, and after I did, he then drained the rest himself while his eyes never left mine.

"Well, I'd say we have another great couple, wouldn't you agree, Barbi?" My trance was interrupted, forcing my disoriented gaze to Chip.

"Yes, I sure would," his wife agreed, eyeing Jude up and down as if she wanted to go away with him herself. If I weren't desperate for money, I would have handed her my ticket. Jude appreciated the attention and winked at her, not caring that her husband was standing next to her, or that his hand was holding mine.

Prick.

Barbi went on, "This is a once in a lifetime experience. We hope you both take full advantage of all the tools we will be supplying to help your relationship grow."

His eyes caught my sneer when I pulled my hand from his. He grinned at my discomfort before dampening his lips with his tongue—the same one that assaulted mine not more than ten minutes ago.

Chip continued where his wife left off. "As your audition paperwork detailed, all your affairs should be in order. From here, you will be driven straight to the Grand Hotel where you will be spending tonight."

My stomach dropped. This was happening. When I looked at Jude, he tossed a look at one of the men I didn't know, who responded without being asked, "Your bags are in my car." Jude didn't say anything in reply, but the anger that radiated from his eyes spoke volumes. He didn't want to be here anymore than I did. I definitely picked the right one.

"Tomorrow morning, a car will come pick you up from the Grand Hotel at nine. You'll still be on U.S. soil, so passports aren't necessary. But you will need a government issued ID with you. Also, any electronic devices, including cell phones, will be collected when you land. You aren't permitted to contact anyone while on the resort, and as you both know, you were to assign one person who is allowed to reach you during your time on St. John for emergencies only."

Jude's eyes narrowed at the guy next to Shelly, who was avoiding him.

"Do you have any questions?"

"Will there be booze on the island, access to firearms?" the other friend asked. When they both started laughing, Jude shut them down really quick with a glare.

"Yes to the alcohol, no to the firearms," Chip responded, as if they were serious. "No worries, though. They will have all the amenities they'll need." He turned his focus back to us. "You'll even be given a thousand dollars in spending money. Just follow the rules, let fate take over, and we have full confidence that with our help your spark will ignite and turn into a roaring flame."

The moment Chip and Barbi left, Shelly said, "Well, this will be great."

Jude and I both shot her a look. The man who had his arm draped over her shoulder chimed in, "I'm Kyle, Jude's best friend."

"Ex-best friend." I almost laughed at Jude's comment, but I didn't give him the satisfaction.

Unfazed, Kyle continued. "This is our other best friend, Luca."

Luca, who was tall, dark, and very handsome, raised a hand, and said, "Ciao." He also had an accent.

Shit, these three were best friends? Kyle was fairer than his friends, but just as good looking in a more wholesome way. I could only imagine the havoc they could wreak on the female population when together. I watched Kyle whisper something to Shelly, causing her to smile. My friend was holding out on me, which could explain why she didn't take this opportunity herself.

I introduced my friends. When Vanessa shook Jude's hand, I couldn't fathom why my stomach twisted. Yes, she was one of the most beautiful women I'd ever met— long brown hair, perfectly shaped body, toned legs that seemed to go on for miles in the short dress she was wearing—but why should I have cared?

"Nice to meet you, Mr. Wrong. I'm Vanessa." It was impossible for me to stifle my laugh, but after Jude gave Vanessa a livid expression, he politely shook her hand, as well as Cassie's and Desiree's.

Des leaned in, and whispered, "If you hurt her, I will find you," loud enough for me to hear.

Jude's snarky smirk faltered a bit before he said, "I'll take good care of her." He winked and the smile that spread over his lips knocked the wind from my lungs.

Fuck.

After the salacious responses to my questions, that kiss, his gorgeousness, and his sexy as sin accent, I second-guessed my confidence that I could handle him. I was in way over my head.

Chapter 5

Jude

KNOWING WE HAD MINUTES LEFT before being whisked away to la-la-land, I muttered, "Excuse us," and grabbed the collar of Kyle's shirt to drag him out of the room. Once in the hall, I transferred my hold to his neck, squeezing until his eyes bugged out.

"Give me one good reason why I shouldn't end you right now."

"You'd be lost without me?" he croaked out before laughing in my face.

"Wrong answer." Not trusting myself, I released him and ran a hand through my hair. "Du inavlad kuksugare."

"Whoa, slow down there, Mr. Swedish Fish. English."

"I called you an inbred cocksucker. Seriously, what the fuck, Kyle? I need to see what you signed my name to. I need to know every detail of this fucking nightmare."

He nodded with enthusiasm. "I put a copy in your suitcase. It's not terrible, I promise. I wouldn't have done this if it were something you couldn't handle."

"You also didn't think he'd get picked." Luca

appeared, counting out the bet he won.

"This is true." Kyle shoved his hands in his pockets and grinned. "You should look at it as a nice, long vacation—which you are long overdue for. You've been looking pretty haggard these days, eh." At my lunge, the jackass laughed harder.

"No outside communication? How can I run my business without occasionally touching base, at the very least?"

"Luca is your emergency contact. He will make sure Soren Enterprises runs without a hitch. I'll be here to make sure your apartment is fine, your mail gets opened, and your secretary handles whatever needs to be handled. We've got this, Jude. Trust us."

"I don't have a choice, do I?"

"Well, you do, but then, thanks to Kyle, you would have to file bankruptcy," Luca answered with a casual shrug.

"There will be no need to file anything. This is the universe telling you to step back, relax, and focus on your people skills." Luca snorted and Kyle suppressed a laugh. "All kidding aside, Jude, she's hot as fuck. It's a no-brainer."

Yes, she was. When I first saw her in that tight-fitting black dress, toned legs, sexy curves, and the long, silky sable hair, I envisioned wrapping those locks around my fist. My visual wasn't making this any easier, but that was beside the point. I thrust a finger at him, and said, "I'm still going to hurt you when I get back."

He mimicked Luca's shrug. "Worth it."

"Luca, promise me if anything happens that needs my attention you'll call me."

"I will." He stepped closer and lowered his voice.

"They'll be monitoring your calls. If I call and say your Aunt Mildred died, that's code to come home immediately. How's that?"

"Okay, good." I pulled out my cell and began forwarding the contact info of my key men. "I'm texting you their cell info, since it's the weekend, and I don't want you waiting until Monday. Call my lawyer, Cleese. Tell him what's going on. Then call my CFO, Morrison, and tell him what Kyle signed me up for. Tell him he's in charge during my absence. Then fill Ruth in. She not only needs to hold down the fort at the office, she needs to give daily journals of all the office activity to Morrison. Once done, call my parents and tell them what Kyle did. Then give them Kyle's contact info and tell them to call him with anything they need. Anything at all." I looked up to be sure Luca was still listening.

His fingers flew over the screen of his phone before he finally looked up. "Got it."

"What do you need me to do?" Kyle asked.

"You've done enough. Just pray nothing goes wrong, and if it does, disappear." Kyle mumbled something I didn't quite catch. "Say again?"

He straightened his shoulders, and repeated, "I said, when this is over, I bet you'll be thanking me." His confidence faltered when I glared at him in response. "Or not."

Shelly poked her head into the hallway with a bright smile. "Jude, are you ready? Your ride is here. You can collect your luggage and meet us out front."

I looked at Luca first, and then Kyle. "Where did you say my luggage was?"

"In my car in the lot. I'll go grab it," Kyle said, bolting down the short hall and disappearing around a corner.

The asshole had to be relieved to make an escape. He was probably counting down the minutes until I left. I really, really, really couldn't believe he did this to me.

"What the fuck was he thinking?" I asked Luca once we were alone.

"Revenge."

I raised my hands, palms up. "This is by far the stupidest thing he's ever done. Playing innocent pranks is one thing, but that fucker took it to an insane level."

"Well, I think a chick with a dick is pretty bad." At my growl, he added, "Hey, don't turn on me. I'm innocent in this. Besides, this is Kyle. He doesn't think things through. Don't you remember that time he thought it would be a great idea to spend our spring break on his parents' sailboat, neglecting to tell us they'd be joining us?"

Christ, that week was a mess. Scrabble, Monopoly, Bundt cake—it was a complete and utter nightmare.

He nodded at my tortured groan. "Exactly. He thought it would be fantastic to have someone steering the boat, cooking for us, doting on us. It is what it is now. Just use the time in paradise to get into her pants and plot your revenge."

"I can do that," I concurred. Luca was right. This was what it was, and I just needed to get through it, try to enjoy the opportunity, and ride this insane wave. One thing Kyle was correct about: I did need a vacation. I looked at Luca and pleaded, "Dude, you must help these six weeks. Please? I won't be able to relax unless I know you have my back."

He walked closer and put a firm hand on my shoulder. "Always."

♡♡♡

Brae

WE DIDN'T SAY ONE WORD to each other on the drive from the club to the hotel. Jude checked us in and our silence continued on the elevator ride up to the first room we would be sharing as a couple. I wasn't sure what caused more of my nerves. The fact that I'd be alone with him in a hotel room all night long, or the fact that a tiny part of me was looking forward to it.

When I glanced at his reflection in the mirror-lined doors, his face was etched with a blend of irritation and what appeared to be anger. I didn't know him well enough to be certain what thoughts were traveling through his head. My sole indicator was the way he snarled at his friend Kyle earlier.

Did he think this was how I wanted to get married? All of my little girl dreams of the perfect wedding flew out the window the moment I signed on that dotted line and committed to this game. A means to an end, I kept telling myself, but the on stage kiss he planted on me made my insides feel like I was on a wild roller coaster ride—one we were now on together.

Jude swiped the plastic key into the black box on the door before holding it open for me. At least he had manners. Right in the center of the room was a king size bed covered in oversized pillows and a fluffy white comforter. A note with our names on it sat in the middle. We set our bags to the side and stared at it.

There was a quick knock on the door and a voice behind it announced our luggage was here. As Jude went to answer the door, I walked over on shaky legs and picked up the folded card, reading it out loud.

> *Jude and Brae,*
>
> *Welcome to the first night of the rest of your lives. Tomorrow, you embark on a journey of love.*
>
> *May the spark you've ignited develop into a roaring flame.*
>
> *Congratulations and have a wonderful time.*
>
> *Love and Sparks,*
>
> *Chip & Barbi*

Cheesy much? With a sigh, I glanced his way. He tipped the bellhop and once again mumbled something in his native tongue.

"If you're going to insult me, please use English so I know how to defend myself."

"I wasn't insulting you, I was contemplating ways I was going to kill Kyle."

"Well, if you end up in jail for a year, that would make our first year together a piece of cake for me."

"Year? It's only six weeks."

"It's in the contract."

Jude unzipped his suitcase with so much force, I was convinced he broke the zipper. Snatching out the manila envelope containing said contract, his eyes darted across the words as he studied it. His brows furrowed as he flipped the pages. Raking his hands through his hair, he began mumbling again in his native tongue. Defeated, he sat with a thump on the edge of the bed. "Did you read this? My jackass of a friend implied we could get divorced once the wedding was over."

"I read it. My friend is a lawyer and went over the details with me. Your friend, the jackass, was mistaken."

"So, you knew you'd have to marry a complete stranger and stay married for a year, and you still did this? Let's not forget the public appearances we're required to do. Is that why your friend called me Mr. Wrong?"

A chill ran up my spine. "Well, technically I didn't know that detail before I signed it. Desiree pointed it out to me afterward, and I don't control what Vanessa calls you, but she knew I wasn't looking for Mr. Right."

"Detail?" he almost shouted, ignoring the back half of my response. "That's what you call this? A detail? This is a major fucking deal. One year of my life is now committed to you."

I dropped the card on the bed and planted my hands on my hips. "It's been two weeks since I received the contract. I'm sure you did as well. So, you can file your complaints at the door. We're in this together now, and believe me I'm more concerned with how we'll survive the next six weeks first. Because at this moment, I'm not sure I will."

"For your information, missy, I didn't have two weeks. I barely had two minutes before I was dragged on stage. So, excuse me if I seem a bit upset by this."

"Well, don't blame me, *mister*, I'm not the one who dragged you on stage. You can blame your ex-friend for that."

"No, but you're the one who picked me." I thought he mumbled something else, but I couldn't make it out.

"What was that?"

"Nothing."

Irritation continued to boil my blood. "No, please. Enlighten me," I said, crossing my arms over my chest.

He stood, his eyes pinned on my folded arms—or maybe it was my boobs he focused on. A very long moment went by before he spoke. "I *said*, lucky me. I did my damnedest to make sure you wouldn't want anything to do with me. Yet, you picked me anyway. Why is that?" He stalked closer, until we were mere inches apart, causing my heart rate to spike. When he folded his arms, mimicking my stance, he was so close, our forearms touched. "I get why you didn't pick tool number two, but tool number one was perfect in every way. So, why me?" At my silence, he prompted, "I was nothing less than a prick on that stage. Maybe you like pricks? Or maybe my answers were right up your alley and turned you on?"

The accusation was clear in his question; the taunt clear in the way he moved even closer and leaned down until his nose almost touched mine. His greenish-brown eyes seared lasers right through mine. It took me about three seconds too long to react, but three seconds was long enough for an arrogant smile to tilt the corners of his gorgeous lips. My tongue betrayed me by poking out to dampen my own lips, causing that smile to spread. Dammit, he irked me with the way he stood staring, but I couldn't get my brain to function in any capacity.

I took a step backward and scoffed. "Oh please. I'm in this for one reason, and you fit the bill perfectly, Mr. Wrong."

"Yeah? What reason is that? A hot, mindless, emotionless fuck? Because that's all I'll agree to."

"Not on your life," came out of my mouth, but my brain thought, *I'm good with that*. Stomping over to my suitcase, I grabbed my toiletry bag and pajamas. "You're an ass, and you can take the couch."

Jude pointed to what was more of a loveseat on the opposite side of the room next to the desk and a small table. "That thing? You want me to sleep on that?"

"Yep." The more I studied him, the more I was certain there was no way he'd be comfortable on it. Here we were together just two hours, and I already sentenced him to the couch. I could offer half the bed, but screw him. This could be the last good night of sleep I'd get for six weeks.

He plopped down on the end of the sofa and yanked his shoes off while speaking in his foreign tongue again.

"I have no idea what you're saying. Is that Greek?"

In a curt tone, he replied, "No, I'm Swedish."

"Do you live in Sweden?" I asked, panicked. If we went to the end, there was no way I was moving to Sweden.

"I'm from Sweden. I live in New York."

I didn't bother hiding my sigh of relief. The scowl on his face deepened. He was insanely handsome, but his anger put his gorgeousness on steroids. The well-defined lines of his amazing physique were visible beneath the white fabric of his dress shirt. Even his fingers had muscles. Everything about the man screamed sex. The way my body automatically began Kegel exercises once again confirmed I was screwed.

Before he picked up on the fact that I stood rooted while staring at him, I stormed into the bathroom with my small overnight bag and slammed the door. As much as I despised him at the moment, he was still getting under my skin. Even the mint flavor of my toothpaste couldn't rid my memory of what Jude tasted like. Everything about that kiss was a mystery. So many questions swirled in my brain.

Why did he kiss me that way? Why did I let him? Would he do it again? However, the one question that had me wondering was: would he want to? Especially after his outburst, there was nothing indicating he'd ever want to again.

Wait . . . why should I care if he did?

Cassie's words, "you're crazy," seemed prophetic. Because now that I was here with a door separating me from the most annoying, conceited, arrogant, gorgeous man I'd ever met, she was one hundred percent correct.

Since screaming at my reflection wasn't an option without my roommate thinking I was certifiable, I continued my nighttime routine. I had a way and order in which things needed to be done. My methods kept me calm. Vanessa would tell me I was OCD, but it was a great system that worked, so I stuck with it. Everything I did had a rhyme or reason. My routine started with my six-step cleansing ritual, a four-step moisturizing process, brushing my hair ten times, and then slipping into my sensible pajamas. Before I opened the door, I grabbed the box of tissues to keep on the nightstand.

Jude was standing just outside the bathroom with his arms crossed in front of his chest. "Took you long enough. What the hell were you doing in there?"

Before I could get a word out, he took a step back and looked at me from head to toe. It wasn't a sly or quick glance. No, he made a production out of it, making me feel self-conscious in my pink pajama short set.

Our arms brushed as he walked past me into the bathroom. He let out a chuckle just before closing the door. Ass. Deciding to expedite the sleeping arrangements, I tossed a pillow and blanket from the bed onto the small sofa.

I sank my head in the plushness of the feather pillow, tucked the comforter under my chin, shimmied on the thousand-thread count sheet, closed my eyes, and prayed Jude didn't snore. They sprung open only a minute or so later when he emerged from the bathroom.

His routine was shorter than mine. He stood wearing nothing but a very tight-fitting pair of white boxer briefs. Through them, the outline of a thick, long shaft was clear as day. His abs were ridiculous, and I counted at least eight. My eyes focused on his unique tattoos. Two simple bands around his right forearm, as well as a line of graduated stars that curved from his armpit down to his happy trail. They were nothing less than an orgasmic orbit of sorts, a beacon guiding me toward the promise of something wonderful . . . and based on the visible outline of that *something* in those briefs, it would be sure to rock my world.

The nail in my coffin would have to be the sexiest happy trail I'd ever seen, and I was a sucker for them. Just the thinnest line of dark hair, perfectly centered in the middle of his abs and extending down over his belly-button before disappearing behind the waistband of his briefs.

I gasped—*yes, gasped* . . . an embarrassing audible puff of air that I sucked down my dry, parched throat echoed in the room. The obvious sound floated from my mouth to his ears. By the time my eyes found their way back up to his face, I was beet red and he was gloating. He leaned against the doorjamb, his arms folded and an obnoxious smirk on his lips over having caught me ogling him.

"Would you like me to turn around so you can get a good look at my ass as well?" he asked on a chuckle. "Or I could just remove these to save you unnecessary eye strain," he added, tucking his thumbs into the waistband of his underwear and lowering them just enough to cause panic.

"No!" I yelped, covering my eyes in case he wasn't bluffing. The chuckle turned into a full-blown laugh as I heard him cross the room. When I chanced a peek, he was standing in front of the tiny couch, his hands on his hips and his back to me. I took the opportunity to go ahead and check out his fine ass, the defined muscles of his back and shoulders, and the peppering of hair on his exposed upper thighs.

"While you were hogging the bathroom, I decided I'm not sleeping on that thing," he said, turning to face me with a scowl. "I'm six-three."

"The carpet is nice and plush. I'm sure it would be comfy for you."

"I've never slept on the floor in my entire life, and I don't plan to now." He snatched his pillow and walked over to the other side of the bed. I sat up, annoyed at his gall while he promptly ignored my scowl. The bed dipped beside me and he punched the pillow a few times before turning his back to me, ignoring the comforter beneath him.

"Night, Sparky." When he reached over to shut off the lamp, the fabric of his briefs dipped into the crevice of his ass. I stifled a moan.

"First of all, it's Brae. Second, you aren't sleeping here." Having the lights out was way too dangerous. I huffed as I got out of bed and stalked over to the bathroom, flipping on the light. "This stays on," I demanded.

When the bright beam hit him in the face, he groaned, "God, you're a pain in the ass. I guess you don't trust yourself?"

"It's you I don't trust."

"Relax. When I make a move on you, you'll be forewarned." He flipped onto his back, putting his right hand behind his head. "But, if you want this," he said, waving his left hand over his body, "by all means, have at it, Sparky. Even if I'm out cold, I invite you to go for it. I love surprises."

"Ugh!" I snatched my pillow and moved to the small couch, repeating my mantra over and over as he chuckled at me in the dimly lit room.

Keep your eye on the prize. Keep your eye on the prize. When I shut my eyes to try to fall asleep, the prize I visualized was a six-foot-three Swede.

Chapter 6

Jude

GREAT, SHE SNORES.

I just had the worst sleep of my life in the most comfortable bed, and the only thing I could attribute it to was the gorgeous buzz saw currently sprawled on the couch. Something kept waking me just as I fell back asleep. At first, I thought there was a cat in the room, but considering I'm allergic to cats, I knew that wasn't the case. No, this loud purring came from my new roommate.

When my eyes focused on her, I did my best to refrain from chuckling. Brae was sprawled out like a disjointed starfish. The blanket that once covered her body now lay on the floor.

Her chestnut brown hair created a veil over her delicate face, wavy strands vibrating with each rumble erupting from her chest. Taking advantage of her comatose state, I walked closer to finally get a good look at her body. I scanned every inch from head to toe, inspecting her like an exotic sports car.

The knit fabric of her shirt outlined her fairly large

breasts, which my hands could handle. A sliver of bare skin on her flat stomach and those gorgeous legs had me growing with excitement. I already knew what her chocolate brown eyes looked like and how her pouty lips tasted. The memory of kissing her along with seeing her sprawled out caused my excitement to worsen.

I really should've taken a cold shower. If she were to wake now, there would be no hiding my hard-on. A quick glance at the clock on the nightstand showed it was eight a.m. It wouldn't be long before those clowns running this show would appear. I debated between showering or waking her, but another loud snore forced my hand. It was time to have some fun with the future Mrs. Soren.

Stepping right beside where her head lay on the couch, I crouched down with my hands on my knees, and yelled, "Wake up, Sparky!"

The way her body comically jolted, forcing her to fall off the couch and land at my feet, was one of the funniest sights I'd ever seen up close. I cracked up laughing, doubling over her body with my own. Gorgeous brown eyes blazing with anger glared up at me. "You're an asshole."

A response wasn't possible; I couldn't stop the hysterics overtaking me. Through my tears, I watched her lift a cushion from the couch. As the cotton connected with my cheek, the sting did little to calm my laughter.

"Oh my God, Sparky. That was hilarious."

"Stop calling me that!" She clamored from between my legs in quite an unladylike fashion into a standing position.

"Okay, I just changed your name to kitten." She folded her arms beneath her ample breasts, shooting daggers at me as she did. "Be thankful I'm not Native

American or your name would be Snoring Kitten."

"I don't snore."

Another fit of laughter erupted. "You just earned yourself a video proving you do. I can't wait until you fall asleep tonight."

In a huff, she spun around, ignoring my comment. The floor vibrated as she stomped her feet into the bathroom just before she slammed the door, again. She did that last night, and ended up in the bathroom for a very long time.

Dammit, I should have peed first. I rapped my knuckles on the door. "Hey, Kitten, before you lock yourself in there for an hour, I need to take a piss."

The door swung open. "You're disgusting. There's no need to be so crass."

I flashed her a sweet smile. "Kitten, I need to relieve my bladder, may I please use the lavatory?" I asked, batting my eyelashes.

"Stop calling me kitten," she snarled. She was one pissed off little cat.

"I'm sorry, do you prefer pussy? Because I know I do."

With another huff, she slammed the door. "Now you can hold it," came from beyond the wooden panel.

"Fuck."

There was a knock on the outside door. Realizing I was still in my boxers with stiff morning wood, I grabbed the blanket off the floor and slung it around my waist.

Barbi stood in the hallway donning her beauty queen look. Her fake eyelashes were so long, I swore I felt a breeze when she blinked.

Her eyes looked down to the small tent below my

waist. "I hope I'm not interrupting."

My dick throbbed with the need to relieve itself. "Is there something I can help you with?"

She pulled out a large manila envelope. "These are your boarding passes. A car will be waiting downstairs in one hour to take you to the airport. Breakfast will be arriving shortly."

"Thank you." I took the envelope from her and hurried to shut the door.

I could hear the shower running. Great. "Brae, I need to come in. Be prepared for me to break this door down or open it now."

The water turned off, and an image of Brae naked suddenly flashed in front of my eyes. In my visual, water droplets rolled from the ends of her hair down her ample breasts toward her navel and over the curve of her pussy. God, she was stunning, even in my thoughts.

"You're such a pain." Brae flung the door open wearing a towel around her body like a strapless dress and a turban on her head.

Without acknowledging her, I pushed forward, raised the toilet seat, and shifted to pull my boxers down. That's when I looked up and saw her reflection in the mirror. "Sparky, I'm not shy. If you want to continue watching, feel free. If not, I suggest you stop staring."

That was all it took for her to turn and walk out, slamming the door behind her. I couldn't remember when taking a piss ever felt this good or lasted this long. It was like the scene from *Austin Powers*. As soon as I thought I was done, there was more to come. What seemed like an eternity later, I finally flushed.

Without asking for permission, I turned the shower on. Steam scented with a pleasant sweet smell billowed around me in the small stall. I figured it to be whatever shampoo or body wash Brae used. It reminded me of her. When I looked on the shelf, sure enough, there was a small white bottle with a green apple on it.

I quickly washed up, dried off, brushed my teeth, and opened the door to join my new roommate. My first instinct was to tease her a bit more, but through the mirror on the wall, I could see the solemn look on her face as she stared out the window.

"Everything okay?" She shifted to look at me. The soft pink dress she wore landed just above her knees.

"Yes, everything is fine. I'm just hoping there are two bathrooms where we'll be staying on the island." All I could do was smile. I wished for the same. "Are you done in there, or do you need to shave?"

Running my hand along my stubbled jaw, I smiled. "No. I'm all set."

"Great, because I need to finish getting ready." She didn't close the door this time, which was fine with me, except I needed to get dressed. I slipped on a pair of tan shorts and a navy T-shirt.

"Room service," came from the hallway, followed by a knock.

Brae rushed out of the bathroom with damp hair and opened the door. Apparently, she was hungry.

A beautiful redhead wheeled the cart in. Her uniform looked like something out of a fantasy French maid catalog. I reached into my pocket for a tip, but when I handed it to her, she wouldn't take it.

"Your tip has been taken care of." Something about that sentence had me thinking of Brae's lips.

"Well then, take another." I slid the bills into the pocket on her small apron.

She bit her lip and then smiled. "I'm Melanie. Will you be ordering lunch as well?"

"Ahem," Brae uttered in a sharp tone. "We will not be ordering lunch since we are checking out. Thank you and have a good day." She stood with her hand on the edge of the door prepared to slam it. Hmmm . . . jealous Sparky was a sexy turn on.

"Yes . . . well, have a nice day." Melanie hurried out, leaving the cart of food behind.

"Jealous, much?"

"You already broke rule number one. While we're together, we are not supposed to hit on other people. It's in the contract." She snagged a strawberry off the platter and bit into it, leaving just the green leafy stem between her fingers.

"Let me guess, you're a rule follower, and I wasn't hitting on anyone."

"Yes, for the next six weeks, I'm following the rules to the letter. I don't want to jeopardize losing the money. Plus, you don't know when they'll be watching us. For all we know, sweet Melanie could be a mole. If you can keep it in your pants, that would be peachy." She ended her request with veiled sarcasm.

Was she kidding? I crossed my arms and forced a laugh. "Sweetheart, technically we aren't on the island yet. As far as keeping it in my pants, trust me, you'll be the one begging for it to come out to play."

Brae

I REALLY SHOULDN'T HAVE BEEN shocked by anything he said. Knowing him all of twelve hours, I had a good indication of his personality. My sense of character was pretty spot on when it came to reading people. My eyes tracked him as he lifted the silver domes off the breakfast plates. He snatched a grape off one of the plates and popped it in his mouth. When his gaze fell on me, a half smile spread over his lips. "Hungry?"

"Yes, but I definitely need coffee first."

"Ah, my kind of woman." He pulled out one of the chairs at the small round table and motioned with his hand. "Have a seat." His gentleman act surprised me. Ambling over, I sat in the chair he offered feeling it hit the back of my legs as he pushed it under me and closer to the table. In a smooth move, he took the linen napkin off the tray and flapped it open. "May I?" he asked, one eyebrow raised in question. On my nod, he gently placed it on my lap. With a smug smile, he sat across from me and poured us each coffee. A chivalrous prick, and there was something very sexy about that.

"Thank you," I murmured.

"You're very welcome." The second smile he gave me was genuine, and absolutely stunning. "Cream . . . Kitten?" he asked, his eyes lighting with the tease of his nickname for me.

And . . . he was back. "Yes," I replied, resisting the urge to roll my eyes. "And please don't call me kitten."

"Okay, no more kitten," he agreed on a nod before shoveling a huge forkful of scrambled eggs into his mouth. "What would you like me to call you, then?"

"Brae. My name is Brae."

"What fun is that?" He chewed thoughtfully, his brows furrowed in concentration as he actually waited for my reply. I got it, he liked teasing me. The more I huffed about it, the more he would.

Ignoring his question, I took a much-needed sip of my coffee and bite of my breakfast. I decided to switch tactics. "So, since we're stuck together, maybe we should get to know each other?"

"I agree. What do you want to know?" He leaned back and spread his hands wide. "I'm an open book. Nothing is taboo."

"Okay, why the graduated star tattoos?"

"Because the 'biggest star' is behind my zipper." He smirked, using air quotes, his brows waggling.

"Can you be serious?"

"I am serious." I rolled my eyes on an exhale. "Fine. I'll tell you. One for each of my sisters."

"You have five sisters? There are six of you?" His response was a shrug. "And the two bars around your forearm?"

"My parents."

I did not expect him to say that. My deer in headlights response must have clued him in on that. "What?" he asked, looking at his egg-laden fork. I watched the food go into his mouth and his lips move subtly as he chewed.

"Nothing. I guess I didn't expect that. You're close to your family?"

"Yeah, I guess. Aren't you?"

"My parents, yes. I'm an only child."

"I couldn't imagine that." He reached for his coffee, his eyes holding mine as the cup tilted upward. "You must have had a lonely childhood."

"I had friends, cousins. It wasn't so bad."

He tipped his head and watched me for a long, hard minute. "What do you do, Brae?"

Crap.

A slow blush spread over my cheeks. "Stripper?"

"What? No!"

"Well, I'm trying to figure out what has you blushing. Lingerie model?"

"Sales."

"Ah, Escort?"

"No, you jerk." I hit him with a glare and left it at that. Taking a sip of my coffee, I asked, "What do you do?"

"No. We're still on you. Why would your position make you blush?" I pictured the many positions I engaged in with my boss, Stefan, the many surfaces in which we practiced those positions, and my blush deepened.

"I'm unemployed." I leaned back and shrugged. "Thus this," I added, waving a hand between us. "All inclusive six-week vacation, plus a nice cash prize sounded perfect for what I needed in my life at the moment."

"Ah, so it's all about the money?"

"For me, it's all about a house, so yes, the money is important. Who would do this to legitimately find love? Why would you be here if not for the money?"

"I got railroaded into it by my best friend."

"The one who's your now ex-best friend?"

"The very same." He quirked a brow and nodded. "You pay attention." His eyes focused on my plate. "Don't you eat meat? Please tell me you eat meat."

"I try to eat healthy."

He snatched a piece of bacon and his jaw worked in small, meticulous circles as he chewed. "Why? Your body is incredible." The slow perusal over my breasts caused my heartbeat to quicken.

"Um . . . thank you, but it's because I do that it is." I pointed to his abs. "Don't you work for those?"

"If I'm in the mood, I'll run. Otherwise, I rely on my sex life for physical activity. Just thirty minutes of fucking burns almost one hundred and fifty calories. Did you know that?" On my eye roll, he nodded. "Truth. As long as you put in some effort, that is. In fact, with you on top, you could probably burn double that. Would you like to know how many calories you can burn giving a blow job?"

My mouth gaped open in shock. "Oh *my* God."

His lips lifted in an amused smirk. "Looks like you have the technique perfected, Sparky." He finished up the last morsel on his plate and helped himself to the rest of my bacon. "Actually, three slices of bacon are about that many calories. Would you like to help me work them off? We'd be done just in time for the car service to arrive." He raised one of his brows in an invite.

"No."

"Why not make the most of our predicament? Six weeks in paradise without sex is going to be challenging. What kind of vacation is that? Not to mention a whole year after that. If you hear moans coming from the bathroom, that's just me taking care of business."

"Anyway . . ." I drawled out, needing to change the subject before I made the insane choice to take him up on that offer. "What is it you do?"

"Finance." The way he sat back and folded his arms meant that was all he was saying on the topic. Well, too bad. I had the right to know details of his life if he knew some of mine. Okay, granted, I didn't reveal why I was unemployed, but still.

"What exactly do you do in finance? Loan shark?

Bookie?"

"Bookie?" he asked in his sexy Swedish accent. "I don't know what that is. Does it involve sex?"

"Is that all you think about?"

"Pretty much."

"You're very evasive. I think I deserve to know what my future husband does for a living."

Jude choked on the sip of coffee he'd just taken. "You're pretty confident we're going to make it to the end without killing each other or breaking the rules."

Did he think I was taking this lightly? He may have been forced into this situation by his friend, but I was forced into it by my circumstances. I needed to get to the end.

"I don't plan on breaking any of the rules, and yes, I most certainly will be able to make it to the end." I picked up the napkin from my lap and placed it on the table. "Our ride will be here soon."

"Yes, dear." When I stood, he took my wrist in his hand. "Forty-two days . . ." his words trailed off, but his grip remained. "Looks like I'll be taking a lot of cold showers."

"Or you can just jump in the ocean." Before he could say anymore, the alarm on my phone chimed. "They'll be here any minute."

Jude stood and stretched, his shirt rising just enough for me to see the lowest star on his torso. He rubbed his stomach. "Good thing jerking off burns up to fifty calories, and after tonight, I'll have that video of you." He grinned. "I'll just keep it on mute."

"You're disgusting, and you're not videotaping me."

"Whatever you say, Sparky."

I went into the bathroom to retrieve my toiletries and

throw my pajamas and dirty laundry back into my suitcase, but he never moved away from the table. His eyes tracked my every move, the expression on his face unreadable.

"Are you going to stand there all day?" I asked, irritated he was staring at me, and being blatant about it. I hated being watched. Now that I knew he watched me sleep, I doubted I'd be able to get a good night's rest with him near.

Without a word, he moved around the room, collecting his things. It took him less than a minute. He waited for me to be done, leaning against the dresser as he continued to watch me. I zipped up my suitcase and looked at him expectantly. "What?"

"Are you done?"

"Yes."

He walked over to the phone on the nightstand and pressed a button. "We need a bellhop to room eight-eleven. Thank you."

I shrugged into my coat and hoisted my purse on my shoulder. And there we stood, awkwardly waiting for the bellhop. I felt his eyes on me the entire time. It seemed like hours passed by the time there was a knock. I wheeled my carry-on toward the door when a large hand skimmed mine as he took the handle from my grip.

"I can handle my own bag," I argued.

"Not so long as I'm around," he said with a wink.

The two sides of Jude Soren were both sexy and frustrating. Something told me there was more to him than just good looks and snarky retorts. Now I just needed to decide whether I should bother to take the time to find out what they were, or spend our time together just tolerating him.

Chapter 7

Jude

FIVE MINUTES AFTER BOARDING THE plane was all it took to conclude that Brae definitely had some issues. Before takeoff, she pulled out every necessity she could need from her purse, which could double as a satchel. A magazine she bought in the airport, gum, mints, a small pack of tissues, hand sanitizer, eye drops, which piqued my curiosity, and even ChapStick. The small items were in a Ziploc bag, which she tucked away in the seat pocket, then she stowed the satchel under the seat in front of her.

"Eye drops?"

"The air is very dry in an airplane."

Good lord. Here we were sitting in first class, and for the first time in my adult life, the mile-high club wasn't even a thought. Thankfully, cocktails were still available. I sipped my vodka on the rocks, feeling her eyes on me. "What?"

"Isn't it a bit early for hard liquor?"

My response was to finish it in one swallow. When the flight attendant came back, I ordered a vodka with orange juice. "There, is that better?"

Brae just rolled her eyes before she turned to look out the window.

We didn't say much to each other on the flight. As Brae dove into her magazine, I immediately purchased the Internet package. Besides wanting to use every minute of the long, five-plus hours to attempt to organize my affairs, I'd have to relinquish my damn phone as soon as we landed.

"We'll be losing our phones soon. Don't you want to take advantage of having Wi-Fi?"

She looked at me as if I'd lost my mind. "No. Besides it being a fortune, I already tied up my loose ends."

Well, good for you, I quipped in my mind, but my mouth said, "Suit yourself."

Even though I already asked Luca to, I still shot off an email to my key people telling them I'd be unreachable for an extended period of time. I gave each of them Luca's contact info, as well as Kyle's. I challenged my secretary, Ruth, to bother Kyle at least ten times a day for every little non-business related decision. I didn't care if she called him to ask if she should order sandwiches for the staff lunches or salads. If salads, with or without dressing. Should she include dessert? If yes, cookies or cake? Every question needed to be a separate phone call. By the time I got back, I wanted him pulling his hair out from Ruth's incessant inquiries. Ruth, of course, would get a nice bonus for her assistance.

While I was at it, my final email was to my mother. Without getting into detail, I explained, because of Kyle, I was involved in a social experiment for six weeks and couldn't be reached. I then said if she needed anything to contact Kyle's cell. I knew that wouldn't sit well with her, and the moment she told my siblings they'd all be bombarding him with questions. What made that plan even better was they all spoke broken English.

Payback, I chuckled to myself.

As we started our descent, Brae sanitized her hands and then smoothed ChapStick over her lips in a counterclockwise motion before reversing directions. I'd never witnessed anything like it, and I had five sisters.

With a thud, the airplane touched down at the airport in St. John. Brae's fingernails may have left a lasting impression on my forearm as she gripped it until we came to a rolling stop. When she finally decided we were safely on the ground, she released me.

"I'm so sorry." She looked down at the half-moon indentations in my skin and winced. "I'm not a fan of flying."

"Or landing," I teased with a wink.

Three dings sounded and passengers started moving about. I retrieved our bags from the overhead compartment while Brae gathered her belongings under the seat.

Felicia, the perkiest flight attendant in the sky, gave me one last flirtatious smile as we exited the plane along with other anxious vacationers.

Hot humid air greeted us like a slap in the face. "Could she be more obvious?" Brae snorted as we walked down the stairs leading to the tarmac. "Bye, Felicia," she added with an eye roll.

"She was just being friendly. It's her job." Pulling our small carry-ons behind me, we entered the slightly air-conditioned terminal and made our way to the luggage carousel.

"If she's so friendly, why did she snarl at me?"

"Maybe it's your sunny disposition."

Her brow puckered for a split second before she sported the annoyed look I'd already grown accustomed to. My veiled insult must have hurt her feelings. Not wanting to start this adventure on the wrong foot, I offered a genuine smile. "I'm sorry."

Brae smiled in acknowledgment as we stood amongst other people. For a small airport, it was a busy place. Most likely people were escaping the cold and looking forward to relaxing. Ironic that we stood next to them as tense as a whore in church and just about as out of place. Tropical steel drum music played through the sound system, which was most likely to get visitors in the mood for what was to come.

An older gentleman held a sign with our names printed on it. We both strolled over to him, and a warm smile spread over his lips. "Mr. Soren, Miss Daniels?"

"Yes," we responded simultaneously.

"I am Pedro. Chip and Barbi would like to welcome you to St. John. We hope you'll enjoy your time here. Once you retrieve your luggage, there will be a blue sedan waiting outside to take you to your cottage. The driver's name is George. I am here to collect your cell phones. They will be returned to you at the end of your stay."

I pulled mine out, mumbling a variety of curse words in Swedish. Brae handed hers over with a smile. Kiss-ass.

Finally, bags started dropping on the moving belt. "That's me," Brae said as she pointed to her large blue suitcase with a bright pink ribbon tied to the handle. She went to grab it, but I got to it first and set it down next to her before waiting for my bag.

"Thank you." She smiled up at me, and the look in her eyes just about knocked me over.

"You're welcome." I wasn't sure whether it was the

way my words were just above a whisper or the flustered look on my face that caused our eyes to connect and hold.

A confusing moment passed between us, and I broke the connection by turning away in haste. Spotting my suitcase, I leaned over and pulled it off the belt. An older man was next to me, trying to reach for his blue and green plaid bag. Without hesitation, I pulled his case off as well.

"Thank you, son." He looked to Brae, and gave me a smile. "You're a lucky man. Hold on to her. She's a beauty." Rendered speechless, I just looked at him. "You kids here on your honeymoon?"

Brae stepped closer and placed her hand on my arm, clearly not wanting to disappoint the man. "No, just a vacation." The way her fingers flexed on my skin followed by her glorious smile made me almost forget the real reason we were on the island.

"You'll love it here. This is where my wife and I came to celebrate our anniversary, marking each decade with new memories. Unfortunately, my Luanna passed just before the holidays, but I couldn't bear to cancel the trip. This would have been our fiftieth anniversary. Luanna would have wanted me to come." His voice trailed off as if recalling a memory, one I was sure involved his late wife.

A lump formed in my throat. Brae released my arm and wrapped the man in a quick hug. "I'm very sorry for your loss."

The old man smiled at us. "Thank you. Well, I better go, but you two enjoy this time together. Believe me, this island is magical."

We stood and watched his plaid case disappear out the

door. Not knowing what else to say, I turned to Brae, noticing her eyes filled with tears. "Let's go find our ride."

She wiped her now damp cheeks. "Okay."

Brae

BLUE WATER, WHITE SAND, PALM trees, and silence. Tranquility was just what I needed after the hustle and bustle of city life. Ever since meeting the older gentleman at the airport, Jude had been particularly quiet. Not that I minded the peace, but for some reason it was worrisome.

When we first got in the car, I observed everything was opposite of how it was in the states and got a bit nervous. "Why do they drive on the left side of the road?" Maybe that question would break the ice since all Jude had been doing was staring out the window.

Jude mumbled, "Because it was previously owned by Denmark."

The driver, George, chimed in, "And because of the donkeys." I caught his smiling reflection in the rearview mirror and smiled back. When I glanced at Jude, he just shook his head.

"Donkeys?" I scooched toward the edge of the seat, trying to get closer to the front.

"Yes. Island folk will tell you that before there were cars, donkeys were the mode of transportation. They traveled on the left side of the road. So, when motor vehicles came to the island, they were forced to drive in the same direction to avoid hitting the animals."

"Wow, what a cool story." I looked at Jude. "Isn't that

a great story? So much better than Denmark."

"Sparky, it's folklore. The real answer is because of the Danish."

"Well, I like George's explanation better." I smiled at George.

"Yes, we will blame the asses," Jude chortled, sarcasm thick in his tone.

"Isn't Denmark near Sweden?"

"Yeah, why?"

"Oh," I drawled with a grin. "You meant the asses with *tails.*"

Jude finally laughed. "Smartass."

George tossed me a wink and I relaxed in my seat, relishing in the fact that I got one up on Jude.

♡♡♡

The place where we were going to be living for the next six weeks wasn't exactly what I had expected. I had a feeling Jude felt the same way since he stood stock-still, staring at the small white home.

George shook his hand, then hugged me and softly whispered, "Good luck."

"Why did he leave?" Jude just stared at the sedan as it pulled away down the narrow road.

"Because we're home, sweetheart." I batted my eyes at him.

"Fuck me."

"No, thank you." For once, I was excited. This little white home was perfect—absolutely perfect. I instantly fell in love with the white shingles, thatched roof, the tiny porch holding adorable white potted plants, and the white picket fence surrounding the property. It looked like somewhere Snow White would live, if she lived in the Caribbean.

"Why is everything white?"

Ignoring him, I stepped closer, staring at all the details in awe. The house wasn't any wider than a doublewide trailer home, but I'd give up everything in New York to live here in a second

Without giving him the chance, I grabbed both my bags and pulled them behind me, clunking up the porch steps one by one.

There was a sign on the door:

Welcome to Ignite Your Spark Cottage.

The place where love ignites into flames.

Jude grumbled and rolled his eyes. "Welcome home, Sparky."

"I wish you'd stop calling me that," I said through gritted teeth.

"Nah."

He reached in front of me and jiggled the doorknob. "Great, we're off to a good start. No cell phone, and we're already locked out."

I dug out the packet and produced a key. "Oops, I

guess that's what this is for."

Jude stared at me like a deer in headlights before snatching the key from my grasp. "There's only one?"

Looking deeper into the packet, I said, "Yup. And I'll take that now."

"Not on your life." He opened the door and shoved the key into his front pocket.

My, "This is beautiful!" was countered with Jude's, "This is a nightmare."

Stepping inside, my heart filled. The home was more like a studio apartment in Manhattan. The white walls were topped with a navy blue crown molding. The one room open floor plan was separated not by walls, but by each corner having its own living space. The dining room, bathroom, kitchen, and bedroom all shared equal real estate. Jude scurried through the small space, opening and closing doors. The only doors aside from the ones leading outside were the closet, a small laundry room, and the bathroom.

"Do you realize there's only one bathroom? And what the fuck is that?"

"It's called a washing machine," I enunciated the words very slowly. "It's to wash clothes."

"Smartass," he grumbled. "This is no bigger than a jail cell."

"Which you need to get used to, according to your plan of murdering your ex-friend. Stop exaggerating. This place is beautiful."

I was truly in love. Navy curtains framed every window, the fabric pooling on the dark wood floors. The doors leading in and out were French, with tiny panes of glass that made it a touch more formal than just a beach house. Even the kitchen was inviting. A small peninsula island was the focal point. White tiled countertop accented in navy matched the color scheme of the room. The white on white cabinets, although few, were delicately designed with etched glass fronts. Even the tiny round table in front of the peninsula with two dark wood chairs made me smile.

Jude contradicted my joy with a grumble. "This gives a new meaning to breakfast in bed. I could just swing my legs over and eat at the table."

I glanced at the quilt-covered bed attached to a fancy wrought iron headboard. My eyes first realized that it was only a full size. *Shit*.

I could tell the size of the bed only just hit him as well. "What the hell. Is that a twin?"

"It's a full. You're assuming you're sleeping in the bed."

Jude's eyes scanned the room. "There isn't even a couch in here. That small couch doesn't count, Miss We Need to Follow the Rules and Share a Bed."

"Oh gee, I can't wait," I mumbled, but he heard me.

"I need air." It only took a few strides until he opened the door leading to the outdoor space. I hurried behind him, excited to see what was there.

My feet were immediately ensconced in sand. I glanced around for a mat or rug. Constantly having sand on those gorgeous wood floors would drive me nuts. A spicket on the side of the house and a hook with a towel hanging off it immediately caused a sigh of relief. Pointing to it, I said, "See that?" His eyes followed the line of my finger. "Please wash your feet and use the towel before you come in the house so we don't have sand everywhere."

He stared at me while blinking. I responded with a

fake smile.

Two mesh lounge chairs were nestled together, creating the perfect romantic setting intended for couples. The cute white picket fence bordering the front of the cottage also wrapped around the back. I let out a sigh, appreciating everything about this home.

"I could live here forever."

Jude glanced back at me. "You just got here."

"It doesn't matter, look at this place. It's paradise."

"It's hell."

"Are you going to disagree with everything I say? If so, this is going to be a very long vacation."

"Vacation? Did you see the TV in the bedroom, or should I just say room? The screen on my iPad is bigger."

"No, I didn't notice. I'm not planning on watching television while we're here." I opened the back gate and spotted a hammock two steps away from us on the beach. Cutting my eyes to his face clued him in to what I was about to do. At the same time, we both lunged toward the hammock, sending it rocking furiously from side to side.

"I call dibs," I said, trying to push him off.

"No way, Sparky. This has my name on it." Without effort, he lifted me by my waist and plopped me down so fast, the bottom of my dress pushed up toward my hips. On instinct, my legs straddled his lap.

The position lined us up perfectly, and I gasped at the immediate contact of his obvious arousal. "Now we're talking, Sparky," he said, his tone husky. Despite his words, there was no humor in his eyes. They blazed in vivid color as he stared right through to my soul. Before he had a chance to blink, I flew off his lap and lost my balance, landing ass first on the sand beside him.

"Shit."

"You're a klutz." He leaned over the side of the hammock and chuckled. "That's twice now that you've landed on your ass in my presence, and we haven't even been together twenty-four hours. Maybe you should consider strapping a pillow to your ass."

"Shut up," I brilliantly responded, dusting myself off and storming toward the turquoise sea. Just staring at the ocean as I crossed the short strip of beach already calmed me. I had a feeling sitting out here while reflecting my bizarre predicament would become a normal occurrence these next six weeks.

Hearing the waves roll in was so peaceful, I debated running back to the house to grab a towel to sit on since I despised the sand, but that would have made my dramatic exit comical. Forcing myself to sit required a pep talk, and my inner voice quipped I was in the freakin' Caribbean and needed to suck it up. With my hands behind me, I leaned back. The ends of my hair grazed my lower back as I relaxed my neck to face the sun. Closing my eyes, I tried to imagine how wonderful this place could be if the person I was with appreciated it as much as I did.

When Jude said he was in hell, my heart sank. Not because of me, there's no way I'd think I was his heaven, but St. John was far from hell. Thoughts of the man we'd met at the airport made me smile. I could see why he came here to celebrate with his wife for their anniversaries. It was a shame she wasn't here now. A seagull squawked and flew overhead. When I opened my eyes, Jude was sitting next to me, his forearms on his knees as he stared out over the water.

"How long have you been sitting there?"

"Not long." Turning his head to look at me, he gave

me a smile that made my heart beat a bit faster—one I knew could get the attention of anyone in its presence. "I've always loved the water." I simply nodded. "I'm sorry I said this was hell."

"Me too." I gave him a feeble grin. "That's twice you've told me you're sorry. Maybe you should consider those words to be your next tattoo." After taking a shaky breath, I offered, "I don't know what type of life you lead, but that house is everything I'd ever want or need. It's simple and beautiful at the same time."

"So, you're a white picket fence sort of woman?"

I hadn't really thought about it too much in the past, but now being in this predicament, it was hard not to. "I suppose I am. I'm guessing you're not?" He quirked a brow. "I know you're not a woman, I meant about the picket fence."

"Two point two kids surrounded by a picket fence has never been anything I've dreamt about, so I suppose my answer is no."

"Then it's probably a good thing we're only in this for a year." Even though I picked the wrong guy for the right intentions, knowing we didn't want the same things saddened me for some reason. Maybe it was because of what I'd been dealing with between Stefan's cheating, my self-induced unemployment, and the endless interviews that went nowhere—rejection in any form wasn't pleasant.

Jude stood and brushed sand off his legs. Everything the man did was sexy. Maybe I should have picked bachelor number two. Then at least I'd know my heart wouldn't get broken.

He extended his hand to help me up and we stood toe to toe, looking at each other. It was a shame he was such an ass sometimes, because he was perfect in every other way possible. How I wish I could call Vanessa or one of my friends to help me out. Okay, maybe not Vanessa. She'd tell me to jump his bones.

Chapter 8

Jude

HUNGER HIT LIKE A FREIGHT train. Realizing we hadn't eaten since breakfast, and the three vodkas I had on the plane weren't really sustenance, I rubbed a hand over my empty belly. "I'm starving. Let's order dinner."

"Order dinner?"

The way she asked made me snippy. "Yes, order dinner." I glanced at my Rolex, and added, "It's only five, but we haven't eaten all day."

She stood with a smirk like the cat that swallowed the canary. "You do realize we didn't see any restaurants or eateries on the way to the cottage, right?"

Come to think of it, we didn't. "So, they're going to starve us? Please don't tell me there's a clause in that stupid rule book that says that boat," I thrust my arm forward and pointed a finger at the little dinghy anchored off shore, "is meant to catch our own meals!"

She laughed, and I was pretty sure it was at me. "The fridge is stocked. They aren't that cruel." As she walked toward the cottage, she dusted the sand off her ass, and my eyes honed in on the motion. Turning her head, she said over her shoulder, "I'll cook tonight. You're welcome."

What the fuck? Cooking? Laundry? Seriously, what the fuck? I rubbed the back of my neck, trying to relieve the tension radiating through me. How was a couple supposed to fall in love when subjected to all this menial labor?

I reluctantly followed her, my hunger making my ire even worse. Two things made me very cranky: lack of food and lack of sex.

I found her removing ingredients from the fridge, humming as she did, taking her sweet ass time. "Do you need help?" I asked to speed things along.

"Yes, can you light the grill outside?" My guess was the very audible sigh I released wasn't what she was looking for as a response. "Never mind. I'll do it."

Ignoring her, I went outside to light the fucking grill. I think I did this once in my life at the frat house. How hard could it be? They all had to be the same, right? I stood before it, almost wishing the thing would spontaneously ignite itself. Maybe it was a female grill? The thought made me chuckle.

"Okay, be nice," I said to it as I turned a few knobs and pushed the button marked start. With a small *whoosh*, the flame sparked to life, bringing with it a smile on my face. I rubbed the hood affectionately. "Thanks, babe. Forced to be here six weeks to ignite my spark, and how ironic if it only ended up being with a grill."

"Who are you talking to?"

I turned to see Brae holding a plate of raw chicken. "How long have you been standing there?"

"Long enough to know the island heat has baked your

brains." She walked over and plunged a fork into one of the breasts before plopping it on the grill.

"Did you season them?"

She furrowed her brows. "Not yet."

"You do realize you need to, right?"

"After they're cooked, I will," she snipped. I knew enough about cooking to know that's not how it worked, but my line of questioning annoyed her enough to thrust the plate toward me. "You're welcome to take over." When I remained still, she nodded. "Yeah, I thought so. You can set the table."

Another sigh caused her to roll her eyes, and I walked back into the shack. After opening and slamming a few cabinets, I pulled out plates, glasses, and utensils. That took me all of three minutes, and then I stood with my hands on my hips while staring into space.

What the fuck was I supposed to do with myself now? I could jerk off, but even that made me cranky. I glanced out the window to see a very vague outline of her body surrounded by white billowing smoke. Part of me felt like I should check on her, the other said *fuck it.*

I walked to the small TV and switched it on. Static. Switch. Static. Switch. Spanish News. Switch. Static. Switch. Soap Opera.

"Goddamn it!" I jerked the knob to turn it off. My eyes darted around the room, looking for something to do. Boredom aggravated by hunger hit me full force, and it wasn't a good combination.

On the coffee table was her girly magazine and a pen. Desperation had me picking it up and flipping it open. The crease in the spine forced open a page that read— *How does your man rate?*

I only managed to read six of her answers, but it was

enough to know she thought I was an asshole. Guilt had me slapping the periodical back on the table when I heard her coming through the door. I made the mistake of glancing at the plate where what looked like three large lumps of coal sat practically whimpering over their condition.

Humming to herself, she seemed unfazed that she cremated our already dead dinner. I continued to watch in disbelief as she put a plate of salad and wilted vegetables on the table beside the chicken.

"Honey, dinner is ready," she said with a saccharin smile.

I was absolutely starving, but there was no way I could eat this meal. God, what I wouldn't do for a Spark's Steakhouse sirloin right now . . . *heh, Sparks*.

She helped herself to a serving of each and started sawing through the charred chicken, oblivious to my gawking. Her eyes cut to mine as she huffed. "Do you expect me to serve you too?"

"Um, I can't eat this." I was sure my prick-ish behavior would further her negative opinion of me, but damn it, I was starving and this wasn't going to cut it.

She waved a hand to the fridge behind us, and said, "There's plenty in there for you to eat. Feel free to help yourself. You live here as well."

My eyes focused on the meal already prepared, then to the fridge, then back. On the one hand, I could eat now, even if it was crap. If I started from scratch, it could be another twenty minutes before my stomach was fed. Flipping back and forth like watching a tennis match, the sound of her knife screeching across the ceramic plate forced my decision.

I stood and stormed over to the fridge, which only

took three steps, and yanked it open. Eggs. That would be the quickest thing to make. Finding some cheese, peppers, and onions, I prepped and made a quick omelet without uttering a word.

Seven minutes later, I was sitting with my edible dinner. She glanced at my plate, eyeing the contents like it was a gourmet meal.

"So, you *can* cook?"

Around a mouthful of food, I said, "I never said I couldn't. You assumed." Pointing to her plate that still held more than half a charred breast, I added, "No wonder you're so skinny. It has nothing to do with not eating meat, you just suck at cooking." Loading my fork up with a healthy bite of eggs and peppers, I lifted it toward her. "Want some?" She leaned away like I was offering her road kill. "Suit yourself." I shoved the forkful into my mouth and moaned in pleasure. "Mmmm, not so bad, if I do say so myself."

"Okay, hotshot. You just earned cooking as your chore for the duration of our stay. Congrats."

"And what is your chore going to be?" I shoved more eggs into my mouth with a smirk. "Keeping your man happy?" I asked with an obvious wiggle of my eyebrows.

"Yeah, no. I'll do the laundry." She pushed her plate away with a shake of her head. "Why are you such a jerk?"

"You tell me." I pointed to where the magazine lay, and said, "You seem to have all the answers."

Her eyes followed, her brows puckered together in confusion. "What answers?"

"Oh, let's see. Question number four, would your man put you before his own needs? You don't know me enough to answer 'hell no.'" I stretched and grabbed the magazine off the end table, tossing it between us.

"So, you're my man now? That's not about you," she quipped.

It didn't occur to me it could be someone else. I mean, why was she here if she was attached? Then again, how could someone like her not be attached? Remorse had me hanging my head and mumbling, "Sorry. I assumed it was." The pained look on her face caused a lump to form in my throat. "You don't have to explain. It's none of my business."

While I stared at my plate, the sound of her chair scraping against the hardwood floor caught my attention. She stormed over to the small kitchen and dumped the contents of her plate into the garbage. Feeling like a heel, I followed to grab a beer from the fridge, also having lost my appetite. The water splashed around her hands as she scrubbed her plate before leaning into the counter with her head down. After expelling a long breath, she turned her head to look at me. "Remember when I told you I was unemployed?"

"Yes."

"My boss was my boyfriend. One day, I caught him cheating on me with his secretary, so I impulsively quit. My love life was a big cliché, I was unemployed, and . . ."

"And?"

"Nothing." Brae turned toward me, her back against the edge of the sink. She crossed her arms in front of her chest, and added, "I know you think a lot of yourself, which is fine, but like you said, I don't know you well enough to judge. Thanks to your vagueness, I don't know much about you aside from you're Swedish and have two ex-friends who seem more like your brothers. Maybe you shouldn't push them away. If you keep up the high and mighty attitude, they might be all you have left one day."

My eyes widened at her response. Sparky was the perfect name for her. "One ex-friend. Luca had nothing to do with this," I said, trying to bring some levity into our conversation.

She wasn't amused, nor was she interested in continuing this discussion, made obvious by the scowl on her face. I expected her to go into the bedroom and slam the door, but since we were technically in the bedroom, Brae surprised me when she pulled a bottle of white wine out of the fridge and one glass out of the cabinet. She uncorked the bottle and poured a healthy serving.

Every movement was like a dance. Her lithe body, which I'd assumed to be tense, appeared relaxed. I wasn't going to apologize again, but I was sorry about her job. Her ex sounded like an ass. I didn't condone cheating. Even though there was a lot I still needed to learn about Brae, I couldn't imagine why any hot-blooded male would cheat on her.

Silence stretched between us. I had no idea what to say to help her feel better. In the defeated way her shoulders sagged, her stunning brown eyes dull and hollow, there was a lot more to her problems than her asshole of a boss/boyfriend cheating and her being jobless.

Before I could ask, or attempt to console her, she slipped out the back door, closing it behind her with a firm click. Through the window, I watched her drag one of the lounge chairs out the gate and onto the stretch of beach. She positioned it facing the ocean and settled on it while staring ahead, nursing her wine.

A lump I didn't understand formed in my throat. Was it pity? Remorse? Whatever it was, I had no idea what to do about it.

♡♡♡

Brae

I COULDN'T BELIEVE I ADMITTED that to him. That look on his face, I knew it well. It was the same look the foreclosure representative from my parents' bank had on his face when he said, *"I'm sorry, Ms. Daniels. You're running out of time."* It was the same look Stefan had when his eyes cut away from her face to mine as he fucked her in his office. It was a look that instantly made me sick to my stomach.

There was no way I needed him feeling sorry for me. I couldn't handle that on top of everything else I needed to worry about. I preferred him being a prick—that, I could fight against. Pity made me defenseless, and that was worse than anger. I'd rather be angry. Over the past few months, being angry at the bloodsucking banks and Stefan became a motivator to get me to do something about my situation.

I'd be damned if Jude Soren derailed my goals just by feeling sorry for me. That alone was enough to force me to make a deal with myself. For the rest of our time together, I'd push the weight of my worries to the back of my mind and focus on the prize. Money was my motivator. Jude was just a means to an end. Even if it meant being the better person—and being nice to him.

My parents raised a strong woman, and once I put my mind to accomplishing something, I did. So, for now, I'd finish my wine, maybe give myself this brief time to sulk, and do my best to enjoy the next forty-one days.

Chapter 9

Brae

"**B**RAE?" THE USE OF MY real name surprised me more than his appearance. He came to stand beside me. His hands shoved into his pockets made him look insecure. It wasn't a trait he normally possessed. "Are you okay?"

I plastered a bright smile on my face. "Yes, I'm fine." Lifting my glass, I drained what was left. "The wine is decent. You should have some."

One corner of his lips lifted in a half smile. "Maybe I will." He took the glass from my hand and walked away without another word. A few minutes later, he dragged the second lounge chair over to where I sat. I couldn't stop another smile—a genuine one this time—when I saw him balancing two glasses of wine in his other hand.

"Here you go. I assumed you'd want a refill." Our fingers touched, and I paused before taking the glass. "I didn't poison it," he teased at my hesitation.

"Good to know. I'm just surprised you're being nice to me, I guess." My stomach twisted when I considered the reason was probably pity. Refusing to succumb to those negative emotions, I took a sip and grinned. "Thank you. That was sweet, Jude."

"My pleasure." He looked out at the darkening ocean as I stared at his profile. Straight nose, firm square jaw, and that damn delicious scruff would be hard to resist if I had met him in the real world. He was just the type I'd be attracted to. Feeling my gaze, he turned his head as I looked away.

"We missed the sunset," I said, forcing his attention away, as if to confirm I was right.

"There will be others. Are you tired?"

"Yes, a little. I should probably turn in soon. It's been a long couple of days." Reminding myself not to be snarky—or sparky, as he enjoyed calling me—I refrained from mentioning the horrible night's sleep I had on the rock hard sofa in our room last night.

"Are you a lefty or a righty?" When I didn't reply right away, he clarified, "Do you sleep on the left or right side of the bed?"

"The middle, but I'm good both ways. You can decide."

"Hmmm. . . . ambidextrous. That could prove to be a very positive trait in our growing friendship."

I couldn't help but laugh. "So, we're friends now?"

"Sure, why not? That'd be new for me, being friends with a hot chick," he placated with a humorous tone.

I laughed again. "I don't know what's more insulting, the fact that you're reluctant to be friends, or the fact that you referred to me as a chick."

"Woman. Sexy woman. Hot, sexy, beautiful woman who purrs. Does it matter how I label it?" He frowned and groaned. "Ugh. I just remembered how much you snore." He pointed to the wine. "Drink up. Maybe that will knock you out and quiet the buzz saw living inside you."

"I don't snore." Before he could respond, I quickly added, "You'll never be able to prove it either. Your grand plan of taping me is null and void since you don't have a phone with you."

"Doesn't mean I don't have a recording device. Well, GoPro. Kyle packed my GoPro. I guess the idiot thought I'd need it to record some mad surfing or . . . something." He chuckled, but didn't explain further.

"Or something?" I prompted.

He cut his eyes to mine with that sexy smirk on his lips. "Do you really want to know?"

Did I? "Sure, why not," I admitted with a shrug.

"The last time I used it may have been to make a homemade movie of sorts . . ."

"Ugh," I croaked, thrusting a firm hand in his face. "Stop right there. On that note, I'm going to unpack and get ready for bed." I swung my legs over the side of the chaise and stopped before walking away.

"Unpack?"

"Yes. You know, you take clothes out of a suitcase and place them in drawers. Some you hang on hangers in the closet." I quirked my lips, mimicking his smirk. "I'm not living out of a suitcase for six weeks, and *neither are you.*"

He rolled his eyes and groaned, as if my statement completely exhausted him. It was clear this man had people in his life to do such simple tasks like packing, cooking, and laundry. If he thought I was going to take on all those roles, he had another thing coming.

"Also, if you need to pee, now would be a good time to use the bathroom."

"Seriously, what do you do in there? You don't need primping." Unfolding his body, he released a long, drawn out groan as he stood beside me. "We need to work out a schedule."

"It's simple. I'll warn you before I start my morning and night routine. The rest of the day, have at it." I took a few steps before stopping again. "Just be sure you clean up after yourself. I've heard using a sock helps," I said, winking, then laughed out loud at the shocked look on his face. It felt good to laugh. "Last chance to get in before I do."

He scurried past me and bolted right into the bathroom. A few minutes later, he appeared and waved a hand. "It's all yours." It was annoying how little time he spent on himself, yet could always look so fucking hot.

"Don't forget to unpack," I demanded before shutting the door behind me. Of course, he left the bathroom a mess. His towel lay on the floor, and cluttered on the counter was an opened tube of toothpaste oozing onto the Formica, a generic tube of hair gel, a comb, an electric trimmer, a razor, and a can of non-descript shaving cream. *Hmmm . . . I wonder if he manscapes?*

His blue glass bottle of cologne caught my eye. I glanced at the shower and noticed the shampoo bottle had the same generic label as his other products.

The man's hair was impeccably styled and he used no name brands? Picking up the tube, I flipped open the cap and sniffed the masculine scent. Did the man shop at a Dollar Tree for his toiletries?

Next, I picked up his cologne. Like an idiot, I glanced behind me, even though I was alone in the small room, pulled off the gold cap, and turned the nozzle to spray it away from me. When the blast of liquid hit my neck, I almost dropped the bottle in shock.

Shit, shit, shit.

Grabbing a towel, I ran it along my neck after placing the bottle back. My reflection in the mirror displayed a red splotchy neck from scrubbing, which blended well with my red face.

After a few long minutes, I took a deep, calming breath, and emerged from the bathroom to find him on the left side of the bed staring into space. My entrance broke his trance, his greenish-brown eyes landing on my face. They didn't stay there long before he dragged his gaze down and back up my body. I purposely packed functional, very unromantic sleepwear. But the way he leered at my sleeveless plaid top and matching shorts made me feel completely exposed.

What was even more disturbing was the way the quilt lay across his lap. It left an unnerving mystery as to what he was wearing to bed. God help me if he was naked. He wouldn't do that, would he? That would be all I needed to make this already uncomfortable situation completely unbearable.

Walking over to the front door, I unlocked and then re-locked the deadbolt. I could feel his eyes on me as I crossed the cottage to do the same with the back door. I refused to look at him as I checked to make sure the burners on the stove were all in the off position, grabbed a steak knife from the drawer, and turned on the microwave lamp.

Tucking the knife under the mattress, so only the handle stuck out, I flicked off the main light and lifted the quilt to slide into bed. It was only then I chanced looking at him. His folded arms and raised brow forced me to involuntarily ask, "What?"

"Afraid we'll be murdered in our sleep? Or do you have plans to kill me?"

"Unlike you, I wouldn't fare well in jail. One can never be too safe." I motioned to the door. "Plus, we're in the middle of nowhere."

"Oh, Sparky, you are one complicated chick." The stunning smile he gave me eased the insult.

"Why do you smell like me?" He leaned over and sniffed. "Yup, that's my cologne, all right." The look in his eyes told me I was busted.

"I was trying to clean your messy side of the counter and it slipped. Can you please put the top on your toothpaste? Is that hard?" There, that should cover it.

Ignoring the second part of my statement, he smirked his sexy, yet annoying smirk. "It slipped and sprayed onto your neck? Or maybe you just like how I smell?"

"No, I was turning it to see the brand and it slipped. Did you make it in your basement?" I changed the subject, again.

"No, but Kyle did." The confused look on my face prompted him to say, "He's a jackass, but the man is a genius when it comes to cosmetics. It's what he does."

"That explains the no frills packaging. I hope he tests his products before you use them."

"Yeah, on me and Luca. Luca already grew a third nut." He cracked up at my wide-eyed expression. "I'm kidding, Sparky."

"Goodnight, Jude," I said, as I rolled over to hide my smile.

"Goodnight, Sparky," he said before rolling onto his side.

There was barely any space between our backsides,

and the warmth of his skin hit mine even though he wasn't touching me. I could already predict being sore tomorrow from having to sleep as close to the edge as possible to avoid him. The thought elicited an involuntary sigh.

"Sparky?"

"Yes?" I responded, prepared to hear a snarky sexual comment.

"If someone breaks in, I'll protect you. You can sleep well knowing that. Sweet dreams," he said, shocking me.

"Thank you." Smiling at his offer, I then added, "You too."

Jude

PURR . . . RUMBLE . . . SNORT . . . WHISTLE.

Purr . . . rumble . . . snort . . . whistle.

Purr . . . rumble . . . snort . . . whistle.

Warm air hit my neck after every snort and whistle. What in the hell? My attempt to move felt constricted. Glancing down, a warm hand rested on my pecs. Further down, her bare leg was laying on mine. If I moved an inch to my right, I'd fall off this bed. But it was the rumbling near my ear that still had my attention. To say she was literally sprawled out would be an understatement.

I glanced at the sliver of mattress I was confined to and then to the petite brunette currently hogging the entire bed.

Purr . . . rumble . . . snort . . . whistle.

Holy cow. I slipped one hand under my pillow, doing

my best not to disturb sleeping beauty. With the GoPro in my grasp, I turned it on and positioned it just above my shoulder, aiming it at her face. While I was at it, I skimmed down her body, stopping at key parts, before moving the shot back up to her head.

The sounds coming from her could rival a lumberjack. If I weren't careful, I knew I'd start to laugh, which would definitely wake the beast. God knew I didn't want to start the day off on a bad note. After what I thought was ample recording time, I clicked off the camera. Rather than stow it back where it was, I stretched to put it in the drawer of the nightstand.

The motion caused Brae to stir and release me. "Is it morning?" Her husky voice was sexy as hell.

I sat up and hurried to close the drawer. "It sure is. Did you sleep well?"

"Mmmm . . ." Her arms stretched over her head, causing her back to arch, *and* her top to lift, *and* her belly button to show . . . *and* my cock started to stretch much like she was.

"Yes, did you?" she asked, turning on her side to hold her head up on her bent arm. Her tousled chestnut hair was a mess and there was a crease in her cheek from the way she was passed out all night on her pillow, but she still looked stunning.

What was the question?

She must have sensed my confusion. "Sleep. Did you sleep well?"

"Oh. Yes, I slept fine. I'm used to sharing a miniscule bed and being left with enough space to accommodate the width of half my ass," I said with a wink before swinging my legs over the edge of the bed.

"Did I hog? I'm sor—" Her words halted the moment

I turned to face her. In lightning speed, her head whipped around to face the other way.

Glancing down at my morning wood, I shrugged. "Sorry. I kind of can't help it."

"You can by wearing more than those tiny briefs." She blindly pointed behind her to my crotch.

"Well, that's not true. It really wouldn't matter what I wore . . . but no can do," I said with a firm shake of my head. If I had to fight every night against a bed-hogging bear, I intended to do it while being comfortable. Little did she know, one day very soon, I would adopt my own sleep routine. "You're actually lucky I have these on. This is way more than my usual."

"More?" she mumbled.

"Way more," I repeated. "I have an OCD of my own. I prefer not to wear anything, but I thought I'd cut you some slack until we're better acquainted." With her head still turned, I took the opportunity to go into the bathroom. Not only did I need to use it, but after waking up next to her, I needed a cold shower.

Using the only time I'd have to myself, I decided to take a bit longer than I normally would—granted, it wouldn't be as pleasurable as I'd like it to be. Warm water cascaded down my body. When I closed my eyes, visions of Brae stretching and rolling mixed with the raspy sound of her voice had me turning the faucet to cold. I wasn't in the mood for a fantasy when the real thing was lying ten feet away.

Even though the streams felt more like shards of glass on my skin, I still couldn't rid the images of what I wanted to do to her. One day, I'd take her in this shower and every other area in this house—maybe even outside. What worried me was how long I was going to last until she let me.

The sound of a doorbell was enough to force me to turn off the water, grab a towel, and sling it around my waist. The cool porcelain sink felt good under my palms as I leaned against it, trying to rid the images in my mind. It was no use, though. The longer I tried, the more vivid they became.

When I pulled the door open, Brae was sitting at the table with an envelope in her hand and a cup of coffee in front of her. Turning, her gaze landed on my chest, then lowered before rising to meet my eyes.

"I forgot to bring my clothes in. But you seem to be appreciating this outfit, so if you'd rather me stay in a towel all day, I'd be happy to accommodate you." She lifted a brow at my snark, but I wasn't going to apologize again. Turning toward the dresser, I noticed the bed was impeccably made. The throw pillows were even fluffed to perfection. "The housekeeper came already? Is she coming back to clean the bathroom and bring us clean towels? Is that who rang the bell?"

"No," she quipped. "I made the bed. They'll only be sending a maid once a week to supply clean linens, towels, and groceries."

"Once a week?" Just kill me now. "So, who was at the door?"

"A messenger." She waved the envelope. "He dropped this off."

"What is it?" I walked over to stand next to her. My waist was practically at her eye level. Watching her blush was quickly becoming one of my favorite things.

"Can you please put some clothes on? And I don't know what it is. It's addressed to both of us."

Leaning down, I whispered, "You should turn your head, or you're going to get an eyeful." With a chuckle, I walked to the dresser and opened one of the few drawers she was so kind to leave empty for my stuff. "Can you read that so I know what to wear?"

She angled herself away from me.

Jude and Brae,

We hope you're enjoying your home away from home. Today, you'll need to work together to steer yourselves down the right course. Use this time to understand each other's strengths and help each other in times of weakness. Just like relationships, your ability to work together will be necessary in order to maneuver yourselves to the finish line. Your ride will arrive this afternoon to take you to Caneel Bay.

Love and Sparks,

Chip & Barbi

I stepped into a pair of navy swim briefs and black shorts before shrugging into a black tank top. Since we were going to a bay, I assumed this involved water. "You can turn around now. That's all it says?"

She flipped the card over. "Yes, that's all it says. What do you think it means?"

"Water sports? Why don't you get ready?" She grumbled something while rummaging through the top drawer before disappearing into the bathroom with a few articles of clothing.

The door creaked open. "I made a pot of coffee. I can guarantee it's much better than my chicken." She smiled before closing the door behind her.

I helped myself, and moaned in pleasure at my first sip. Thank God it was good. Not knowing how long we'd be gone, and not wanting to repeat the hunger pains I had last night, I scoured in the fridge for breakfast.

Nothing appealed to me, until I saw pancake mix in the small pantry.

She was in the bathroom long enough for me to make a large stack of pancakes, cut up some fresh fruit, and fry some bacon. I couldn't resist.

I could smell that green apple shampoo she used before I saw her. She turned the corner and smiled. Her simple lilac sundress wasn't sexy in any way, but the visible deep purple string around her neck sure as fuck was. Goddamn, I could only imagine what she looked like in a bikini. And in a short while, I'd be finding out.

"Smells delicious." When she stepped beside me to snatch a berry from the bowl, I had to resist leaning in to sniff her hair. "Is all this for you, or are you sharing?"

"I guess I'll share," I mumbled, pretending to be put out by doing so. I lifted a piece of bacon and hovered it near her lips. "Pork?"

She clenched her mouth into a tight line and leaned backward. "No thank you."

"Suit yourself." I snapped a piece off with my teeth and released an erotic groan while I chewed. Her face tensed as she did her best to contain a smile.

One day, I'd make sure she'd devour bacon. So long as I was making guarantees, one day I would devour her. I had sex with women I liked a lot less than Brae. Compared to her, they were Fords when she was a Rolls. So, who could blame me for wanting to test drive before I committed?

Chapter 10

Brae

"**W**ELCOME TO TODAY'S ADVENTURE," A very handsome man greeted us as soon as we arrived on a different part of the island. He was a few inches shorter than Jude, but just as muscular. Where Jude was drop dead gorgeous, Roberto, as the nametag on his tank top read, was handsome in a free-spirit kind of way, with longer hair and darker skin.

Roberto's chocolate brown eyes were on me, mine were on him, and I could feel Jude's eye's drilling holes through the side of my head.

"I'm Roberto, and I'll be your kayaking guide here at Caneel Bay."

"Kayaking?" I asked, panicked.

Jude sensed my apprehension through my tone and appeased me by saying, "Don't worry, Sparky. I was on the rowing team at Yale."

Of course he was.

"Together, you'll navigate the beautiful bay where you will see colorful coral and an abundance of marine life, including some of the most spectacular turtles in the Caribbean."

"Are they snapping turtles? I'm not wearing a cup," Jude snorted, and I elbowed him in the ribs.

"Be respectful," I said, but internally laughed at his joke, immediately remembering his jockstrap comment during the game show. "This is his home, and he's proud of it." He muttered something in Swedish, and I could only imagine what it was based on the grin he sported.

Unfazed, our guide continued. "You can stow your clothing in the foot locker by the palm tree. Once you're ready, meet me by the yellow kayak."

Before I knew it, Jude lowered his shorts to reveal a European cut bathing suit American men didn't wear. As if my eyes were paralyzed, I couldn't stop staring when he pulled his tank over his head. His body was like a work of art. Each muscle moved with purpose, and his tattoos made him even sexier.

"Are you just going to stand there gawking or do you plan on kayaking in that dress you're wearing?" Jude chuckled at his joke before he threw his clothes haphazardly into the locker and shoved his sandy shoes right on top of the pile.

I felt my face heat with embarrassment at being busted. As quickly as I could, I stripped down to my bikini and stowed away my neatly folded dress on top of his mess, putting my sandals away on the shelf at the bottom.

When I turned and saw him now gawking at me, I immediately assumed he was making fun of my OCD again. Just as I was about to defend myself, he said, "Purple."

"What? Purple is my favorite color." I folded my arms, waiting for the insult.

"Purple . . . looks . . . good on you." Our eyes met and

held.

"Um . . ." Using the small backpack I brought with me as an excuse to change the subject, and never having been in a kayak before, I looked to Jude for advice. "Do you think I can bring this with us?"

"Do you need it? What do you have in there?" Taking it from my hand, he pulled the top apart, widening the opening. "Do you really need all this stuff?" He reached in and pulled out a tampon. With his sexy leer, he asked, "No sex tonight, dear?"

Mortified, I snatched the bag away from him and closed it. "I'll just ask Roberto."

"Screw Roberto." He stepped closer, taking the bag from my hand. "You don't need this. We'll only be gone an hour or so." Taking control of the situation, he put the bag in the locker and slammed it shut.

"Wait, I need my sunscreen." I flipped open the locker again, grabbed the tube, squirted a glob of lotion in my palm, and rubbed it over my exposed skin. "Would you like some?"

I added a dollop to his palm, and in a swift motion, he smoothed some over his face and arms. My eyes feasted on his toned skin that now glistened in the sun. On instinct, my tongue moistened my lips. Even the way his muscles contracted when he pushed the locker closed affected me. "We good now?" He cocked his lips to the side.

At my nod, he took my hand and led me to the yellow kayak of death waiting for us. I couldn't even allow my fear to fester. All I could think about was my hand in his. It wasn't the first time, but it wasn't any less thrilling.

We came to stand beside Roberto, and Jude positioned himself between us. Roberto handed each of us a bright red life vest. Jude dropped my hand to put his on, and I followed his lead. The problem was, he snapped his black straps easily into their receivers, and mine had at least four inches between them. Glancing up, his eyes danced as he laughed at me.

"Mine doesn't fit."

"Sparky," he said, his tone scolding. "You need to adjust the straps to accommodate the girls."

Roberto moved closer to help, but Jude intercepted, saying, "I've got it." The snark in his tone was unmistakable, but again, Roberto seemed oblivious. The man must have taken a happy pill.

Jude came toe to toe with me, his hands first releasing the tension on the top strap and then the bottom. As he concentrated on my vest, I stared up at his face. If I just lifted on my toes, my lips could be on his. My eyes honed in on the way his lips parted just enough for me to see his tongue pressed against his front teeth while he concentrated. His green-brown eyes followed the movement of his large hands. By the time his fingers closed the pieces together across my boobs, my entire body was pulsing.

"There, now they're safe and sound." He took both hands and patted the padded vest right over my boobs, an obnoxious grin on his face. Then, he did it again, keeping them there the second time.

"Are you done?" I arched a brow.

"Yep," he said with a prideful nod.

Roberto witnessed the whole exchange with a smile. "You make a very beautiful couple."

"Thank you," we both responded at the same time.

Jude's eyes connected with mine and held—again. Whenever he did that, stared at me in that way that made me feel like he wanted me desperately, my brain always malfunctioned. I barely listened through the instructions Roberto recited. I did hear him say, "To complete your challenge, you must kayak out to the red buoy and back. Do you need accompaniment?"

I then heard Jude say, "No, we're good."

That snapped me back to reality. "Good?" My heart pounded in panic. "I've never done this before."

"Trust me, I've got us." I glanced out to the bay we would be navigating, completing a mental check. No waves, thank God. No obstacles to maneuver around. Really, it was just one big, open, calm pond. This shouldn't be too hard.

Minutes later, there we were cutting through the calm waters. I held my paddle in a way where neither end touched the surface. We picked up speed, and the gentle breeze blew my hair away from my face.

I tilted my head up toward the sun, enjoying the ride, until he barked, "You plan on helping me, Sparky?"

"You seem to be doing a good job. You don't need me."

"Yes, I do. Because if I take a break, this is what will happen." He stopped paddling and the kayak bobbed and tipped dangerously. With trembling fingers, I gripped my paddle in a false sense of security and gasped.

"Okay, stop shaking it. I'll help." He chuckled and caused even more rocking. "I said I'll help!" I yelled, my veins humming with anxiety.

"That's what I thought. Now, do what I do. Sweep."

"Sweep what?"

"Your left. Sweep, then right is draw. Sweep. Draw." Confusion caused my body to freeze like a mannequin. I startled when he barked, "You're not listening."

"I have no idea what you're talking about." I turned to glare at him, the motion dipped us to the right, and before I knew it—splash!

Beneath the surface, I heard him yell, "Knulla!" I came up sputtering beside him.

Once I caught my breath, I quipped, "Is that another rowing term, Mr. I Was on the Yale Rowing Team?"

"No, it means fuck! As in what the fuck! Good job, Sparky," he scolded.

"You can't bark orders I don't understand. I've never done this before." By the way he stared at me, I could tell he wasn't listening. He reached over with his thumb and pointer finger and touched my lips, picking something off them. I swore I felt it everywhere.

The cool water did little to cool me off. He lifted his fingers, and said, "Seaweed."

There was nothing remotely sexy about having a piece of seaweed stuck to my lips. But holy hell, my brain shut down without warning. Every part of me in comparison sparked to life. I felt myself sinking, and his arm wrapped around my waist. The damn vests kept our chests apart— too far apart. His long legs dangled with mine beneath the surface. With each move he made, I could feel his manhood brush against my thigh.

I held onto his vest, gripping the edges near his bare arms. "Sparky, don't look at me like that."

"Like what?" My words were barely a whisper. His gaze moved to my lips, then back up to my eyes. "We need to get back on," he said in a sexy rasp. His warm breath fanned my face. Without moving a muscle, he added, "I'll lift you first."

I'd rather stay right where we were, until something not human brushed against my leg. Just as he placed his hands on my waist, I shrieked and bucked enough to send the kayak floating away from us.

"You're killing me, Sparky." With a hand on my vest, he towed me toward the kayak and steadied it with his other hand. "I'm going to lift you. Don't touch the kayak with your hands or you'll tip it again. Keep them on your vest." I did as I was told as he turned me to face the kayak.

That was when two large hands grabbed my ass cheeks before stilling. When it didn't look like he'd be moving them, I said, "The only reason I'm allowing this is because I want out of this water. Can you get on with it?"

"In a minute. I'm having too much fun." He chuckled at my glare. "Hey, cut me a break. It's the little things." He flexed his fingers, getting a good grip on my ass, and pushed me up.

Forgetting everything he said, I reached out with a hand, tilted the vessel to the right, and sent it spiraling away from us.

"Sparky! I said not to touch the side." His brows pulled together in an annoyed expression.

"I'm sorry."

Instantly, his features softened. "Please, let me do this or we'll be here all day. And I really don't want to find out the hard way that there are snapping turtles in here." Repeating the steps again, his vest hit the side, causing it to flip upside down.

"I swear I didn't touch anything."

His only response was a sigh. After a few more failed attempts, I was beginning to think we'd never get out of that water. Where it was pristine and gorgeous when we started, it suddenly turned murky. Things kept touching my legs, and I was getting the heebie jeebies the longer we were submerged.

Jude glanced toward the shore. "Can you swim to the shore?"

I followed his gaze, and shrieked, "Hell no! Are you nuts? That's like a mile."

"It's like fifty yards, but fine. We'll get in this fucking banana one way or another. I'll hold it still. Climb me and get in."

"Climb you?" My thoughts immediately went to Vanessa and how she told me to climb him like a tree. My nipples pebbled, and it didn't have anything to do with the water surrounding us.

"Yes," he said like I was a five-year-old. "Hold my vest, put your foot on my thigh, then the other, and climb into the kayak."

Doing as I was told, I found myself sitting just where I was supposed to be. Flashing a smile he couldn't see, I bragged, "Yay, I did it."

"Good girl. Now, don't move," he threatened. "It's going to rock. Just sit still." I sat stone still as he retrieved our paddles from nearby and handed them to me. When the kayak leaned dangerously close to the surface of the water, my heart stopped. My gut instinct was to scream and jump, but his voice repeated, "Don't move!"

I barely blinked for fear of getting in trouble, and waited until he situated himself behind me. He released a very audible breath, and said, "Okay. Let's try this again. Sweep."

"Are you kidding me? Just say left or right."

"Fine, Sparky. Left." A moment later, he deadpanned, "Your other left."

☆☆☆

Jude

I'D NEVER BEEN SO HAPPY to see dry land. Once we removed our life vests, Roberto raked his eyes over Brae while smiling wide as we approached him. He took our vests, and asked, "Did you have a good time? You looked like professionals once you got the hang of it."

"Thank you. It was just wonderful." Brae smiled with pride as if she just rowed the English Channel. "It was spectacular. Such smooth, clear water. Kayaking should be something everyone tries. I'd do it every day if I lived here." I shook my head in disbelief at her exaggerated reply.

Roberto clapped his hands together. "You are welcome anytime, and if your boyfriend is busy, I'd be happy to go with you."

"Thank you. I'll remember that."

Did she just bat her eyes? She had to be one hell of a sales person. She had me sold even though I experienced that disaster with her. There wasn't a question whether Roberto was also sold on her. His eyes kept roaming her body and a perpetual smile lifted the corners of his stupid mouth.

Brae laughed. "As soon as I understood what sweep and draw meant, I did much better."

Roberto grinned. "You can just think left and right. The idea is to relax your mind and enjoy the ride."

Cutting her eyes to mine, she smiled sweetly, "We'll remember that next time, won't we, honey?"

Honey? Hello, green light. "You better believe it, sweetheart." In one swift motion, she was in my arms.

Just like in a dance, I dipped her backwards, making a production of it, and stared into her eyes like a long lost lover. The hollow of her neck pulsed as she worked down a swallow. When her lips parted in an attempt to say something, I closed the small gap between us.

As the kiss progressed, so did my want for her. With one hand on the back of her neck, I could feel her pulse pound beneath my fingers. My other hand, having a mind of its own, gripped her thigh and brought her leg up to wrap around my hip. The more we made out in front of that tool, Roberto, the more I wanted to stretch her out in the sand and really give him a show.

Brae's hands squeezed my biceps. This move could have been interpreted in a couple of ways. She either, A, wanted more of me, or B, was signaling for me to stop. Naturally, I chose option A, but of course I was wrong.

She mumbled something into my mouth. Her tongue stopped moving and the firm grip once on my arms was now planted on my chest. When I finally released her mouth, she sighed. Our eyes connected and if it weren't for Roberto clearing his throat, we probably would have continued to stare at each other.

Something about this woman intrigued me, but my feelings confused me. Part of me still wondered what could make her so desperate to be willing to go away and marry a stranger for money. The other part, my ego, felt protective. Roberto looked at her with interest. If Luca or Kyle saw her in a bar, I would bet my left nut they'd make a play for her. Of course, I would have as well, but that was beside the point.

"Let's get out of here." I released the hold I had on her leg and pulled her upright. Her flushed skin mixed with the sun we got today made her glow. Taking her hand in mine, I strode away from Roberto while he stood, subtly adjusting himself.

"Thanks, Roberto," I called over my shoulder.

"Why did you do that?" she asked as I tugged her along.

"You never know, Roberto could be a mole."

She turned her head to look at him. "You think?"

"Maybe." I had to suppress a chuckle. This mole theory could work to my advantage. Hand in hand, we walked to the locker to gather our belongings and got dressed. Her stomach growled, making me laugh. "Are you hungry, Sparky?"

"I am." She reached into her bag and pulled out a granola bar. My stomach chimed in and internally kicked me for not bringing one for myself. That's when she handed it to me and pulled out another.

"Thank you." I peeled the foil wrapper back and took a bite.

"My pleasure. Call it an appetizer. What do you want to eat?" She slid the bar in her mouth and took a healthy bite.

Between her lips wrapping around the bar and her question, my first instinct was to say, "*You.*" Instead, I said, "Lady's choice."

"You're being awfully kind. First you saved me in the water, even though it was your fault we tipped, Mr. Sweep then Draw." She laughed. "And now you're letting me choose what we're having for dinner?"

"You're right. I've been too nice. Forget I asked. Now, move your ass because I'm hungry."

Rather than the snarl I normally received, she let out a hearty chuckle. Damn, this woman was going to drive me crazy. I just couldn't wait to get my head between her legs so I could repay the favor.

Chapter 11

Jude

"YOU'RE A REALLY GOOD COOK. If all else fails in the finance world, you could open a restaurant." Brae sat back in the chair with her hand on her stomach and a satisfied look on her face.

"Thank you, but I think I'll stick to finance." What did this woman eat at home? Frozen dinners? All I did was grill steak and bake a potato. Just as I was about to relax outside, there was a knock on the door.

Both of us stood to see who it was. That's when we noticed a piece of paper lying on the floor. Great. Another note. I retrieved it and began to read it aloud.

Jude. "Hmmm, this one is just for me."

Brae sidled up beside me to read it, but I spun around, holding it above my head. "Let me see!"

"No. Ever hear of privacy laws?" I cupped it in my hand, shielding her away from it with my back. As my eyes scanned the words, my brain had trouble following.

Jude,

You shall provide an act of chivalry in the form giving. In this exercise, Brae is the sole recipient. You are the giver. This act cannot revolve around household chores and needs to be more than holding a door open—although, that's always a nice thing to do.

Did they think I was raised by wolves?

Just remember, this is all to please Brae.

Love and Sparks,

Chip & Barbi

Well, pleasing a woman was my specialty.

"What does it say?" Brae stretched her neck as far as she could in an attempt to see around me.

Putting her out of her misery, I told her, "It says I need to pleasure you." I licked my lips. "Finally, something to look forward to."

Her eyes widened in shock. "No, it doesn't. Give me that." She ripped the note from my hand and I watched as her eyes frantically scanned the words. "You're such an ass. It doesn't say pleasure me. It says you need to please me."

"Meh, same difference." With each step I took toward her, she took one back. "What's the matter, Sparky? You look nervous."

She flicked her hand back and forth. "Don't be ridiculous." She then raised that shaky hand up to rub the back of her neck. "Um . . . I'm getting tired. I'm going to clean up the dishes and then go to bed."

"I've got this. Why don't you go take care of your nighttime ritual so we both can get to bed before midnight?"

Brae smiled at me. "Are you sure you don't mind? I'd like to take a shower. I feel very stiff all of a sudden."

Humph . . . stiff. Welcome to my world, sweetheart. "No, go ahead. I'll take one when you're done."

✩✩✩

There was no way in hell I was going to be able to sleep. Between the scent of apples, her moaning, and lack of sex, I was doomed. "Can you please stop moaning? It's after midnight."

"I'm so sorry. My shoulders are killing me and I can't get comfortable." Brae rolled over, laying on her stomach in her signature X form. Her short pajama shorts hugged her ass like a fucking glove.

I studied her for a moment before getting the best idea I'd ever had. Reaching over to the nightstand, I grabbed the complimentary bottle of lotion. Sparky shifted just as I sat up and straddled her upper legs.

"What the hell are you doing?" She craned her head back, then groaned.

I leaned forward to whisper in her ear. "I'm going to please you now. Call it a Swedish massage." My dick got the wrong idea. He woke up, ready for action, but, sadly, this was going to be all for her tonight. Glancing down at my cock, I whispered, "Next time, buddy."

"What?" Brae spoke, my dick flinched, and I moaned.

The cotton of her top provided a barrier, but it wasn't enough, nor would it suffice. With a dollop of cream on my hand, I reached under her tank top and began to rub her soft skin. "Mmmm . . . that feels amazing." With each movement I made, my now rock hard dick rubbed up and down her ass.

"Shhh, try not to talk. Just relax." Knowing this was going to be impossible for her to accomplish, I readied myself for her to keep talking.

With gentle pressure, my thumbs rubbed each side of her spine from her waist to her neck and back down, each stroke firmer than the last. My fingers got in on the action as they rubbed her sides. Her skin felt like silk under my palms, which continued to caress every inch of her back.

In a long glide, my hands went from the top of her ass to the base of her neck. Her eyes were closed, her lips curved up, and her face was relaxed. The more I rubbed, the more she moaned, so I kept repeating the motion. In her defense, her back was tense. The muscle just above her shoulder blades had a large knot in it, which I worked with my thumbs. Inching my way down her body, I stared at the waistband of her shorts. If I attempted to pull them off, I knew she'd flip out, so I just took a chance and rubbed her over the cotton. This woman must live to do squats. The tone of her ass was perfection in my hands.

I skimmed my hands around her hips to massage her lower abdomen. She lifted slightly to allow me better access, and I took the liberty, rubbing close enough to her mound so if she had hair there, I'd feel it . . . but she was fucking bare.

God help me.

Moving back around to her ass, my thumbs continued exploring. Now, under her shorts, they moved up and down, but never hit pay dirt. I couldn't without asking, "Brae? Is this okay?"

"Feels wonderful." Her voice sounded euphoric. "Don't stop."

"Are you sure?" If my dick could punch me or tell me to shut the hell up, he would have.

"Yeah, I'm sure. I'm so tight."

Fuck me. I knew she was talking about her muscles from rowing today, but hearing her moan and using words like "tight" and "don't stop" was killing me.

I shifted off her to get more lotion before positioning myself between her legs. With a hand on each thigh, I began to move, up and down, squeezing with each gentle motion. Every part of this woman was perfection. Even her pink-painted toes, which I was now working on one by one. When my fingers rubbed the arch of her foot, she flinched and almost kicked me in the head.

"Sorry, I'm ticklish," she giggled. "I'll try not to do that again."

Moving back up her legs, I angled myself on my stomach, so my face was in line with her ass. How I wanted to kiss, bite, and own it. Maybe one day, but for now, I'd pleasure her, and not because that damn card told me to. Mainly because I wanted to. Yes, this was supposed to be for her, but I'd have to be dead not to also get pleasure out of watching her come at my hand.

In a slow motion, I rolled her over, shifted the fabric covering her pussy I now knew to be bare to the side, and waited for her objection. None came. Perfectly pink, glistening with wetness I no doubt caused, it beckoned for me to touch it. Who was I not to comply? I paused for a moment to glance up at her face. God forbid she'd fallen asleep and I took advantage of her, but she wasn't sleeping. Her eyes met mine. Her breasts rose and fell in rapid breaths. She wanted this. Thank fuck.

Her pajama shorts were hampering my plans. With our eyes pinned, I dragged them off her legs, leaving her exposed. Again, I waited for her to stop me, but she never did. Unwilling to give her a moment to overthink what was happening, I repositioned myself and blew a stream of air onto her bare flesh, watching it twitch in acceptance. My fingers hovered over it, aching to touch, but knowing once they did, they wouldn't stop until she came all over them.

Using just my right index finger, I ran it alongside her opening. My left hand firmly held her thigh as I spread her open just a bit. I licked my finger that had just touched her and practically came in my shorts at the taste of her.

With my finger now wet, I gently slid it inside her. Her ass bucked up a bit, but I ignored it. Not wanting this to end right away, I took my time—stroking it in and out, then around her clit and back in again. Each of my movements caused her to jolt, as if my touch was electric. My lips were so close. Touching her was one thing, but tasting her would be entirely different. Yet, being where I was, there was no way I could stop now.

Moving forward, I flicked my tongue against her clit before flattening it against her opening. Having the evidence of her arousal on my mouth spurred me to focus on that one spot. Without moving my head, I continued to apply pressure with my mouth while my hands spread her thighs farther apart. Her arousal on my tongue tasted even sweeter than it did on my finger, as I knew it would. What I hadn't expected was how satisfying this actually was. Not that I was a selfish asshole when it came to pleasing a woman, but generally speaking, I'd get some satisfaction out of it in the form of an orgasm. Oddly, I wasn't thinking about myself getting off, just Brae.

"Jude . . ." Brae's hands landed on my head just as her legs shifted, squeezing my body. Her fingers grabbed my hair, giving it a gentle tug.

"Shhh, I'm just getting started. Please don't stop me." Brae stiffened for a moment before she relaxed, letting her arms fall to the side.

Alternating my finger, thumb, and tongue caused her to tremble. Knowing she was getting close, I slowed. Yes, this was supposed to be for her pleasure, but I wasn't ready for this to end, no matter what my cock was telling me. Reluctantly, I removed my mouth from her pussy and climbed up to lie by her side.

"Jude," she repeated, but the way she said my name this time was more like a plea to keep going. Her next command confirmed it. "Please."

"Patience, Sparky." I slipped my fingers back inside her to resume my efforts, using my thumb where my tongue had been. With my free hand, I lifted her shirt and cupped her breast. Her pebbled nipple hardened further under my palm.

"Yes, just like that." She moved her hand on top of mine and applied pressure to it. Holy shit. Sparky had a naughty side.

"I've got you, Sparky. Just relax."

Her hips bucked against my fingers as I curled them up just enough to find the one spot that set her on fire. Pinching her nipple with one hand while fucking her with my other brought her to her peak.

"Oh my God!" Her entire body trembled under my touch.

I claimed her mouth with mine. My tongue mimicked the movements of my fingers as her pussy pulsed around them. She broke the kiss to say my name before her body relaxed.

A sheen of sweat coated me as I rolled onto my back. All I could do was stare at the ceiling. If I looked at her, I knew I'd want more. The bed shifted when Brae sat up.

"Jude." I glanced at her, and my hand instinctively covered my hard cock. The way her skin flushed and lips parted further worsened my condition.

"Are you . . ." She looked down at my boxers. "Do you need me to . . ."

"I'm fine, Sparky. I'm just going to go take a quick shower."

Brae simply nodded. "I know what the card said, and that's why you did what you did, but . . ."

"Sparky, the only thing the card said was to do something nice for you, thus the massage. The rest was me taking the opportunity. I'd been wanting to touch you since we got here. I'm a man, it's what we do."

A tight smile crossed her face. "I see."

Without another word, I retreated into the bathroom. With a door now separating us, I was able to breathe. The water from the shower did little to satisfy me, and after seeing the look on her face, jerking off wasn't even an option. The desire was gone—deflated, if you will.

Five minutes later, I was towel dried, back in a clean pair of boxers, and climbing into bed. Brae lay on her side facing away from me. I climbed in behind her, not knowing whether she was awake or not, and pulled her into my arms. While I was gone, she put on her pajama shorts and was tucked under the covers.

She immediately stiffened against me, contradicting the way she responded to what I did to her a few minutes earlier. Surmising she must be feeling embarrassment, I tightened my hold in an attempt to comfort her. With her back pressed against my chest, I whispered into her ear, "Goodnight, Sparky. Sweet dreams."

Brae didn't say anything, didn't even flinch. But goosebumps appeared on her arms. She definitely heard me, and that was all that mattered.

Chapter 12

Brae

EVERY BONE AND MUSCLE IN my body protested my movements. Morning sunshine beamed through the windows. As I rolled over a bit, I realized I wasn't in the bed—the place where Jude made my body come alive and then dismissed it as if it didn't happen. Which was why I was on the sofa.

I sat up and looked at him, all comfortable in the center of the mattress, his backside exposed since he slept over the comforter. He groaned and shifted his body a bit. That groan. The same one I heard last night when he brought me to one of the most intense orgasms of my life. Ironically, I remembered his response to my question. *What was the last gift you gave a woman? The best orgasm of her life.* But just like a man, he acted like it didn't matter.

For most of the night, I stared at the ceiling fan above the bed. I watched it spin, counted the rotations, and tried to fall asleep with no luck. At least not while I was lying next to him—not while replaying his words. I had a feeling he had a line for every situation, and by the talents he showed last night, he'd probably used them before. I was sure I had just become another meaningless conquest.

Coffee. That was what I needed to clear this fog out of my head. Once I had my cup in my hand, I turned to stare at Jude. God, why did he have to be so perfect in every physical way? Suddenly, Jude stretched out his arm as if he was searching for something.

"Sparky?"

I didn't bother replying. I just took my coffee and headed outside to my happy place. Once lying on the lounger, I took a deep breath and started to relax. As I watched the water roll in, caressing the shoreline, I thought of the real reason I was here. My mantra—*keep your eye on the prize*—sounded off in my head. Yes, that was all I needed to do. Make it to the end without getting attached and take the money.

"Sparky?" He stood beside me, wearing those tiny swim briefs—and, of course, no shirt. "We got another note." I swore, if the man could walk around naked, he would.

"Did you want me to read it through osmosis, or are you going to tell me what it says?" My snippiness was clear in the tone of my voice. Jude cocked one brow as he studied me—or more precisely, my boobs. "Well?"

"Sorry, Sparky." His brows furrowed, probably wondering why I was cranky. When he sat on the side of his lounger while studying me, I snagged the note from his hand and began to read it out loud.

Jude and Brae,

We hope you're enjoying your time together. Today, you will be participating in one of our favorite activities. It's sexy, sensual and much better when doing it with someone else ..."

"Finally!" Jude abruptly cut me off.

"Finally, what? I haven't even finished reading it."

Before I could read another word, he said, "Sex. I wonder if it's some island ritual or live porn."

Rather than being completely offended like a rational human being, I just stared at him. After last night, he has the nerve to say that to me? It was official. I was in hell.

"Can I continue please? I highly doubt that's what it is."

Jude shrugged, nonchalant. "Fine, go ahead."

After I let out a long breath, I picked up where I'd left off.

It's sexy, sensual, and much better when doing it with someone else. Please head down to the beach just beyond the fence at seven this evening for your first Rumba lesson.

Love and Sparks,

Chip & Barbi

"What the fuck is Roomba? Isn't that a vacuum? We're going to clean the beach? What the hell kind of vacation is this?" He threw his hands in the air.

Was he serious? "No, you idiot. I said Rumba . . . rum, like the alcohol. It's a dance."

"I'm in. You had me at sex and alcohol."

I sighed. "I never said sex."

"No, Chippy did."

Realizing this was getting us nowhere, I got up to get another cup of coffee. "You're ridiculous." He followed me to the water spicket and miraculously mimicked my ritual without groaning about it. Once inside, he stood behind me to grab a cup out of the cupboard. When he held it out to me, I set the coffee pot down. "Fill it yourself." His eyes widened at my reply, but he filled his cup just the same.

"Why did you sleep on the couch last night? You should have stayed in bed, you'd be less cranky. Was it your snoring?" He glanced over the rim of his cup as he took a sip.

I balked at his cluelessness. Was I supposed to stay in a bed with a man who made me feel cared for and wanted, which was something I hadn't felt in a long time, only to find out it was because of a note he received? What did he say last night? *I'm a man, it's what we do.* So, with that in mind, it had nothing to do with the me and all to do with the note.

"I'm going to go shower." Bringing my coffee with me, I closed and locked the door, knowing full well I'd be using all the hot water.

Feeling a bit more relaxed and refreshed, I thought about everything that transpired last night. Hell, his penetrating gaze alone was enough to send me over the edge. But his mouth on me, his fingers in me, the memory of all he did to me, caused my insides to clench. There was no denying my body came alive under his touch . . . nor was there any denying I wanted more.

The pale yellow sundress I picked out for today would be perfect for what was planned later. Dancing with Jude would prove to be difficult. The Rumba wasn't a fast dance, nor was it one where dancer's bodies didn't touch. I knew this from a couple sources. One, I was an avid watcher of Dancing with the Stars, and two, I took ballroom dancing as an elective in high school. Naturally, Jude wouldn't know either one of these facts.

When I stepped out of the bathroom, I didn't see him. Expelling a breath, I wasn't sure what to do. It wasn't as though this was a large home and there'd be various places to escape, but I still wanted some alone time. When I peeked outside, I saw the deck was unoccupied.

Warmth from the island breeze soothed me as I relaxed on the chaise lounge. I couldn't help but wonder where Jude was. Not because I missed him, but because we weren't supposed to be apart for more than an hour or we could be disqualified.

My heart raced a bit in fear. I'd kill him if he screwed this up for me. Maybe he didn't need the money, but I did. Hell, the man didn't know what a washing machine was. That fact alone piqued my curiosity, but right now, I just needed to know he didn't bail on me.

I closed my eyes to gather my thoughts when I heard breathing—no, panting. Did a stray dog find its way here? When I opened my eyes, Jude was bent over at the waist, hands on his knees—and, of course, *shirtless*.

He glanced at me before snagging a towel off the railing. I quickly slid on my sunglasses to mask my indifference toward him.

"Did you have a nice shower, Sparky?" Even the way the man wiped sweat off his body was tantalizing. "You could have let me use the bathroom first to take a piss at least." My nose crinkled in disgust, but I remained silent. "No worries, though. The palm tree just outside the fence and I are now closely acquainted."

"That's nice. I hope you two will be very happy together." I leaned over and picked up my *People* magazine. "Although, next time you decide to leave, can you please let me know?"

"Awww, were you worried about me?"

I lowered the magazine with a bored expression and narrowed my eyes. "No, I was worried someone from Ignite Your Spark would come here for one of their surprise visits and I wouldn't know what to tell them."

Jude quirked his lips to the side. "I like to go for runs in the morning. I just haven't been able to do that. But, if it makes you happy, I'll leave a note from now on. You've made it clear you don't trust me. Did you think I packed up and left?"

God, that thought saddened me more than it should have. "I didn't know what to think. I don't know you."

He nodded once before leaning toward me. Each muscle in his torso constricted. "I don't run from commitments. I'm here, and that's all you need to worry about." When he stood, his strong body shielded the sun from my eyes. "I'm going to go shower now."

Commitment. He said that word with such conviction, it made me relax just a bit, but not enough to forget he had yet to acknowledge what happened between us last night. The best plan would be for me to act just as unaffected.

Jude

I COULD STILL TASTE HER. Neither of us spoke about last night, and I wasn't sure why. So many times, I thought about bringing it up, but even being in this small house, Brae managed to keep her distance until it was time to go to our dance lesson. Fabulous.

An older woman wearing a red shiny dress stood on a makeshift dance floor sitting on the beach. To be honest, this was ridiculous. This fucking dance was going to be the death of me.

Brae stood about three feet away from me. Every so often, she'd glance at me from the corner of her eye. Aside from that, I was invisible.

"Welcome to the dance of love. I am Belinda, and I will be your instructor today." Humph, dance of love my ass. "The dance is flirtatious, fun, and very sensual." She handed Brae a sexy pair of heels. "Put these on, darling, and you'll be able to move better. Your hips will line up with his."

"Are they really necessary?" Brae dangled the shoes off her fingers and crinkled her nose.

"Yes."

With a huff, she fastened the shoes on her feet. Belinda wasn't kidding; they added about four inches to her height.

Belinda took us each by the hand until we faced each other, but Brae refused to look at me. The seagulls appeared to be circling nearby as if they didn't want to miss the show.

"Brae." Her eyes cut to mine in an instant.

"Jude." Fantastic. Her tone mimicked the way she stood—stiff as a board. This was going to be a blast.

"Kids," Belinda addressed us. "I have instructions that if you two come together as a couple—a team, if you will—the prize will be a couple's massage. Isn't that wonderful?"

"It sounds glorious." Slight sarcasm laced my statement, "Brae loves massages." That earned me a glare.

"Fabulous." Belinda clapped her hands together. "Now then, the Rumba. It's a sensual dance. Flirtatious and fun. Let me set the scene for you." Our instructor placed my right hand just under Brae's shoulder blade, her left hand on my shoulder, then put our free hands together. "Jude, you are trying to win Brae's affections. You will flirt with her, and she will reject your advances."

Without thought, I let out a chuckle. Considering that wasn't far off the mark, this should be a piece of cake. Naturally, my partner snarled at me.

Belinda turned on a slow song with a Latin vibe that sounded like something out of a bad porn movie. "Bend your knees and do a box step." She demonstrated the moves as if she had a partner. "Brae, these are your steps. Move your right foot back first—slow, quick, quick, slow, quick, quick, slow, quick, quick, back, side together, forward, side together, back, then repeat."

Brae stared at her feet while moving in the same pattern, her hips swaying just like Belinda's. Then, it was my turn. The steps were the same as Brae's, but I started going forward rather than back. Seemed easy enough—it wasn't.

By the tenth time of stepping on Brae's feet, Belinda jumped in between us. "Jude, watch me and Brae."

Sounded great to me. I could use a little girl on girl action to get the creative juices flowing.

I probably should have been looking at their feet, but when their hips closely gyrated together, I was transfixed on each movement. Sparky had moves. Clearly, she was holding back on me. "Okay, I think I have it now. It's vertical sex."

"Oh my God." Brae rolled her eyes as she started to turn away.

I snagged her by the arm and pulled her into my chest. My lips close to her ear so Belinda wouldn't hear me, I said, "I want that massage, so dance with me the way you just did with her and we can get out of here. You do want to make it to the end of this farce, don't you?" Yes, maybe I pressed my lips farther into her ear with each word. Yes, maybe by the last word I pulled her lobe in between my lips. And yes, maybe I pushed my growing excitement into her hips suggestively . . . but I wanted that damn massage.

I straightened, pinning my eyes to hers. "Ready, Sparky?"

Rendered speechless, she nodded before turning to Belinda. "Can you please start the music again?"

With a bright smile, she did as Brae asked, then counted off starting at five. Why did they always do that? Anyway, we heard, "Five, six, seven, eight," and began to dance, honest to goodness dancing.

Our bodies were in sync and perfect rhythm with the porn music. Then Sparky's hip grazed my dick and all bets were off. He sprung to life and decided to join the party. My palm on her back pulled her close so there wasn't even space for sand to come between us.

My hand moved up to the back of her neck. With a

swift movement, I pulled the clip out of her hair and cast it aside. Gorgeous waves cascaded over her shoulders. The scent of apple assaulted me, practically beckoning me to inhale it, which I did. I speared my fingers into her hair and pulled her close enough that we were breathing each other's air.

Our Rumba turned into a scene from *Dirty Dancing*. Brae's dress hiked up, almost exposing her ass as she practically rode my thigh. My dance partner let her inhibitions go, just as she did when I went down on her last night. She mumbled something about a prize as she bent backwards, causing her hair to brush my feet and her tits to point to the sky.

Holy fuck.

Chapter 13

Brae

BELINDA BEGAN TO APPLAUD JUST as the music ended. Jude never released the hold he had on me. Once he pulled me up, my head spun, though I wasn't sure whether it was the sudden movement, the feeling of his erection on my hipbone, or the way his eyes darkened as he stared at me.

"God, Sparky, you're beautiful."

This was all bad. I was at a complete loss at what to do. That's when Jude licked his lips and I remembered why I was annoyed with him. "You can let me go now." I pushed my body away from his.

Jude furrowed his brows and looked at me with concern. I turned to Belinda. "Did we pass?"

"Oh, honey, you more than passed. I've worked with many couples, some of whom were taking lessons in preparation for their wedding reception. In most cases, these people had known each other for a very long time, but you two put them to shame. I never witnessed such chemistry before. Chip and Barbi are going to be pleased as punch."

Punch. I liked that word. In fact, I'd love to punch the smug look off Jude's face.

"Thank you, Belinda." Jude placed a chaste kiss on the back of her hand.

She blushed before reaching into a bohemian style bag to retrieve an envelope. "Here is the information for the massage." She pulled me into a hug. "Congratulations, sweetie, he's a dream."

Yup, sure was. Jude Soren was every woman's dream. Wow, did he have them fooled. My guess would be he didn't stick around long after he got what he wanted to find out whether he was, in fact, a dream or a nightmare. How was he not thinking about what happened last night? Now, if only I could forget it. The problem was, I didn't know if I wanted to. The bigger problem was I wanted him to do it again. I was so screwed.

As soon as we walked into the house, Jude took his smug ass into the shower. When the water turned on, I was able to let out a breath. Being on pins and needles all day was exhausting. Of course, the prick who put me in this mood was completely unaffected.

How was it men could do that? It was like they had a switch connected to their brain like a remote control, and with just a flick, they could change the channel. I'd love to get off the all-Jude-all-the-time network.

I flopped down on the bed and bounced slightly along with the small throw pillows. A nap would be lovely. Maybe that was what I needed to rid my brain of all things Jude. God knew I didn't sleep much last night. As soon as I closed my eyes, I heard him singing. Seriously? The pillow that bounced toward me now was being used to muffle the sound of his voice.

I couldn't help but notice what song he was belting

out beyond the bathroom door. Was he even serious? I Touch Myself by the Divinyls? He even changed the lyrics to include my name.

Frustration grew, and for once, I disliked how small this house was. That's when I remembered the prize we won. Yes, a couple's massage sounded perfect. I opened the envelope containing a card we needed to fill out with our preferences and leave in the basket on the porch.

I glanced at the bathroom. The door was still closed and Jude was still singing. Taking a pen from my bag, I began to fill out the form. We needed to tell them what types of massages we wanted based on the choices given. So, for Jude, I picked deep tissue, which sounded awfully painful, and for myself, a relaxing reflexology massage. Also, whether we preferred a male or female masseuse.

Tapping the tip of my pen on the table, I contemplated the best answer for this. Hedging my bets, I picked both. If the guy was good looking, I'd take him. If he was older and creepy, Jude could have him. Then again, if the woman was gorgeous, I'd take her since Jude would make a field day out of it. All I could do was hope for a hot guy and an older woman named Helga to show up.

♡♡♡

All my sleeping habits changed since I started sleeping next to Jude. He was always eager to let me know I snored and hogged the bed. Occasionally, I'd feel my foot brush against his leg or my hand graze his chest. That was when I squeezed a pillow between us as a barrier.

However, most of the time was spent staring at the ceiling. It had been three days since his act of kindness, or whatever he called it. Seventy-two hours, and still no mention of the way he touched me, kissed me, and made my body feel things it never had before.

We'd wake up, have breakfast, chat about the weather and what we were going to do for the day. It wasn't easy pretending anger when all the man did was walk around half-naked. Clearly, to him, it was nothing special—just another woman under his Swedish spell.

I stared at the window, waiting for the sky to lighten. Jude grumbled something I couldn't understand. When I turned to look at him, he had a grimace on his face. Maybe he was having a bad dream. Rather than waking him, I got out of bed, grabbed my robe, made a cup of coffee, and sat on the deck. A gentle, warm breeze blew across the beach. I tucked my knees under my chin and stared out at the waves, waiting for the sun to rise.

It was probably a good thing we were getting our couple's massages today. That thought put a smile on my face. Not only could I use a good rubdown, I was curious to see if my requests would be carried out. Granted, it all could backfire, but a girl could dream.

"You're up early." Jude's deep voice echoed in the still morning air. He walked up to the chaise next to mine and sat down. Of course, he only had a pair of boxer shorts on.

"You know, wearing shorts isn't against the law." I took a sip of my coffee before enjoying the sunrise.

"I am wearing shorts." When I glanced at him, he smirked.

What was it about this man that made him get under my skin? Right before I was going to give him a witty reply, my inner voice reminded me of why I was dealing with this nonsense. *Eye on the prize . . . eye on the prize.*

"I'm going to go shower. Don't forget our masseuses

are coming today." I stood, and Jude's eyes raked up and down my body. The way they fixed on my robe, I almost thought he had superhero powers and could see through it. That was enough to spur me to move faster.

Damn that man. Resting my hands on the bathroom vanity, I looked at my reflection in the mirror. "Don't fall for him, Brae. He's just a means to an end." I nodded at my own words and decided I needed to find that magic switch in my brain. Turning off how his presence sent a spark through every cell within me wasn't going to be easy, but it had to be done.

I pulled the shower curtain closed, hoping the hot water would soothe my nerves. After I washed up, thoughts of his hands on my body plagued me. *Dammit, I should have picked number two.*

Jude

BRAE WAS TALKING TO TWO people out on the deck. They didn't look like a couple. The woman looked like she could be the guy's grandmother. Maybe they were out on the beach for a walk. We hadn't really seen a lot of people over the nine days since we'd been here.

"Good afternoon." I stepped outside and all heads turned toward me. With an extended hand to the woman first, I introduced myself, "I'm Jude."

"I'm Svetlana." Her strong Russian accent mirrored the grip on my hand. Damn, she could shatter bones. My eyes landed on her chin. More specifically, the long hair protruding from a nasty mole.

Suppressing a grimace, I said, "Nice to meet you." She released my hand. "This is Blase." Svetlana motioned toward the man standing next to Brae, who had a wide smile on her face.

"Blaine?" I reached out my hand.

"No, Blase. Like a hot fire." Brae was all too eager to correct me. "Svetlana and Blase . . ." she put an extra emphasis on his name, "are here for our massages."

No way. Just as I was about to say exactly what I was thinking, the Russian woman grabbed me by my forearm and said, "You with me." Her broken English was almost as terrifying as her grip. She pointed at Blase. "He take care of her."

Brae giggled at something preppy boy said before he handed both of us a white cotton robe. "We'll be back in fifteen minutes. Please, go change, and then get under the sheet. You can leave your undergarments on—or not." He winked at Brae, and I saw red.

Back in the house, I set the robe on the chair while Brae went into the bathroom to change. Not giving a flying fuck if she saw me changing, I decided to strip down to nothing before putting on my robe.

"Are you ready?" Brae's hair was now pulled up into a knot on top of her head. Her sleek neck looked extremely inviting. "I'm so stiff, I could use a good rubdown. I hope Blase likes using oils," she quipped, a glint in her eye.

Just like always, she knew how to get to me. Not wanting to have a tent form under my robe, I thought of Svetlana's mole and all was good. I knew what Brae was doing. Well, two could play at that game.

A thin white sheet covered both tables, which were three feet apart from one another. This wasn't like a spa. Being out in the open, hearing real waves rather than manufactured ones . . . it was relaxing.

"This is lovely." Brae said before releasing a calming breath. We stood between the tables, facing each other. She cocked a brow. "Do you mind?" Swirling her finger in a circle, she added, "Please turn around."

It wasn't long until I heard the creak of the table. That's when I turned, caught her eye, and dropped my robe onto the sand. Standing in all my glory without a care in the world, I smiled at her. Her eyes raked up and down my now naked body, and I almost did a jig at seeing her jaw drop a bit.

Rather than saying anything right away, I stood there so she could get a good look, stretched my arms above my head, and twisted the upper part of my body toward the ocean, then back toward the house. "Nothing like enjoying a bit of nature." With my hands now on my hips, I cut my eyes to Brae, assuming she'd be face down in the donut style headrest, but she wasn't. Sparky was studying me. Her eyes were level with my dick, which was starting to show signs of life.

Svetlana and Blase came around the corner and stopped dead in their tracks. Both—yes, both of them—stared at me. "You get on the bed and cover up. I not give happy endings."

Brae giggled, and I did as I was told. With the sheet barely covering the top of my ass, Svetlana rubbed her hands together before squirting something on my back. It smelled like flowers and was warmer than the sun beating down on us.

"What type of massages are you giving us today?"

"Looks like you picked the deep tissue, and this pretty lady picked the reflexology." When I glanced up, Blase loud-whispered to Brae, "Great choice, by the way."

"Hold on a second. I didn't pick anything." Before I

could stop what was happening, Svetlana rubbed me so hard, it felt as though her fingers were under my muscles and in my ribcage. I grunted in distress, and begged, "Can you please switch mine to the Swedish massage? I heard they give the best ones."

Svetlana let out a "pfft," but changed her method—thank God. Finally relaxed and ready to doze off, I heard groaning. Then moaning.

"Mmmm . . . ahhh . . . ohhh . . . yes . . . mmmm . . . just . . . like . . . that . . . mmmm."

What the fuck was he giving her, an orgasm or a massage? "You okay over there, Kitten?"

"Mmmhmm. You have great hands, Blase. So strong. So intuitive. It's like you know what my body needs and how to satisfy it. Sooo gooood."

"I was all-star quarterback. Wait, did you just call her kitten?"

I lifted my head and glanced over Mr. All-American. "That's right, I did. She purrs in bed."

"Is that so?" Dickhead smiled at me. "Sounds like a great story."

"Don't pay attention to him," Brae said, her voice sounding like a porn star's.

Without giving me anymore thought, Blase resumed his ministrations on Brae's back, which was now glistening. I wasn't fond of this feeling coursing through me. I wasn't sure what it was exactly, but if I had to guess, I'd say jealousy—which was completely and utterly ridiculous.

Svetlana started using her elbows rather than her hands, and it felt like she put all her body weight behind each push. I bet she weighed more than I did and stood just as tall. Rather than my muscles relaxing, they did the opposite and stiffened in pain. Between that and Brae's orgasmic taunts, it was time to put an end to this.

"I think we're done here." I sat up, stood up, and wrapped myself in the robe. "Thank you, Svetlana, but I'm tired. I haven't been sleeping well."

"Oh, okay. Maybe go inside and take nap. Sleep is just as good for the muscles as is massage."

"Yeah, thanks." With that, I left Brae outside and went in to cool down. The sounds she made coupled with that tool she was flirting with having his hands all over her bare skin pissed me off . . . and that confused the fuck out of me.

Chapter 14

Brae

WALKING INTO THE HOUSE AND seeing Jude lying on his side with the quilt barely covering his boxer shorts wasn't what I expected. Guilt started to settle in my chest when I realized I'd ruined his massage. Yes, it was my intention because the man just infuriated me, but that made me no better than him. Why couldn't he acknowledge what happened between us?

Rather than shower, I decided to lie down. Every muscle in my body felt like a wet noodle. Blase had amazing hands, he truly did. I changed into a T-shirt and a pair of boyshorts. As slowly as I could, I pulled the covers back and slid into my side of the bed.

Jude's body shifted just as I laid my head on the pillow facing him. God, he was beautiful. Every inch of his skin was toned and perfect.

"Sparky?" I smiled at his nickname for me. I'd decided it was much better than kitten since I knew I didn't snore. With his eyes closed, he stretched his arm out, his hand landing on my hip. His lips curled up in a sweet grin, but he didn't say anything. When his eyes opened, they settled right on mine.

"Yes?" I asked, curious about what he was going to say.

"Did you have a good massage?"

"I did. It was amazing."

I prepared for an insult to come, or a snippy or snide comment, but with his eyes still pinned to mine, he simply nodded before saying, "I'm glad."

"Are you hungry?" I asked, trying to hide the shock in my voice over his civility. "I can make spaghetti. I'm pretty sure you can't botch spaghetti." By offering the gesture, I was hoping I wouldn't have to say I was sorry . . . loophole.

"Well, I'm sure *you* can find a way to, but I'm starving, so I'll take my chances," he teased with another sweet smile.

Jude was even more gorgeous when he smiled. The kind of gorgeous that literally knocked the wind from your lungs, left you speechless, rendered you stupid. I knew I should have moved my ass off that bed, yet there I remained, lying on my side, still staring at him while smiling right back.

The smile slipped off his face. The butterflies in my stomach felt like bats flapping their wings the longer I stared. Electricity bounced between us as if it was a living, breathing thing. He flexed the hand still laying on my hip. It was on the move, skimming my side, slinking under my T-shirt and around to my back, before it rested right above the curve of my ass. His touch was warm. Wondering what he was going to do next both scared and intrigued me to the point where I waited, stone still.

"Sparky?" he repeated, his tone much huskier this time, much lower than a few minutes ago. The levity was gone, replaced with a heated, penetrating gaze.

"Yeah?"

He closed his eyes, and I watched his brows pull together. "Stop me," he said, refocusing on my face.

"Stop you from what?"

As I waited for my answer, he shifted his entire body closer, eliminating the distance between us. His arm was no longer stretched straight, but slackened just enough, allowing him to rest his hand at the apex of my thigh and ass. His lips were so close, the slightest lean on my part would result in contact. I debated, argued even, whether I should or shouldn't. He had taken the liberty a few times now. It would only be fair for me to. Before I could act on my stupid rationale, he made the decision for me.

"From this," he said before pressing his lips to mine. The first few seconds were soft, sweet, tentative. When no resistance came, when the argument I should have voiced failed to find its way out of my mouth, he changed the kiss to something entirely different. Both hands now met on my lower back, his knee slid between my legs, and when his tongue skimmed over mine, back and forth, he tortured me in the best of ways.

I should have been embarrassed by the moan I released into his mouth, but it really couldn't have been stopped. And hearing it only seemed to fuel his determination. He pulled me into his body, causing the curve of his thigh to press perfectly against me. It provided just enough friction to cause an involuntary humping on my part. Again, I should have been embarrassed for shamelessly using his leg to try to get off, but I wasn't at all. When his moan came, and he followed my motions with his hips, it fueled me even more.

I tangled my fingers in his hair, holding him to ensure

the kiss continued. His hands moved up my back, one stopping in the center, the other sliding around and cupping my breast.

That was all it took. One simple cupping, a skim of his thumb over my hardened nipple, and I could feel the shocks of a small orgasm rippling through me. It wasn't nearly as intense as the first one he gave me, but it was just as satisfying.

He broke away, his breaths coming in short, forceful pants as he gauged my reaction to what just happened. Through my haze, I considered the orgasm score: two Brae—zero Jude. Even with my mind thinking out of sorts, I knew I needed to do something for him.

The silence between us became deafening, making my heartbeat even more amplified than it was. I removed my shaky hands from around his neck and slid them down his bare chest. One of his hands fell away from where he held my breast, landing with his knuckles pressed against the skin below my belly button. His lips parted ever so slightly as my nails traced over every bump and ridge of his abs. I could feel his eyes pinned to my face, but I wouldn't dare to look. If I was going to do this, I needed all the courage I could muster.

During our heated make-out session, the lightweight quilt shifted between his feet. With an impatient hand, I tossed it to the floor. Holy hell, every inch of this man was sexy. His feet, his calves, the way the muscles defined his thighs—every part of him was all male.

The fabric of his briefs left nothing to the imagination. My eyes focused on the outline of his erection as it impatiently pushed toward his waistband, desperately wanting to be let out. It pointed right toward the star tattoo closest to it, his tip causing a slight gap in the elastic running around his hips.

When I glanced at him, Jude looked angry. I knew him well enough now to determine it was also the same look he got when he was turned on. The way his nostrils flared, the way his brows tilted toward the bridge of his nose, were all effects of what little effort I'd already put into this crazy plan. I could only imagine what his face would look like once my mission was accomplished.

Refocusing on his lower half, I used my fingertips to peel away his underwear. Instantly, he sprung free. Without barriers keeping him confined, he stretched proudly toward his belly button. It could have been my tiny gasp, or the way my eyes bulged, or even the way my fingers halted their movements that caused Jude to say my name. Or, it could have just been his way of saying, *please don't stop*.

There he was in all his Swedish glory. God love a Swede. If I had a Swedish flag, I'd wave it with pride. If I knew his parents' address, I'd send them a thank you card.

My manscaping question was answered in the neatly trimmed hair showcasing his beautiful penis. I saw him outside before our massages, but it only now registered he was cut. "So, wait . . . you're circumcised?" I blurted out, then clamped a hand over my mouth.

He looked down and smirked. "Wow, look at that, Sparky. It seems I am."

"Very funny." My entire body flushed from head to toe. "You're European. Doesn't that mean you wouldn't be?"

"My dad's a surgeon." After a long, uncomfortable pause, he said, "Do you want me to formally introduce you?"

"Wait, to your dad?"

"No, Sparky. My cock."

"I'll take care of that introduction." The smug look on his face intimidated me, but I'd gotten this far, there was no way I'd turn back now. I dragged his briefs down his legs and repositioned myself between his spread thighs. Being so close to his manhood almost made me giggle with thoughts that maybe I *should* introduce myself. A quick glance at his face caused the giggling instinct to immediately fade. Sporting his sexy angry face, his greenish-brown eyes drilled right through mine. Just as I placed his tip on my tongue, he groaned and bucked his hips, wanting more.

A sudden surge of courage controlled my actions. Keeping my eyes pinned to his, I trailed my lips up and down his length. I gripped him at the base and stood him straight up, pointing toward the fan rotating above our heads. The first few seconds, all I did was tease him, working him up with every long swipe of my tongue. I had yet to cover him with my mouth, and the anticipation he felt was obvious in the way he flexed his fingers into the sheet beneath him.

I covered the head of his cock with my mouth, and he hissed at the contact. The angle of my body between his legs wasn't working well, so I lifted to my knees, allowing myself the access I needed. I took him as far into my mouth as I could, my hand working the part of him that wouldn't fit. I tightened my lips around him as I slowly moved down toward my fist, then loosened them as I dragged my tongue back up his underside toward his slit. Hard and firm going down, loose and teasing going up . . . over and over.

He dug both hands into my hair and had a firm grasp on my head. If any other man ever did that to me, I would have immediately stopped and walked away, but having

Jude do it caused a delicious clenching deep within me. I was as turned on now while pleasuring this beautiful man as I was when he pleasured me.

The moans coming from his mouth, the way his fingertips tightened on my head, and the way his thighs flexed beside my knees all told me he was dangerously close to reaching his breaking point.

"Brae, I'm coming." With his admission, he tried to pull my mouth away from him. I removed one hand from his base, and slid it under his thigh to anchor myself to him. He didn't argue. He didn't try to stop me again. Instead, he clutched the pillow behind his head, his eyes closed shut. I took the opportunity to study his reaction. His abs flexed, showing their definition through every bump and crevice. The muscles of his arms bulged as he white-knuckled the pillow. And then, his lips parted just as he released into my mouth with a guttural groan.

Never had I been so eager for a man to finish as I was in that moment. Never had I wanted to accept every drop he offered without wanting to flinch away once I did. For the first time in my life, I enjoyed every goddamn minute of a blow job.

"Holy fuck," he said when he opened his eyes. I remained on my knees, leaning back on my heels. "Brae." He reached for me, and I accepted his hand to lay beside him on the bed.

I waited for him to say something, anything—and once again, he frustrated me with his silence. I tried not to let my anxiety bubble to the surface, but the longer I lay there, the harder it was. He tilted my chin upwards with his thumb and index finger. His face searched mine before he asked, "Are you okay?"

"Yes, I'm fine," I rushed out, my eyes deceiving me by cutting to the side.

Based on the confused look on his face, he clearly wasn't buying it. But he obviously didn't care enough to say anything else. What was I expecting him to say, anyway? *Oh hey, thanks for doing a stellar job sucking my dick.* No, but something like "that was amazing" would work. I knew he enjoyed it, that was blatantly obvious . . . but it would have been nice to hear that he did.

While still holding my chin, he leaned closer and kissed me. Before it could progress, I pecked him back and darted to the bathroom. "I'll be back," I called over my shoulder.

With the door firmly closed, I stared at my reflection and sighed. A soft knock preceded an even softer, "Brae?"

"I'll be right out." I needed time to think, and quickly jumped into the shower to buy that time.

As I figured it, I had three choices. Go out there and pretend it meant nothing, just as he did. Go out there and talk to him about it. Or, go out there and tell him off. If there was one thing I wasn't good at, it was pretending. My parents always teased me about how my feelings were always so visible on my face. So, option one would probably not work well for me, and option three wouldn't work well for him.

Either way, I couldn't hide in the bathroom forever. After drying off, combing out my hair, and dressing back into what I had on, I opened the door, expecting to see him lying on the bed, his eyes focused on the door. What I found was an empty place where his stunning body had just been.

The sound of pots clanging clued me in. I turned the corner and there he was in his briefs preparing dinner. Just as he flung a dishtowel over one shoulder, he looked up and smiled.

"I can do that," I said, coming closer to take the pot from his hands. "I did offer to cook tonight."

"No, I've got it. Go relax. It's the least I can do after you . . ." He glanced up, and upon seeing my face, stopped mid-sentence. "Um . . . did my laundry yesterday," he finished with a devilish smirk.

"Okay." He raised a brow at my lack of a comeback. Undeterred, I poured myself a glass of wine and went outside to my happy place.

☆☆☆

Jude

I WAS DETERMINED TO FIGURE her out. It was frustrating as all hell. Just when I thought I had, she threw me off once again. I'd teased her before, both verbally and physically with random kisses and touches, but never had she responded like she did today.

When she pushed herself against me as we were kissing and humped my leg to climax, my initial thought was that masseuse riled her up. However, when she blew me as fucking fabulously as she did, I knew it had to be me who riled her up.

So then, why the hell did she run yet again? Why was she looking at me the way she was? These questions ran through my head like a puzzle begging to be solved. Brae Daniels was one of the most complicated women I'd ever met. But, being the man I was, I loved a challenge. And the one I was currently living with was most definitely a doozy—albeit, a hot one.

As I prepared our meal, my thoughts replayed the last twenty minutes. Maybe she was PMSing, and that was the reason for her mood swings. I knew enough about women to know not to dare mention that. Growing up with five sisters, I knew to back away slowly and shut the hell up.

I opened the back door and called for her before plating our pasta. If I waited until then, by the time she ran through her feet cleaning routine, it would be cold.

She appeared a few minutes later, just as I placed our plates on the table. "Smells good. What is it?"

"Spaghetti Carbonara. I hope you like it."

She quirked a brow when I pulled out her chair, but sat without a word, allowing me to push her closer to the table. Aside from my random comments, conversation was brutally awkward between us. The more she simmered over whatever she was angry about, the more I wanted to call her out on her mood.

"That was so delicious. Thank you." She surprised me and spoke before pushing away her plate. "My plan for spaghetti was to open a jar of sauce and smother it over the noodles."

"Yeah, no. That's awful," I shuddered.

"Well, I'm impressed you managed to whip up a carbonara sauce in less than thirty minutes."

"And I got you to eat bacon," I bragged shamelessly.

"Yeah, well, I was too hungry to argue. And the way you chopped it up into the tiniest of pieces made it impossible to pick out," she said with a raised brow.

"You can pretend all you want, Sparky. I know you loved every tiny piece of it." A *swoosh* had us both glancing at the door. There on the hardwood floor sat another envelope. I flew to the door and yanked it open, but to no avail. "I'm going to catch that fucker one of these days," I said with a smirk.

I lifted the envelope and read out loud, "Brae and

Jude." Her groan caused a chuckle. "What's wrong, Sparky?"

"I'm dreading what they'll have us do next. Diving for pearls? Swimming with sharks?" She stood, taking our plates to the sink.

"Nope. Sand castles."

A grumble and a few inaudible words preceded a sigh. "What are you griping about, Sparky?" I came to stand behind her, watching her take out her frustrations on the poor dish. "I think this is clean enough." Leaning over, I pulled it free from her slippery fingers. "What's wrong with sand castles?"

"I haven't exactly hidden the fact that I despise sand. It gets everywhere, and it itches."

"We're living on a beach, Sparky. It's kind of unavoidable." Another chuckle from my lips worsened her scowl. "You are by far the strangest woman I've ever met."

"Stop making fun of me."

"That would make things boring." I tossed the card on the counter. "It's a reward challenge, so like it or not, we are kicking ass for this one. We get five days to practice. We'll start in the morning."

"Great," she mumbled. "I'll design it, and since you're so good at everything, you can build it. Something big and annoying, I'm sure you can think of the perfect design." She mumbled something else I didn't hear.

"What's that, Sparky?"

"I said, maybe we should consider a donkey for the locals. You're familiar with them, right?" The snark in her voice was obvious.

"That's it." I turned her as the water still poured from the faucet and held her upper arms to keep her from running. "Okay, now tell me what really has you all pissed off." She thinned her lips and folded her arms in defiance. "Well?" I prodded. Still nothing. I slammed the faucet off and hoisted her over my shoulder.

"Put me down, you jackass!"

"No."

Her wiggling while trying to get down was in vain. With one arm wrapped around the back of her thighs, I guaranteed she wasn't going anywhere. For good measure, I added a hand on her ass beneath the fabric of her shorts and nearly moaned when my fingers felt a thin scrap of lace.

"Hey!"

"Oh please. Now you're getting modest?" I asked as I carried her out to the beach toward the ocean.

"What are you doing? I just showered, Jude. Have you lost your mind?" Ignoring her, I flipped one shoe off her foot, then the other. Replacing my hand on her ass, I kicked off my own shoes while never breaking stride. The closer I got to the surf, the more she struggled in my arms. "Jude, stop. Okay, I'll talk. I'll talk!" she squealed.

I stopped when my toes reached the water, tightening my grip on her thighs and ass. When she said nothing, I took another step. "Okay! What do you want to know?"

"Let's start with why you're angry."

"I'm not angry!" Another step had her saying, "I'm just annoyed."

"At me?"

"Yes."

"Why?"

Silence. Another step.

"Because."

Another step.

"Stop! I'm talking," she gritted out through clenched teeth. I couldn't see her face, but I laughed anyway at what it must have looked like. That earned me a two-fisted punch to my ass.

"Ow. Talk faster, Sparky."

"Maybe most of the women you seduce are okay with your 'love them and leave them' act, but I'm not."

"Love them and leave them? I know English is my second language, but what the fuck are you talking about? I haven't left, I'm right here."

"Ugh, I don't mean literally. It doesn't matter. Put me down."

Step. The waves now hit above my knees, splashing the bottoms of her feet.

"Jesus Christ. Jude!"

Step.

"I'm now doubling my steps if you don't talk. The sun is just setting and the surface of the water is shimmering with golden highlights. It's a shame you're missing it, Sparky, and being forced to stare at my ass instead."

Silence. Two more steps. The water was now to my waist, soaking her feet. She kicked up a leg, drenching us in the process. "You're already so wet. I may as well finish this."

"No! Okay, after you did . . . you know, to me."

"Ate you out?"

"Must you always be so crass?"

I lifted my leg dramatically and she squealed. "Wait. Stop. Yes, when you ate me out. You ruined an act of kindness by making it all about you. Don't do me any more favors, I'm fine *without* your acts of kindness."

"You didn't enjoy it?"

"That's not the point."

"No? Then fill me in. I'm still lost here. I made it all about you, yet I still enjoyed every minute of it. I can still taste you on my tongue. I can still hear your moans in my head. So, explain how you interpreted all that as a bad thing." She squirmed against me, forcing a satisfied smirk on my part.

"You acted like it never happened." She went very still and her hands loosened around my waist. "And then you walked away without a backward glance." The last part she said so quietly, I barely heard her.

I turned and walked back toward the beach stopping to slide her down the length of my body. She wouldn't look at me, but her pink-tinged cheeks deepened in color the more I stared at her face. Forcing her to meet my eyes, I asked, "I thought you were embarrassed for letting me do that to you, and for enjoying it. I didn't want you to feel uncomfortable. I never meant to hurt your feelings."

"You did it again, earlier. It took a lot for me to . . ." She looked away again, and I gripped her chin, turning her face back to mine. "For me to do that to you. I don't even know you well enough. I wanted to please you, and I also enjoyed it. Probably more than I should have, which caused even more confusion on my part. But then there was nothing but awkwardness between us. No 'thank you', no kind words on your part. I'm not the type of girl who engages in casual sex." Her eyes shimmered in the dusk. She blinked a few times and shrugged. "So, now you know."

I had no idea my actions affected her as much as they had. Now that I knew, it fucking hurt to know I hurt her. There was no logical explanation; it didn't make sense.

Yet here I was feeling bad regardless. It was obvious the more time I spent with her the more I liked her. This, though, went way beyond like. As I stood staring at her beautiful face, I realized I cared about her. This woman, who I was thrown into a very unorthodox situation with, was beginning to make me care. And it went beyond just caring about a friend. I'd never felt this way for anyone I was friends with.

Friends. Were we even friends? We went from strangers to roommates. Now we were roommates with benefits. What the fuck did I get myself into? Fucking Kyle. All these foreign feelings were his fault, and now I needed to deal with them while trying not to hurt Brae or myself in the process.

I raked my hand through my hair before pulling her into my arms. She remained wooden against me, until I said, "I'm sorry, Brae." At my words, she relaxed against me. Once she did, I tightened my hold on her.

After a few long seconds, she sniffed and pulled away. "You okay?" I asked, now afraid anything I said or did would hurt her feelings.

"Yeah. I'm sorry. I guess I'm not handling this all that well. I can't be good at everything," she quipped with a lopsided smirk. Her admission made me smile.

"Well, I can." She shoved me playfully, causing me to laugh. "Hey, I'm not handling this any better than you. So, I guess we'll have to figure it out together."

Chapter 15

Brae

WE CROSSED SOME SORT OF threshold in our relationship. I began to feel like I overreacted. He really wasn't a bad guy. It was obvious in the tiny little things he did that often showed his true colors—like making me dinner, even after I said I would.

After he forced my confession, he led me to our lounge chairs and helped me to sit. Then, in a very sweet move, he pushed his chair flush against mine to eliminate the gap between them.

The rest of our evening was spent lying side-by-side while drinking wine and talking. For the first time since we met, we had a real conversation about his likes, and mine. He shared stories from his days at Yale, and had me in tears over hearing the trouble he and his friends had gotten into.

"Tell me about you, Sparky." Even in the moonlight, his eyes sparkled when he used the nickname he assigned me.

"What do you want to know?" I took a long sip of my wine. Something told me I would need some liquid courage.

"Ever play twenty questions?" He flashed me a cheeky grin. "Aside from the questions you asked the night I met you."

I laughed at the memory of his answers that night. "That reminds me, could you have been any cruder?"

"Oh, trust me, the answer is yes. Don't change the subject. Ready?"

"No, but why do I have a feeling I don't have a choice?"

Jude let out a chuckle. "You're learning. Okay, I'll go first."

Draining what was left of my wine, I handed him the glass. "Refill first."

He leaned over and grabbed the bottle sitting beside him on the sand. Once my glass was replenished, I took in a few cleansing breaths before nodding. "Okay, ask."

"How old were you when you lost your virginity?"

"Wow, you're not wasting any time." His eyebrows arched, waiting for my reply. "I was eighteen." His head bobbed forward, assessing my answer. "What about you?"

"Fifteen."

"You were young."

Jude shrugged. "She was older. I went to a party at a sorority house and hooked up with someone. She may or may not have known my real age."

"So, it was meaningful, and a felony." I wasn't sure whether it was my nerves or the wine, but I was the one laughing now. "Sorry, that was rude."

"Was yours?"

"Was mine what? A felony? No."

"No, Sparky. Meaningful?" I thought about my first time. It was sweet, gentle, but I wouldn't say it was meaningful. He gauged my shrug and nodded, thankfully not prodding further.

"Okay, next question." He narrowed his eyes, and asked, "Have you ever kissed a girl?"

God, how I wanted to lie and tell him I did in college just to get a reaction out of him, but I couldn't. "Not in the way you're imagining."

"Shame, that would have been an awesome visual."

"I'm sure it would have. Sorry to disappoint you." I suppressed a laugh, but he didn't. God, even his laugh turned me on.

"That's okay, I have a great imagination." He winked at me. "Were you attracted to Blase when he touched you?"

Where the hell did that question come from? "That's two questions. Blase did have great . . . hands," I said with a waggle of my eyebrows. He grimaced at my comment, and now it was my turn to laugh. "No, Blase isn't my type."

"Who is?"

I shook my head. "Nope, it's my turn to ask. Did Svetlana turn you on?"

"More than you know." We both laughed. "You set me up, didn't you? What did you do, fill out a questionnaire asking for a manly woman with brute force to come over?"

"Not exactly." I took a long sip of my wine, feeling his eyes on me.

"Yeah, yeah. Nice try. I'm on to you, Sparky."

"You have no proof."

He shook his head, amused. "Are you close with your parents?" he asked, changing the subject.

"Very. They're really all I have aside from the friends you met." Thinking about everything my parents had been through over the past few years, the hardships they've endured, saddened me. It also fueled me to see this through to the very end. "Does your family live here or in Sweden?"

"Sweden." His lips turned down. "I miss them."

"How often to you visit?" I asked, wondering if I would have to spend time in Sweden. It didn't matter. I'd visit Timbuktu if it meant winning the money.

"A few times a year. During the holidays and usually in the spring," he said with a faraway look on his face.

"You said you had five sisters. Where do you fall in the lineup?"

"Youngest, but we're all very close in age. Two of my sisters are twins. My parents were busy making babies for about a dozen years."

"Wow, five girls, one boy, all about two years apart? That must have been fun when you were growing up."

"More so chaotic," he admitted on a chuckle. "Dad worked around the clock. I already told you he was a surgeon . . . thoracic. He lived at the hospital for most of my childhood. It was up to Mom to hold down the fort."

"Was?"

"He retired." Jude refilled my wine glass without request.

"Thank you." I stared at the burgundy liquid, contemplating my next question. "How mad were you when I picked you?"

He raked his hand through his hair, practically

scrubbing his scalp. "I'll admit, I was pissed. Especially since I tried my damnedest not to be picked," he said with a sideways glance. The cords in his neck tensed as he worked down a swallow. "This is nothing I'd ever sign up for. I have a business and being out of touch with the real world is the worst part of this game. I pray every day it's not imploding while I'm stuck frolicking in the Caribbean with you."

Stuck? I turned away to hide my disappointment. I knew how he felt about being here . . . and really, I felt the same. Regardless, it stung a bit hearing him voice it out loud.

"Are you sorry you chose me?" he asked. "Spark number one was pretty perfect."

"No. I'm not sorry." My cheekbones rose with my smile. I didn't want to rehash my motive for picking him. Bringing up the reasons I chose him would open a can of worms. I dropped my gaze to my hands before meeting his eyes again. "So, now that we're here, are you sorry I picked you?"

Without hesitation, he said, "Not at all." His immediate admission lessened the sting of his earlier comment and left me wondering why it meant so much to hear.

We sat back in comfortable silence, nursing our wine and staring at the ocean. I let out a yawn and rested my head on his shoulder. "Is this okay? I'm getting sleepy."

"Of course. But if you're tired, we can call it a night and head inside." He wrapped his arm around my shoulders and placed his hand on the small of my back.

"Maybe in a little while. I'm too comfortable to move." Closing my eyes, I let the sound of the waves take over all the thoughts swirling around in my head. With a gentle touch, Jude's hand started rubbing my back. The warmth from his palm soothed me through my cotton shirt. After a few minutes, I lifted my head and looked at him. "Thank you."

"For?"

"This."

He placed a sweet kiss on my forehead, causing a shiver to run through me. "Let's get you inside. You're cold."

I nodded, although the reason for the goosebumps pebbling my flesh had little to do with the ocean breeze. We stood and Jude gathered the wine bottle and our glasses. Everything seemed different tonight. Even the air in the house seemed lighter.

"I'll wash the glasses while you go do what you do in the bathroom." He turned the faucet on and laughed. "You're something else, Sparky."

I wagged my finger at him. "Don't mock my nighttime ritual." Turning to get ready for bed, I paused. "Jude?"

"Yeah?" He wiped his hands on the towel before laying it over the handle of the stove.

"It was nice getting to know you better." Before he could reply, I smiled and headed into the bathroom.

Closing the door behind me, I looked in the mirror. "I think you just made a new friend." That thought alone spurred me to go through my nighttime steps a bit quicker than normal.

Jude was standing with his back to me, gazing out the window. "It's all yours."

"It's about time." He walked by me and smiled.

The bed sheets were cooler than the air. Nestling myself in, I rolled onto my side and gathered the quilt around my neck while staring at Jude's side of the bed.

My eyes slid shut before I heard, "Scooch over, Sparky." Jude stood behind me, lifting the covers to squeeze himself on the small space of mattress.

"What are you doing? This isn't your side of the bed."

"Does it really matter? In about two hours, you'll commandeer the entire mattress." His hand snaked around my waist as he bent his knees behind mine, causing my ass to rub up against him. "I'm being proactive."

"Is that what you call it?" Letting out a playful huff, I wiggled against him, and he stiffened behind me, groaning out my name. "What?"

"Truth is, I just want you in my arms tonight, but if you move your ass like that again, I can't be held responsible." The huskiness in his voice was hard to misinterpret. His hold tightened on me as the fine hairs on his legs tickled my bare ones. I laced my fingers with the hand pressed against my stomach. I felt his breath fanning my neck—something I was sure I could get used to.

"Jude, can I ask you a question?"

"Sure."

"Do you still feel like you're in hell?"

His response was immediate. "Not in the least."

I smiled even though he couldn't see it. "Goodnight, Jude."

He kissed the back of my head before replying, "Goodnight, Sparky."

To most, living day after day in a tiny cottage on the

beach with absolutely nothing to do would get old quick. And if we hadn't turned the corner in our relationship five days ago, I may have been one of those people. But truth be told, I was enjoying our time together. His incessant teasing no longer bothered me. I wasn't as uptight over his sexual innuendos, and I often gave back my own dose of clever comebacks.

With barely any outside human contact this past week, we could have gotten on each other's nerves, yet that hasn't happened.

When a new feisty housekeeper came by for the weekly cleaning of the cottage, her grumbling over the fact that there was nothing to clean caused Jude to laugh at my expense. The others before her were much more polite than Muriel. She pulled the knife from under the mattress, and in her heavy Caribbean accent, asked, "What is this?"

"Security," I said with a shrug. She rolled her eyes and mumbled something that sounded suspiciously like "wacko." Hearing him cracking up caused my own fit of giggles. The more she glared at us, the more we lost it.

When the groceries for the week were delivered, Jude told me to stay where I was lying in the sun and he'd go put them away, only to come back with a can of whipped cream behind his back and stage an attack of epic proportions. He chased me around our beach, spraying me the entire time as I screamed and giggled. By the time the can went dry, we were both covered in a white sandy stickiness, which we washed off in the ocean.

And when he took us out for a ride in the little dinghy, he surprised me with a packed lunch of peanut butter and jelly sandwiches. As we floated on the turquoise sea, he serenaded me with the Swedish national anthem, claiming he really didn't know all the words to any other songs except the one by the Divinyls. The man could have been saying the crudest things to me, and I wouldn't know it. Every so often, he grinned, and I wondered if he was indeed changing the words to his benefit. Either way, hearing his native tongue in any form was sexy as hell.

Today was our sand castle competition. Walking hand in hand up the beach to our destination, he smirked down at my drawstring bag and shook his head. "What's in your backpack, Sparky?"

"Nothing."

He narrowed his eyes with suspicion. "Tell me what could you possibly need when we're only twenty feet from the house."

"No, you'll make fun of me."

"You are too much." He laughed at me and shook his head. "Ready to make a kick ass castle with me?"

I nodded enthusiastically. Wow, have I been abducted by aliens? Not once did I think about the sand I would be digging into with my bare hands in just a few minutes. Not once did I consider all the places sand would end up. All I thought about was his hot body in that tiny European cut bathing suit while he used muscles sure to put on a spectacular show.

The visual made me giddy, and he noticed. "What's so funny?"

"Nothing."

"I can always tickle it out of you," he threatened just as an older man, who really shouldn't have been wearing a Speedo, clapped his hands and hooted.

"Heelloo, lovebirds. How are we on this fine, fine day?" He bounced up and down on his little legs, causing things to jiggle. I immediately averted my eyes as Jude snorted. His jovial demeanor and Humpty Dumpty physique had Jude and I fighting to hold in our laughter.

Our babysitter for the day then said, "I'm Felix, and I'll be judging your work today. Ready to get nice and sann-deee?" he asked, stretching the word out to six syllables. Without breaking eye contact, Jude squeezed my hand, which caused a giggle to erupt.

To cover for my silliness, Jude cleared his throat, and said, "We're ready."

"Okay, let's get started," Felix whooped. "You will have one hour to create your masterpiece. You'll be judged on teamwork, communication, and creativity. But there's one catch." He walked to a small table containing the variety of tools available to us. A small handheld shovel and things that looked better suited to be in a child's sandbox were scattered across the surface. From the clutter, Felix lifted a pair of handcuffs. "You must complete your castle while being handcuffed—together."

"Hell yes," Jude said, just as I said, "Seriously?"

He leaned down and whispered into my ear, "I may swipe those for later."

I was sure he was kidding, but the idea both terrified me and thrilled me regardless.

"Are you two ready?"

"One question. What is the reward?" Jude asked with a grin.

"Sorry, it's a surprise." Felix shook his head. "But I will tell you it will be quite delicious. Any other questions?" We shook our heads simultaneously. "Excellent." Motioning us closer, he asked for our wrists. Jude repositioned himself to my right, offering his left wrist.

I wrinkled my brows. "What are you doing? I'm a

righty."

"So am I, and it's more important for me to use my right hand than it is for you."

I put my hand on my hip. "Is that so?"

"Yes, Sparky. It is. I predict I'll be doing most of the work, therefore I need my good hand. Am I wrong?"

I huffed. "No."

"Good." Taking the cuffs from Felix, Jude snapped one side onto my right wrist and the other to his left. The cold metal sat heavy on my skin. That combined with the warmth of his arm pressing up along mine caused goosebumps to riddle my flesh.

Felix then clapped his hands once, and said, "Okay. Go!"

Without warning, Jude lunged to the table, dragging me behind. He grabbed two buckets and then marched down the beach toward the ocean without breaking stride.

"Ow," I whined, practically jogging to keep up. "I'm going to bruise."

"Sorry, but you need to move your ass faster, Sparky. We only have an hour. I'll rub it better later." He looked down at me and his heated gaze caused my bikini bottoms to dampen.

Jude was the only man who could annoy me and turn me on in the same breath. He was also the only one I'd want to.

Chapter 16

Jude

WHO COULD HAVE PREDICTED ROLLING around in the hot sand with a bikini clad brunette beauty would have been absolute torment—in a salacious way? Every time her smooth thigh pressed against my leg, or my left hand brushed her boob, it was pure torture.

Hiding the effect she had on my cock wasn't easy while wearing nothing but a small swimsuit. Bending forward while working on our masterpiece turned out to be a huge blessing in disguise. It wasn't for fear that she'd see my cock hardened to painful proportions, but more so that if she did and unintentionally gave me a welcoming response, I couldn't guarantee I'd be able to ignore it.

On the one hand, taking her right there on the beach beside our medieval castle may have won us this stupid game. On the other, when the day came that I took her, it wouldn't be in the sweltering heat on a sandy beach with a rotund man looking on.

Felix came over with a tiny silver key and unlocked our cuffs. Brae began rubbing her wrist while moaning in relief. Taking her hand, I resumed rubbing the red welt marring her skin. Her eyes looked up into mine just as she bit her bottom lip.

"Congratulations," Felix said while our eyes remained locked in some sort of a trance. "I was most impressed with your teamwork, communication skills, and final results. You have achieved a very high score in all categories. Your reward will be delivered tonight to your cottage." When we still hadn't looked his way, he cleared his throat, and added, "I'll give you some privacy."

His last comment caught Brae's attention. "What did he say?"

"He said he'd give us some privacy."

Her head twisted from side to side. A few people were scattered way up on the beach to the left, sunbathing and swimming in the ocean. No one was nearby, nor were they paying attention to us. It would have been very easy to act on my urges.

"So, we won?"

I nodded while staring at her lips. "Yes, Sparky. We won."

In an abrupt move, she stepped away, pulling her wrist from my grip. "It feels better now, thanks," she said, avoiding my gaze. With the distance between us, there was no hiding my hard-on any longer. When she looked back into my eyes, she appeared nervous.

"What's wrong, Sparky?"

"Nothing." Turning her head, she focused on our castle, but the rosy tinge on her cheeks gave her away. She was just as turned on, just as wired as I was. "I did a great job," she quipped, tilting her head slightly to give me a sideways glance.

"*You* did a great job?"

"Yes." She pointed to the tiny flag she stuck in the highest tower. "That was my idea. And that moat, it's perfect. But what I think won it for us was the detail I put into the brick façade. You're welcome."

The look on my face and my hands on my hips caused her to break out into a fit of giggles. The sound of it, the look of pure unguarded happiness on her face, and the way her hot body looked in that damn royal blue bikini was what had me propelling toward her. She froze for a moment before she took off running down the beach. I caught up quickly, lifting her and dropping to the sand with her in my arms.

Pinning her arms above her head, I said, "Admit I won us this contest." She shook her head in defiance. "Sparky, last chance," I warned, a gleam no doubt in my eyes.

"No," she retorted, her lips twitching.

I switched my grip into one hand and used my free one to tickle her relentlessly. "Stop, Jude!"

"Say it, Sparky!"

"No. I won." She squirmed beneath me, giggling while twisting and turning, trying to break loose. The more she wiggled, the more our bodies lined up perfectly. The moment my cock pressed against the nylon fabric of her bikini bottom, she immediately halted her movements, her eyes darting to mine.

We were completely covered in sand, and that fact confirmed she was as preoccupied as I was. Because instead of insisting I let her up so she could brush it off, she lifted her head and kissed my lips.

That one move caused a chain of events that started with us writhing in the sand while making out and ended with her on my back as I sprinted us back to the cottage.

"Wait, I forgot my bag."

"Fuck your bag."

On a mission, I bounded up the few steps to the cottage. "Wait! We're all sandy."

I halted my steps and turned to look at her. "Seriously, Brae?"

She tightened her grip around my neck. "Let's go for a swim. Please?"

The woman was a fucking tease—intentional or not. The way she said that against my ear and the way her pussy pressed into my lower back as her thighs tightened around my waist was fucking me up. With a sigh, I turned and bolted for the ocean. When I got to the water, I twisted her around my body until she straddled my front. Pausing with my hands holding her up by her ass, we came nose to nose. The look in her eyes made me want to fuck her right then, right there.

Salty waves splashed up at us, but the coolness of the water was not helping my disposition in the least. The nylon fabric of her top now looked as if it was molded to her body. My thumbs grazed the sides of her tits, coming very close to her pebbled nipples. I focused on her lips and moved in closer, surprised to see her tilting her head back. Our eyes met again before hers darted around the beach. Even though I knew no one but the two of us were present, it didn't prevent me from looking as well.

"Jude, we can't." All the playfulness that had been in her voice vanished. From the time we were rolling around in the sand to then, she must have snapped back to her senses. The lust that had been visible a few minutes earlier was now replaced with apprehension and fear. It wasn't the right time . . . she wasn't ready.

Reluctantly, I set her down, the water now resting just

below the top of her bikini. All I could do was stare at her. Maybe I'd been reading the signals wrong, or maybe it was my dick doing the thinking lately.

"Are you okay?" She worried her bottom lip.

No, I'm not. I need to fuck you. I need to feel you, was what I wanted to say. But we still had a few weeks left together. If I spewed my thoughts, she might be turned off completely and I could be left sleeping on the hammock.

"I think I'm going to stay out here for a bit. I won't be long."

Brae's eyes searched mine as she nodded her head. "Okay. I'm going to go take a shower. I have sand in places it shouldn't be," she said with a forced laugh. "I'll leave a towel for you on the porch."

"Thank you."

I watched her hot body walk away and adjusted myself under the water. I needed to reel in my shit and figure out what was going on in her head. Taking advantage of the water, I dove in under a gentle wave and realized I needed to figure out what was going on in my own head first.

As the water supported my back, I looked up at the sky. This would all be so much easier if I'd met her at a club, picked her up—because I definitely would have—and had a one-night stand. But here, neither of us could leave after we had sex. The problem was, if she felt awkward afterward and shut down on me again, I now knew one time with her would never be enough.

My feet hit the ocean floor, and I looked at the home we were currently sharing. Fuck, I was so confused. What I did know for sure, Sparky was different than other women. Now I needed to figure out what to do about it.

Just as she promised, a nice clean towel was waiting

for me on the railing. I dried off and washed the sand from my feet, chuckling to myself as I did. Boy, did she have me whipped.

When I walked into the house, there was a note sitting on the table addressed to both of us. Since the envelope was opened, I read it. We were being awarded a gourmet dinner for winning the sandcastle challenge. Our instructions were to dress for a fancy dinner, which would be held on the beach behind the cottage, at 7:00 p.m.

Brae's hairdryer turned off just as I was looking through the clothes hanging in the closet. Thankfully, I had appropriate attire for this evening. The bathroom door swung open and my mouth went dry at the sight of her. She looked gorgeous. Her skin had taken on a golden color, which glowed against the pale pink strapless dress she had on. The soft fabric hugged every one of her curves, making me jealous of a dress.

"Oh. I didn't hear you come in." Her fingers clenched and unclenched at her sides. She glanced at the clothes I'd laid out on the bed. "I gather you saw the note?"

"Yes." I took a step toward her. "You look stunning."

"Thank you." A blush crept up her cheeks and a shy smile spread over her lips.

"Are you done in there?" She nodded as her eyes focused on my chest for a moment. An awkward silence passed between us, one I didn't particularly care for. "Okay, then, I'm going to take a shower."

"Okay," she said as I walked past her. Before entering the bathroom, I looked back at where she still stood with her back to me. She hung her head before her shoulders visibly relaxed. Feeling dejected, I closed the door behind me and prepared for yet another cold shower.

The sun had begun to set, making the ambiance as romantic as they'd intended. Candles were on the white linen covered table set with crystal glasses and dishes that looked like fine china.

"Wow, they outdid themselves." Brae's voice was a hair above a whisper.

"Yes, they did." I pulled out her chair, and when she sat in it, her dress rose higher on her thighs.

A bottle of champagne sat in a chilled bucket to the right of the table. After I sat, I pulled it out and poured us each a glass. Her eyes studied the bubbles dancing to the top of the flute. Right as I was going to raise my glass to toast, a deep voice bellowed.

"Welcome." An older man approached us wearing black pants and a white suit jacket. "I'm Allesandro. It will be my pleasure to serve you this evening. Tonight, you will be enjoying a lovely five-course meal, which has been prepared with you in mind. I see you already found the champagne, so now take a moment to revel in this wonderful view." He motioned toward the horizon as the sun was setting. "A beautiful evening for a beautiful couple. I will be back shortly with your first course." With a bow of his head, he left us.

When I looked at Brae, her eyes were fixed on where the sun just set. Something needed to relieve the tension I knew I created, so I broke the ice. With my glass in the air, I cleared my throat. "I'd like to make a toast."

Her eyes cut to mine. She lifted her glass, but not before shifting in her seat a bit.

"To getting to know one another, for making it through our first few weeks, and to handcuffs." I wasn't going to say the last part, but her face was so stoic, it made me edgy.

With a weak smile, she said, "Cheers."

Normally, I wasn't a big champagne drinker, but this went down in one smooth sip. "Brae, can I say something?"

With a nod, she set her glass down. "Of course."

"I'm sorry for what happened earlier. I didn't mean to push you. It's just . . . this is all weird for me."

"What is? Being with a woman for more than a day?"

Pouring myself another glass and topping hers off, I shrugged. "No. Wanting to be with a woman for more than a day. You intrigue me, and sometimes I feel like I really don't even know you. We share a bed, share a home, and I've collectively spent more hours with you than I have with any woman I wasn't related to." I reached across the table and placed my hand on hers, which was fiddling with the salad fork.

"Believe me, this isn't how I planned on spending my time. But I need to be here. It's important that I see this through to the end, and I know I've been acting on edge . . . it's just that you scare me."

Not knowing whether I should pull my hand away, I did the opposite and squeezed hers a bit tighter. My thumb made gentle circles on her soft skin. "I didn't mean to scare you. Just say no and I'll stop any of my advances. Maybe you should consider a scuba suit when we have water activities. You in a bikini makes me lose my mind."

That compliment earned a genuine smile. "You don't scare me like you're going to hurt me. I'm just all over the place. This is all so irrational." She took a sip of her champagne, draining the glass. "If I didn't—"

Before she could continue, Allesandro was back with

our first course. "The chef has prepared gorgonzola stuffed figs wrapped in prosciutto and drizzled with honey." He set the platter down. "Enjoy."

I couldn't help but laugh as she bit into one of the figs. "You know, prosciutto is Italian bacon."

"Yes, I know that, but it's not fried, so the caloric intake is less," she shot back, smirking. Wiseass Sparky was coming back to me.

"True." I took a bite myself. These were delicious. A drop of honey sat in the corner of her mouth and without thinking, I reached over and gathered it with my thumb before placing it in my mouth. "Can you finish what you were going to say? If you didn't what?"

Wiping her mouth, she said, "If I didn't need the money, I wouldn't be here, but you know this."

"Why do you need the money so badly? I know you said you were unemployed, but you seem intelligent and should be able to get a job."

Her lips turned down as she expelled a long breath. "The money isn't for me—not really. And even in our vast city, replacement jobs aren't easy to come by."

What the hell was she talking about? Why would she put herself through this? What could be so important? "Who is the money for?" I asked, then my heart sank, thinking maybe one of her parents was ill. "Is it one of your parents?"

Tears shimmered in her eyes. She quickly picked up her glass and took a sip. "It's for both of them."

Holy shit. "Are they sick?" *Please say no.*

"No." Thank God. Now I was the one exhaling. "The bank is getting ready to foreclose on our family farm. They fell on hard times and had to take a second mortgage. I've been helping, but now that I'm out of a job, I can't make the payments."

"I'm sure they'd understand if you told them," I said, my eyes sliding to the side as Allesandro approached to clear our plates.

When it was just us again, she said, "They didn't know I was helping. Since I took over the books when my dad fell ill, I'd made a deal with the bank. I gave them a percentage of my earnings and they applied it toward the debt." Brae dropped her head in her hands. "I can't believe I quit my job. How selfish of me."

"Selfish? No, you're anything but selfish." She looked up and smiled, and my heart clenched at the sight of it. "So, you need the money in order to keep the bank from foreclosing on your parents' farm, which they know nothing about?"

"No of course they know but they didn't know my part in it. My parents think they have more time."

"Can you borrow money from a friend?"

She scoffed with a short sarcastic laugh. "My friends offered, but they don't have that kind of money. Even if they did, I'd never accept that from them."

How much do you need and I'll write you a check, I wanted to say, but knowing she would never accept it, I said, "Then it looks like we're in this together until the end." At least being here with her gave me the opportunity to help.

Music started to play off in the distance and I stood, holding out my hand. "Dance?"

With her hand in mine, we took a few short steps to the makeshift dance floor. Brae eyed me up and down. "You clean up nice. I like you in blue."

Apparently, Kyle did something right when he packed my lightweight navy suit, white shirt, and pale blue tie.

"Thank you."

Taking her in my arms, we began to sway to the music. Having her chest pressed against mine, my right hand on the small of her back and my left one holding hers felt right. No, it felt perfect. I was once again consumed with a foreign feeling. All I wanted was to hold her and make everything better. All her worries, I wanted to take on myself.

Fuck. I was falling for this woman. What the hell was I going to do now?

Chapter 17

Brae

BEING HELD BY JUDE FELT right. We moved as if we had danced together for years. Allesandro arrived with our main course—grilled lobster tails with drawn butter and lemon—and replaced our empty bottle of champagne with a fresh one.

We sat back down and Allesandro took the liberty to refill our glasses before walking away. "Wow, Jude, I can't believe you drank that entire bottle."

"Me?" He pointed toward my glass. "You're the one who appears to love the bubbly." I ignored his comment and took a sip. He cocked one brow. "I rest my case."

Jude dove right into his lobster, dipping a piece he'd cut off into the melted goodness while I squeezed the lemon wedge on mine.

"No butter either?" He chuckled. "It's the best part."

I could feel my nose crinkle. "Do you know how many calories are in butter? If I ate everything you did, I'd be a ball with limbs. You gain muscle like a freak of nature, whereas I'd grow cellulite."

"You're insane. You really don't realize how beautiful you are, do you?"

His words hit me straight to my core, automatically commencing my Kegel exercises. "Maybe if I ate what you recommended, I wouldn't look this way, ever think of that?"

Jude chuckled while dipping another piece into the butter filled ramekin. "Like I told you before, there are ways to burn off those calories."

More clenching. At this rate, my hoo-ha was going to be in the best shape of its life.

"Just try it." He extended his fork across the table, small droplets of butter landing on the linen tablecloth. "Open wide."

With a hard swallow, and trying not to look like someone who wanted more than what was on the fork, I licked my lips before taking his offering into my mouth. In the most seductive way, I pulled the succulent bite off with just my lips. A moan escaped me as I began to chew. It was mouthwatering, just like him.

"Mmmm. . . . it is delicious."

His gorgeous eyes darkened. "Please don't do that."

"What did I do?" Feeling embarrassed, I dabbed my lips with my napkin.

"You moaned. You have no clue what that does to me."

Needing to change the topic before my muscles squeezed the hell out of my vagina, I asked, "So, I know you come from a large family, you're Swedish and clearly a successful business man, but what I don't know is why you're here aside from the fact that Kyle signed you up. Why would he do that?"

Jude shook his head. "Because he's a dick."

I couldn't help but laugh, but that didn't answer my question. "And . . ." I prodded.

"Kyle, Luca, and I have a habit of pranking each other. This is his payback. A while back, I set him up on a blind date and she turned out to be a he. Well, I knew his date was a man, but Kyle didn't. In my defense, Randi was better looking than some of the women he had gone out with. Personally, I thought I did him a favor."

Jude broke out in a laugh and I followed suit just picturing it. "That's awful."

He shrugged. Then his words sunk in. "So, you're here because of a prank?" Sadness lined with fear hit me square in the chest. I was here because I needed to be and he was here because . . . of a joke? The smile fell from my face. "This isn't a joke to me, Jude. Based on your perfectly tailored suit, your Ferragamo shoes, and everything else about you, I can tell you don't need the money."

Suddenly losing my appetite, I set the fork down and leaned back in my chair, feeling utterly defeated.

"Sparky, I'm not going to abandon you. Just because my ex-friend thought this would be funny, I know you need to finish this to help your parents. I won't let you down."

"I want to believe you, I do. It's just . . . lately, being let down seems to be the norm for me. I'm not trying to turn this lovely dinner into Brae's pity party, I'm just stating a fact. Please don't make me regret picking you." As soon as the words escaped my mouth, I regretted them.

Jude's eyes narrowed on me. "I just said I won't let you down. Even though you're this complex woman who clearly loves to drive me crazy, I also know you wouldn't allow me to help you outside of doing this together."

"Thank you. I'm sorry. Let's talk about something else."

Before we could say more, Allesandro was back to clear our dinner dishes. I hadn't even touched my asparagus or baked potato, but it was hard enough finishing the lobster, and I loved lobster.

Rumba music started playing—the same song we danced to during our lesson. Jude looked at the small wooden floor. "Shall we?"

I smiled and took his hand. Aside from our hips pressing together, we didn't dance the typical Rumba. We just moved together in an intimate way. Being there in his arms caused an immediate swell of desire—enough to throw my steps off kilter. Tightening his grip, he looked into my eyes. "Are you okay?"

"Yes. I think the champagne is going to my head," I fibbed . . . kind of. I was feeling the effects of the alcohol, but it was Jude who had me all discombobulated. I felt like every cell in my body was electrically charged. I wanted this man desperately, yet worried it would change everything between us. "Mind if we sit?"

"Of course not." He led me back to the table just as Allesandro appeared again. I was stuffed. There was no way I could eat another bite. That was, until he placed a chocolate lava cake drizzled with salted caramel in the center of the table. Two forks leaned up against the plate. I dropped Jude's hands like they were on fire.

"Let me get this straight," Jude eyed me as I dug in with my fork, "you won't eat bacon or butter because they're fattening, but a chocolate cake is okay?"

I shrugged. "Dark chocolate is good for you." The gooey sweet confection danced around my taste buds, soliciting another moan from me. Did I always moan when I ate?

"You're killing me, Sparky."

Jude hadn't tasted the cake yet, so just as he did with the lobster, I took a piece with my fork and held it out to him. He cocked a brow before taking my fork in his mouth. A smear of chocolate rested just under his bottom lip, and without conscious thought, I got out of my chair, sat on his lap, and licked—yes, licked the chocolate off of him.

His eyes widened and his hand on my hip tightened when I fused my lips to his. I pulled away, and seeing the smoldering look in his eyes caused my head to spin. "Chocolate is a terrible thing to waste. It's also an aphrodisiac."

"How drunk are you, Sparky?" I wasn't that drunk, just tipsy. But I suppose this was out of character for me. When I released a hiccup, he laughed. "I think it's time to go inside."

"Can we make-out?" Before he could decline the offer, I kissed him again. No sooner did I pull away, he stood up, grabbed the champagne, and carried me in his arms into the house.

"Still want to make-out?" He set the champagne bottle on the nightstand.

And then some, I wanted to say. Instead, I nodded. He lowered me until my feet hit the floor and began to remove his clothes. Was it possible that he got hotter as the day wore on? When he pulled his shirt over his head, exposing those sexy stars, I answered my own question with a "yes."

"I'm going to show you my favorite way to drink champagne." His voice was merely a growl.

"How's that?"

"Ever hear of body shots?"

"Of course. I'm not a nun."

"Lose the dress."

In just his tiny dark blue boxers, which I appreciated even more since they matched the suit now laying on the floor, he laid down on the mattress.

He repeated in a deep seductive command, "Sparky, take off that dress or I'll take it off for you. If you like it, I suggest you do it, because I'll be ripping it off."

Knowing how much I spent on this tiny piece of fabric, I took it off myself. Jude's eyes widened when he saw the pink lace bra and matching thong.

"You've been half-naked all night?"

I looked down like an idiot, confirming that I was indeed half-naked. "Looks that way." A jackhammer now took up residence in my chest as his eyes raked over every inch of my body. Part of me thought this was wrong—the tiny sober part. Naturally, I ignored the little angel in my head, reached around my back, and watched my bra hit the floor. Before I could lose my nerve, I removed my thong.

"Jesus, Brae." Jude's hand went to his crotch as he adjusted himself. "You're fucking gorgeous."

My nipples immediately went hard. I could actually feel my skin stretch into tiny peaks. "Why am I the only one naked?"

Without hesitation, he took off his boxers. Even though I'd seen his penis before, I still gawked in the most unflattering way. "Why are you all the way over there?"

"Is there any part of you that isn't toned and

spectacular?"

"Nope." He smiled. "Now, grab that champagne and get your sweet ass on this bed."

The glass bottle was cool to the touch. Then as provocatively as I could, I slid onto the mattress. Jude sat up, took the bottle from my hand, and drank. He then held my head and kissed me, forcing the cool champagne into my mouth. I didn't think I would ever be able to drink champagne from a glass again.

"More?" he rasped.

"Yes," I said with baited breath.

After another swig of Jude flavored deliciousness, he instructed me to lie down.

"Too bad we don't have those handcuffs." Jude's eyes never left mine. "I'd love to cuff you to this bed."

All I could do was blink. Doing my best to get the handcuff visual out of my brain, I admitted, "Yeah . . . too bad."

"We'll just have to be creative without them." Jude took a sip from the bottle before releasing the cold bubbly liquid onto my stomach. It pooled in my belly button and slid down my sides onto the sheet. My body shifted as I watched the bedding darken from the liquid.

"If you're even thinking about the sheet below you, it can be washed."

I rolled my lips between my teeth. This man knew me better than I thought. "I wasn't thinking that."

He shook his head. "Just like you believe you don't snore. Keep lying to yourself."

Again with the snoring. Before I could defend myself, I felt his tongue. Warm, wide, smooth strokes lapped up the champagne from my body. Jude took another sip and released it into my cleavage. My back automatically arched, causing it to flow onto my neck.

Jude leaned over and licked me clean again. "I want some," I said, my voice a heavy sigh.

He smiled and tipped the bottle toward me. "No. I want to drink it off you."

We switched places. Jude was now on his back, I was on my knees at his side, and his dick was looking at me. God, how I wanted to lick it. Rather than take a sip like he did, I tipped the bottle and watched a small stream trickle onto the ridges of his stomach and each nook filled. Starting at the highest star tattoo, I licked my way down. My chin hit his hardened tip, a groan burst from his lips.

Leaning back again, I took a sip of the champagne and swallowed it. "You're not sharing . . ." All at once, I took him in my mouth. "Sparky, shit . . . Brae . . . God . . . damn . . . you have to stop . . ."

After one long drawn out lick, swirl, and suck, I released him. "I'm sorry, I just wanted a taste."

"Don't apologize, but . . . I won't be able to hold back." Surprising me, he started trailing his lips across my chest before latching onto a pebbled nipple.

"Jude."

"What? I also just wanted a taste." He briefly looked into my eyes. "Is that okay?"

"Yes, I was going to say don't stop." A stunning smile spread over his face before he resumed the path he took with his lips. To my disappointment, he traveled north instead of south. From my breast, he skimmed his tongue over my skin until he reached my earlobe. My disappointment didn't last long when I felt his hand roam down over my belly to right between my legs.

At my long, guttural moan, he said, "Sparky, you know what that does to me." Without stopping his hand, his mouth found mine and he swallowed my next moan.

My legs automatically fell open for him, my hips lifted with each stroke of his finger, and when he slowly slid one inside me, I felt it in every part of my body. His mouth never left mine and he mimicked the movements of his fingers with his tongue.

I tried to reach for him, wanting to hold him in my hand, but as quickly as the thought entered my mind, it flew out. All I could do was lie there and try to remember to breathe through one of the most erotic moments of my life. How strange that all the times I had sex or even fooled around with a man, none compared to how hot it was kissing him as he fingered me.

He pulled away for a moment, and I grabbed his head, forcing him to continue. I needed his mouth right where it was as I clenched around him during a fucking fabulous orgasm. The teasing between us all day caused the sexual tension to literally explode, the epicenter right between my legs.

"Shit, Sparky. You're so tight," I heard him say.

"Kegel," I heard me say.

He nibbled on my neck as his fingertips gently stroked my clit. If I weren't so tired, he would literally be igniting my spark all over again. *Hehehe*, I thought to myself. That would make a great ad campaign for this competition. My eyes slid shut, and then the last thing I heard him say was, "And Kitten is back."

Chapter 18

Jude

PURR . . . RUMBLE . . . SNORT . . . WHISTLE.

Purr . . . rumble . . . snort . . . whistle.

Purr . . . rumble . . . snort . . . whistle . . . growl?

I rubbed the sleep out of my eyes before realizing my kitten had turned into a tiger. Once she passed out on me, I finished the rest of the champagne by myself. I loved getting her off, and would never tire from watching her come, but the severity of my blue balls was becoming a problem. Remnants of all the champagne I drank last night made me feel sluggish.

The need to take a piss and a bigger need for aspirin forced me to attempt to roll out of bed, but I was stuck. My head pounded as I lifted it slightly to see what had me pinned. Apparently, even when passed out, Brae could commandeer the entire mattress.

Her leg hitched around mine like a vine on a tree. It took me a minute to figure out where she started and I ended. With a few more blinks, I was able to decipher between us. Lifting her leg, which still felt tacky from last night's body shots, I gently set it on the mattress.

She groaned right before rolling over onto her stomach. The sheet rested on her lower back exposing her sun-kissed skin. Giving my dick his morning adjustment, I headed into the bathroom.

After a quick shower, I downed an ibuprofen with a large glass of water. A few minutes later, I was back under the sheet next to Brae. God, she was stunning. Part of me wanted to grab my GoPro to capture her beauty, but I decided to pull her into my arms instead.

You'd think holding a sleeping woman would be easier, but of course, even Brae made this a challenge. I pulled her toward me, only for her to try to roll the other way. All I could do was grip her tighter and laugh.

"Mmmm . . ." Brae's mouth opened and closed a few times before her eyes squeaked open. "Did I eat cotton?"

Her body shimmied against me, causing her tits to rub against my chest. She craned her head back a bit and smiled. "My orgasmic orbit. Stars are my favorite." With another soft rumble, her head was back on my shoulder and she was out cold.

All I could do was stare at her. Sparky was definitely a natural beauty. I ran my thumb along the arch of her eyebrow, then kissed it. I did the same to her cheekbone, her jawline, and just below her ear.

"Jude?"

"Good morning, Sparky."

Arching her back, she stretched her one free arm up and let out a moan. God, how I wanted my mouth on her chest, to give equal consideration to each breast, to suck her nipples into hardened buds until she exploded. My hand decided to go for it, skimming up her bare torso until the weight of her left tit was in my palm.

"What are you doing?" She looked down. "Why don't

I have clothes on. Did we? Oh my God? We had . . . um . . . did we?"

I smiled at her. "No, we didn't. We had a lot to drink and when we do have sex, I don't want it to be because of liquor."

Brae laughed. "You said lick her." *Was she still drunk?* Suddenly, she yanked the sheet with two hands and wrapped it around her as she bolted out of bed, leaving me completely exposed.

"What are you doing?" It was my turn to ask.

"I have to pee, and brush my teeth, Mr. Minty Breath who also showered." She touched her neck. "Oh my God, I'm a sticky mess."

"Give me that sheet back."

"No and when I'm finished with it it's going in the laundry." At the bathroom door, she stuck out her tongue. I pretended to jump out of bed and the door slammed shut with an adorable giggle behind it. This woman was making me crazy.

After ten minutes passed, I sighed in frustration. Based on the amount of time she ended up spending in there, there was no way she was just peeing or brushing her teeth.

When thirty minutes went by, I called out, "Sparky, what the hell are you doing in there?"

The impatience in my tone was obvious, but I didn't care. There I was lying on a bed with my cock at half-mast and he and I both had the same resolution in mind. We had nothing to do today. The idea of walking around bored out of my mind with yet another serious case of blue balls was not on my agenda. One way or another, we were getting off. If not with her help, then I needed to get into that bathroom.

Finally, she opened the door with a coquettish smile—until she saw my cock. While my eyes raked over every inch of her, hers darted around the room, avoiding my hard-on. The sheet was still twisted around her body, her hair still looked like she just woke up, and her lips still looked like they'd been kissed for hours.

When I still hadn't spoken, she asked, "Are you covered?"

"No. You've seen me naked, Sparky. What the hell do you do in there? I seriously don't get it. You look just as hot as you did when you walked into that bathroom, so for the life of me, I can't figure out what takes you so long."

"Girl stuff."

"Is that like guy stuff? Did you touch yourself, Sparky? Because that isn't fair when you left me in this condition," I motioned toward my little friend. *Well, not little.*

"First of all, no, I did not." Her cheeks flushed pink as her eyes moved south on their own accord. "Secondly, that's not my fault," she said, pointing a finger at him, which caused him to jerk. Her eyes widened before she quickly looked away.

"Oh, yes it is."

Our eyes connected and held. Nervously, she changed the subject. "Um . . . do you want breakfast?"

"No. It's too early for breakfast. Come back to bed." I patted the sheet beside me.

She hesitated for only a few seconds before climbing back onto the bed while still wrapped in the sheet. "Why are you wrapped up and I'm naked?"

"Again, not my fault," she quipped, keeping a deliberate space between us. I wanted the way we were when we woke up back. I wanted her warm, silky skin pressed up against me, her breasts pushing into my side. I wanted my hands on her. Determined to bring us back to that point, that moment when she'd cave to my desires, I peeled away the sheet before moving her to my side.

"Much better." Now that her head rested in the nook of my shoulder, and my arms were back where I wanted them to be, I sighed in contentment. "I like holding you, Brae." I was shocked by my admission. I'd never considered just holding a woman while we were naked in bed. Sure, I wanted more, but with time. That also shocked the fuck out of me. Patience was not something I had in regard to sex.

She looked up and smiled. "I like it too." While her face was tilted toward me, I couldn't resist touching her lips. They parted when my thumb ran over her top one, then her bottom.

Her hand ran up and down my abs as her gaze slid to my tattoo. "I love these stars." I watched as she traced the biggest star with her fingertip. My body flinched from her touch. She hit the one spot that was ticklish, plus her proximity was fucking torture.

"Are you ticklish there?" She giggled and did it again, clearly fascinated by her discovery.

If I admitted I was ticklish, I knew her well enough to know she would aim for that spot on a regular basis. If I admitted it was also a fucking major turn on, maybe her touch could turn into more. Before I could respond, she popped up on her elbow, causing her tits to bob with her movements. "How did you sit for a tattoo if you're ticklish there?"

"Probably because I didn't find a needle rapidly hitting my skin while leaving a permanent image funny. And probably because I was fully dressed as a big scary dude drew it, not naked with a hot chick like you touching me there."

"That doesn't make sense. Dude or not, a needle right here . . ." she tapped the star with a knuckle and I bucked, "you could sit still for, but if I do this . . ." She traced the star with her fingernail, causing me not only to flinch again, but to suck in air through my teeth. At my reaction, the corners of her lips lifted in a devious smile.

"Don't look at me like that, Sparky. I know your weaknesses too." The hand I had on her waist flexed, while my other began to roam.

She stiffened, and pleaded, "Okay, don't tickle me. I'll be good."

"I wasn't planning to. We should hope you never fall into enemy hands, Sparky. All they'd have to do is this . . ." Unable to resist, I let loose on her, tickling her relentlessly as she squealed and squirmed against me. My plan to torment her somehow morphed into her tormenting me. When her thigh grazed my engorged cock, all thoughts flew out of my head except for the one that had consumed me for days . . . I needed her.

She went stone still in my arms, understanding what had made me immobile.

Without further thought, I speared my fingers into her silky hair and crushed her mouth with mine. Her lips parted and I took that as an invitation. Just a taste wouldn't suffice, but it would be a start. Our tongues touched like long lost friends needing to get better acquainted.

Brae let out a sweet moan, and her fingers flexed on my back before moving to the nape of my neck. My cock was getting harder by the second. I pushed my hips forward to try to get some friction just as she wrapped her leg around me.

As if on autopilot, my hand grabbed her thigh, massaging and squeezing it. It trailed up to cup her ass. Brae moved her hips against mine, and I groaned at the pressure. That small move made my need to sink into her even more evident.

With our mouths still fused together, my hand found and palmed her breast, giving it the same attention I'd given her ass. She broke our connection to let out a moan.

"Jude. God, that feels so good." She arched her back, forcing more of her soft flesh into my hand.

Both of her nipples pebbled, begging for attention, and who was I to deny them? I took her nipple into my mouth, licking, sucking, and then giving it a gentle bite. While ravishing her other tit, I dragged my hand down the length of her torso, resting it right above the apex of her thighs.

Brae rolled onto her back, giving me full access to her body. Every inch of her was pure perfection. I moved over her, my entire body pressing hers into the mattress. Like magnets, our mouths connected again, her arms wrapped around my neck, her legs around my waist. Fuck, we were on the fast track too soon, and I needed to slow things down. So long as we were on the same page, I was going to take my goddamn time with her.

I slipped both hands behind her back, forcing her up as I moved into a kneeling position. Her legs fell from my body so she could mimic my stance. My cock rested at the seam of her thighs, wanting in—wanting all of her. Forcing myself to break away from her lips caused her to groan, "No."

"I'm not going anywhere." She looked up into my eyes, her chest heaving with every breath. With my eyes pinned to hers, I trailed my hands down to her breasts, holding them, running my thumbs over her nipples. I only paused briefly before their downward trek to her thighs. My gaze shifted to her lips, watching her tongue poke out and drag from side to side.

When I reached her thighs, I slipped my hands between them, forcing her to spread her knees on the bed. With her now open for me, I moved my right hand to her pussy, my left to her ass. She released a gasp the moment my finger skimmed her clit. Taking my time, I stroked her from front to back. Her eyes slid shut as she moved herself against my hand and flew open when I stopped.

Before she could speak, I twisted around, laid on my back, and guided her hips above my face. I could feel the moan that erupted from her lips travel through her body. My mouth found her clit and held on for a long ride.

I had no warning to prepare me for the hot, wet silk I felt closing around my cock. Bucking upward at the contact of her mouth on me, she made sure to quickly catch me up to the level of ecstasy I had built up within her. By gripping me tightly with both hands and by sucking on my tip, she managed to make me forget what I was doing to her. She never stopped, even though I had. My balls tightened, my hips lifted, and just as I came, I covered her with my mouth, licking and sucking until she came with me.

"Jesus Christ, Sparky." I kissed the inside of her thigh and flipped her around to face me. My lips caught hers once more before she slid off my body.

"You have a great mouth." She placed a chaste kiss on my jawbone.

Turning my head toward her, I smiled. This woman made me happy—and not because she just sucked me off. Everything about her was fascinating.

"My mouth is nothing in comparison to yours. I don't even want to know how you got so good at that."

Brae giggled. "A woman never reveals her secrets."

I licked my lips, wanting the taste of her to stay, but I needed more. "You don't need to tell me your secrets. Just tell me you're ready for round two."

"Don't you need time to reload?"

"No. I'm good to go. Are you ready?"

Thankfully, there was no hesitation before she nodded. "This is going to change everything. You know that, right?"

"I'm counting on it." Her eyes widened at my admission. "Brae, being with you, no matter how unconventional, has been interesting to say the least." She went to say something, but I placed my index finger over her lips. "What I mean by interesting is I haven't wanted to pull my hair out. Yes, we got off to a rocky start, but who wouldn't in our situation? The fact of the matter is I think we're good together." I kissed each of her fingertips one by one.

"Are you going soft on me?" Her smile was radiant.

I glanced down at my cock. "Nope, just the opposite."

"Lucky me." Brae moved her fingers along the line of hair running down my abdomen. "I love this." She looked up at me. "You're a sexy man, Jude Soren."

Rolling my body on top of her, I took her mouth with mine. She spread her legs and the tip of my cock slid against her wetness. My hands held her head as I looked into her eyes. "Are you ready for this?"

"I am," she responded confidently. "I want this, Jude."

I shifted my hips as I said, "Obviously, you can feel that I do too."

"Yes, I can. All kidding aside, I just want you to know it's not casual for me. I can't pretend it won't mean something."

Her admission hit home. I knew it wasn't for me either. I might have been confused in regards to our relationship, but I also knew what we shared was not meaningless. "Brae, despite what you think, nothing we've done has been casual for me."

"Thanks for telling me that." She bit her bottom lip before her mouth turned up into a shy grin.

"Do you have a condom?"

"I do." Not wanting to, but needing to, I rolled off her to grab a condom out of my bag in the closet.

"So, I was a sure thing?" My heart stopped as I tried to work down a swallow. Shit.

I put my hands up in defense, exposing the two packets in my palm. "I didn't think that. Blame Kyle, he's the one who packed my bag."

"And how many did Kyle pack?"

My gaze landed on the closet containing a carton of them. "Um . . ."

At my fumble, she laughed and crooked her finger. "Come here and remind me to thank him when I see him again."

Sparky was spunky. "I'll be sure to do that." Climbing back on the bed, I asked, "Now, where were we?"

Chapter 19

Brae

MY HEART POUNDED WITH SUCH force, I was sure he could hear it. The confidence I exhibited was a ruse. If he knew how very nervous I was, he'd never stop teasing me. I was a grown woman, not a virgin by any stretch of the imagination, and in a few weeks, I could be married to this man. I'd had sex with men I knew a hell of a lot less than Jude, and was a hell of a lot less attracted to.

This shouldn't be a big deal . . . so why did it feel like it was?

What was it that caused my freak out to the point where my palms sweated and knees trembled? Now that he was right there, lying beside me, it was harder to act cool. I was mesmerized by the way his sexy hands ripped open the foil packet. The way he watched me watch him roll the condom onto his length sent my heartbeat into overdrive.

Actually, I did know why I was spiraling in a vortex of uncertainty. I couldn't believe we were really doing this.

Reaching over, he pulled my lip from between the

confines of my teeth. "Are you okay? Brae, we don't have to . . ."

"No, Jude. I want this," I repeated, and it was the truth. There was no way I would turn back now. I've had this man in some very intimate ways, and this was the one way I wanted more than anything. Even though a tiny nagging voice in the back of my mind reminded me of my goals, I pushed it aside, arguing this was only helping me reach my goals. But was it? Would it help if things didn't end well? Again, I pushed the negativity out, refusing to go there.

He studied my face before nodding. "I do too. You're a beautiful woman, Brae. And I don't only mean your appearance." He paused, his brows pulling in, making it seem like he was deep in thought. I waited for him to say something else, but he didn't. Instead, he held my face between both his hands and bent his head to kiss me softly. It wasn't passionate by any means, and it wasn't the explosion of heat that usually detonated on contact, but it was by far the most meaningful kiss he'd ever given me.

His lips traveled over my face, stopping to kiss each of my eyes and my forehead before moving back down to my mouth. He placed a few more soft kisses against my lips, then he was on the move again, this time kissing my neck, below my ear, and the hollow of my throat. The way his scruff left a delicious bite of pain below my chin caused my thighs to clench.

After a few moments, he lifted his head to stare into my eyes. I desperately wanted to know what he was thinking, yet at the same time, didn't. If his thoughts weren't on the same wavelength as mine, I couldn't pretend it wouldn't hurt.

But what he said next gave me all the confirmation I

needed for now. "Brae, I think I've wanted you from the moment I kissed you on that stage." He positioned himself between my legs, pausing so his tip pressed against my clit. "I also think we've waited long enough."

His eyes fixed to mine, he found my hands and laced our fingers before raising them above my head. Right when my heart swelled from the emotion etched on his face, Jude slid inside me . . . one . . . damn . . . inch . . . at . . . a . . . time. The way he filled me was nothing less than perfection.

"Fuck, Brae. You feel amazing." I swallowed on a slow nod. Words failed me. In fact, if I didn't concentrate on my breathing, I'd probably start hyperventilating over the swell of euphoria that engulfed me. Having him deep inside me, staring into my eyes, and holding my hands in his grip was erotic on so many levels. Even the way his thumbs ran circles over my palms as he pushed into me had my muscles deliciously contracting.

It could have easily been a quick fuck, but he was making it so much more. Whether it was his style or me crossed my mind. Jude would be the type of man to make every woman he fucked feel special. Deep down inside, the romantic part of me that was sick of worrying about foreclosures and money, desperately wanted it to be me who brought this out in him.

Unfortunately, young in life, I learned romance was a fairy tale only found in storybooks or movies. My real life forced me to do something as crazy as this social experiment, devaluing the sanctuary behind true love and marriage. That reality kept me grounded most of the time—until now. With him, I literally felt like I was soaring, as insane as that sounded.

My eyes welled as he tightened his grip on my hands and positioned his hips so perfectly against mine. With each slow drag, the emotions within me battled, causing them to spill out in one tiny tear. He watched it roll down my cheek.

"Brae," he whispered my name with so much emotion, I smiled despite the conflict I felt inside—the divide between wanting this and not wanting to want this. My smile seemed to comfort him into returning one of his own.

"It just feels so good," I admitted the first thought I could that wasn't a lie. It did feel good. He didn't need to know it also felt both right and wrong at the same time.

My impending climax came closer with each thrust. The way he struggled to hold back was etched in every facet of his face. Forcing myself out of my own head, I lifted one of my legs to wrap around his hip. The position caused his eyes to slide shut on a guttural moan. He released one of my hands and gripped the back of my thigh, holding my leg against his body.

This man was the epitome of perfection. The mess of wavy hair on the top of his head from constantly running his hand through it, the seductive curve of his lips, the strong angle of his scruff covered jaw—these were all minor details in his appeal. It was more so the way his greenish-brown eyes drilled right through me, like he wanted to devour me. The way his breath came quick and fast, fanning across my face. The way he said my name as if it was the most important word in his vocabulary.

"Brae, I'm close," he said, his accent thickening on my name.

"Me, too. Don't stop, Jude."

"Never, Brae."

Without conscious thought, the sound of his voice and the way his body skillfully manipulated mine combined to push me over the edge whether I was ready or not.

Jude

EVERY MUSCLE IN HER PUSSY gripped at my cock as if it was meant for her. I almost forgot my own name. Somewhere along the line, it went from hot sex with this woman to so much more. Unprepared to feel something while fucking, other than what I normally felt in my cock, stole any coherent thought I had floating in my head.

One tear escaped from her eye, they remained glassy with emotion. I wanted to know whether it was sorrow that caused her to well up or if what she admitted was the real reason. Remembering how I acted after our first encounter, and our second, which caused her to withdraw was why I cupped her face tenderly. I wasn't good with words during sex, and on instinct, my brain wanted to shout out crude comments. It was just the way I was wired. Yet, with Brae, it felt wrong.

She said nothing as she came so perfectly around my cock. I, however, uncharacteristically, said just what I was feeling. "I mean it, Brae. I never want this to end." I pushed harder and faster through my climax, enjoying every goddamn second of it, memorizing everything I was feeling, until I released every ounce I held deep inside her.

A random thought of doing this one day without a condom, of owning her in a way I'd never owned a woman before, lengthened the duration of my orgasm.

"Fuck, Brae. You feel so fucking perfect," I huffed while spearing her, over and over again.

Her fingers gripped my back, and she whispered my name as I buried my face in the crook of her neck. The apple scent of her hair and silky texture of her skin beneath my lips overwhelmed me, confused me, and scared me all at once.

God, this woman was exquisite. It wasn't fair for me to have her shoved down my throat when I wasn't looking for anything she represented. I wasn't searching for that *one* person. Yet, now that I knew her, I couldn't remember why my sex life prior to now was anything special.

Fucking Kyle. What the fuck did he do to me?

She remained quiet as I practically crushed her body beneath mine. It felt too good to move. But I knew I had to, and I had to say something. The longer I waited, the more I'd inadvertently hurt her.

I lifted my head to stare into her eyes. What stared back was an unsure beauty battling her own onslaught of confusion. I skimmed my knuckles across her cheek with a smile. Her expression mirrored mine.

"That was perfect, Brae. You're perfect." Before she could respond, I kissed her soft lips, pressing mine against hers for a few long seconds. Her arms tightened on my back, and while still inside her, I realized how badly I wanted the moment to go on. My normal urge to flee, to distance myself and run, was nowhere to be found. Just the opposite—I wanted to stay just as we were. It felt right.

When I finally pulled out of her warmth, I shifted to her side and laid my head on her chest. Her fingers continued to caress my skin. I wrapped my arms around her waist, clutching her. I may not have spoken much after we were done, but through touch, I let her know I meant what I said, and she let me know she felt the same.

Without words, we communicated that we were both feeling exactly the same way.

After a few long minutes passed, she said, "I'll be right back." Nodding against her breast, I loosened my hold and watched as she left our bed to walk to the bathroom. Stopping at the door, she asked, "Do you want me to throw that out?"

It took a minute for me to realize she meant the condom, and damn if that wasn't hot as fucking hell. How stupid was it that her asking and then taking it with her to dispose of turned me on? Damn, I was losing my mind.

It was Brae. She really was making me crazy—in a good way and bad way. The way she walked away, glancing over her shoulder with a shy smile, made me to want to take her again. I was used to that kind of response to a woman. It was besides that, the part where she was also getting under my skin—that was the crazy I didn't know how to deal with.

Taking it one day at a time was all I could do.

A few minutes later, she emerged, and my breath hitched in surprise at her being back so soon. With a stunning smile, she climbed back onto the bed and settled against my side. "That must be a record for you, Sparky."

She looked up and smirked. "What is?"

"You were only in there for a minute." I gripped her ass and pulled her even closer to my body. Just as I did, her stomach rumbled. "Holy shit," I said on a laugh. "What was that?"

She giggled adorably. "I guess I worked up an appetite."

"Well, I guess it's time for breakfast. You need your strength to get through the rest of the day."

"Really? Did we get another note card?" She looked around for the evidence. "What now, cliff diving?"

I shook my head, tightening my hold on her ass. "Pleasing your husband-to-be."

"Oh, is that so?" she asked with a wide grin. "And will he be pleasing me?"

"In every way possible." I placed a tender kiss on her lips before smacking her ass, causing her to yelp. "But food first."

☆☆☆

Giving her the tasks of setting the table and making coffee was no accident. I was too hungry to involve her with the actual cooking of our meal. It baffled me how the woman couldn't even make toast edible.

Her forte may not have been in the kitchen, but I wasn't complaining in the least. It could have been the way I leered at her as her hot, naked body moved around the tiny space, causing her to throw on one of my T-shirts.

"You're no fun," I grumbled when she came up behind me as I fried the bacon.

Her arms wrapped around my waist as I felt the cotton fabric press up against my back. My cock immediately responded knowing she was naked beneath it. "You're brave frying bacon while naked."

"If I burn myself, you'll just have to kiss it better." I twisted and stepped us to the side, away from the splattering grease. She did have a point. My hands slipped beneath the fabric so I could grip her hips. Lifting onto her toes, she kissed me before reaching for a piece of bacon off the plate. I watched her take a bite, then another.

She offered me what was left of the piece, and I closed my mouth over it until my lips touched her fingers. "Yum. Only thing better than bacon is being fed bacon by a hot chick."

"Yes, you keep calling me that," she said on a sarcastic laugh.

"Did you not hear the compliment behind that?" I grinned unabashedly, and she grinned in response. A loud pop sounded from the pan, forcing my attention back to the stove. "Let me finish this so we can eat. Then, I can eat you." My eyes shifted from her eyes to the way her teeth bit down on her bottom lip. "How does that sound, Sparky? Can I eat you for dessert?" I reached under her T-shirt and cupped her pussy. "I know for a fact you're tastier than bacon and eggs."

"You definitely have a way with words, Mr. Soren." Her voice sounded winded, and when I curled one finger and slid it inside her, her eyes closed on a breathy sigh.

I pulled my finger from her and she opened her eyes in time to see me slip it into my mouth. "Delicious." That one word and that one move on my part instigated a heated groping and make-out session that went on for a full ten minutes. The burnt smell of bacon and sudden haze of smoke finally made us step away from each other.

By the time we sat down with our charred pork side dish, burnt toast, and rubbery eggs, she shook her head at my accusation that she ruined our breakfast. "No way. That was all your fault. I refuse to be blamed this time." She reached over and snatched the only surviving piece of bacon from my dish.

"Hey. You don't like bacon, remember?"

"I do now," she said on a wink.

"Oh, Sparky. Watching you eat my bacon is one of the

hottest things I've ever seen." The force in which I pushed my chair back caused it to topple over behind me. Darting toward her, I pulled Brae from her chair and carried her to the bed.

"What are you doing?"

"It's time for my dessert."

Chapter 20

Brae

EVERY DAY WAS BETTER THAN the last. It had been four days since our relationship turned. Actually, it had been four days since we became a couple in every sense of the word. He wasn't kidding when he said he preferred to sleep naked, and he preferred I did now as well. The bed wasn't the only place we had sex, and we managed to christen the shower, couch, hammock, and beach. My favorite part was waking up to warm kisses and falling asleep in his strong arms. Our new connection was something unexpected, yet at the same time, it was perfection.

Today was the day of our mid-point interview. *Ignite Your Spark* was sending one of their representatives to check on our progress. Jude and I hadn't talked about what potential questions they'd ask, or even how we'd answer them.

While we were getting ready for our interviewer to arrive, Jude seemed a bit on edge.

"What's going on in that head of yours?" I trailed my fingers down his bare shoulder until it rested on the waistband of his shorts.

"Just thinking about how we're halfway through this."

The way his brows furrowed made me believe there was something more to it, but I didn't pry. Maybe it was the business he'd been away from. It was clear he had a lot of responsibilities back home that I didn't. I didn't even have a plant to water.

Smiling up at him as he pulled a white T-shirt over his head, I said, "It should all be downhill from here, right?"

He fixed his perfectly coiffed hair before giving me a swift kiss on the cheek. "Let's hope." With another smile, he took my hand and led me out to the deck where we relaxed and cuddled in the chaise lounge before our guest arrived.

His hand settled on my thigh—his favorite resting place, I'd come to realize. "How are you feeling about being questioned today?" Hearing him ask that made my pulse pick up its pace. "Are you nervous?"

"I wasn't until you just asked me that." I shifted my body away a tad, just so I could look at him. A glorious smile greeted me. "Are you nervous?"

"Nope." His hand moved to the ends of my hair, which he started fiddling with. "If this interview was last week, I might have different feelings about it, but now it just seems like a no-brainer."

Hearing his confidence gave me some of my own. Finally releasing a genuine smile, I said, "I'll agree with that assessment."

That was the God's honest truth. I'd never forget the first time he referred to himself as my future husband. We were going to really do this. So far, everything was working out better than I'd ever dreamed.

♡♡♡

We sat in our living room, Jude and I on the small sofa, Penny, the representative from *Ignite Your Spark*, across from us in one of the dining chairs. She clicked the top of her pen, opened the notebook on her lap, and smiled.

"First, all of us affiliated with *Ignite Your Spark* are very pleased you've made it this far. By the body language you two are exuding, I'm assuming all is well."

"Your assumption is correct," Jude said, lacing his fingers with mine. Penny's eyes saw his gesture and her lips tipped up into another smile.

"Well then, let's get started. Jude, if you don't mind stepping outside while I interview Brae, that would be great."

My fingers gripped his tighter. I had no idea this was how it was going to be.

Penny must have sensed our confusion. "I'm sorry, let me explain how this is going to work. First, I'll interview Brae, then you, Jude . . ." She batted her eyelashes at him. On a normal day, that little gesture would make me uneasy, especially since Penny was a very attractive woman, but today, it did little to dampen how I was feeling. "If I find it necessary, I'll bring you both back in to question you together."

Jude gave me a tender kiss before standing to walk out. Once the door clicked closed, Penny sighed. "Wow, you two have really hit it off, haven't you?"

I glanced at the door, watching Jude disappear onto the beach. "Yes, it's been very nice." Nice? Great, I was going to screw this all up. I needed to be sure my word choices were better.

"I can sense you're a bit nervous, but believe me, this

will be painless." She smiled, and I relaxed into the couch cushion.

Her pen poised and ready to start writing, she asked, "How has living with a stranger been?"

After I cleared my throat, I replied, "At first, it took a bit to get used to, but once we began understanding and getting to know each other, it's been great."

She smiled and jotted down my response. "That's wonderful. Did you think you'd feel that way when you signed up for this?"

I couldn't help the small laugh that escaped me. "No. When I signed up for this, money was my sole motivator." Penny's nose crinkled at that reply. "Having feelings for someone wasn't in my plan."

"I see, so you had a plan?" She started scribbling in her book.

"Well, initially, I suppose so," I scoffed. "Finding your true love in six weeks seemed a bit far-fetched. Plus, I really didn't know about this until a friend of mine told me. I've always felt when two people meet, they first get to know each other before diving in with two feet. Never did I imagine being thrust on an island with a stranger would be the way to go."

More scribbling. "Has your opinion changed?"

Penny's eyes met mine, and I couldn't help but smile. "Yes, it has. Jude is a wonderful man, and although my initial reasons for selecting him that night may have been wrong, I now know I made the right decision."

"I was there that evening, and to be honest, I didn't understand why you picked him. I would have picked number one. Granted, Jude is a very attractive man, but you couldn't see him."

Attractive? The man was a fucking god. "Like I said,

I wasn't looking for my soulmate, I was looking for a means to an end." More scribbling. I held in a groan as my heart started to race. I was screwing this up. "Look, Penny, my original reasons for picking him don't matter. What matters is how I feel about him now. Maybe it was fate? Does your company believe in that?" That last part came out a bit snarkier than I intended, but her demeanor was putting me on the defensive.

"Yes, we believe when two people are destined to be together, they just need a little push to realize that. Having to spend six weeks with someone is a true test of what can be. Obviously, either one of you can leave and call it quits, but I have a feeling you're not going to do that."

I swallowed hard, still unsure if she thought my reason for not leaving was the monetary prize. But, truth be told, my motive going in didn't break any of their rules. The experiment itself supported the theory that a spark could be stoked into a flame with the right tools. I pretty much was proving Chip and Barbi's point.

Surviving a year of marriage either provided eternal love or a monetary consolation prize. Jude was now worth more to me than the money. I'd grown to need him just as much. In the end, this was all to help my family, and I needed to remember that. Marrying the man would be an added bonus—a dream I never knew I wanted come true.

"I'd never leave, and it's not just because of the prize. I've found something I didn't know I was looking for." Penny smiled up at me and nodded. "Jude captured a piece of my heart, and I couldn't be happier."

Penny beamed at my declaration. "We at *Ignite Your Spark* couldn't be happier. You've expressed exactly what we've known to be true. Taking out the social aspects and life's interruptions allows the couple to solely focus on each other, therefore they have an understanding and trust that might normally take months or sometimes years to find."

"Sometimes people don't find that at all."

"You're right. You and Jude are very lucky. Why don't you send him in now, then we'll see if I need to interview you together?"

Before I walked out, I shook her hand, surprising the both of us. I laughed. "Sorry, too many job interviews lately. I'll go get Jude now."

Jude

BRAE LOOKED COMPLETELY FLUSTERED WHEN she walked outside to get me. If Penny weren't waiting for me, I'd pull her into my arms and hold her until she felt better. Since I didn't have the time, I settled for, "Did you tell her you snore?" trying to add a needed bit of levity.

She laughed. "No, because I don't."

"Whatever you say, Sparky. I might have evidence to prove otherwise." Before she could reply, I shot her a wink and walked inside.

Penny greeted me as I sat down with my ankle resting on my opposite knee and my arm slung on the back of the couch.

"So, Jude, tell me how the past three weeks have been."

I smiled, thinking about how the past four days had been. "Surprisingly, they've been great."

"Hmmm . . ." She started writing something in her notebook. "What has been surprising to you?"

Wasn't it obvious? "Well, the fact that I've been stranded on an island and forced to live with a woman I didn't know for starters." I flicked a piece of imaginary lint off my shorts.

Penny laughed. "Yes, well, that was the point of the experiment and what you signed up for, so it couldn't have been that surprising."

An image of Kyle behind bars popped into my head. "True, I just didn't think I'd get picked."

"Yes, your answers were very blunt, to say the least. One would think you didn't want to be selected."

"I was just being myself." I shrugged. "We were told to be truthful, right?"

Penny nodded. "How do you feel about your relationship with Brae?"

A genuine smile grew on my face. "It's better than I expected it to be. She has her quirks, but I've come to like them. Being with her day in and day out has allowed us to become great friends."

"That's good." She wrote something else down before clicking the top of her pen a few times.

"It's what your company wanted, right?"

"Well, it's what we hope for, but it's not for us, it's for our clients. In this case, you and Brae. Speaking of companies, you're a successful businessman, correct?"

What the hell did that have to do with any of this? I folded my arms across my chest. "Yes, but why does that matter?"

"Well, I'm just wondering why you're here. You didn't think you'd get picked, yet you signed up for the experiment, and I'm guessing, being successful, you don't need the money like Brae does. I'm just wondering what your motivation was."

Shit. Did Brae tell her she just wanted money? Does she know I'm wealthy? "One can never have enough in the bank. Plus, most women in my experience have been gold diggers and not much of a challenge—I'm always up for a challenge. As you said, I'm successful. Once a woman knows my net worth, they often put that before anything else and it becomes their sole focus. It's nice to be with a woman who doesn't expect to be courted with expensive dinners and getaways."

"I can imagine how difficult that would be." *No you can't.*

"Yes, well, now that I've met Brae, she's the only prize I'm focused on."

Penny sighed. "That's lovely. Brae is a lucky woman."

"The way I see it, we both are."

"One more question." Penny rolled her shoulders back. "Do you see yourself leaving the island with a wife?"

A wife. Mrs. Brae Soren. My heart jackhammered in my ribcage as I imagined me on one knee and the most gorgeous diamond adorning Brae's petite hand. There was only one way to answer that question. "Yes."

Brae was back inside just as we were when we started this interview. Our fingers laced together and a sudden calm washed over me when Brae squeezed my hand.

Penny smiled at both of us and closed her book. "Let me say how wonderful it's been getting to know the both of you. Just knowing this experiment is working makes me very happy. I can't wait to report back to Chip and Barbi."

"Don't you need to interview us together?" Brae's voice was a bit shaky, making my insides twist.

"No, I think I have everything I need. We've been monitoring your progress. Actually, Belinda, your dance instructor, works for us. She boasted about the chemistry you two had."

"Wait," Brae leaned forward, "Belinda was a spy?"

"Well, we don't call her a spy."

I chimed in. "So, an informant?"

"We refer to them as a love liaison," Penny boasted.

"Them?" Brae's question was immediate. "There's more than one?"

"I'm not at liberty to say. Just know, you are both on the right track."

This Penny chick was getting on my nerves. Losing my patience, I raked my fingers through my hair. "What track would that be?"

"Happiness." She stood and adjusted her flowing skirt a bit. "It was wonderful meeting you both. Since this was a success, tomorrow you'll be taken into town where you can hang with the locals, shop with the allowance you were given, and spend the day somewhere other than this small part of the island. I suggest you take advantage of it."

Brae and I stood to walk her to the door, and Penny turned before leaving to look at us. "You have something wonderful. Keep the flame burning and don't lose your spark."

We both exhaled when Penny drove away. I pulled Brae into my arms. "Are you good?"

She bit her bottom lip. "I've been told I'm amazing."

"That you are. But you know what?"

"Hmmm?"

I lifted her off the floor, forcing her legs to wrap around my waist. Pinning her against the door, with the weight of my body supporting her, I held her hands above her head. "I think you need to remind me how amazing you are."

Her breaths came in short pants as I licked and nipped at her neck before dragging my tongue up to her earlobe. When I took it in my mouth and pulled on it with my teeth, she let out one of those moans I loved to hear.

"Jude. I want you."

"Sparky, you have me."

Chapter 21

Brae

TODAY WAS GOING TO BE a great day. To say I was excited would be an understatement. Going into town was just what I needed. Being all alone with Jude was beyond anything I had imagined, but now I was going to be able to hold his hand while strolling the streets in town.

Not knowing what we'd be doing other than shopping, I opted to wear a cute short white sundress with spaghetti straps paired with my favorite flip flops. Jude, on the other hand, looked as though he was ready to strut down the runway in a Ralph Lauren fashion show. His loose-fitting navy shorts, untucked, white, short-sleeve, button-down shirt, and slip-on white sneakers made him look downright edible.

We stepped outside to wait for our ride. "What are you looking at?" Jude asked, looking down at himself and then to me.

"You. How is it that no matter what you wear, you always look model perfect? Even your hair. It's hot and humid today and your hair looks like you just had it styled. Meanwhile, I had to pull mine into a ponytail so it wouldn't puff out like Chinese noodles."

Jude let out a laugh right before grabbing me by the waist. "I love when your hair is like this." He wrapped my ponytail around his hand and tugged my head back. His lips landed on my neck, followed by his tongue. Pressure started to build between my legs. "Leave it like this." He whispered in my ear. "I plan on using it later."

Kegel. I was back to those damn exercises. This man was going to make me combust. Just then, a Jeep pulled up to bring us into town. I did my best not to clench my legs together as I walked, but that was easier said than done.

The town we went to was quaint. Multi-colored building façades made everything seem more tropical than it already was. A cruise ship had just docked, unloading hoards of tourists. Families and couples filled the streets. Jude linked our fingers together as we strolled down the sidewalk and window-shopped. Women of all ages eyed my guy, and I couldn't fault them. He was a wonderful specimen of a man.

We stopped at an art gallery where a local artist had some photographs for sale. "Wow, look at this one, Jude." It was a stunning picture of the sunset just after a storm. It was titled, *Settled by the Storm.* I had a thousand dollars to spend, but this picture alone would take half of my money.

"Do you want it, Sparky?"

A voice came up behind us. "I'm sorry, that piece just sold."

We nodded and stared at it a bit longer before walking away. It was for the best. I couldn't imagine spending that much. My plan was to buy a souvenir or two, then keep the rest of the money. There wasn't a rule stating I had to spend it all.

"There are other galleries, maybe you'll find something else." Jude sensed my disappointment, but I was also relieved.

"Yes, maybe. Let's keep shopping."

As we made our way down the streets, weaving in and out of a sea of tourists, one man kept looking at me. I thought maybe it was my imagination, but even Jude noticed.

"Do you know that guy?" I'd never heard him sound so stern before.

I shook my head. "No. Maybe he was looking at someone behind me." Then I let out a laugh. "Maybe he's looking at you. Don't think I haven't noticed the ladies have been eyeing you."

"Very funny, but his eyes are definitely on you." Jude possessively slung his arm over my shoulder as we continued on our way.

"Oh! Look, this store has handmade items. Can we go in?" I bounced on the balls of my feet.

"Whatever you want, Sparky."

I loved boutiques like this. "There are so many cool things in here," I said, making my way from case to case, looking at ornate baskets to handcrafted jewelry. "Wow, this is stunning."

Jude looked over my shoulder into the glass case I was eyeing. A salesman appeared. "Would you like me to take it out for you?"

"Yes, please," Jude answered for me.

The man unlocked the cabinet and took out the most unique bracelet I'd ever seen. It looked like sterling silver, but what caught my eye was the pattern etched into it. A line of abstract stars that reminded me of Jude's tattoos. The salesman explained it was designed after the yellow elder flower.

"Would you like to try it on?" I extended my hand to him in answer, and he put the bracelet on me, clasping it with a small hook.

"Wow, it's beautiful. How much is it?" I turned my arm in different directions to get views from various angles.

"That piece is a one of a kind and retails for six thousand dollars, but for you, fifty-eight hundred." The man acted as though he just did me a huge favor by knocking off two hundred, but in all honesty, he could have lowered the price by two thousand and it would still be too much. "It is eighteen-carat white gold," he added, trying to further persuade me.

I smiled at the man and unfastened the bracelet. "Thank you, but that's a bit out of my price range." He looked up at Jude, but there was no way he was buying it for me. "Thanks, again."

With my hand in Jude's, I quickly led him out of the store. "Brae . . ."

I hated the tone in his voice. He sounded like the banker ready to foreclose on my house. I wasn't poor, but I was frugal. "So, are you hungry?"

Jude gave me a tight grin. "Yeah, there's a place across the street that looks good."

"Great, because I'm starving."

A few minutes later, we were seated at an outdoor table on the sidewalk of a quaint restaurant. The aroma of Caribbean spices and citrus filled the air. A waitress welcomed us and offered the rum based house cocktail to start. It was early in the day, but when in Rome—or in this case, St. John.

"Everything sounds so good." The menu was filled with seafood and other foods I'd never heard of before. "What is conch?"

Jude grinned. "It's a mollusk. It's good. We should order the fritters. Anything tastes better fried."

The waitress was back with our drinks, and since I had no clue what to order, Jude took the liberty of ordering what sounded like half of the menu for us to share.

"I'm going to gain so much weight. I can't keep eating like this."

"Sparky, how many times do I need to tell you, there are ways to burn calories." He shot me a wink, which made me laugh. "You've probably burned close to two-thousand over the past few days, so eat and be merry."

A witty retort was on the tip of my tongue when the man we spotted before walked past us, slowing down right next to me.

"That's it," Jude said, tossing his napkin on the table.

My heart raced. I'd never seen that look in his eyes before. The saying, "If looks could kill," came to mind.

Jude

WHAT IN THE EVER-LOVING fuck? I was about to stand and ask this fucker what his problem was, but Brae put her hand on mine to calm me down. A sense of possessiveness mixed with protectiveness filled me. My eyes tracked the fucker as he walked down the street and turned the corner.

"So, this drink is tasty, isn't it?" Brae slipped her lips around the straw of the fruity concoction and took a long sip.

Knowing she was trying to change the subject, I took a deep breath and tasted it myself. "Holy shit, this is all sugar." My taste buds grimaced. "I need a beer, you can have mine." A large group of ship-goers entered the small establishment, blocking my view of the waitress. Not seeing that asshole on the busy street, I added, "I'm going to head to the bar. Will you be okay for a minute?"

"Yes, of course. Don't be silly."

I needed a beer to calm the anger that prick caused by looking at my girlfriend. That word stopped me in my tracks and I looked back to where Brae was sitting. Yeah, she was my girl, all right.

My eyes scanned the room full of tourists in tropical shirts. Steel drum music played over the speakers, drowning out some of the chatter from patrons. I waited a few minutes at the crowded bar. Once I ordered my beer, I paid and made my way back outside.

As soon as my foot hit the sidewalk, my eyes landed on the cocksucker who had a hard-on for my girl sitting in my chair at the table with Brae. Dude had balls, I'd give him that. The closer I got, the more my blood began to boil. Brae's back was to me, but I could tell she wasn't comfortable by the way she shifted in her chair.

Weaving my way through the throngs of people, I finally got to her. "Everything okay here?"

Brae's eyes went wide. "Yes," she immediately replied, her voice shaky.

"You shouldn't leave such a beautiful woman all alone." The stranger's words caused my grip on the bottle of beer to tighten as my free hand clenched.

Figuring he was about my age and size didn't deter me from protecting what was mine. "Get lost," came out of my mouth on a growl. I set my beer down on the table, but the dickhead didn't move. "Now."

Finally, he got up. We stood toe-to-toe. "Brae here was . . ."

"How do you know her name?"

"I heard you calling her that."

This fucker was lying. I'd been calling her Sparky all day.

"So, Brae was telling me this was your first visit to this restaurant. I was just informing her how trying new things was a way to experience life."

I quickly cut my eyes to Brae, who was twisting her napkin in her lap, before looking at this guy. "I don't know what game you're playing, but you've been eyeing my girlfriend for hours. Now, walk away before you can't."

A crooked smirk grew across his face. He took a few steps forward, passing Brae, but then took one back and whispered something in her ear. I didn't give a shit if he was telling her the time and temperature. No one was getting that close to her. Without further thought, I grabbed him by his shirt collar, brought my arm back, and punched him square in the jaw before tossing him onto the pavement. He wiped the corner of his lip with the back of his hand, smearing the drops of blood onto his cheek.

"Chill out, I wasn't going to kiss her."

Just the thought of his lips on hers provoked me to reach down and pick him up by his shirt. "Jude, don't. He's not worth it." Brae's panicked voice stopped me from kicking this guy's ass. "All he said was I was pretty."

My face millimeters from his, I said, "Get the fuck out of here. If I see you even looking in our direction, I'll finish what I started. Do I make myself clear?" I shoved him back, knocking him into the waitress who was bringing us our lunch, which was now on the sidewalk. Well, this turned into a complete cluster-fuck.

Brae shot out of her chair at the sound of the plates crashing to the ground. Her hands held my face until my gaze focused on her. "Jude, ignore him." She looked at me with glistening eyes and pressed her lips against mine.

Once we separated, I helped our waitress pick up the evidence of my fury. "I'm so sorry. Let me clean this up. Can you please just bring us our check?"

Another waiter came out and started to help. I felt like an asshole, but what the fuck was with that guy? All I could think about was what if he pressed charges. I'd be in jail in a foreign country. However, no one seemed to be upset, as if this were a daily occurrence—either that or islanders were naturally calm people.

A portly man came outside. "Sir, we'd be happy to bring you a new order." When I looked around, the other patrons were going about their business, totally ignoring what just went down.

I took Brae's hand in mine before pulling her close to me. "I'm so sorry for ruining our lunch. What do you want to do?"

She craned her head back to look at me before kissing me, but this time, without abandon. Her fingers fisted my hair, pulling me as close to her as possible. My hands were firm on her back. Finally breaking the kiss, I looked down at her, only to see her smiling.

"That was the hottest thing I've ever witnessed." She picked up my right hand in hers and kissed my red knuckles. "And I'm still hungry."

I asked the waiter to bring us a new order. Annoyance still coursed through me. Brae placed her hand over my clenched fist resting on the table. "Let's just enjoy the rest of our day." She looked up at the sky. "I love it here. The sun is always shining."

I knew what she was doing, and it worked. My entire body felt relaxed by the time our meals were set in front of us.

We finished our lunch without further incident and although they comped our check, I left the waitress a hundred-dollar tip.

Brae and I continued our excursion, tasting frozen mango ice at a local stand before heading into a souvenir shop. I bought us both T-shirts that said, "Keep Calm and Enjoy the Island." Naturally, Brae picked them out, finding it to be appropriate attire—especially for me.

I had a feeling Brae wasn't going to part with her spending money. The woman was as frugal as they came. We walked in and out of galleries and shops until my feet started to ache.

It was almost time for us to head back when we turned down a street off the beaten path. It was much different than the colorful one we'd been on. Brae spotted a building that looked out of place, the sign in front claiming it was an orphanage. Kids were playing in a broken-down playground on the side of the building. The swing set looked rusted and as old as I was—definitely not safe.

She walked toward the fence surrounding the play yard and just watched the kids. "This is so sad. They don't have parents."

An older woman walked up to where we were. "Do

you kids need directions?"

Brae shook her head. "No. Do all of these children live here?"

The woman smiled. "Yes. But these are only half of them." We both looked at the building, which didn't look much bigger than the house we were staying in.

"How many kids live here?" Brae asked without taking her eyes off the little girls playing with old dolls in a sandbox.

"Right now, there are twenty-seven. They range from four years old to sixteen. Once they become adults, they can leave. Unless, of course, they're adopted, but that's very rare with older children."

I watched Brae as she worked down a swallow while fighting back tears. "Do you take donations?"

The woman smiled. "We rely on them. As you can see, we don't spend what we have on entertainment items. Since our funds are limited, we use it for food and medical supplies."

Brae reached into her small handbag, took out the envelope containing the spending money we were given, and slid it between the bars of the fence. "Here, this is for you."

The woman looked at me before taking the envelope from Brae. When she looked inside, her eyes went as wide as the sun. "Sweetie, this is too generous."

Reaching through the fence, Brae placed her hand on the woman's. "No, it's not. I wish I could do more. Thank you for taking care of these children. Family is very important to me, and it breaks my heart that they don't have any."

I put my arm around her and kissed the top of her head. My girl was the best. Before we left, I reached into my wallet and pulled out a wad of bills. Without bothering to count it, I handed them, along with my business card, to the lady. Both women gasped. "Please use this to buy new playground equipment. If it isn't enough, call that number on the card. I'll be back in the office in a few weeks. My name is Jude, and this is my girlfriend, Brae."

"I'm Virginia, and thank you both from the bottom of my heart. May God bless you." A bell sounded from inside. "I need to get the kids inside. The little ones need naps."

We headed back to where our ride was going to pick us up. "You're an amazing woman, do you know that?"

"You're pretty amazing yourself." She rolled up on her toes and kissed me. "How much money did you give her?"

"I'm not exactly sure, but it doesn't matter."

Brae's eyebrows rose to her hairline. "Wow, what's that like?"

"What's what like?"

The Jeep pulled up. "Not having to worry about money? That's all I seem to worry about. It's been my sole focus for years."

Just hearing her admit that after she made the donation proved she was someone special and different from the rest.

"Money isn't everything." I now knew that for a fact. Opening the door to the Jeep, I added, "Hop in, Sparky. I have a date with your ponytail."

Chapter 22

Brae

BARRELING INTO OUR ISLAND HOME, I couldn't keep my hands off Jude or the burning need to rip his clothes off. His alpha male display at lunch coupled with his large, carefree donation made him sexier than he already was—something I didn't think was possible.

Our lips were fused together, forcing our bodies to angle away from each other in order to take off our clothes. We broke our connection for all of five seconds for Jude to lift my dress. Braless, my boobs sprang free and Jude pounced. We ravished each other, practically panting out our desires.

"I need you so bad, Sparky." He toed off his shoes while palming my breasts.

"Jude, you have no idea what you did to me today. My panties are soaked."

"Holy fuck," he growled before placing his hand between my legs to confirm my statement. "Jesus Christ." He pushed aside the cotton and slid a finger inside me. "All mine. You understand. This is all for me."

"Just you." Without much grace, I unbuttoned his

shorts and shoved them down his legs. He kicked them off to the side, and in a swift move, I wrapped my hand around his considerable length over the cotton of his boxers, which were the next item of clothing to hit the floor.

I heard fabric ripping and felt a tug on my hips as I watched what was one of my favorite thongs fall to the floor.

"Hey, I liked those." I pouted.

"I'll buy you a dozen more—and more after that. I intend to rip your clothes off you on a daily basis."

His finger continued to move in and out of me as my hand stroked him up and down. My thumb rolled over his engorged tip, finding a delightful bead of wetness there. Remembering how good he tasted, I almost went to my knees, but Jude lifted me up until I felt my back hit the mattress. All the while, his fingers never stopped teasing me.

Those damn stars on his body were like beacons. Every ridge of his torso combined with the most delectable happy trail was too much for me. I needed to touch him. Reluctantly, I released his stiff shaft from my grip and ran my fingers over his abs, memorizing every dip and valley before resuming my place on his dick.

Jude hissed. "I need to be inside you."

"I'm on the pill. I have no idea why I blurted that out. Not that it isn't true, I just didn't want anything between us. Technically, we'll be married soon and foregoing protection would be inevitable . . . oh my God." His eyes widened as I babbled. "I just meant I'm clean, I promise. I was tested."

"I've never gone without one. Are you sure you're okay with this?"

Mortified at my forwardness, but not enough to stop, I dropped my knees to each side in invitation, and simply said, "Yes."

"Sparky, you surprise me at every turn . . . and I love that you do." Jude held himself, dragging his tip up and down my wetness with one hand while wrapping my ponytail around his other to keep my head still. "I need to see you when I'm inside you. Keep your eyes on me."

Just as he started to slip in, there was a knock on the door. Both of our eyes cut to where the annoying sound originated, but when it stopped, we resumed where we left off. Again, the knock sounded, and then again, louder.

"Go away!" Jude yelled from the bed, making his dick bob and me laugh.

Clearly, the person was on a mission because the knocking never ceased—it just got louder and more determined.

Jude got up and grabbed the sheet to wrap it around his waist, leaving me completely bare. Scrambling toward the quilt, I wrapped it around me in a makeshift dress and huffed. It wasn't as though we lived in a house with many doors.

He flung the door open. "What the fuck are you doing here?"

Upon hearing Jude's angry words, I rushed beside him to see the man from lunch . . . although, now he had a swollen lip and bruised jaw. I hoped he wasn't here to press charges. The man looked at Jude, then me.

Jude pushed me behind him. "Are you that stupid? Did you come back for more? Do you have some sort of death wish?" Even wrapped in a sheet, Jude was ready to fight. When he took a step forward, the sheet dipped in the back, exposing the top of his ass. I probably should have been focused on the fact that Jude was ready to beat the shit out of this stranger rather than his ass, but he had a great ass.

The man put his hands up in surrender. In one hand, he had an envelope with the *Ignite Your Spark* logo on it. "I'm Toby, and I work with Chip and Barbi. My job is to gauge couples' reactions when their union is tested. I'm pleased to announced you both passed." His words came out rapid fire, most likely to thwart any move Jude was ready to make.

"Both?" I stepped out from behind Jude, clutching the quilt to my chest. "What do you mean, both? Wait, that's how you knew my name?"

"Yes. When I sat down with you, never once did you give me any indication that I stood a chance. All you said was you were with your boyfriend and I was in his chair." He looked at Jude. "And we don't need to discuss your reaction."

Jude ran his free hand through his hair. "You mean to tell me you go around hitting on other guy's women for a living?"

"The point is, you both passed with flying colors. This is for you." He handed Jude the envelope. "Have a good rest of your day, and I'm sorry if I interrupted."

Toby closed the door and I started laughing. "If he interrupted?"

"Can you believe that guy?" Jude was clearly frustrated. Once again, he ran his hand through his sexy as fuck hair.

"Jude?" I dropped the quilt just as he turned to look at me. "Where were we?"

"Fuck," he said, releasing the envelope and letting it

float to the floor.

In a flash, he dropped his sheet, scooped me up, and sat me on the kitchen table. This wasn't exactly where we were, but I liked where this was going.

He pushed my bent knees apart, sat in a chair, and lowered his head. A mewl escaped me as his tongue met the hardened bud between my legs. The rough scruff on his face scratched the insides of my thighs in the most delicious way.

"You are the best meal I've had on this table." Jude licked, nipped, and sucked until my entire body began to quiver.

"God . . . yes!"

"That's right, babe, let it go." Jude thrust two fingers inside me, curling them just enough to hit my hot button . . . and I came. Before I could come down from my climax, he carried me to the bed and positioned us just as we had been before the interruption. "You're sure about this, right?"

"Get inside me. Please, for the love of everything holy, I need to feel you—all of you."

Jude

RESUMING MY POSITION, HER HEAD nestled between my hands, my body between her legs, I looked into her eyes as I slid inside her. It wasn't a hard, quick thrust. No, this I needed to savor. Skin on skin, heat on steel, the way she molded around my cock sent a surge of electricity down my spine and into my balls.

Buried deep inside Brae without anything between us was heaven on earth. Her breath hitched as I started to move. She wrapped her legs around my waist, giving me even deeper access.

"Fuck, you feel fantastic." Her eyes glistened at my words. She tilted her head back as I thrust forward. My hand moved down to cup her ass, squeezing as we both moved simultaneously. I kissed her without abandon. Our tongues mimicked the movements of our hips.

Not wanting this to end, I flipped us around so she was straddling me. Looking up at this woman, I felt as though I'd known her all my life. In reality, I hadn't even known her for a month.

"Mmmm . . . Jude . . ." She arched her back as she slid up and down my cock. My hands instinctively grabbed her tits while she teased my balls with the tips of her fingernails.

I began to massage her clit with my thumb, applying just a bit more pressure each time she moved forward. Every time I did that, she rubbed my balls. I wasn't going to last. I needed to come inside her. The exquisite feel of her tightening around me and the way she said my name, over and over again like a chant, caused spots that looked like fireflies to flutter under my closed eyelids.

Before I came, I looked up at her. Noticing her eyes were closed as well, I instructed her to open them. When she did, they locked with mine.

"Brae, don't stop looking at me." She nodded. My hands gripped her hips. Doing my best to keep my eyes pinned to hers, I felt her tremble and came harder and deeper than I ever had in my life.

☆☆☆

I made us a simple dinner, then we moved outside to relax in the hammock, her head nestled in the crook of my shoulder. "Remember how we fought over this when we first got here?" Brae's sweet voice made me smile.

"Yeah, when you fell on your ass?" Chuckling at her pout, I placed a quick kiss on her lips. "That seems like a long time ago, doesn't it?" I stroked her arm with the tips of my fingers, relishing in the softness of her skin.

"Yes, it does. Sometimes, I feel like I've known you forever, and other times, I don't feel like I know you at all."

I smiled. She felt the same way I did. "What do you want to know, Sparky?"

She turned to look at me. "How old are you?"

"How old do you think I am?" I smirked at her, but she just cocked a brow. "I just turned thirty on December nineteenth. How old are you?"

"I'll be twenty-seven on June ninth."

"Ahhh, you're a baby." I beamed at her. "Okay, what else?"

"You've told me a little about your family, tell me about your business."

Just thinking about my business stressed me out. Not having been there for so long and being without contact was driving me insane. "I own a financial company. When I was at Yale, I'd watch the market and invest money for myself and friends. It became a game. Some of the fraternity guys would play poker and I'd play the market. When they realized I wasn't losing money like they were, they would give me their money to invest. I'd take a small commission and it became quite lucrative. Luca and Kyle, who you met the night I met you, acted like my salesmen. They'd spread the word and drum up business." I let out a laugh.

Brae's eyebrows lowered. "Why is that funny?"

"Because Kyle being Kyle would concentrate on the

sororities and female population who had zero interest in investing. And he had more interest in sleeping with them, so he basically sucked at his job. Luca, on the other hand, focused on the technical and business majors. They saw the long-term potential, and some are still my best clients."

"Kyle sounds like he'd get along with my friend Vanessa. I'm sure that's what she would do too. Well, not the sororities, but she'd hit up the football team."

"I'm sure they'd get along famously, for a night or two." I couldn't help but laugh. Fucking Kyle.

"Isn't he dating Shelly?"

"The chick who got you involved in all of this? I highly doubt they're still together. Kyle doesn't do girlfriends."

The sun started to set and we walked to the beach, not wanting to miss it. Naturally, I had a large towel in my hand for Brae to sit on. God forbid she got sand on her ass.

"From what I remember, you don't do girlfriends either." Brae nudged me with her shoulder.

"Correction, I didn't do girlfriends." Not wanting to dredge up my past, I continued with my story. "Anyway, Luca still works for me. He's holding down the fort while I'm gone."

"Luca works with you?" she asked, surprised.

"Yes. He's one of my right-hand men. I trust him implicitly."

Brae nodded, but otherwise didn't respond. When she sat up and wrapped her arms around her knees, pulling them into her chest, I wondered what went through her mind. Her eyes studied the pink and orange sky as the sun lowered out of sight. "I love it here," she said, changing the subject.

"What about you? I know you're unemployed, but what is it you want to do?"

A warm breeze picked up the ends of her hair, forcing the scent of apple to waft past me. She was absolutely gorgeous. I'd been with and seen many beautiful women in my day, but Sparky was in a league all by herself.

"I loved my sales job. It was something I was good at, which had nothing to do with my upbringing. I grew up in upstate New York. As I told you, my parents have a farm. It's a dairy farm. So, my mornings started very early with tending to our chickens and cattle. It's a lovely piece of land. They own fifteen acres." She lowered her head and closed her eyes. "They can't lose it."

Oh, how I wanted to pull out my checkbook and pay off the debt just so Brae could breathe a bit easier, but I knew she wouldn't want me to do that. What blew me away was the donation she had made to the orphanage.

This conversation was getting her down, so I changed my direction of questioning, knowing she needed it. "Where do you want to live when we leave here for the year we're together?"

Her shoulders slumped a bit before she shrugged them. "I have a one-bedroom in SoHo I love. It's rent controlled, so I can afford it. We could live there. I'm not prepared to give up my home."

"My place is a two-bedroom on the upper east side. You'd love it. It has a gourmet kitchen and everything you'd need to make your man dinner." We both laughed at that comment, knowing the only thing she'd be using in that kitchen was the microwave—and even that was a stretch.

We both fell silent, lost in thought. After a few long

minutes, she asked, "What do you think the next card will say?" That's when we both remembered Toby, the pick-up artist, brought us one we had yet to read.

After a few more minutes, we went inside and found it under the table.

Jude and Brae,

Congratulations on passing yet another test. For your reward, we are allowing you one phone call to a person of your choosing. Two phones will be delivered to you within the next few days. Each will have a total of ten minutes of cellular time.

Choose wisely. This will be the only call you will be able to make.

Love and Sparks,

Chip & Barbi

I let out a loud breath. "Well, that's a great reward."

"It's going to be nice to talk to a friend. Do you know who you'll call?" Part of me wanted to tell her I was a friend, but I understood what she meant.

"I'll probably call Luca. Kyle will waste the ten minutes talking about the last chick he laid. What about you? Will you call your parents?"

Brae's body tensed. "No, I'll most likely call Desiree."

"Do your parents know you lost your job or that

you're away?"

She shook her head. "Not exactly. They know I'm away on business. Desiree is covering for me. If they knew what I was doing, they'd sell the farm to help me out. It's bad enough they don't know I've been helping them."

This woman amazed me. Not only did she give the orphanage all her spending money, it appeared she sacrificed for everyone.

"You're a good woman, Sparky."

"I know, and don't you forget it." Her smile was as bright as the sun we watched set.

"Never."

Chapter 23

Brae

SINCE LEARNING WE WOULD BE allowed to make one phone call in a few days, the unknown weighed heavily on my mind. We've been comfortable—oblivious in our own little bubble. Fear rushed in and I was scared something from the outside would pop it.

It didn't help my situation when my time of the month arrived just as these insecurities did. The early morning sun shimmered on the ocean, almost blindingly, yet still mesmerizing. It was times like then when I could just stare into space and think. Without him close to distract me, it was easier to remember the purpose of this madness.

I came in not wanting any chance of a relationship, yet here I was in one and enjoying every minute of it. Most of the time Jude made me feel like I was the only woman on earth for him. Of course, being stuck here with me had a lot to do with it. But if he could change so much in just a few weeks, what would happen after a year? And more importantly, what would I want to happen after a year? What would he want?

I honestly couldn't answer those questions, and that terrified me.

After lying awake most of the night, plagued by thoughts, I slipped out of our warm bed and went to my happy place in an attempt to channel my goals and refocus. Once I was settled on my chaise, it did little good. All I'd been thinking about while sitting out on the beach was Jude.

His smile that could change my mood in an instant. Every touch affected me. A few weeks ago, I was able to come out to the beach and contemplate my situation. Now, it didn't matter whether I was lying next to his naked body or sitting out on the beach alone, I still felt his presence and could no longer think clearly.

Funny, when I started this whole thing, my mantra to keep my eye on the prize often got me through, especially when he was being his charming prick self. Somewhere along the line, I subconsciously bulked him in as part of the prize.

I was screwed.

Taking a sip of my now lukewarm coffee, I sighed and tightened the towel I carried out as a blanket around me. The morning chill felt much cooler than it actually was. Just as I closed my eyes on another sigh, a pair of warm lips on my ear said, "Want to have sex on the beach?"

Jumping and spilling coffee on my legs caused him to chuckle at my startled response. "Oh my God! You scared me." I used the towel to wipe up the droplets that sloshed over the side of my cup.

"Sorry, Sparky. Didn't mean to scare you, but who else would be whispering about wanting sex in your ear?"

"I was just lost in thought."

"Why are you out here so early?" He reclined on his

chaise facing me. Once again, he was practically naked in his tight boxer briefs, displaying every ridiculous bump and dip of his abs. "How long have you been out here?"

"A while. I couldn't sleep."

A sly grin spread over his face. "Next time, wake me up." He waggled his eyebrows, then frowned. "You didn't answer my question. Sex on the beach?"

"No." I dismissed him with a wave of my hand.

"Ouch. Have your period? For the record, we could do other things." My open-mouthed gape caused another chuckle. "Ah, you do. I knew it had to be coming. You've been quiet, and last night you were very weepy and restless."

"I was?" I was a bit taken aback that he noticed. I had been lost in thought the past few days, but tried very hard to camouflage my mood. We fell asleep wrapped in each other's arms, only for me to toss and turn the rest of the night.

"Yes. You mumbled a lot. Cried even, and I knew something was wrong when you didn't snore."

"Shut it, I don't snore."

"Okay, Sparky. I have to provide my evidence soon." He skimmed his hand over one bare leg, eliciting goosebumps. "Is this from my presence, or are you cold?"

I shook my head, frustrated at his ability to flip back and forth between the caring, sweet Jude and the sexual, arrogant Jude who never failed to rile me up—and even more frustrated at my inability to hide how much he did. "I'm cold."

"Liar." When he turned around and pulled me into his warm body, that move almost caused tears to well. "Talk to me, Sparky."

I looked away, trying to hide my emotions, but I couldn't hide them for long. Everything I did, every way I acted, was on display for this man to see. Rather than making excuses for what had me so somber, I played on the one thing he picked up on. "It's just how I get every month. No worries, woman problems."

"How can I improve your mood?" He nuzzled my neck and skimmed his lips across my skin up to my ear. The lower half of my body immediately sparked to life from his touch. Trying to push my gloom aside, I turned my head and captured his lips with mine. His low moan single-handedly erased my doubts, and with each kiss after that, he managed to distract my thoughts.

Uncharacteristically, he was the first to break away. "Let's get inside and have breakfast. Are you okay now?"

"I'm fine. Don't mind me." A genuine smile spread over his perfect face. He stood and held a hand out for me, which I immediately took. Together, we walked back to the cottage and he amused me through my sand removal routine.

Once inside, Jude went into the kitchen to whip up something to eat. He no longer even asked for my opinion, and just took it upon himself to make whatever he was in the mood for. Most of the time, I was absolutely fine with his decision.

Just as I began to set the table, a knock sounded on the door. "It's so freakin' early. How do they even know we're up?" he grumbled while I heard the first piece of bacon pop and sizzle from the pan. Him and his bacon.

"I'll get it," I said, walking toward the door. "I wouldn't want you punching someone this early in the morning. It'll delay my breakfast." I threw him a devilish grin and he reciprocated with his own.

"I love how the smell of bacon now turns you on. I can see it written all over your face."

"I'm just hungry." I opened the door to a small box sitting on the ground and looked around, but no one was in sight. Lifting it, I pulled the card off the top, and read, "Jude and Brae."

What is it?" he asked as he flipped another piece of bacon. At my short pause, he looked over, catching me ogling his work-of-art body. The combination was hot as hell. What was it about a practically naked sexy man cooking that caused my crotch to clench in an instant? Damn it, I couldn't take him right there on the floor with the bacon popping above us on the stove.

"Would you rather I take my shorts off, Sparky? You'll get eyestrain."

"Shut up." No longer phased by his conceit, I resumed the simple task of walking back to the table and ripped open the package. I read the note out loud.

Jude and Brae,

Your phones are included in this package. You can make your ten-minute phone calls at any time during the day. Use your minutes wisely.

Love and Sparks,

Chip & Barbi

Lying at the bottom of the box beneath two very outdated flip phones, was another note I, again, read out loud.

Jude and Brae,

We will begin preparations for your matrimonial ceremony taking place two weeks from today.

Our eyes instantly met across the room. "What else does it say?" he asked, his voice barely above a whisper.

I looked down and continued.

Arrangements have been made. One week from today, Brae will be picked up for her bridal gown fitting at one p.m., and Jude will be fitted at the cottage by our tailor for his tux. During the next week, please use the stationary included to compile your guest list for the ceremony. In total, you are allowed ten guests. You'll have to work together to decide who they will be. Other details of your wedding day will arrive over the next two weeks.

Love and Sparks,

Chip & Barbi

With his back to me, I saw him grip the counter top on each side of the stove, his head bowed in thought. This was getting very real, very fast, and with that one little note, the fairy tale we'd been living these past few weeks became a scary reality.

Jude

OUR BREAKFAST WAS SILENT WHILE we ate, each of us lost in thought. She pushed away from the table, and said, "I'll be back," before walking into the bathroom without another word.

Chalking her mood up to her hormones, I cleared the table, impatiently tossed all the dishes into the sink, grabbed one of the phones, and walked out onto the deck.

Maybe that notecard freaked Brae out **as** much as it did me. Shit, how did the one part that made this all too real sneak up on us so fast?

I stared down at the phone for a few long minutes before flipping it open and dialing his cell number. On the second ring, he answered, "Luca Benedetto."

"Luca."

"Well, if it isn't Mr. Spark!" In his deep Italian baritone voice, he added, "Didn't expect to hear from you. How's it going in paradise?"

"It's fine. I only have ten minutes. How's my company doing?"

"Um . . . okay?"

My hackles rose at his nonchalant answer. "What do you mean, um . . . *okay?*"

Luca cleared his throat. "We have a situation with Waldon Industries. He's been giving us a hard time over your absence."

"How hard of a—"

Luca went on to speak over me. "I personally didn't

think you'd last this long, but things must be going well with that hot piece of ass you're stuck with. Did you do her yet?"

"Shut the fuck up, Luca."

"Wow. What the hell is going on over there? Did you fall for this chick?"

"No." The more I waited to explain things, the worst it would be for me. "I care about her is all. Just focus, please. They only gave us ten minutes of cell time. I have more important things to worry about. How hard of a time is he giving us? I need you to tell me what Waldon said."

"There was a tiny dip in his stock last week and he's claiming it's because no one was watching his portfolio . . . which is a fucking lie." The ten silent seconds that stretched between us were ten wasted seconds.

"Luca, spill it."

"He's threatening to walk. We've been able to stall up until now, but our tactics are no longer working. We're meeting with him tomorrow."

Fuck. Howard Waldon was my biggest client, and my biggest pain in the ass. Since his portfolio was thriving, I had hoped he'd be content while I was gone.

"I planned to hear him out, and if he was serious, I was going to call to say your aunt died. Anyway, during my call with him this morning, he said he wants to speak to you directly. He's not buying the fact that you can't be reached."

Shit. Shit. I needed to think. I glanced at the phone and watched the time tick ominously. "Okay, listen carefully. One week from today, we have our fittings for the wedding."

"Wedding! Shit, Kyle just won back his hundred bucks."

"Luca, focus," I said through gritted teeth. "Get online, quick. Look for flights arriving that afternoon."

"Okay." I heard Luca's fingers flying over the keyboard. "There's a flight arriving on St. John at twelve forty-five."

"Perfect. Fly here with those contracts. Before you take off, arrange a taxi to pick me up at twenty-two Beach Haven Way at one-thirty. I should be there by the time you disembark. I'll meet you at baggage claim and we will call Waldon and assure him I support what you guys have suggested. Make sure you schedule that call with him at two p.m. sharp for no more than thirty minutes."

"Got it."

"My time is up. If anything goes wrong from now 'til next week, call via the emergency ruse that my aunt died."

Just as Luca was saying, "Is there anything you need me to bring . . ." the call went dead.

My head pounded with an oncoming headache that had all to do with the helplessness I felt regarding my pride and joy. I knew going in this could happen, but denial and being swept up in this fantasy with Brae had dulled my logic. Lesson learned: lust always trumps logic.

I walked my aggravated ass back into the cottage, sandy feet and all. She'd just have to deal with it. I found her at the sink cleaning the dirty dishes I dumped before calling Luca. At my entrance, she turned her head and frowned.

"You made your call already?" she asked, shutting the water off and wiping her hands on a dishtowel.

"Yeah. I called Luca."

Gauging my expression, she asked, "Is everything

okay?" Her eyes widened a bit with concern.

"Yep." My clipped response caused a frown to pucker her forehead.

In the way she stood staring at me expectantly for a few seconds, it was obvious she wanted a better explanation. When it was clear I wasn't offering one, she asked, "You look upset. Are you sure you're okay?"

"I'm fine. Don't worry about it. It doesn't concern you."

She nodded with a tight smile before snatching her phone off the counter. "I might as well make my call now." Without a backward glance, she walked out the door, slamming it shut behind her.

Why was it her ten minutes went by a lot slower than mine did? When she walked back into the house and avoided eye contact with me, I wondered if she received bad news as well.

"Who did you call?"

"Desiree." Without looking my way, she busied herself by making the bed.

"Everything okay at home?"

My question caused her to twist her head in my direction while sporting a scowl. "No. But I have nothing to hide, so I'll tell you. I need to sign something from the bank. Des is having it faxed over tomorrow. If you see it before I do, I'd appreciate it if you could be sure to find me asap."

"That shouldn't be hard. You'll probably be in the bathroom," I quipped.

Her livid expression cut me to the quick. "Screw you. I meant if I was on the beach."

Leaving the bed half made, she walked past me toward

the door, stopped abruptly, and looked down. "Can you please clean up the sand you tracked in?"

"Yes, dear." With a disgusted shake of her head, she opened the door and walked onto the deck. The echo of the door being slammed yet again shook the glass cabinet fronts.

"What the fuck did I do now?" I grunted out loud to myself, and walked outside to find her staring at the ocean. Her arms were folded tightly across her chest. "Did I do something to piss you off, Sparky?"

Without turning her head, she said, "Nope. Nothing at all."

"No? So, this little hissy fit you're throwing just has to do with your period?" Her lip curled up in a snarl before I dragged my leg behind me as I hit the shallow the water.

She crossed her arms and snapped, "What are you doing?"

"Just trying to get used to the ball and chain clamped around my ankle," I called out with a smirk. "I get it, you're stressed out. Well, so am I. Too bad I can't take off to a bar and drink with my buddies to release my own stress. Instead, I'm stuck here like a fucking prisoner."

The moment I said it, I regretted it. Her expression went slack, and her face paled. Without a word, she turned and walked back to the cottage. I called out to her, but she ignored me.

It was more than the aggravation I felt over my business that caused me to feel sick to my stomach. It could have been the wedding talk or our phone calls that triggered our moods—the list went on and on.

But one thing I knew for sure as I sunk to my knees in the wet sand feeling like the world was imploding around me, Brae Daniels had gotten under my skin, and

I hated that I cared so much.

Chapter 24

Brae

HEAVY FOOTSTEPS SOUNDED OUTSIDE OF the bathroom door, followed by the slamming of drawers. What the hell was he doing? After taking a much-needed breath, I pulled the door open to see Jude jerking on a pair of jeans over his bare ass.

"Where are you going?"

His eyes narrowed as he looked at me. "For a walk. I need air. Just like you need everything to be neat and tidy, I need my space to think."

"You know you can't be gone longer than an hour." That's all I needed was for him to get sidetracked and us to get busted.

"Don't worry, Miss Rule Follower, I'll be back in time. So, just calm your tits. I wouldn't want you to lose the prize money. After all, I know that's your main reason for being here."

My mouth dropped at his words. Of course, that was my main reason, but now he played a large factor in it too. Did he think we were just playing house all these weeks? That I'd just sleep with him because he was available? "You're an asshole."

"So, I've been told." With that, he turned and left out the back door. Even though I was furious, I couldn't help but watch his toned body walk away. His worn jeans hung low on his hips, cradling his ass in the most delectable way. God, I hated that man. It was a shame he held a solid place in my heart.

Him giving me a few minutes to myself was a good decision. With my blood boiling to dangerous levels, I filled a tumbler with ice and topped it with the chilled white wine we opened yesterday.

Forfeiting the hot chaise on the beach for a shadier spot, I made myself comfortable on the hammock. Wave after wave rolled in, but the sound of the surf, which usually calmed me, failed. All I heard was him calling me his ball and chain as I took a large gulp of wine. It was becoming clear he didn't want to get married. His entire demeanor changed as soon as we received our instructions regarding wedding attire.

It would appear I was back to square one of being here for my original reason. But things changed, and it'd be hard to block out the effect Jude had on me. His need to keep that phone call private, even after I told him all about mine, was very telling. Something was going on and it was stressing him out. Part of me wanted to ask him if it was his time of the month, but I refrained.

Not knowing the exact time, my nerves began to spike. It was then movement caught my eye. Jude strutted down the beach looking sexy as hell. Those damn tattoos. His skin glistened with sweat and his bare feet kicked the sand with each step he took. The washed-out denim defined every inch of his long, muscular legs. And from twenty feet away, Jude Soren, managed to spike my temperature quicker than the island sun ever had.

Even though I couldn't see his face, his actions painted a clear picture. When he ran his hand through his hair while staring down at the sand, I knew his short walk didn't do him much good.

He stopped when he saw me relaxing in the hammock. Neither of us spoke for a short moment, but it felt longer. Not since we first started this dating adventure has the tension been so high between us. I grew accustomed to his jokes, nicknames, and incessant teasing. The thought of all that being gone saddened me.

"Did you have a nice walk?"

"I did. What have you been doing?"

Taking a sip of my wine, I relished in the ice hitting my lips, temporarily cooling me down. "Sitting here thinking about all we've been through the past few weeks. We got another note. Three days before the wedding, we'll be picked up and taken to a jeweler to pick out rings." His jaw tensed, and I quickly changed the subject. "You look hot, would you like something cold to drink?"

"You still think I'm hot, Sparky? If we're exchanging compliments, I think your tits look amazing in that tank top."

I rolled my eyes, but secretly loved his retort. Maybe he was feeling better. "So, that's a no to the drink?"

"I think a shower would be better. Care to join me? I'll let you wash my back. I'd be more than happy to take care of your front."

"As you keep reminding me, I am on my period. Plus, don't forget we're supposed to be mad at each other."

"I'm sure you've heard of make-up sex." He took a step toward me, the expression on his face one that said he wanted to devour me. "Besides, do you think your period is going to stop me?"

My mouth gaped open in shock. Holy shit. I've never in my life had sex during my time of the month. Was he suggesting what I thought he was?

"I see your wheels turning, Sparky. You think too much." In one fell swoop, he tossed me over his shoulder, sending the hammock swinging and my wine glass crashing to the sand.

"Jude! Put me down." My legs kicked, but it didn't deter him. Each of his movements caused the waistband of his jeans to gap. Once again, my eyes were fixated on the top of his ass. I purposely fisted my hands to keep myself from slipping them in to cop a feel. "You can't fix everything by having sex."

"Do you know me at all?" Setting me down in the bathroom, he turned the shower on before sliding the metal button through the hole of his jeans. His eyes pinned to mine, he lowered the zipper until they fell to the floor. There, in all his glory, stood an infuriating man. "Ready to make up, Sparky?"

"I don't know. Should I make up with you? I'm not sure what a ball and chain would do." I planted my hands on my hips and stared up at him.

Jude smiled smugly, unfastened my shorts, and pushed them down until they rested on my feet. His hand went between my legs, over my panties, causing me to gasp. Shit. There was no way I would let him touch me there, not today, not for a couple more days. He tucked his thumbs under the elastic of my panties and slid them down.

Two gentle tugs on the pink string hanging between my legs practically caused an instant orgasm. "Do what you need to do, Brae, but I will be inside you. Either you take care of this, or I will." His lips found a spot on my neck that had clearly become his favorite to nibble on. My entire body tensed. *Could I do this with him?* I thought as steam filled the small room.

With every flick of his tongue on my skin, he convinced me in less than five seconds. Tilting my head to the side so he could continue, I whispered, "Get in. I'll be right behind you."

He lifted his head with a wicked grin. "I'd rather be behind you, but that could be round two."

The moment he turned his back, I rushed to remove the only barrier stopping him from taking me on the spot. I glanced his way, and was thankful he kept his back to me until I finished what I needed to do.

I joined him in the small shower, and between the pounding spray of warm water and his proximity to my body, there was no hiding how turned on I was.

Jude

I'D NEVER WANTED A WOMAN as much as I wanted her right then. That confirmation seemed far-fetched, especially with my sexual history. But wanting to fuck someone wasn't nearly as all-consuming as wanting to own someone. I didn't merely need to be inside her; I needed to mark her, take her, and possess her in every way.

I took half a step closer until every part of me pushed against every part of her. One more step forward successfully sandwiched Brae between the stone wall and me, the rock hard man in front of her.

"Jude, I've never done this before," she said,

panicked.

"Neither have I, and that makes it even hotter. Lift your legs, Sparky," I demanded without giving her an option. She held my shoulders and did as she was told. I gripped the back of her thighs to help her along. Without the slightest hesitation, I slid my entire length into her pussy in one deliberate thrust.

"Oh, fuck." The euphoria of being buried balls deep in her warmth was immediate. I didn't think I'd ever tire of her, or how she so perfectly surrounded me.

My movements were anything but gentle as I pounded my hips against hers, a growl marking each move. She dug her fingers into my hair and tugged, causing me to hiss against her lips.

Her penetrating gaze held me hostage. I couldn't look away, and when she came nose to nose with me while tugging harder on my hair, I practically came. "You're still angry, Sparky. I can tell."

"Congratulations, Captain Obvious." Her labored breathing, glare, and the way her pussy gripped me were all telltale signs that she was beyond turned on.

"Angry or not, you're also hating the fact that you like me fucking you hard in a shower." I pressed my fingertips into her thighs, pushing up against her even harder with each move I made.

"Enough talking," she gritted out before crushing her lips to mine.

We swallowed each other's grunts; consumed each other's ire. With our mouths cemented together, our bodies joined as one, her anger and my frustration took on a life of their own. Together in that shower, we used an act of primordial fucking to douse the fire raging within us.

I pulled far enough away from her face to demand, "Get there, Sparky." She stared back at me in defiance, but otherwise ignored me. Taking it upon myself, I shoved my hand between us to fondle her.

The river of water flowing over and between us felt hot to my skin. The pressure in my balls begged for release. I couldn't hold back any longer, and gave one final warning. "I'm coming, with or without you."

I drove into her with three more thrusts before every molecule of stress, anger, frustration, and ecstasy I was feeling poured into her. With that, she buried her face in the crook of my neck and clamped her teeth into my shoulder as her pussy clamped my cock in a death grip.

"Fuck," I hissed again while a never-ending climax almost dropped me to my knees.

Out of necessity, I slowed my movements and loosened my hold. She lifted her head to look into my eyes. Streams of water cascaded over her head and down her face, but I could still tell she was crying.

"Brae," I whispered, but something clogged my throat, preventing me to say any more. She didn't respond; just continued to stare sadly. I brushed her hair back off her face and pulled her head down to rest against my shoulder. "I'm sorry."

"Me too," she said without hesitation against my skin. Her arms tightened around my neck, yet her body submitted against mine. I held her, once again trying to comfort her through actions, not words.

☆☆☆

After I washed her hair and she washed mine, we dried each other tenderly, dressed, and slipped into bed. I buried my nose into her damp hair, not getting enough of her sweet shampoo.

"Jude? Do you really feel I'm acting like a ball and chain?"

"No, Sparky. I'm sorry I said that. And to be honest, I don't know what a ball and chain feels like." I tightened my hold on her and sighed. "Talking to Luca threw me off. We have a lot going on this quarter and since I wasn't prepared to leave, I dumped a lot on my team. When I leave town, which isn't often, I hold team meetings and contact any clients who may need me. Granted, my employees can hold down the fort, but it's very easy to have things fall between the cracks, and those things can cost me millions in revenue."

"I understand, and I'm sure it's stressful. It would have been nice if you talked to me about it, though."

"I'm sorry. I wasn't sure you'd understand."

"I guess we're in opposite positions. If you're here, you could lose money. If I'm not here, my parents could lose their farm." Her body shifted, but my hold didn't loosen. "We only have two weeks left. Will things be okay until then?"

Would they? That was a question I wouldn't be able to answer until after I met with Luca. Not wanting her to worry, all I could say was, "I'm sure everything will be fine." Trying to alleviate the stress, I chuckled, "You don't happen to know anything about the market, do you? Maybe I could hire you when we get home. We could have hot desk sex."

"The only market I know is the supermarket, and even that's limited to produce and frozen foods."

"So much for that idea." I kissed the top of her head. "We'll figure things out, okay? Trust me?"

After a pause that made my heart twist and wishing she didn't hesitate, she finally said, "Okay. And I do trust you, Jude."

"That's my Sparky." My fingers traced lazy circles on her arm.

Once I heard Luca's news, I didn't harp on the wedding part of this day and pushed it to the back of my mind, but it was still there nagging at me. We hadn't talked about what would happen in less than two weeks. I supposed they'd allow us to separate at some point to give us a chance to get organized, and I'd have to take that time to fix everything that's fallen apart while I've been gone. I assumed she'd do the same with her parents' situation.

But then?

Living in a small apartment in SoHo did not appeal to me in the least, and I had a gut feeling it wouldn't be easy to talk her into moving in with me.

After a few long minutes of her remaining silent, I thought she fell asleep. "Sparky?" I whispered.

"Yeah?"

"I know you don't want to give up your apartment, but would you consider moving into my place? It's plenty big for the two of us and you would love the building. We have a pool and gym, and it's minutes away from great shopping on Fifth."

She chuckled against my chest. "I can't afford great shopping on Fifth, Jude."

"I can." She stiffened against me, and I rushed on before her snark appeared. "You're just going to have to get used to the fact that I have money. I live a very spoiled lifestyle."

"I knew that the moment you stared at the washer and dryer like they were aliens."

"Nonetheless," I said, stretching out the last s, "I

work too hard to change my ways. It would be much easier for you to adapt to my lifestyle than for me to adapt to yours." She lifted her head, her eyes blazing again. "What did I say now?" I lifted my free hand in defense. "I can't help it if I'm a diva."

Her furious expression couldn't hold and a slow smile lifted the corners of her lips. "If you admit to getting manicures and pedicures, I'm walking now."

"No, smartass. But I do get weekly massages."

"By a hot woman?" I looked away, and she huffed. "Yeah, that ends."

"Wow, Sparky. Bossy much? Does that mean I have to fire every hot broker who works for me?"

All levity in her expression vanished. "Jude, I know this isn't real to you and we have an expiration date, but I won't be able to handle you sleeping with anyone else while you're sleeping with me."

I didn't know whether I should be insulted or angry at her accusation. To be honest, I hadn't thought that far ahead, but with the way things were progressing between us sexually, I didn't want or need extracurricular activity. Choosing my words carefully to avoid another fight, I shook my head, and said, "I'd never do that to you, Sparky."

She nodded, and said, "Thank you."

"Same goes for you. You've seen my jealous side."

"Your hot jealous side? So, I can't egg you on?" I raised a brow and offered a tight-lipped smile just before I smacked her ass. "Ow. I'm kidding. Ditto, Jude. All my orgasms are reserved for you."

"As they should be." I kissed her lips, pulled away, and kissed them again . . . and again . . . and again. Before I knew it, I was hard as a rock. "Want to go for a swim with me?"

"Now?" she asked, wide-eyed.

"Yeah, now. Put your suit on, and forget the tampon. I'll meet you on the beach." With a persuasive shove toward the bathroom, she took my hint and shockingly followed my direction without argument.

Chapter 25

Brae

"**R**EALLY, I LIKED THE SECOND gown the best." A pouf of white tulle looked even worse than I thought it would. All I could imagine was Jude's expression since I looked like a wedding cake topper.

"Brae, darling, this is your wedding day. You should look like a glamorous bride." She cocked her head to the side. "Let's try a few more."

My shoulders slumped at those words. I couldn't help but think of my mother. Oh, how I wished she were here. There was no way I'd be trying on these ridiculous dresses. The thought that the dress I selected today may not be my only wedding dress saddened me. Jude and I never discussed what would happen after the first year.

"Barbi, I like the second one. Silk organza would be perfect for the beach. Plus, it's simple and sand won't get into the fabric. If I wear tulle or one with a long train, it will look dirty by the time I make it down the aisle."

She waved her hand back and forth. "Nonsense. You won't be walking on the sand, hence the fabulous shoes." White beaded pumps dangled from her fingers. "These are spectacular, as your dress should be."

I sighed. Part of me wanted to just agree and buy this monstrosity of a gown, but rather than do that, I agreed to try on a few more. I bet Jude was relaxing in the hammock, all done with his fitting. Men had it so much easier.

Finally, after five dresses, and an Italian seamstress who was pin happy, I was on my way back to the house. Barbi and I agreed on a strapless, white lace, sheath dress. No train, no veil—another argument I needed to win.

"Let's go inside. This home is so charming, isn't it?" This woman was driving me crazy, but since her company just paid for a five thousand dollar dress and three hundred dollar shoes, how could I not at least offer her iced tea? Hopefully, Jude was dressed.

The room was empty and very quiet. "Jude must be out back. I'll pour us some tea." I scanned the counter and tabletop for a note from Jude, but there wasn't one.

"You two are a wonderful couple." I smiled at her words. "He's quite the catch." She walked to the glass door leading to the deck and peered outside. "Where is that handsome man of yours?"

Handing her the iced tea, I pulled open the door. A wave of heat hit me, but it was eerily silent outside. "Maybe he went for a run."

We both took a few steps toward the beach, but didn't see anyone. "Hmmm . . ." Barbi's face twisted into a scowl as she looked at her watch. "I'll just wait until he comes back."

Dread suddenly consumed me. Where could he have gone? When I looked back inside, I saw his bag in the closet, so I knew he didn't leave me. There had to be a logical explanation.

"Do you think he went out with the person who came to fit the tux? Maybe they went to the store?" I set my glass down on the table.

"Eduardo doesn't have a shop here. He makes custom tuxedos in his home. Jude's fitting should have only taken half an hour. She sat down at the table, pulled out her cell phone, and started texting someone. God, how I wish I had mine.

Not knowing what else to do, I began to pace. Forty-five minutes dragged by as I peeked out the window every time I walked past it. Barbi's phone dinged, and my heart jumped.

"According to Eduardo, Jude's fitting took twenty minutes. He said he seemed as though he was in a hurry."

In a hurry? All I could do was stare out the window. More time passed and Barbi's phone dinged again. This time, she stood. When she looked at me, her lips curled down. "I'm very sorry, but it appears Jude has breached the contract."

My eyes lowered in an attempt to disguise the tears forming. "Breached? Are we going to be sued?"

"No, you won't be sued. But you're no longer eligible to receive the prize money. As the rules clearly stated, you were only allowed to be apart for one hour. Granted, I'm the reason you weren't here today, but he was to stay on the property." She walked away to make a call.

He left me. All his promises, and he broke them. Tears finally escaped the corners of my eyes and I didn't bother to wipe them away. No, they could fall just like I did for a liar. What a fool I was for believing he'd stay. Now, I was in worse shape than when I'd left New York. I've lost time where I could have been looking for a job.

Nausea set in. I was going to be sick. His words

replayed in my head as if in a loop, *"I won't let you down. You can count on me. I promise. You can trust me."* The ache in my chest was real. It was official, Jude Soren broke my heart.

Even Barbi's skin looked pale. I needed to ask, what did it all mean, but couldn't formulate the question.

She stood next to me. "You must pack your things and leave the island. The contract is now null and void." Barbi placed her hand on my shoulder. "Such a shame, I thought you two were a wonderful couple. I'll send a car for you in thirty minutes to take you to the airport. I just confirmed a six o'clock flight for tonight. It's the last one off the island until the morning. The driver will have your cell phone with him."

With shaky legs, I stood and nodded. "I'm very sorry about this. Are you sure we can't give him a bit more time?"

"Rules are rules. If you'd like to try again, you have our card. I'm sure your Spark is out there. I'll cancel the wedding gown. I'm very sorry, Brae. Some men aren't wired for relationships." With that, she walked out the door. Not wired? My breath caught in my throat at how true her words were.

Without much time, I forced myself to get my luggage out of the closet. Anger started to replace the sadness as I emptied my drawers. Rather than fold everything, I started to throw my clothes in my cases, not caring about them. Part of me wanted to leave everything here. Once I shoved everything in, I walked into the bathroom to get my toiletries.

"Honey, I'm home," came from the living room. I walked out of the bathroom, eyes red-rimmed and tears staining my cheeks. "What happened?" Jude's eyes went from me to the luggage on the bed.

"You! You happened, you lying asshole. How, Jude? How could you do this to me? God, you knew how badly I needed this, and what did you do? You left. Five weeks into this charade . . ." I flung my hands out to the side, "this farce of a relationship, all to help my family. But that didn't matter to you, did it? No, not Mr. Upper East Side. What do you care if my family loses their measly farm? Why would you give a shit that you broke my heart? Maybe I should be thankful that it happened now. God forbid we got married and you had to be with me for twelve whole months so I wouldn't have to pay the money back." I shook my head. "What a fool I was."

Our gazes connected and the pressure of fresh tears built behind my eyes, but I refused to cry in front of him.

"Brae, I didn't leave you." He took a step toward me, but I held my hand up. "Let me explain. I needed to see—"

"Don't. I don't care who you needed to see, or what you needed to do. All I know is my ride is coming to take me to the airport so I can catch my flight." I zipped my bags shut and yanked them off the bed to land on the floor with a *thud*.

He ran his hand through his hair. "I'll talk to Chip and Barbi. Once I explain—"

"You don't get it, do you? Barbi was here when you weren't. She's the one who gave me my walking papers. It's over." I motioned my hand between us. "We are over. To think I was trying on wedding gowns today." I shook my head in disgust. "You know what?" His eyes lowered before rising to meet mine again. "I started this thing determined to find Mr. Wrong, and how apropos that I succeeded."

"You're wrong. I'm not wrong for you. We are perfect together." His dull eyes pleaded with me.

"Having mind-blowing sex does not make a couple perfect. Compassion, putting the other person first, and communication are needed ingredients. That's where you showed your true colors." Grabbing my bags, I wheeled them to the door. The sound of a car horn alerted me that my ride had arrived. "I never, ever want to see you again. When we get back to the city, don't try to contact me."

"Brae." Jude lunged at me right before I grabbed the doorknob, placing a firm grip on my arm. "I had to go meet Luca. We had a client who needed to talk to me. I planned on being back before you came home, but the client was late for the meeting. His business is worth millions. This wasn't supposed to happen. I had no way to let you know I was running late."

"You knew you were going, you could have told me about it." I glanced down to where he was holding my arm. "Let me go, Jude."

"No, you need to hear me out. When I talked to Luca the other day, we had this planned perfectly. I'd never hurt you, or break my promises to you."

"You just did." I wrenched my arm away from his grip and walked out the door.

The driver put my bags in the trunk and opened the door for me. Before he could close it, Jude ran to the car. "Please, don't leave. I'll work this out. You can't leave me."

The pain in my chest hurt like none I'd ever felt before. "Let me go." Ignoring my demand, his hand flexed on the edge of the door. "Now, Jude. I don't want to miss my flight."

Jude's eyes glistened as he leaned forward. "I'm sorry."

I had no more words for him. He pushed the door closed and I drove away from the man who owned my heart before shattering it.

☆☆☆

Jude

WHAT THE FUCK JUST HAPPENED? Goddammit! I slammed the front door shut before looking around the room. My fingers speared my hair, tugging on the roots. Son of a bitch. I swung my foot, sending a wicker basket flying through the air.

There was a knock on the door. My heart slammed in my chest. *She came back.* I flung open the door, ready to beg for forgiveness, only to find a messenger. He handed me two envelopes and my cell phone.

When he left, I looked inside to see I was on the first flight in the morning. I needed to get to the airport to try to talk to her. If we were on the same flight, she wouldn't be able to avoid me. As fast as I could, I packed my shit and searched for a cab company to take me to the airport. By the time the cab would arrive, she would be on the plane.

I slumped on the couch and stared at my phone. I'd never felt so defeated in all my life. I didn't even have her number. There was no way to contact her—not that she wanted me to. Maybe Kyle could get her number from Shelly.

Even though the second envelope had Brae's name on it, I opened it anyway. Maybe it had contact information for her. When I pulled out the tri-fold paper, I saw it was a fax from Desiree with a letter from the bank attached. Shit. This was what she had been waiting for. As I scanned the document, it stated it needed to be signed today and payment needed to be sent in order for the note on her parents' farm to stay active.

As quick as I could, I dialed the number in hopes to leave the agent in charge a voicemail since it was past closing time.

"Hello." When the man answered, I was surprised.

Fumbling with my words, I responded, "Hi. My name is Jude Soren, is this Mark Jackson?"

"Yes, how can I help you, Mr. Soren?"

"My girlfriend, Brae Daniels, received a letter from your bank, but she's traveling and can't contact you in regards to her parents' farm."

"Oh, I was unaware Brae had a boyfriend." *What the fuck did that matter?*

"The reason for my call is, I'd like to know where to send the payment to clear the debt?"

"Sir, I'm not at liberty to discuss her personal finances with you."

"Let me rephrase. Give me the routing number so I can clear the debt on the Daniels' account. I happen to work in finance and know quite a few people. If you'd like me to contact your superiors, I can do that."

"Did you say your name was Soren, as in Soren Enterprises?"

"Yes. I'm Jude Soren. Do you have any more questions or can we complete this transaction?"

"I'll text the routing number and the amount to clear the note to your phone."

"Thank you."

My phone alerted me to his text and with a few keystrokes, the Daniels' property was secured. I was sure

Brae would be pissed, but it was the least I could do. I then texted Luca, instructing him to pick me up tomorrow afternoon at the airport.

Looking around the house, there wasn't a shred of evidence she had ever been there. My eyes focused on our bed—the one we shared as a couple in every sense of the word. That stupid steak knife she used to feel safe poked out from under the mattress. I wasn't kidding when I told her I'd keep her safe, yet I failed.

I remembered how happy Brae was when we arrived and what a prick I was. She loved it here. It didn't matter that it was a small, modest home; it made her smile.

Unable to bring myself to sleep in the bed we had shared, I stretched out as best I could on the small couch and stared at the ceiling. Every time I closed my eyes, I saw her—the way she looked at me right before getting into that cab. I hurt her.

I tried to picture her smiling, laughing, even the way she'd stare into my eyes when we were intimate, but all I could see was the sadness and hurt when she left me. Remembering my GoPro, I got up and took it out of the nightstand and pushed play. I saw her beautiful face on the small screen and couldn't help but smile when I heard her snoring.

Sitting back down, I clutched the camera to my chest replaying the video over and over again. The image blurred through my unshed tears. "I'm sorry, Sparky."

☆☆☆

New York greeted me with a blast of frigid air. I was surprised I felt it since my entire body was numb. Dragging my bags behind me, I spotted Kyle's car out at the curb.

"Well, look who's back." Kyle greeted me with a bro

hug. "How are you doing?"

"Fine. Where's Luca?" I tossed my bags in the trunk of his car.

Kyle, the dork that he was, put his hand on his chest. "I'm hurt. Aren't you happy to see me?"

"No." With a shake of my head, we both got inside. "I'm still plotting your horrible death."

"Screw you. I had to endure at least a dozen phone calls a day from your assistant, Ruth! And a few a week from your mother, and each of your sisters as they all babbled in broken English interspersed with Swedish. Seriously?"

"You got off easy. Fuck, it's freezing." A shiver ran through me.

He turned the heat up in the car. "That's what you get for spending time on an island while the rest of us suffered through this shit. Luca had a meeting. Did you want to go to the office?"

I cut my eyes to him. "No, I need a shower first. And really? You're the one who started all of this. Now, I'm back with nothing to show for it except a tan."

"What you mean is, you lost the girl. Luca filled me in." Kyle shrugged. "I can't believe you made it as long as you did. Granted, she was hot a fuck, but still."

My fists clenched. "Don't talk about her that way."

"Wow. You're pussy whipped."

All I could do was remain silent. I had nothing else to say. It was true, I was. She hated me, but at least I knew the stress of losing her family's farm was off her shoulders. Thankfully, I was able to send the money from a business account. God only knew what she'd do if she found out it was me. And it wasn't something I did to try to win her back. It was something I did because she needed help. Brae wasn't a gold digger, she was an honest person who worked hard. Never once did she ask me for help. Maybe that's why I did it without thinking.

People filled the streets as Kyle drove me to my apartment. "Thanks for the ride."

"It's the least I could do." He parallel parked his car along the curb. "I am sorry it ended up this way. In all honesty, I never thought you'd be this serious about her."

"Me either. She was fun once I got past her quirks, and even they were cute." I smiled at the thought of her nighttime ritual, even though I still didn't know what it was, and the way she made the bed even though we had maid service. How she couldn't cook and wouldn't eat bacon until we started to burn calories. Everything about her made me smile. Everything except the fact that I might never see her again.

I reached for the door handle. "Can I ask you something?" Kyle lost all humor in his voice.

"Sure."

"Would you have married her like the rules stated?"

That was an easy question. "Yes."

"Would you still?"

Kyle's question didn't shock me. I'd asked myself the same thing more than once. Admitting to him how I felt would only cause me more grief. So, I ignored his question, but in my head, replied, *Fuck yes.*

Chapter 26

Brae

GRAY SKIES GREETED ME YET again. Not much had changed since I'd been home. People still filled the city streets, horns still blared, sirens sounded, and I was still looking for a job. But, first things first, I needed to get to the bank. Since I left St. John so quickly, I never got the fax. However, a certified letter was waiting for me at the post office, and when I read it, my heart dropped.

The deadline had passed. Now, I needed to rely on the bank's compassion to give me just a few more days to figure things out. The problem was, they didn't have compassion. I was such a fool to try to take the easy way out. What a joke, the easy way. Being on that island, living in a fantasy world, was the worst idea I'd had. Scratch that. The worst was falling for a man who was clearly self-centered and one hell of an actor.

Every man I passed on the street didn't hold a candle to Jude. How could they? He was the most handsome man I'd ever seen up close and personal. The way his body was sculpted like a statue was unsurpassed. And those damn tattoos. I knew I could never look at stars the same way again. Maybe I'd just never look at the sky. Then again, even the sunsets reminded me of him. He ruined things for me. Things I loved. Now they were tarnished like old silver.

A man held the door open for me when I arrived at the bank. I spotted Mr. Jackson's office, but my heart sunk when I noticed the lights were off. Another bank employee approached me. "Hello, I'm Mr. Allen. May I help you?"

"Yes, can you please tell me when Mr. Jackson will be in?" I fiddled with my purse strap knowing I'd have to wait until he returned to beg him for yet another extension.

"He's on vacation for the next ten days. Is there something I can help you with?"

Vacation? Ten days? Without another choice, I'd need to start schmoozing Mr. Allen and play on his sympathies. I'd been told time and time again this wasn't personal, yet to me, that's all it was. Yes, I knew banks loaned money and expected prompt payment, but I needed them to believe this was a temporary setback. Maybe I should apply to the bank for a job and handover my paycheck right to the source. Clean their bathrooms even?

Giving him a smile worthy of a beauty pageant queen, I said, "Yes, I need to discuss a loan."

Mr. Allen nodded, immune to my forced charm, and motioned for me to follow him into his office. Once inside, my heart began to thunder in my chest. What if he didn't care? This could end up with me crying like a fool in front of a stranger.

"Here is the account number." I handed him the certified letter. He began keying things into his computer.

With each new keystroke, his brows would lower, then raise, then he looked questioningly at me. Before he could say more, I spoke up. "I know I'm late. I was away and missed the fax that was sent to me. Is there a way I could just have one more month? I have a lead on a job and it won't be long until I'm able to make a payment." That was all a lie. Although, I had passed a hiring sign on the restaurant down the road. I supposed I could waitress.

"Ms. Daniels, this loan is cleared."

"What? What do you mean cleared?"

"It's been paid in full."

I tapped my finger on the letter sitting on his desk. "Can you please look at that again. There must be some mistake." A little voice told me to say thank you and get the hell out of there while the getting was good, but I didn't listen. There was no way possible it was paid.

Mr. Allen tilted his monitor toward me and pointed to the zero balance. "There's no mistake. This is the account, and it's clear."

"How? Who paid it?"

There was more clicking and tapping on his keyboard until he found what he needed. "It says here it was paid in full by SFS, Inc. Do you know who they are?"

I shook my head. "No, do you?" Jude popped into my head, but he had no idea where the loan originated, so it couldn't have been him. I needed to search SFS, Inc. and figure out who they were.

He beamed. "I'd say they were your fairy godmother. But, according to the notes on the account, Mr. Jackson was the one to speak with them." Mr. Allen pushed a button and the sound of a printer came to life. He handed me a piece of paper. "Keep this for your records."

Rather than the usual high number I'd been used to seeing in the balance column, this one just had three zeros. "Thank you." I stood and shook the man's hand before leaving his office.

♡♡♡

"Wait, you mean to tell me the loan is paid off?" Cassie sounded as surprised as I did. Music filled the air at José Ponchos where I met my friends for drinks. I nodded and took a sip of my margarita.

It was my third, and the knot in my chest was finally loosening. I filled the girls in on the basics of what had happened over the last five weeks, and it only took about five sentences to do so.

"Do you think it was him?" Desiree asked.

"Yes. I searched his name, which led to his company, and this SFS, Inc is a subsidiary of Soren Enterprises. So, it's him. He's so arrogant, I'm surprised he didn't want me to know he paid it to get back in my good graces," I admitted with a scowl. Desiree mumbled something inaudibly. "What did you say?"

"I said, unless he didn't want you to know because he knew how you'd react." My eyes flared and I opened my mouth to argue, only to be stopped by Desiree's palm facing me. "Let's face it, Brae. You're a proud woman. We've all offered to chip in and help, but you declined. If you guys are as close as you said, he would know that too. Maybe this was his way of apologizing."

Desiree's words rattled around in my brain. I didn't care what his reasons were. As far as I was concerned, now I had another debt to pay. I didn't want to owe that man anything.

Vanessa waved her hand back and forth. "Who cares? Our girl is debt free. I'm more interested in hearing more details of what happened on the island of sin."

We all looked at her with wide eyes. "Please don't call it that."

"What? I'm sorry, but, sweetie, that man was delectable. Plus, you told all of us you didn't want to end up with the man, just a way to pay off the loan. If I were stranded with him, I know I'd be climbing him like a monkey on a tree."

"Well, be my guest, because he's an asshole," I hissed with a sneer.

Desiree put her hand on mine. "I'm so sorry he hurt you."

I just shrugged. Hurt? The man crushed me. Hurt would be easier to get over.

"Now, tell us what really happened." Vanessa leaned forward, intrigue written all over her face. When I cocked one brow, her lips turned down. "I'm sorry. I didn't realize how much he meant to you. If you want, I can hunt the bastard down and cut his balls off."

Trying to suppress a smile didn't last long. The four of us started to laugh. It felt good to be with my friends again. How I wished I could have had them with me on the island. So much could have been different.

"Okay, I'll tell you. But then I don't want to talk about him anymore. Deal?" They all nodded while taking sips of their drinks. "Jude wasn't exactly like the man who answered those questions. Don't get me wrong, when we first got there, he was a Grade A prick, but the more we got to know each other, the more I saw the real Jude Soren." I smiled at the memory. "He was kind and attentive. He'd cook for us, since you all know I can barely make toast." They all nodded, but remained silent. I could feel the pressure of tears starting to build. "He made me feel things I didn't think I had in me."

"Wow, you fell hard for him," Cassie interjected before waving for the waitress to refill our drinks.

"Jude Soren ruined me." All the hurt, all the pain, and even all the wonderful parts rushed through me in a sudden surge of emotion that settled as a lump in my throat. Three sets of eyes were on me, and I needed to take a few deep breaths before I could continue.

Desiree reached over and caressed my arm in support. "Are you okay, sweetie?"

"I'm fine. I just need to figure out how to forget him. You'd think it'd be easy, since I only knew the man barely over a month. But . . . it's not. Being with him day and night wasn't scary or intimidating. It was comfortable. I'd never spent so much time with a man before. Every hour of every day for the past five weeks was spent with him. How could I not have feelings for him?" I choked back a small sob. "Except the only feeling I have for him now is hate. I hate that he broke the rules. I hate that he had such little regard for my feelings. I hate that he didn't care enough about me. He knew the purpose for me being there and about my parents, and he still left when he shouldn't have." When I looked up all my friends, including Vanessa, they had tears filling their eyes. "What I hate most is how much I miss him."

Jude

RUTH SAT AT MY DESK, rattling off my meetings for the day. This was what I was used to. Constant meetings, phone calls, and staring at the stock market ticker on the bottom of the plasma screen hanging in my office. This was my sanctuary. That was, until I met Brae. Now, this felt like my hell.

By now, she knew her loan was paid off. At least she no longer had that burden. Part of me felt like she hadn't figured it out yet, otherwise I would have no doubt heard from her. If she did know, her silence was even more telling. She hated me.

"I need a favor." Before Ruth walked out of the office, I reached into the top left drawer and took out a small wrapped box. Right before I left the island, I had the cab driver stop in town so I could buy her that bracelet she loved. I'd never forget the look on her face when she modeled it in the store. I wanted to give it to her in person, but I had a feeling that wouldn't happen anytime soon.

"Yes, Mr. Soren?"

"Can you please have this messengered to the address attached?" I handed her the small package.

"Would you like a card added?"

"No, I put a note inside, but thank you." I leaned back in my leather chair and rubbed my temples with my fingertips.

"Sir, are you okay? I don't know what happened when you were away, but if you need me to free your schedule, I can do that." Poor Ruth looked like her dog died. She has worked for me since I started and knew this wasn't my norm.

"That won't be necessary. Just please have the package delivered, and if you could send Luca in, I'd appreciate it."

With a nod, she was gone.

"What's up, my brother?" Luca bounded into my office and dropped his ass on the chair. His chipper disposition didn't help my current one. In fact, it had the opposite effect.

"We need to go over the financials for the Lamen Foundation. A few money market accounts split overnight and we need to decide where to allocate the funds to increase their profits while the prices are low."

Luca just stared at me. "You look like hell."

"Thank you. Once you're done critiquing my appearance, can you please pull the necessary recommendations? We have a lot of work to catch up on. Tell me what else is going on."

He started firing off dollar figures, percentages, and fluctuations. All the things that would usually get my blood pumping, but today, it all sounded like a big burden. I spun my chair a bit and stared out the window, looking down at the people milling about on the sidewalks. Brae was in this city and even though I had her address, going there wouldn't be an option if I wanted to keep my balls.

Luca started knocking on my desk. "Earth to Jude, are you listening to me?"

"Yeah, fluctuating markets. I heard you."

"Dude, you didn't hear anything I just said. It's clear you're not focused. Why don't you go home? I can't even blame jetlag. You're Brae-lagged." I threw him a livid expression and he raised his hands in defense. "Kidding."

"I need to be here. There's nothing for me at home." Dismissing his suggestion, I tried to focus.

"You mean, aside from your palatial surroundings? Call someone to keep you company."

He couldn't be serious. "Are you suggesting I go home and get laid?"

His hands flew in the air again and his Italian accent

thickened. "No. Did I say laid? I said to keep you company. Call Kyle, he'll come over. I'll stay here and take care of things. Technically, you weren't supposed to be back in the office yet. You're of no use here. Try again tomorrow."

"I'll be fine." I cleared my throat and started the meeting again, pushing all thoughts of Brae to the back of my mind.

My apartment had never felt so empty. Even though Brae had never been inside, I still expected to see her coming out of the bathroom. We'd talked about living here after we were married. *Married.* I was completely ready to say "I do" to her, yet here I was, alone.

Pouring myself a couple fingers of whiskey, I sat on my couch. My GoPro was across from me on the coffee table. I kept telling myself, over and over, to stop watching the video I took of her. It was becoming a problem. My snoring kitten was like a lullaby when I slept.

A knock at my door caused me to groan. I didn't need to even look through the peephole or ask who it was, I knew. When I opened the door, I was right. Luca and Kyle stood in my hallway with pizza, chips, and a twelve pack.

"The Knicks are on. We thought we'd come over and watch it at your place."

They meant well, I knew they did—hell, maybe a guy's night would help me get my head on straight. "Sounds good." I stepped aside, letting my two buddies in.

At halftime, the pizza was gone, as was most of the beer. "So, I talked to Shelly today," Kyle said as he popped a chip in his mouth. "She gave me Brae's phone number."

"I thought you weren't seeing her anymore," Luca chimed in, chuckling. "You said she was too clingy for your taste."

He shrugged. "I happened to run into her while I was having lunch."

All I could do was stare at him. Kyle had her number. Did I want it?

"Anyway, I'll text it to you." Before I could stop him, my phone dinged. Looking down, I saw the number, and my heart sped up at the thought of hearing her voice again. "Do with it what you will, but you're acting like a pussy. Where's the cocky guy we all know and love?"

They were right. Maybe all of this sulking was the worst thing for me. Rejection would just add to my demeanor, so I probably wouldn't call. Not today anyway. A loud buzzing came from my television. It was time for the second half, and time for me to get my head out of my ass.

Chapter 27

Brae

WHEN THE MESSENGER DELIVERED THE package yesterday, I was afraid to open it. There was no return address, but thankfully, after batting my eyes a few times, the young messenger gave up that information. I'd guessed who it was from even though the address meant nothing to me.

There it sat next to my cup of coffee. Teasing me. Baiting me to open it. I finally gave in and picked it up. I shook it a few times, but it barely rattled. With shaky fingers, I unwrapped it. When I pulled the cover off, there sat the bracelet from the store on St. John—the six thousand dollar bracelet. I couldn't believe he'd done that. An involuntary wave of heat warmed my entire body from head to toe.

My fingers trembled as I took it from the cotton and stared at it for a moment. A note rested in the box.

Brae,

I remembered how much you loved this bracelet. How your face lit up when you saw it for the first time, and how beautiful it looked on your arm. I wanted to buy it for you that day, but I knew you'd say no.

Please forgive me. I know you hate me, and rightfully so. I let you down. You trusted me and I failed you—failed us.

I'll never forget our time together.

I'll never forget you.

    Always yours,

     Jude

Tears I finally thought I was done shedding free-flowed down my face. My heart lodged in my throat as I read his note over and over again. No matter how much I cared about him, this wasn't going to work. He made it clear his company was the most important thing in his life, and I couldn't live with that.

There was no way I could accept this gift. It didn't matter that he was wealthy—it was too much.

I put it back in the box, wiped my tears away with the back of my hand, grabbed my coat, and headed out the door.

When the cab pulled up to the tall building, my heart raced. Warning bells sounded in my head. He was inside.

My plan was to leave it with reception and hightail it out of there.

The elevator rose at a snail's pace, stopping at what felt like every floor between the lobby and the fifteenth, where I was headed. Finally, the number fifteen lit up with a ding and the doors slid open. I stepped out, and my eyes caught the silver lettering on the mahogany-covered wall. The script read, Soren Enterprises. And right there beneath it, read, SFS, Incorporated. Even knowing it was him, seeing it in silver staring at me like a beacon felt like a slap to my face.

"May I help you?" I turned my head toward the voice, my eyes landing on a pretty, young woman sitting behind a large desk matching the wall.

"Yes." I reached into my bag and pulled out the box. "I'd like to leave this for Jude Soren."

She smiled at the mention of his name. Not that I could blame her. I could only imagine what he looked like in the office. His confidence had to be off the charts sexy.

"Let me buzz him. Can I get your name?"

"No need." I set the box down. "Just please make sure he gets it. He'll know who it's from."

I pivoted on my heel just as a door opened beside the elevator bay. A familiar looking man walked out and stared at me before looking back into the room he was leaving. He said something in an accent and I realized it was Luca.

A sly grin grew across his face as he stepped aside to make room for someone.

Jude.

Our eyes locked and my pulse pounded in my ears. He looked devilishly handsome in his charcoal suit, white shirt, and thin black tie. Naturally, his hair was perfectly messy and his five o'clock scruff appeared to be thicker. But it was his eyes that got me.

With a tentative smile on his face, he said, "Sparky?" In just a few long strides, he was in front of me. His arms wrapped around me, yet mine just hung at my sides.

He must have sensed my apprehension and realized this wasn't a reconciliation visit. When he released me, I instantly missed his warmth, his scent. All memories flooded through me like a tsunami. I reached over to the desk and grabbed the small box away from the woman who was now staring at us.

"My name is Brae, not Sparky, and I can't accept this." I held the box out for him to take. Instead of taking it, he wrapped his hand around the top of my arm and escorted me toward the office he emerged from.

"I can't stay. I have a job interview." I twisted away from his grip.

He leaned down until his nose practically touched mine. "You can walk to my office and give me five minutes of your time, or I can carry you in there. Your choice. You have ten seconds to decide."

My eyes scanned the plush office, a blush creeping over my cheeks when several of his employees stopped in their tracks and were now watching us. He straightened and waited, the look on his face challenging me. In his mind, he was probably counting down the clock.

There wasn't a doubt he'd follow through, and the only thing that had my feet moving in the direction we were heading was a visual of my ass in the air as my body was flung over his shoulder.

Upon the click of the door, my skin prickled under

the wool of my sweater. "Okay. I'm here. What do you want? Like I said, I have an appointment, so make it quick."

"You look good." I rolled my eyes and moved toward the door. "Wait. How have you been?"

Before I could even entertain giving him an answer, something needed to be said. "Thank you for paying off the loan. I know you did it out of guilt, and as soon as I get a job, I'll be paying you back with interest."

"How did you know?"

Not bothering to explain, all I said was, "I don't want your money."

"Consider it a gift. It was the least I could do."

His offending comment sent me over the edge. "The least you could do?" I seethed. "You just paid off four hundred and twenty-five thousand dollars without blinking an eye, and in the process, made me feel like a whore."

"Don't fucking say that." His pained expression and the way he clenched his fists at his sides almost broke me. "I never have or would treat you that way," he said, his voice barely above a whisper.

"But you did," I responded with the same determination. "We spent five weeks sharing the same bed, same home, fucking, and my consolation prize was almost a half-million practically left on the nightstand as you walked away. Oh, how proud my parents will be when they hear why you gave me the money. I don't want your gifts or your money, but keeping your promise would have been nice." My muscles tightened as I threw my hand in the air.

"I did keep my promise. My intent was never to leave you. Besides, what was the difference if the money came from me or some stupid social experiment?"

"Because winning the show would have meant earning the money. I guess you felt I deserved compensation for the stellar blow jobs. Maybe if I threw in a few more, you would have made it an even five hundred grand." Not wanting to be near him, I placed the box containing the bracelet on an end table near the door.

"You're so wrong, Brae." His greenish-brown eyes bore into mine and the faint gray circle that rimmed the irises still mesmerized me.

"How am I wrong, Jude? Now you've forced me to owe you, and if you knew me at all, you should have known that would bother me. Clearly, getting to know me on a personal level wasn't on your priority list."

He raked his hand through his hair, walked over to his desk, and hung his jacket over the back of his chair before loosening his tie. "I'd think losing your parents' farm would bother you more than thinking you owed me money. I just did it to help you." He went from being hurt and upset back to the sardonic man I'd met so many weeks ago.

His patronizing tone made my chest heave with frustrated breaths. "Of course, Jude to the rescue. Now I'm indebted to you, right? Was that your plan? To have that over me? What was your motive? What I think is you chose to live with me in every sense of the word, use me, and then throw me the money right after you threw me away. How is that different than being your whore?" I jutted my chin out.

"Because . . ." He sat slumped in his chair. "You know what? Never mind." He flipped open a file on his desk before lifting his angry eyes to focus on my face. "Obviously, nothing I say will convince you otherwise.

Are you done making me out to be the bad guy?"

"Honestly, you could have saved us both the time and paid it off right after I told you, then you could have come back to the city, taken care of your company, and all of this could have been avoided."

"I didn't have the account number or a way to contact the bank or I would have," he seethed through gritted teeth.

I let out a dejected, "Wow." Our eyes locked and remorse instantly altered his livid expression. If I didn't walk away now, I knew I'd be a mess of tears. The skin on my face prickled. I had to leave. My hand gripped the door handle, and my eyes landed on a framed children's drawing that said, *"Thank you, Mr. Soren, for our new playground."*

The tears I held back swelled at the memory of that day and how generous he had been when we stumbled onto that sad orphanage. My chest constricted in pain over the conflict I felt between wanting the good guy I knew he could be, and pushing away the one who kept breaking my heart.

The raw pain won the battle. I turned to look at Jude one last time. "When I left the island, I asked you not to contact me. Although I know how hard it is for you to adhere to your words, please try to, and don't ever think of me again."

"Brae . . ."

My lips rolled between my teeth. This was exhausting me. I wanted to go home. Without another glance, I opened the door and left. Salty tears blurring my vision, I hustled toward the elevators, not noticing Luca until I barreled into him.

"Hey, are you okay?" He reached out, trying to steady

me.

"Yes, thank you." As quick as I heard the ding of the elevator door, I slid in and escaped all that was Jude Soren.

Jude

THE SMALL CRYSTAL GLOBE ADORNING my desk met its demise as I hurled it against the wall. Luca walked in at the exact moment it crashed to the marble floor and shattered into a million pieces.

"I liked that thing," he said with a frown. Ignoring his comment, I sat back in my chair. That woman infuriated me like no one ever has in my life. My blood simmered in my veins as Luca sat staring at me with an arrogant smirk. "What the hell did you do to her?"

"What did *I* do to her?"

His eyes trained on my face, he nodded. "Yes, that is what I asked."

"She . . ." I scrubbed my hand through my hair. "You know what, it doesn't matter."

"Really?" His arrogance grew, along with the smirk on his face. "She runs out crying hysterically. You throw objects against a wall. But, you're absolutely right, it doesn't matter."

"I have work to do," I said, dismissing him with a wave of my hand. Pretending to read over the Waldon file, I ignored his eyes on me.

When it was clear he had no plans to leave, I glanced up, watching as he crossed the room to help himself to a water out of my mini fridge. Looking like he didn't have

a care in the world—which, compared to me, he didn't—
he assumed his comfortable position in the chair facing
my desk.

"I'm serious, Luca."

"So am I. You can pretend to be studying that file, but
I'm on to you, Soren."

"Really? What exactly are you on to, Benedetto?"

"That you're not the same man who left here almost
two months ago. I watched you these past few days, and
you can't fool me." He twisted the cap of his bottle
before taking a long, deliberate drink. "I know you've
changed."

"You don't know shit." I turned my attention to my
computer screen and stared at the *NYSE* homepage, but
only saw Brae's face instead. "I don't have time for your
stupid theories," I grumbled, not bothering to hide my
frustration.

"Yes, it is just a theory, I'll give you that. To be honest,
I have no idea what the hell *has* happened to you. Maybe
you got bit by a mosquito in the tropics and are infected
with the Zika virus," he said on a chuckle that turned into
a laugh when he met my glare. "So . . ." he continued,
clearing his throat in an amused sort of way, "my theory
is . . . that woman got under your skin. Never having been
in love . . ."

"Love? Are you fucking insane?" The words felt like
acid as they passed my lips.

"Whatever. Love, lust, bubonic plague . . . whatever it
is you're suffering from. I have no idea how or why that
could happen in a few short weeks, but . . ."

"Five weeks, to be exact," I interrupted. "Thirty-five
days, night and day, all day long, just her and me, with
nothing to do for hours and hours."

His eyes widened, along with his grin. "Do you know the exact amount of hours?"

Eight hundred and forty-two.

With a bored expression, I folded my arms to wait him out. I knew my friend well enough to know when he had something to say, he'd make sure he was heard. Unlike Kyle, who babbled like a woman at times, Luca was a man of few words. And there wasn't a doubt I would be forced to wait for him to enlighten me.

Those words of wisdom came almost a full minute later when he said, "You look like shit. You act like your best friend died, which I know hasn't happened since I'm sitting right here. Whatever it is that she did to you, you got it bad."

Sweat poured down my back as I beat the shit out of the seventy pound Everlast victim hanging from a chain mounted to the ceiling. Not many were there at the ungodly hour of six a.m. My normal appearance would have been at least two hours later before I went to the office to begin my twelve-hour day.

Getting to the gym at the crack of dawn became my new norm these past few weeks. The early morning crowd wasn't interested in interacting, and that suited me just fine. Those who were there ignored me. I guess when your body language said, *don't fucking talk to me,* people apparently listened. The scowl on my face, the earbuds in my ear, and the way I aggressively pounded the punching bag most definitely helped to ensure they didn't.

During the hours before the workday, or right after, meant the gym was more like a social gathering. I wasn't interested in socializing, or flirting with the women who made working out a way of life, or talking business with the men who thought the bigger the weights they lifted, the hotter the chick they'd land.

The only thing I was interested in was taking out my frustrations while trying to forget. Only when my muscles screamed for me to stop did I step away to reach for the towel I draped around the chain-link.

"Hey, Jude. How've you been?" With my back to her, she was spared the eye-roll I made at the sound of her voice.

"Hey, Lanie. Good. You?" I turned, the biggest fake smile I could muster plastered on my face.

"I'm awesome. I landed that modeling job I told you about. It's been surreal."

"That's great," I said with the same amount of enthusiasm one would use when hearing they were fired.

Her ruby red lips spread into a salacious grin. The sports bra that doubled as a top stretched over her ample boobs—the same ones I'd sucked on. Her tiny spandex boyshorts molded over her pussy like a second skin. Her platinum blonde hair screamed bottle. In fact, everything about her screamed fake. Who wore false eyelashes to a gym?

Brae wouldn't dare . . .

Fuck.

"I'm sorry, what did you say?" I schooled my features to hide my boredom.

"I said I haven't seen you around in a while. Traveling for business?"

"Um . . . yeah. I've been swamped." I grabbed the bottle of water I placed on the bench against the wall, and her eyes ravished me as I took a long gulp. I followed her tongue as she swiped it across her bottom lip. It instantly reminded me of the night she dragged it up my cock, leaving red lipstick all over me like a crime scene. Even the way she glanced around the gym, as if contemplating dropping to her knees to suck me off right then and there . . . did nothing.

"I'm glad I ran into you. A few of us are going to Claw Hammer tonight to celebrate Sapphire's birthday. Why don't you guys meet us there. You remember her, right?"

I had to bite my tongue to stop from laughing. Instantly, I remembered the bouncy, annoying redhead who wanted Kyle's cock.

"Yes, I remember. Well, we wouldn't want to disappoint . . . Sapphire. Maybe, we'll see you guys there."

She squealed, causing me to blink. "Yay. Okay, we'll see you later. Be sure to bring Kyle. Sapphire would love to see him."

"Oh, no worries, Lanie. He'll be there." If I had to duct tape his arms and legs and carry him in, he'd be there.

Revenge.

Chapter 28

Brae

WITH A SIGH, I TOOK a long gulp of my drug of choice for the evening. Numbing myself, that would help me get through. Although, I preferred to do so while at home in my cozy apartment, I really wasn't given a choice. And now that we were here, this evening seemed to be turning into an intervention.

Making the decision to move back home wasn't made in haste. I'd been thinking about it for a while. Even though I loved my apartment, and loved living in the city, I could save three thousand a month if I moved upstate with my parents. Actually, I'd save more than that by living off the farm and mooching off my mother's cooking.

But my friends weren't going to let me go without an argument.

Aside from living expenses, I had a bigger debt to pay off. Yes, I could use my savings to pay a small chunk of it, but it would take the rest of my life to pay Jude back. Staying in my apartment would just delay it. Until my debt was paid, I'd be tied to him, and that was the last thing I wanted or needed right now. It was hard enough trying to get over him without having money looming over my head. Now that I knew he was behind the loan, it was damn near impossible not to think about him every day.

I couldn't shake the feeling that he owned a piece of me. He took away what little control I had over the situation, which really pissed me off—especially since Jude knew I hated not having control. Part of me wondered if he did it to alleviate his guilt or to help me. My heart wished it was the latter, but my brain told me otherwise.

The worst part was having to tell my parents I'd been helping them. When I admitted I'd participated in a game show to try to win the money, my mother wasn't pleased. Then she was even less pleased when I told her I was out of the country.

After I apologized profusely for lying, she thanked me for trying. Naturally, I left out what type of game show and that it involved a man. That would have sent her over the edge and I would have been living with parental guilt for years. It was bad enough living with the feelings I already had. Once she heard my version of the truth, my mother understood why I did it, but wasn't very happy given my current situation.

When she questioned how the balance was paid, I told her I met an investor who helped me. Not a complete fabrication of the truth, and even though she couldn't see my fingers, which were crossed behind my back, at least I was able to answer her questions.

So, here we were, in José Ponchos, which wasn't helping my migraine since the noise level was through the roof. The bodies jammed together along the bar looked like one large orgy in motion—albeit a clothed one. "This place is getting too popular," I grumbled over the rim of my margarita.

"Aren't we in a great mood, Miss Mary Sunshine," Desiree chastised with a raised brow.

Vanessa refilled my glass without invitation and lifted hers, giggling as the slushy liquid spilled over the side. "Oops. Okay, a toast. To our Brae-Brae. May she find a hot, overall-wearing farmer to milk her teets . . . tits." She looked at us confused. "Tits or teets?"

Ignoring our tipsy friend, Cassie's smile warmed me when our eyes met. Since the whole spark flame nonsense, she'd been almost weepy over my situation. My girls knew it all, and I held nothing back when I gave them every detail. And true to their personalities, they each responded differently.

Vanessa wanted every sordid detail involving me doing Jude. Desiree was more interested in the possibility of suing *Ignite Your Spark* since technically we weren't together when Jude left. She was sure there was a loophole, and I was letting her stew over that. And Cassie, my sweet friend, was concerned for my broken heart.

She reached for my hand and squeezed. "Can I make a suggestion?"

"Of course." I looked down into my cocktail. If I saw sadness of any kind, I couldn't guarantee I wouldn't bawl right there in José Ponchos. "Sweetie, move in with me for a while. You can save some money and pay him what you would be paying for rent. Take some time, then go home. There's no rush now that the banks aren't hounding."

"There's an even bigger rush for me to leave this city where I can run into him at any moment." Three sets of mascaraed eyes stared at me. "I fell in love with him." I stunned them silent, and quickly moved on. "But thank you, Cassie. I appreciate it. The quicker I get home, the quicker I can get the farm up and running to how it was in its heyday. Besides, it's a hell of a lot more gratifying than waitressing at Sunbeam Diner."

"Those retro uniforms are adorable," Vanessa quipped. "You'd get a lot of propositions, no doubt." The three of us stared at her. Unperturbed, she shrugged, and said, "We need more." Taking the empty pitcher with her, she beelined toward the bar.

"Just one day in my life I'd love to be as carefree as Vanessa," I voiced my thoughts.

"Anyway . . ." Des said on a sigh, "Cassie's right, Brae. Rushing upstate now seems rash. You need time to decompress before you take on the stress of running a farm."

"I just had three weeks to decompress." I wanted to add that during that time I'd done nothing but reminisce, stew, and cry over him. I literally flip-flopped between missing him desperately to hating myself for wasting the energy.

Vanessa came back way too soon to have waited in that huge bar line. Holding a fresh pitcher of margaritas in one hand and dragging Shelly behind her with the other, she grinned, and said, "Look who I found."

"Brae!" Coming to my side of the table, she pulled me out of my chair into a gripping hug. "I feel so guilty. I'm so sorry. I really am. I—"

"Shell, it's fine." I patted her back, reversing the roles and consoling her. "I knew going in what the risk was. No one forced it on me. It's totally fine."

"I know, but still. All that aggravation and torment."

Torment.

Was it? I couldn't say it was until the last hour. Even in the beginning when he drove me nuts and teased me relentlessly, it was never a torment to be with him.

"Water under the bridge." I smiled as genuinely as I could. "Join us?"

She nodded, the guilt she felt was written all over her face. Determined to steer the conversation to safer topics, I mentioned the drink specials, sat back, and listened as my friends chattered and laughed around me. With each funny story and glass we consumed, I was able to forget who Jude Soren was for the time being.

Jude

WITH THE EXCUSE OF NEEDING to get drunk, it didn't take long to convince Kyle and Luca to go to the bar Lanie invited us to. But five minutes in, revenge was no longer that important to me. The place was nothing less than a meat market, filled with scantily clad women on the prowl and successful single men watching the hunt.

Lanie, Sapphire, and . . . I won't even pretend to remember her name, surrounded us seconds after we entered the bar and led us to their table. The only way they could have spotted us that quick in a crowd that size was if one of them was playing lookout.

Kyle's ass was barely planted on the seat when Sapphire wrapped herself around him. "Dance with me," she shrieked loud enough to be heard over the blaring music. The color of her ruby red hair was the exact shade of her cocktail. She placed it on the table and yanked on his arm.

"Oh, I want to dance, too." Lanie turned toward me and I shook my head before she could ask her question.

"Maybe later, I need a drink first."

Luca and I left to get the much-needed alcohol. The look on Kyle's face as Sapphire mauled him on the dance floor helped to at least soothe my bad mood for a few minutes. Unfortunately, that quickly wore off and I was back to scowling.

"How about we ditch him?" Luca suggested after we ordered our drinks.

"Brilliant. Right after this Belvedere." I lifted the short tumbler and downed it in one gulp. Luca followed suit with his whisky before slapping a fifty on the bar. "One more," he said to the bartender, who eyed me up before doing the same to Luca. When he delivered our second round and leaned over the bar to check out the bottom half of my body, I met Luca's eyes and we hightailed it back to the table, downing our drinks along the way.

"Seems not only the women in here are on the prowl," he said, motioning toward the jammed dance floor. Upon closer inspection, there were men writhing together, some women lip-locked in similar positions, and then there was Kyle between Sapphire and an Asian woman who had a five o'clock shadow.

Luca and I busted out laughing and shifted direction. We almost made it out the door before Kyle spotted us.

"Assholes!" he said when he caught up.

"What?" Luca lifted both hands in his Italian way. "We're just getting some air."

Just as we walked out the door to flag a cab, Kyle's phone dinged. He pulled it out and a rueful smile grew across his face. I'd seen that look before, and after what just went down with Sapphire, I knew it was directed at me.

A yellow sedan pulled up to the curb and we all got in. Kyle and Luca took the backseat, while I sat upfront with the driver. As soon as I began to rattle off my address, Kyle shouted a different one from the back.

"Dude, I'm going home." Again, I attempted to tell the driver my address, but this time, Luca chimed in and repeated what Kyle had said. When I turned to look at my idiot friends, Luca was reading the text Kyle had just received.

"Jude, trust us." Luca nodded in agreement.

I couldn't contain the sarcastic chuckle that escaped me. "Trust you? Did you just say that to me?"

Luca chimed it. "It's her."

Her who? Brae? My girl was texting Kyle? What the fuck? "What the hell are you talking about?"

"Shelly just sent me a text saying she's having drinks with Brae and her friends at some Mexican bar. I say we go check it out."

Kyle's words, while tempting, didn't bode well with me. If I saw Brae getting hit on by someone, they were going to end up in the hospital. All I could think of was the feeling I had when Toby hit on her while we were having lunch and he wasn't really interested.

"No, it's not a good idea. She hates me." I ran my hand through my hair. Just as I looked out the window, I saw a green, yellow, and orange sombrero flashing in the near distance. Fuck.

Luca swiped his card and once he was out of the sedan, opened my door. "Come on, man, give it one more shot."

"Yeah, give it the old college try." Kyle swung his fist

in front of him. "What do you have to lose? If she blows you off, I'm sure there are others in there who would just want to blow you. So, it's all good." He slung his arm around my shoulder, ignoring my glare.

"Kyle, shut the fuck up." Luca shoved him away from me. "Just go in there and get her back."

Music blared as soon as we pulled the door open. The place was packed. My eyes tried to focus on faces to see if I could find her, but it was to no avail. The lighting sucked and people who weren't dancing or sitting at a table were occupying every inch of the wooden floor.

Luca pointed to the right side where the bar was located. "There are a couple stools at the bar." We followed him, weaving our way through the crowd.

Once we sat down, I continued to peruse the patrons. I did a double take anytime I saw a brunette, but none were her. Scrubbing my jaw with my hand, I said, "This is ridiculous. Let's just leave."

"Patience, my dear friend." Kyle slapped me on my back, then motioned to the bartender and we ordered the same drinks we had at Claw Hammer.

Kyle's phone buzzed on the bar top and it was like a defibrillator to my heart. A second later, he shouted above the music. "They're at a table on the left side of the dance floor." He slid off his stool. "I'm going to go say hi to Shelly, and you're coming with me."

On my nod, Luca said he'd wait for our drinks and make sure no one took our seats. That told me he wasn't very confident we'd be invited to sit with them. As soon as we passed a group celebrating a bachelorette party, I saw her, and my feet stopped moving, causing a waitress to bump into me.

Kyle turned and lowered his brow. "Dude, you're

causing a traffic jam."

Shelly spotted Kyle first, and when she raised her hand in the air to wave at him, all eyes were on us. Then, all eyes were on me. Her friends were pissed. I didn't know them, but the look they had in their eyes assured me Brae didn't have kind things to say about me. When I stepped closer, a brunette I remembered from the night of the game show eyed me up and down before giving me a smile. Cutting my eyes to Kyle, I noticed he wasn't looking at Shelly. He was eyeing the brunette who had just eye-fucked me.

"Hi, Brae." She threw me a bored expression, then looked away to resume her conversation with one of her friends.

"I'm Vanessa." The flirtatious brunette held her hand out to me, then Kyle. "It's nice to officially meet you." Kyle mumbled something and took a bit longer to release her hand. Didn't he realize Shelly was staring at him? Idiot.

My ribs felt as though they were squeezing my heart like a vise. She couldn't even look at me. This was a mistake. Before I could turn to go, another friend of hers said she needed to go to the ladies' room, which must have been some type of chick code because all of them got up—except Brae. It was clear they all didn't need to go to the bathroom. She just glared at them over her salt-rimmed glass as they made a hasty retreat.

Kyle asked Vanessa to dance, which she accepted . . . and that left two.

I sat down sideways in the chair next to Brae. As always, she looked gorgeous. Her hair was resting over her shoulders, she had on a light pink V-neck sweater, which was made for her body, and a pair of dark jeans.

"What are you doing here?" Her eyes were sad, but her words were strong. Fuck.

"I came to see you." What's the sense in lying? "Shelly told Kyle you guys were here, and I needed to see you."

"Why?" She pivoted toward me. Our knees touched and it took every ounce of willpower I had not to take her hands in mine.

"Because I miss you." Her eyes narrowed at me. Loud music drowned my words. Not wanting to yell, I grabbed her hand and pulled her behind me until we were out the door.

"Jude, it's freezing out." I stopped long enough to take off my leather jacket and place it over her shoulders.

Leading her around the corner of the building, I boxed her in against the concrete wall. "I'm sorry, I didn't want to yell." My ears were ringing, and as far as I knew, I was still shouting. "You asked me why I'm here, and I said it's because I miss you."

Her shoulders slumped as she dropped her head. Lifting her chin with my index finger, I stared into the eyes I've been longing for. "Sparky, I haven't slept well in weeks. My body misses yours. When I go to make dinner, I don't want to just cook for one, I want to cook for us. Everything reminds me of you. I can't look at an apple without thinking of how sweet your hair smells. I can't eat bacon without thinking of how to burn calories. I stand in my bathroom trying to figure out what took you so long at night."

"Jude . . ." she said on a sigh, her warm breath appearing as a puff of smoke in the frigid air.

"No, I need to finish. Every night before I go to sleep, I watch the video I took of you sleeping just so I can hear you snore. It plays over and over again. At first, it calmed me, but now it makes me anxious. I don't sleep in my bed because you're not beside me." I rested my forehead against hers. Her warm breath felt like a balm on my skin. "I need you to forgive me. If I could change things, I would. Do you realize how much you mean to me? I made a mistake, and if I hadn't, you'd be Mrs. Soren right now."

Looking up at me, she pulled her head away from mine, her eyes glistening. "Don't you think I know that? You were everything I've ever wanted in a man. The way you touched me, looked at me, and made me feel was all new and invigorating. I fell hard for you. My entire heart was in it. And now, you're standing here telling me all these sweet things, but what you forgot to say was, 'I'd be Mrs. Soren if you would have put us first.' You put work first. Where did that leave us?" Before I could attempt to answer, she did it for me. "I'll tell you where. Broken, because that's how I felt that day. It's how I've felt every day since. You broke more than my heart—you broke me." Tears rolled over her cheeks, and she looked away, breaking my heart in the process.

"I'm sorry," I said with an ache in my throat.

"You've said that. If I forgive you, will you leave me alone?" The look on her face, the sound of her voice, and the slouch of her shoulders said she was utterly defeated.

"No. I can't leave you alone. Weren't you listening?"

"Let me make this easier for you." I watched as she worked down a swallow. "I forgive you, and I'm moving back in with my parents."

What the fuck? She's leaving? I raked my fingers through my hair. "You're lying. I know you don't forgive me, and I'd rather you stay and fight with me than move away. Don't do this to us."

"Jude." She placed her hand on my chest right over the spot that ached. "I'm not doing this to us. There is no us. We left us in St. John."

"The fuck we did." I crashed my lips on hers, pinning her body against the wall with mine. Every ounce of frustration poured out of me. Brae tilted her head, allowing me full access to taste her. When my tongue touched hers, all sense left me. Spearing her hair with my fingers, I pulled her closer to me.

The woman needed a reminder of how good we were together. If she was dead set on leaving, I'd prove to her why she shouldn't. Then it dawned on me. Did her parents need her there, or was she leaving for other reasons?

Not wanting to break our kiss, but needing answers, I released my hold on her. "Tell me why you're leaving. Are your parents okay? Is it your father?"

"My parents are fine. I'm leaving because I can't afford not to." She pulled the lapels of my jacket tighter around her body.

Money. Everything boiled down to the all-mighty dollar. Something I had more than enough of, and something that caused Brae to struggle. It's what brought us together, and ironically, what tore us apart.

"You're not moving."

"But I am. Jude, everything comes easy for you. You don't get it. You don't have to get it."

"I get it perfectly, Brae. What good is all my money if the person I love won't share it with me?"

She blinked a few times, but said nothing.

"I'm sick of our bullshit. We were more honest with each other when we were strangers. I'm done. I love you. Plain and simple. I can support you, and I will. If you think I'll just sit here and let you move away after all we've been through, you don't know me very well."

The same expression kept her face frozen in shock. I leaned in until my lips pressed against hers. "Cat got your tongue, Kitten?"

"Jude." Her chin lowered to her chest, forcing me to lift it so she had nowhere to look but into my eyes.

"This is me, Brae. I speak my mind. I don't hold back. That alone should speak volumes. I love you. Fuck *Ignite Your Spark* . . . fuck Barbi and Chip . . . fuck it all. Me wanting to be with you has nothing to do with a goddamn spark. It has nothing to do with you needing the money, or jackass Kyle setting me up. It has to do with me not functioning without you. I'm not the same person I was, and it's because of you."

Fresh tears welled in her eyes as she stared up into mine. I held my hands against her cold cheeks and pushed my body into hers. "Brae Daniels, you'll marry me one day."

"Are you serious?" She laughed through her tears, and now it was my turn to blink.

"Completely."

"First of all, you never even wined and dined me. You didn't have to date me, or work to get me."

"Date? No fucking way. I hate dating. I don't do dating. We lived together for fuck's sake."

"Regardless, if you think I'm going to stand here and make it easy for you, you can kiss my ass. I'm still mad at you, Jude Soren. And you have a lot of groveling ahead of you," she proclaimed with a devious smile.

"So, does that mean you forgive me?"

Even in the dim lighting, I could see her blush. "Hmmm . . . I don't know. We'll see." I jutted out my lower lip in a pout and looked at her with puppy dog eyes. "Really, that's what you're going with? Sexy Jude Soren, what has happened to you?" She let out a laugh.

I laughed along with her, kissing her over and over. "Fuck, I love you. Every pain in the ass inch of you." After one long, hard kiss, I took her hand and led her toward the street. "We're going back inside to tell your friends better plans have popped up." She looked up at me as I gave her an arrogant smirk. "It's time to have make-up sex, Sparky."

Chapter 29

Brae

AFTER OUR EPIPHANY, WE TALKED things out in length. He helped me understand what occurred that had him leaving the cottage that day, and even had Luca corroborate his true motives. As far as paying off the loan, I tried to get him to understand where I was coming from. We discussed his very generous donations to the orphanage, and during our conversation, I better understood him. In turn, he empathized with my situation. Communication was key in our healing and moving forward in our relationship.

I have now been with this spectacular man lying next to me for sixteen weeks—minus the three we were apart. Since our brief separation, we've hardly spent much time without each other. Of course we weren't hermits. There were nights I'd hang out with the girls while he hung out with his friends, but we've yet to hang out as a group. Jude wanted all of us to spend time together and I promised him one day soon, we would.

Thinking about how far we'd come from the first time we walked into the small cottage to the day I walked into his two-level apartment made me happy.

When I first saw the fireplace, gourmet kitchen I'd never use, and spiral staircase leading up to the glorious master suite, it completely overwhelmed me. If it weren't for Jude's housekeeper, I doubted it would be as neat as it was. The space was large enough for both my SoHo apartment and that tiny house I loved to easily fit inside.

Despite the luxury surrounding me, it was the man who made me feel as though I'd hit the lottery. His witty banter and dirty jokes coupled with his brilliant mind enthralled me.

And sweet lord, looking at his gorgeous face and magnificent body wasn't any easier than it had been the moment he stepped out from behind that screen. And hearing his sexy as hell Swedish accent whenever he opened his mouth to speak hasn't lessened the way my heart kick-started.

I leaned on my hand, a ridiculously plush pillow squashed beneath my arm, and stared at him long and hard. Taking in his straight nose, square jaw, and that mouth-watering scruff instantly sparked activity in my crotch. Lashes most women would kill for rested on his upper cheek as his sexy man lips parted with each breath. I wanted to catch him snoring just once, but it never happened.

I really couldn't examine him while he was awake since he always called me out on it and usually embarrassed me for my blatant ogling. But when he was still sleeping beside me every morning, I got to truly enjoy admiring every inch of him.

It wasn't hard to do, since the man slept naked and the sheet or blanket we started with more likely than not ended up on the floor somewhere in the middle of the night. He claimed it was my fault, that my annoying thrashing about in his king size bed created a tsunami of cascading linens to tumble to the ground. He was full of shit.

I had my theory, and when I accused him of pushing them away from us so he could ogle me as I slept every night, his returning smirk spoke volumes.

Either way, I wasn't complaining. A sheetless Jude gave me the unfettered opportunity to eye-fuck the rest of his body, his abs, his happy trail, his beautiful cock. Yes, I called it beautiful, because it was. Perfectly proportioned, smooth skin, no ugly veins, or discoloration—a perfect penis.

I often pondered all that we went through to get here, and then quickly thanked the powers that be for bringing this perfect man into my life. Of course, I was blinded by love, because he was far from perfect. I had yet to admit that I loved him, even though I think I fell in love with him the day we went kayaking in St. John.

The way he would relentlessly tease and taunt me to say those three little words was fun—unless I was mad at him. Then it took all my energy not to kill him. Most of the time, Jude was relaxed and easygoing. But when it came to his business, the fun, joking Jude went into hiding. I've heard many one-sided conversations as he went off on one of his employees over the phone, and he liked those people, so I couldn't imagine what would happen when he unleashed his financial-fueled fury on a stranger.

He stirred beside me, rubbing his eye with the back of his bent finger while releasing a sleepy moan. One eyelid slid open to reveal one perfect greenish-brown eye. He stared right at me, a slow, devilish grin spreading over his lips. "What are you looking at, Sparky?"

"Nothing."

"Liar. You know my rules. If you are going to eye-fuck me, you need to follow through."

"Who said I wasn't planning on following through?"

Moving over, I straddled his hips and his morning erection nestled against me. On contact, his scorching skin caused my flesh to pebble with goosebumps. The smile fell from his face, and the look he gave me sent my heart pounding into overdrive. Some would think he was angry, but I knew him better than that. It was the same look he got when he was beyond turned on. Seeing it now forced my hips to slide back and forth over his length. My wetness coated him with each movement. He felt good between my folds, like he belonged there, because he did.

Our eyes connected and held, his livid expression deepening with every shift of my hips. His mess of hair begged for my touch. I ran a hand through his thick locks, scratching his scalp with each stroke. Predictably, his eyes slid shut as he moaned. He loved when I did that, especially if my naked pussy was near his dick at the same time.

"Don't tease me, Sparky."

"Uh huh," I said, bending to kiss his firm lips with one hand still buried in his hair. In turn, he dug his fingers into my hair, holding the back of my head to manipulate my movements. Jude liked being in charge in bed, and I liked him being in charge.

He pulled my head away. "You brushed your teeth already?"

"Of course," I said with a shrug. "Don't you know me by now?" Since moving in with him a few weeks ago, I've been getting up earlier to get bathroom time. He thought it was to run through my crazy OCD routine, when in fact, I didn't want to miss him waking up. That moment his eyes slid open often set forth the fantastic sex we started our day with.

I resumed our kiss, and his hands gripped my hips with each swipe of my tongue along his. He then lifted me until he was able to enter me in one continuous motion, not stopping until his pelvis pressed against mine.

"Feel me, Sparky?"

I nodded slowly, words failing me at that moment. Making love to Jude always caused my brain to malfunction. I often said the stupidest things and then blushed profusely when he'd chuckle and ask me to repeat it. Having his cock deep inside me was as effective as a truth serum administered through my pussy. Once Jude became aware of my eagerness to spill my guts during the throws of passion, he used it to his advantage.

A slow smile spread over his lips when he recognized the phase I had entered. "Love me?"

"No."

He lifted my hips until he fell free from my body, his penis landing on his tattooed abs with a *thump*. I tried to push down, but he shook his head. "Love me?"

"I like you a whole lot."

"That's not good enough, Sparky." Why was he so adamant today? Usually he'd ask and move on when I said no. The look on his face and ironclad hold on my hips indicated he wasn't continuing. "Last chance, Sparky. Love me?"

I paused to stare into his gorgeous eyes. He was everything I wanted. Deep down, he knew it, and so did I. Even I had become frustrated with my stubbornness. We both knew I'd cave into him just like I did when we were on the island. Not wanting to prolong the inevitable, I finally spoke the words he longed to hear and I needed to say. "Jude Soren, I love you more than anything on this earth."

The most magnificent smile lit up his face as he moved my body back onto his. "Was that so hard to admit, Sparky?" he asked, pulling me over his chest as he began pumping his hips in slow, deliberate thrusts.

I shook my head, but failed to remember the simple two-letter word I needed to say as a response. He flipped us, stealing my control. With one hand buried in my hair, the other held my thigh against his hip. His lips latched around my nipple, and he started my day in the same way he had for the last two months—with a mind-blowing orgasm.

More times than not, I was able to come a second time by the time he got to his first. His stamina marveled me as he tirelessly pumped into me longer than a porn star.

"You know I'm going to marry you one day, right?" He swirled his tongue around my right nipple. "I need you to be mine permanently." His attention was now on my left breast. "Knowing you belong to me and me to you, makes me hard as steel." In a swift move, he thrust into me harder than he had been, accentuating his words with his dick. I let out a squeal as my entire body started to throb, pulse, and shiver with each word he spoke. His words coupled with his movements were beyond compare to anything I'd ever experienced. The fact that he loved me and wanted me to have his name created such a sense of purpose. Yes, we belonged together—he knew it and so did I.

A wrinkle formed between his brows and he grunted my name as he came deep inside me. Smoothing it away with my fingertip, I leaned up to place a tender kiss on his lips. "I love you, Jude."

"I know you do, Sparky. I love you too. Ask me again."

"Ask you what?"

"Ask me again how I'd propose."

My heart stopped when I realized what he was referring to. On a nervous swallow, I asked, "Spark number three, how would you propose?"

Releasing my thigh, he slipped his hand under the pillow and pulled out a small black velvet box.

My open-mouthed gape caused him to chuckle. "Every night, I slip this under my pillow, just in case."

"Seriously? You're asking me to marry you while you're still buried deep inside me? We'll never be able to share the story of our proposal."

"What better time? I have you right where I want you, and you finally admitted you loved me. Fuck everyone else, it's none of their business."

"I guess I should have guessed based on your response to my question the night we met."

He frowned, trying to remember. "What did I say?"

"We'd fly to Vegas and I'd get your name tattooed on my ring finger, because you didn't do jewelry. Then Elvis would marry us."

"I like the real version better. Me buried in you after you finally admitted you loved me. Although, I would love for you to get my name tattooed somewhere on your body." He kissed me and opened the box with one hand. Pulling the ring from its velvet bed, he held it at the tip of my finger, and asked, "Brae Daniels, will you marry me?"

The brilliant smile on his face and the way his eyes

gleamed with joy made my heart overflow with love. "Yes. Jude, I would have married you in St. John."

"If I hadn't fucked up, I would have married you too, Sparky." He skimmed the back of his hand over my cheek. "You know how sorry I am. I most definitely fucked up, and I'll never fuck up with you again."

Those words almost meant more to me than his proposal. I nodded, gripped his face in between my hands, and kissed him to the point where he hardened within me. Our connection, both physical and emotional, may have started with a tiny spark, but has since transformed into a raging inferno.

Lifting my hand, I cupped his face. The single, brilliant cut solitaire set in platinum caused tears to instantly swell. It was simple, just like me. "I love this, Jude," I said, twisting my hand to catch the sunlight filtering in through the window.

He caught my hand and kissed the ring. "I love you."

Jude

THERE WAS SOMETHING TO BE said about waking up with the person you were destined to be with. Not wanting to sound like a pussy, but each day was better than the last. The only thing that would make it perfect was if she agreed to come work with me. Not even for me, but with me. God knew she was one hell of a saleswoman and could drum up business, but she emphatically declined each time I made an offer. It didn't matter what salary I offered her, I'd still get a resounding no. Even Luca tried, but he just said she had a harder head than I did.

Ruth called telling me I had a visitor. She adored Brae and I could tell by the singsong in my assistant's voice she was the one who wanted to see me. I shuffled some papers around in an attempt to tidy my desk, since that drove her insane, and stacked them in the corner. I'd even offered her a job as my organizer, but she said there wasn't enough money in the world to pay that salary. The thought made me smile.

"Hey there, handsome." She looked fabulous in a sleek, navy, long-sleeve dress that looked like it was made for her. Brae's curves made my blood pump right down to my cock. Fuck. Having her in my office was the biggest turn on. Stocks and watching the ticker used to excite me, but not like the vision standing in front of me.

I raked my eyes up and down her body. From her brown hair, which was pulled into a knot on top of her head, to her come-fuck-me heels. "Don't you look particularly gorgeous today?"

Her beautiful smile caused my breath to hitch in my throat. "You like?" Brae pivoted slowly, giving me enough time to appreciate her ass before facing me again.

"I like a lot. Not that I didn't like the way I left you this morning in nothing but my T-shirt."

A blush crept up her face. I loved that I could do that to her. "Well, thank you. Actually, this might be my lucky dress. Mr. Graham liked it too. Well, I don't know if he liked the dress, but he sure liked me."

Who the fuck was this Graham character? I'll beat the fuck out of him. Walking toward my desk, she dragged her fingernail along the teak wood before settling herself in front of me, resting her ass on the edge. My hands instinctively went to her hips.

"So, this Mr. Graham, do I have something to be

worried about?"

Brae giggled. I'm glad she found my need to want to pummel someone comical. "I don't think it would be a fair fight considering he's old enough to be my grandfather." She lifted herself onto my desk and crossed her legs, making her dress rise, along with my dick. Leaning forward, she said, "I got a job today."

"What? I didn't even know you had an interview." I stood and wrapped my arms around her. "This is so great, Sparky. I knew you could do it. Why didn't you tell me?"

We released each other and I sat back down so we were closer to being at eye level. "I was tired of getting my hopes up." She shrugged. "So, I went in thinking I'd be leaving the same way I entered—jobless. But he loved everything I had to offer."

I raised my brows and she smacked my arms. "Soren, you have a one-track mind. I'll be selling airtime at a radio station. It's not far from what I was doing before, but the benefits are so much better, as is the salary."

"Congratulations. I'm proud of you. I love that you never gave up."

"You should know better than anyone that I never give up."

"That's one of the things I love most about you." I rolled my chair closer to her, but she stopped my movement when she hopped off the desk and headed for the door. My brows furrowed, wondering where she was going. That's when I heard her tell Ruth to hold my calls.

Her body was now pressed up against the door she was locking. "Do you have any meetings to get to?"

I shook my head. "Nope, not until after lunch."

"Mmmm . . . lunch." She took purposeful strides

toward me until she reached where I was sitting. Placing her hands on the arms of my chair, she turned it toward her.

"Are you hungry?"

"Famished." Brae went down to her knees, causing my dick to jump beneath the fabric of my suit pants. She quickly made work of my belt and the button before I heard the teeth of my zipper lower.

"Sparky, what are you doing?"

She looked up at me with her beautiful chocolate eyes. "If you have to ask, I must be doing it wrong." Brae grinned before pulling my dick free from my boxers. Holy fuck.

First, her tongue teased my tip swirling around it as if she were eating an ice cream cone in ninety-degree heat. She moved her fist lower on my shaft and took me into her mouth. Her diamond—our diamond—sparkled on her hand as she pumped me.

A hiss escaped me and I pulled the clip from her hair, then watched her sable tresses cascade down her shoulders. My fingers gripped into her soft waves again as she moved her warm mouth up and down my rock hard shaft. Goddamn, this woman was going to make me explode with just a few sucks.

The vibration from her moan sent a bolt of lightning through me. With her hands now resting on my thighs and my fingers threaded through her hair, I scooted forward on my desk chair and began to thrust my hips.

"Sparky, you're going to make me come." Her eyes rolled up to meet mine as she smiled around my cock. Rather than slow down, her pace increased. Watching her cheeks hollow with each movement made my balls tighten. That was the moment she grazed her teeth against my skin. "Fuuuuckkkk," I said as I came in her mouth. I bit down on my lip, not wanting Ruth to unlock the door or anyone else to think they needed to come to my rescue. Brae was my rescuer in more ways than one.

She stood, a proud look on her face as she dragged the pad of her thumb along her bottom lip. With as much confidence as she started with, she tucked me back into my pants after giving the tip of my cock a chaste kiss.

"May I use your bathroom?" I nodded, and she vanished through the door in the corner. When she came back out, her hair was back the way it was, her rosy lipstick was fixed, and she looked even more beautiful than when she entered my office.

Brae picked up her bag from where she set down by the door and flung the strap over her shoulder. "Where are you going?"

"Home. I have laundry to do. Celebrate tonight?"

"But I didn't get to have my lunch and it looks delicious. Are you going to leave a starving man?" My hand went to my chest. "I'm crushed."

She snickered. "How about I let you have a midnight snack later?"

"Fuck the snack, I'm having a feast."

Chapter 30

Jude

THANKFULLY, BRAE AGREED TO FOREGO José Ponchos and we headed to Dispatch, which was a low-key bar in Midtown. Our friends were meeting us there and we had a lot to celebrate. Brae had been chomping at the bit, and on her fingernails, anxiously waiting to tell her friends about our engagement.

Her excitement coupled with her sexy smile made me want to devour her in the back of the cab. "So, what do you think your friends will say?" I squeezed her hand, which was in mine. "Will they approve? What do you think their reaction will be?"

"Of you?" She grinned, then thought for a brief moment. "Yes, of course they will. Their reactions will be a bit different, though."

"How so?"

"Well, Cassie, the romantic of the bunch, will want to be our wedding planner. Desiree, the level-headed one—"

"She's the attorney, right?"

"Yes, the attorney who thought I'd lost my mind the day I signed the Spark contract without reading the fine print—or worse, without consulting her. She will be happy, but will have a ton of questions about the prenup."

"There isn't going to be a prenup." Brae had mentioned this a couple times before—sometimes casually, other times when we were discussing finances.

"Jude."

"No way, Sparky. What's mine is yours. A prenup may as well be a declaration that we're planning to break up. I'm never letting you go, so no." Every time she brought up that damn legal document, I wanted to scream. "What about Vanessa who keeps calling me Mr. Wrong?"

Brae let out the sweetest laugh. "She's is your biggest fan and an enabler. I believe her mantra goes something like, 'fuck 'em before you date 'em.'"

"I like her more already."

"Of course you do. Vanessa is the last one I'd see tied down. She likes to go out and have fun. Oh, and she loves to embarrass me, so be prepared."

"Just like Kyle."

"Well, from what I know about him, they are very much alike. Tell me more about Kyle and Luca."

"They're both assholes."

She laughed, and I smiled, even though it was the truth. The sedan slowed to a stop and I paid the fare before helping her out of the car. "Sparky, before we go in, there are a couple of rules I need to put in place."

Her eyes went wide and her eyebrows shot up to her hairline. "Oh no."

Shrugging, I said, "First rule, don't listen to a thing

Kyle or Luca tell you—unless it's that I'm pussy whipped over you. Second rule, if you're doubting something either of them says, refer to rule number one." I gave her a chaste kiss, and before she could question what they could say to cause her doubt, I grabbed her hand and led her inside.

Dispatch was a great bar. A place where people of all ages gathered to watch a game or just unwind with their friends. This bar started out as a hangout for the police and firefighters who protected our city, hence the name. It has evolved into a yuppie hangout. Low murmurs, laughter, and sounds from the TVs mounted on the walls filtered through the dimly lit bar. High-top tables filled the small center space flanked by a long bar on each side.

Spotting my friends, I laced my fingers with Brae's and walked toward them. Of course, Kyle was hitting on Brae's friend Vanessa. Maybe if he was trying to impress her, he'd lay off embarrassing me.

"There's the man." Luca stood and gave me a high handshake before pulling me close to bump shoulders.

Vanessa's face lit up like the fourth of July. "Hi, sweetie!" She pushed me out of the way and hugged Brae.

"Hi, V."

Her eyes met mine, and she nodded. "*Hello*, Mr. Wrong."

"It's Jude, thanks." Once the friends broke apart, I asked Brae, "Sparky, what do you want to drink?"

"Sparky, that sounds interesting." Vanessa interrupted. "Wax play?"

Brae rolled her eyes and ignored her, although that sounded like something we needed to do. "Champagne please."

Ever since St. John, my girl loved the stuff.

Exchanging a private moment, I leaned closer and moaned in her ear, remembering how I drank from her body. Her returning grin almost caused me to drag her back out of the bar and say fuck it to celebrating in public.

As I handed her a filled flute and took my Belvedere, Vanessa told Brae they had a table reserved. After a few steps, Vanessa stopped and turned to look at Kyle. "Aren't you guys coming?"

Kyle met my eye and grinned. "Yes, we're coming." He sniffed after the dark-haired beauty, looking like a dog in heat as his eyes focused on Vanessa's ass sashaying toward the table. Luca was the last to move, walking behind them while shaking his head.

Once we all sat around the table, Brae reintroduced her friends and I did the same. "Brae, you remember Luca and my ex-friend, Kyle. These two clowns are the ones you've heard so much about." Both said hi. Kyle had that gleam in his eye that meant trouble. And if he were sitting closer to Brae, I'd bet he would've leaned over to kiss her.

"Your accents are so worldly. A swede, an Italian," Vanessa said, pointing to first me, then to Luca. Turning to Kyle with a smirk, she added, "And a . . . ?"

"Canadian."

"Oh, I'm so sorry." The disappointment on her face caused Luca and me to laugh while Kyle frowned. Undeterred by his scowl, she lifted her martini, and asked Brae, "So, how's the upper east side? Better than pulling on tits, I bet." Kyle, Luca, and I all choked on our drinks. This girl was a riot.

"You go both ways?" Kyle spouted off, directing his comment to Brae. "That's hot as fuck." He turned to me. "Congrats, my man."

"No, you dickhead. She means at her parents' dairy farm." I looked to Brae for assistance. "That is what she meant, right?"

"Of course that's what she meant!" Brae gasped with an exaggerated eye-roll. While still shaking her head, she lifted her champagne to take a sip.

"Oh my God. Oh my God! Is that an engagement ring?" Cassie's voice went shrill, and Luca, who was closest to her, jammed a finger inside his ear.

"Yes!" Brae exclaimed. "We're engaged!" The women all screeched at the same time.

"Jesus Christ. You're getting married?" Kyle looked like I just told him Santa wasn't real. He looked to Luca. "Did you know?"

"Yeah," he said with a shrug.

"Are you sure you want to commit to one chick?"

"Lyle." Vanessa smacked him on the arm. "Are you kidding right now?"

"It's Kyle. Ky . . . with a K . . . Kyle. And yes, I was kidding." Frustrated, he took a sip of his beer. "This guy owes me huge. If it weren't for me, he wouldn't have met the love of his life." He rubbed his arm. "And don't hit me. Damn, that hurt."

"Whatever. This isn't about you." Vanessa was back to gawking over Brae's ring. She let out a whistle. "Nice job, Jude. I knew you'd be a winner. I was rooting for you the whole time."

"Thank you. That must be why you call me Mr. Wrong."

"Wrong never felt so right," Brae interjected.

I looked down into Brae's eyes, and added, "I completely agree."

Vanessa snatched Brae's hand from mine and tilted it back and forth. "Damn, that's a beauty."

"Again, I couldn't agree more," I responded, my eyes pinned to Brae's. She cupped my face and pulled me in for a kiss right before a chorus of awww's came from the female side of the table.

"So, when's the wedding?" Desiree asked in a faint South American accent.

"Des, we just got engaged. Probably in a year or two."

I stared at my fiancé like she sprouted antlers. "A year or two? We are not waiting a year or two."

"You need to book a proper venue, and flowers, music, the photographer—these things take time," Cassie argued.

"Then we'll elope in Vegas. Do the Elvis thing." I tightened my grip around her shoulders and she giggled at my reference. "Invite strangers instead of our annoying friends."

"What's the rush, dude? Did you knock her up?" Kyle asked, laughing at his own joke.

Brae stared up at me wide-eyed as I said, "No, jackass."

"Slow swimmers? It's all those times you sat in the sauna at the gym. I told you the heat kills the swimmers. Those dumbass bathing suits you wear don't help either. Too tight. You need board shorts, nice and roomy to air out the bat and balls, eh." He lifted his beer and toasted his own stupid logic. Cassie cleared her throat, and my ex-friend suddenly remembered we were among company. "I'm sorry, ladies. Excuse my crude comments."

"Oh my God," Brae said with an eye-roll. "How did we get here?"

I leaned closer and placed my lips on her ear. "Welcome to my world, babe."

♡♡♡

Brae

JOKES AND JABS WERE IN abundance as we all got to know each other. Obscenities and sexual innuendos continued to fly around the table, mostly by Kyle and Vanessa, who both seemed to have met their match.

"Do you think they'll end up doing it or killing each other?" Jude's question made me laugh. His warm breath tickled my ear.

Taking a moment to glance at our outgoing friends, I smiled. "Both. She'll kill him in the act."

Jude pulled me closer to him and started laughing. "God, I love you."

"Do your parents know?" Desiree's question came as no surprise. Of course she'd be the one to ask. The others were occupied with joking around. Cassie and Luca were easily humored by Vanessa and Kyle, so they were hardly paying attention—that was, until Des mentioned my parents.

"Not yet." I glanced at Jude. "We decided we're going to call them tomorrow."

"I've been thinking we should tell them in person. They are your parents, my future in-laws. I need to ask your dad for permission."

Kyle's chuckle gained our attention. "It's a little late for that, isn't it?" He looked at Luca and cleared his throat. "Sir, may I please have your daughter's hand in marriage?"

Luca chimed in. "No." he said in a deep baritone, attempting to mimic my father.

Their roleplay continued. "But, sir, I must marry her. We've been living together and your daughter is great in bed." Kyle's last comment caused my friends to gasp and Jude to shoot daggers at him.

"Well, then, yes, by all means, make an honest woman out of my daughter." Luca and Kyle tapped their beer bottles and took a sip.

Jude shook his head. "Can you believe these assholes are my best friends?"

"In all honesty, no."

The waitress came by to deliver another round of drinks. The champagne was starting to go to my head and all I kept wanting was Jude to lick it off my body—and me off his.

He nuzzled his nose in my hair as I took a sip of the effervescent liquid. "Just watching that slide down your throat is making my cock hard."

A blush rose up my body. "I was just thinking about how I'd rather lick it off you."

The growl that escaped him made a rush of heat pool between my legs. "We need to get out of here soon."

I nodded as Kyle asked, "Hey, lovebirds, we're all in the wedding right?"

We hadn't discussed even having a bridal party, but of course we'd want them to stand up for us. Jude looked at me, and I shrugged then nodded.

"Do you think you'll be able to keep your antics to a minimum on that day? I swear to God, we'll elope." Jude was dead serious. It wasn't the first time he said he'd whisk me away and make me his wife.

Kyle's eyes went wide. "You're worried about me? What about Jezebel over here?" He hitched his thumb, motioning toward Vanessa.

Jude dropped his head, and grumbled, "Idiot."

"Did you just call me Jezebel? You don't even know me, you arrogant ass." Vanessa chirped as she looked at me. "You know I'd never do anything to ruin your big day."

Desiree shook her head at them both while Cassie laughed.

I looked at our five friends and frowned. "It's uneven."

Kyle glanced at Jude, then back to me with a cocked brow. "Bummer, dude."

"You're such an idiot. I believe Brae is referring to the fact that she'd have three bridesmaids and I'd have two ushers."

"I'm good with a threesome. Wouldn't be the first time." Kyle raised his hand to high-five Luca, but it just hung in the air.

Cassie noticed my furrowed brow, and said, "Don't worry, sweetie. We'll figure it out."

Kyle ignored Cassie's comment, and prodded. "So, best man. Who's it gonna be, eh? Romeo over here, or me?"

"I can't deal with you two clowns, I'll just flip a coin."

"We can't wait to plan your bachelor party. Luca and I will handle everything."

My entire body tensed as I shot my friends a worried look. Vanessa, of course, rescued me. "Don't worry, sweetie. I dated a stripper and he still does private parties. We'll have a great time."

"There will be no bachelor or bachelorette parties with strippers in attendance." Jude looked at me, determination in his eyes. "Agreed?"

I nodded. "Agreed."

"The only woman I want to see naked is you." He speared his fingers into my hair, which seemed to be one of his favorite things to do, and pulled me toward him in a heated kiss. "I'm taking you home."

"Thank God."

Grabbing my hand, Jude offered a, "Bye," as explanation for our quick exit. The more the gripes and complaints came from the peanut gallery, the faster Jude dragged me through the bar and out the door.

The cab ride was torture, and by the time we stumbled into our apartment, we were already half naked, since my fiancé decided to use the elevator as our personal changing room. He was damn lucky it was late and it didn't stop on any of the other floors.

We tossed the clothes from our hands to the floor and Jude made quick work of removing my jeans. In one swift motion, he grabbed my ass and hoisted me up. My legs wrapped around his torso, high enough for me to still reach between our bodies and unfasten the buttons on his button-fly jeans. Of course, I paused to touch the tattoos I loved so much.

His pants dropped to his ankles and he unshackled his feet out of the denim one by one without missing a step. My man was commando. God, I loved him. The tip of his hard dick settled under me.

"Fuck, you're wet. I need to taste some of that." Lowering me to the bed, he stripped me out of my white lace bra and panties. "Fucking beautiful." Jude placed his hand between my breasts and dragged his palm down my body to cup my sex. "All mine. This is all mine."

"Just yours." The more he spoke, the less patience I had.

He dragged me to the edge of the bed until my ass hung off the mattress. When I saw him lower to his knees, watching the stars on his torso vanish one at a time, my body squirmed with need.

"I've got you, Sparky." He lifted my legs until they were on his shoulders and spread me wide with his thumbs. "So gorgeous." That's when I felt his tongue. Oh, how I loved his tongue. "You're going to come in my mouth."

"God, yes!" I exclaimed as I fisted the sheets. My head craned back so far, I could see our cream fabric covered headboard.

Soft, gentle licks tortured me. Of course, it was the best form of torture, but I needed more. He was so low, I couldn't reach his head. The highlights in his hair would appear and disappear as he moved.

He stopped, and I groaned in frustration. "Patience," he said as I groaned louder. Now using his fingers, he circled my opening, starting at my clit and then back around, but not inside. I bucked my hips, needing more. Once again, his mouth was on me as he moaned, licked, and nipped, all while teasing me with his fingers. When he plunged two of them inside me, my entire body started to tighten. Anticipation grew and I was ready to detonate all over him. That's when he stopped.

"Please, Jude. I can't take it."

"Shhh." His one hand held my hips down while his other flirted with my clit, his tongue still deep in my sex.

In and out, teasing and licking, his hands now gripped my ass. My fingers ready to pull the sheets off the bed, I arched my back and came. Bright lights appeared beneath my eyelids as the most intense orgasm rang through my body.

Jude's face finally appeared, his lips glistening with evidence of my orgasm. When his tongue licked them clean, he smiled, and I almost came again.

"I want you inside me." I leaned forward, grabbed his arms, and pulled him on top of me. "Now, Jude."

Holding my face between his palms, he looked deep into my eyes, the gray rim of his irises practically pulsing with desire. "I love you, Sparky."

"I love you too, Mr. Wrong."

Jude's eyebrows rose. "Mr. Wrong?" He thrust inside me, never breaking our eye contact. "I thought I was Mr. Right."

"Trust me, you are."

Chapter 31

Brae

I WAS SCHEDULED TO START my new job in one week, so Jude cleared his schedule and we decided to go stay with my parents for a few days. I felt guilty because we weren't going to see his, but Jude said we could Facetime them and we'd go as soon as I could get away.

When I called my parents to tell them I was bringing my boyfriend to meet them, they were both surprised. Jude was insistent on asking my parents for permission to marry me.

"Are you nervous?" I asked as we turned down the road to my parents' farm.

He glanced over with that sly, sexy grin I'd grown accustomed to. "Me? Nervous? Who can resist this charm?"

"I'm being serious. We need to tell them about the loan."

"Leave that to me."

"Jude, my father's a very proud man. You can't just say you paid off their debt because you're fucking his daughter." I meant it as a joke, but when he turned, the anger on his face was obvious.

"Brae, quit saying that. I mean it."

"I'm sorry. I guess I'm just nervous. I wanted to prepare you, so you'd know what to expect."

"I don't need to be coached. Okay? Trust me." His face remained tense as he gripped the steering wheel while staring straight ahead.

"I love you."

At my words, his face immediately softened. "I love you, too." Our eyes met and he gave me my favorite smile. "You do realize I can't stay mad at you, Sparky."

"On that note, would now be a good time to let you know my parents are extremely religious and old-fashioned, so don't be surprised when we sleep in separate rooms. Also, we need to get up by five so we can tend to the cattle. You'll need to learn to milk the cows, and then we'll need to clean the barn. We use the manure for fertilizer, so that will also need to be collected and stored."

Beads of sweat formed at his temples. "We can't sleep together?"

"Did you hear me? You, Mr. Money, will be shoveling cow dung." I poked his rock hard abs to emphasize my point.

His jaw ticked. "Yes, I heard you. Did you say we can't sleep together?"

A loud laugh escaped me as we turned onto my parents' driveway. "Seriously, Jude. You kill me."

"It's not funny," he grumbled miserably. "Sparky, we're supposed to be here for four days. If I would have known we weren't going to be sleeping together, I would have rented a huge ass SUV." He got out of his BMW and circled it while mumbling in Swedish.

"What?"

"Look at the fucking mud covering my baby!"

"I thought I was your baby."

"This is no time for jokes, Sparky. No sex, my car's a mess—I'm not in the mood for your sass." He got our bags out of the trunk and pulled me in for a kiss I felt down to my toes, using its open position to shield us from peeping eyes in the house.

"Are you sure this is a good idea?" I asked against his persistent lips. Pushing my hips against his, I could already feel the effects of our kiss on him as well. "Getting all riled up for nothing could be a huge mistake."

He must have agreed when he took a half a step away to adjust himself. "That's it! I refuse to agree to four days of no sexual activity."

Again, I laughed at his tantrum. "The four days will be over before you know it. And just think how hot our reunion will be. Stop pouting."

"Pouting? You can't just spring such devastating news on me like that." Forgetting his current predicament, he pulled me hard against his body again and nuzzled my ear. "I'm sure there are plenty of places in the barn where I can fuck you. Actually, let's go there now before they know we're here." When I gawked, he added, "What?"

I slapped his stomach, which was like hitting a wall of muscle. He slammed the trunk closed while still sporting a scowl. Just as I was about to tell him we'd find a way, the door swung open.

"Oh, you're here!" My mother flew down the path toward us and immediately threw her arms around me, rocking me back and forth.

"Hi, Mom."

Her eyes focused on Jude. "Well, you must be Jude. It's a pleasure to meet you."

Jude shook her hand. "It's very nice to meet you too, Mrs. Daniels."

"Please, call me Ellen." Was my mother blushing? I tilted my head like a puppy. She was. Her cheeks were actually turning pink. "You have an accent, where are you from?"

She walked toward the house and held the door open, giving us access to the foyer. "Sweden," Jude answered as he took a step in.

"Oh, Brae's favorite candy is from there." I closed my eyes and shook my head as Jude chuckled under his breath.

Before I could correct her and tell her Swedish Fish weren't from Sweden, my father walked in from the kitchen. Not much had changed since I last left. He still sported a flannel shirt and his Wrangler jeans.

"Walter, our baby is home." My father eyed Jude up and down before giving me a hug.

"Sweetheart, we're so glad you're here." He released me, then sized Jude up again. I knew that look. It was his *don't hurt my daughter or I'll string you up by your balls and hang you in my barn from the rafters* look. Of course, he wouldn't do that, but more than one boyfriend had been scared off by that look alone. Dating sucked. "I assume you're the boyfriend?"

"Daddy, this is Jude Soren."

"Nice to meet you, Mr. Daniels." Jude extended his hand, which my father took in kind.

"Let's sit down." My mother led us all into the family room. The blue and white checkered sofa had a bit more wear and tear to it, but I knew my parents were more concerned with keeping the farm from foreclosing than the decor. "I'm going to get some lemonade. Is that okay with you kids?"

We both nodded and sat down on the center cushion of the sofa, even though there were two empty ones on either side of us. My father sat across from us in what was known as "his chair."

A very long minute passed as my dad continued to measure Jude up while Jude pretended to act cool. I knew better, though. In the way his thigh stiffened beside mine, the sheen of sweat on his forehead, and how he refused to touch me, all meant my man was nervous. He doesn't get nervous, my ass. I wasn't fooled.

Finally, my dad spoke, and asked, "Where are you from?"

"Sweden, sir."

"What the heck are you doing here?"

"Daddy!"

Oblivious and bubbly, my mom entered carrying a tray of glasses filled with lemonade and setting it on the coffee table. "So, tell us how you kids met." She took a seat in a chair next to my dad's. I felt like we were back on the island getting questioned.

I laced my fingers with Jude's, which was like a magnet to my father's eyes. "Yes, I'd love to hear how you met my daughter." His eyes pinned Jude, who tightened his clammy grip, almost making me yelp.

"Well, sir, your daughter . . . um, I mean . . . we were at an event and got to know each other." He leaned into me, and whispered in my ear, "Is it hot in here?"

I almost laughed as I shook my head. I needed to help him out. "Here's the truth. I told you I went on a game

351 ☆♡

show, right, Mom?"

"Yes."

"Well, it was a dating show, and Jude was one of the contestants." My dad's eyebrows lowered. "He didn't want to be, but he was." Oh my God, I was screwing this up.

Jude released my hand and stood. "Mr. and Mrs. Daniels, I'm in love with your daughter. There isn't one thing about her I'd change—not even her snoring."

I clicked my tongue against the roof of my mouth in disgust. "She's done that since she was a baby," my mother said, offering her unsolicited information.

"How do you know my daughter snores?" My father tapped his fingers on the arm of the chair as he stared at Jude. "You two have had sex?"

Like my ass was on fire, I sprang up and stood next to Jude. "Daddy!"

"It's okay, Brae." Jude gripped my hand again. "Um . . . as I was saying . . . I'm in love with Brae, and I realize it may seem soon to you, but I'd like your permission to marry your daughter. There isn't anyone else I would want to experience life with. She owns my heart and soul. I'd do anything to make her happy."

A tear rolled down my cheek. When I looked at my mother, she was all teary eyed too. My dad stood, crossing his arms, and my mother's hand was on my father's arm in a flash.

"What is it that you do, son?" *And let the inquisition begin.*

"I own my own business, sir. I'm in finance and do very well for myself. Brae will never want for anything."

After a few more questions and answers, my father stroked his chin with the side of his hand. More beads of sweat formed on Jude's forehead.

"Do you love him, honey? Does he make you happy?" my mom asked with a warm smile.

"Yes, very much." I glanced up at Jude, and added while staring at him, "I've never been happier."

His hold on my hand tightened. With his eyes pinned to mine, he said, "I feel the same way. Your daughter is the best thing that has happened in my life, and I've been blessed with great things." If I could have thrown my arms around his neck and made out with him right then, I would have.

My parents gave each other a knowing look before looking back at us. How could my father find fault with Jude's admission? We could see the fight literally leave his expression as it softened with a small smile. "Welcome to the family, Jude."

A long breath escaped Jude. "Thank you, Mr. Daniels." The two most important men in my life shook hands.

My mother clapped in excitement. "Brae, sweetheart, you can have the wedding this fall. You know how beautiful the farm looks when the leaves turn. We have the room, and it would make your father and I so happy."

I looked toward Jude, wondering if he would sign up for this. My fiancé would probably want our wedding to be at St. Patrick's Cathedral and our reception at The Plaza. But once again, my guy surprised me by smiling and saying, "Thank you for the offer."

We all celebrated, toasting with champagne that replaced our lemonade. I was so relieved that my parents accepted our engagement. While my mother and I gushed over the beauty of my ring, Jude and my father talked about the Yankees versus the Mets. Thankfully they were both Yankees fans.

True to my dad's personality, he broke the jubilation, and said, "Brae. I know you're engaged, but you will be sleeping in separate rooms."

Jude raked his hand through his hair, and said, "I wouldn't want it any other way, sir."

My dad chuckled. "Sure you wouldn't." And I thought the same.

Jude

AFTER THREE DAYS, I WAS about to finally fuck Brae. Her parents never left us alone for more than ten minutes at a time. Even at night, they were sure to put me in the farthest room in the house, and I didn't think it was an accident that the door squeaked louder than that damn rooster.

With luck, they stopped arguing about us joining them at Sunday Mass. Her father glowered at me before they left the house, obviously on to the fact that I'd be like a kid in a candy shop. I wasn't proud to prove him right, but lust trumps logic, and by the time their Buick pulled onto the main road, Brae was naked in the middle of their living room floor while I ate her pussy and pinched her nipples.

"Oh Christ. Oh my God. Jude. Don't stop!" she called as I latched onto her clit and sucked like my life depended on it. In a way, it did. If that man came home because he forgot something, no doubt he'd shoot me dead.

She came with a scream that caused the chickens outside to all start cackling at once. "Shhh, Brae. Be quiet."

"I can't, Jude. You know that." I kissed my way up her body until my cock settled against her pussy. "This is so wrong," she said, contradicting herself by grabbing me and guiding me inside her. "We're fucking on my mother's rug while she's at church!"

"Don't think about it," I said through thrusts. "You called to God a few times. We're good." I grabbed her ass with both hands, and like a man on mission propelled us both into a quick yet satisfying release. I wasn't about to take any fucking chances by prolonging this. Besides, my cock was thrilled with the quickie.

By the time they returned, we were primly and properly making lunch together in the kitchen. Her father stood staring at me as I mixed the chicken salad while Brae attempted to make toast. "Brae didn't make that, did she?" Her father pointed to the bowl I was stirring. All the stress I had bottled up inside came gushing out in the loudest laugh I couldn't control.

"It's not funny," she said as she pulled out the sixth piece of blackened bread.

"Good luck to you," Walter said as he grabbed an apple off the counter. "Her cooking skills are lacking, son."

"Yes, sir. I've experienced her version of barbeque chicken."

Brae glared at me, but the moment she saw my dazzling smile, she cracked. "I say that with love, Sparky."

"Sparky?"

"Oh . . . um . . . it's just a nickname." His eyes met mine and I slowly saw the ire leave as a calm replaced it.

"You know what, I just came from church. I really don't want to know. Let me know when lunch is ready."

"It's ready now, Daddy."

A few minutes later, we all sat around their kitchen table to eat. Conversation revolved around neighbors and friends they ran into at church as her mother listed all the people who asked about Brae.

It didn't take long to finish our meal. "That was delicious, Jude. Thank you," Ellen said with a smile.

"It was my pleasure." Brae's spine stiffened. Several times during the meal, she nudged her leg against mine, trying to get me to say what I needed to say. The one other thing since arriving I needed to mention was the loan.

We were leaving the next day, so it was basically now or another visit, and the thought of coming back so soon caused panic to swell for obvious reasons.

"I'll be in the coop," Walter announced before pushing back his chair to stand.

Brae raised her brows as she looked up at me, but it was the pinch she gave me on my side that had me blurting out, "Sir!" so loudly, her mother jumped in her seat. He stopped and turned expectantly. "Um . . . can you sit for a few more minutes?"

With no expression on his face, he sat back in his chair and folded his arms while staring at me like I was one of his cows that had escaped their pen.

"Um . . . well, as you know, I said I loved Brae very much." I paused, realizing it was in vain when I didn't get a response whatsoever. I swallowed to bring some moisture into my mouth, but was met with more cotton. Why was this so fucking hard? Brae patted my leg in encouragement . . . or maybe it was her way of saying move it along. "Um . . . well, I know how much this farm means to her. So, as a wedding gift, I paid off the loan."

Her mother gasped, as he said, "You did what?"

"I, um . . . your farm is no longer under the bank's control."

Ellen reached for Brae's hand. "Is this true, sweetheart? I thought you said it was an investor."

Brae glanced up at me with a smile before nodding at her mother's question. "Yes, Mom. Jude is the investor."

"Brae didn't know I was the man behind the payment." I paused a moment to look down into her eyes. She'd come a long way in accepting what I did, but still, she struggled with it. When she squeezed my thigh, I finally felt her consent. I took her hand in mine and squeezed back. "She was upset with me when she found out. I think she now understands why I did it. Again, I love her. I can afford it, and I won't sit idly by and allow the woman I love to stress over something I have the ability to make go away."

As I predicted, her father said, "I can't accept your money. That's not the kind of people we are, Mr. Soren. Taking charity is not something I've ever done in my life, and I'm not about to start now."

"I understand, sir. But I did it for Brae." I lifted her hand and kissed it softly. My eyes pinned to hers, I added, "I meant it when I said I would do anything to make her happy."

"I intend to pay you back."

"I won't have it, sir. Again, I did it for Brae."

"Walter," Ellen said with a raised brow. The two communicated through the look in their eyes, and I sat worrying over what it all meant. By some sheer miracle, or maybe it was the fact that Jesus was still present in his soul from that morning's mass, he nodded over and over before offering his hand. I accepted it in shock, wondering if he had too much wine at communion.

"That changes things. I can respect a man who would do anything for his love." His eyes met Ellen's and the first genuine smile I'd seen in days spread over his thin lips. "I worked two jobs when we were engaged to help her father keep this farm."

My mouth dropped at his admission, and so did Brae's. "Daddy, I never knew that. I thought you and Mom took it over once Grandpa got sick."

Ellen came around the table to wrap her arm around her husband's waist. He kissed the top of her head. "No one knew, sweetheart. Your grandfather was a proud man."

With that one admission, I understood. History was repeating itself through his daughter.

☆☆☆

Every morning, that goddamn rooster scared the shit out of me. Upon hearing him, I'd reach for Brae in a panic, only to remember she was nowhere near me. Nope, she was on the opposite end of the house separated by two very noisy creaky doors.

Today, I flipped that cock the finger. Today, I didn't mind the ungodly hour we'd all be sitting down to have breakfast together. Today, Brae and I were leaving to go back to our world in Manhattan—a world where waking up naked together was our norm, and the only cock involved was mine. A perfect world where my perfect fiancée loved morning sex more than I did.

Life was going to be good again.

I stretched my achy muscles and walked over to stare at the darkness outside my window. My body felt like someone took a baseball bat to me while I slept. I was in great shape, but fuck, farm life was hard work. My visit to the farm gave me a newfound respect for how my eggs, milk, and bacon made it to my table.

By the time Brae and her parents appeared in the kitchen, I was dressed, bags were sitting by the door, and breakfast was ready. I wasn't a dummy.

Ellen patted my arm with a warm smile. "You're spoiling us, Jude."

I should have felt guilty since the real reason I made breakfast had little to do with pleasing them and all to do with hitting the road as soon as possible. But fuck that— I had to milk a cow yesterday.

Brae laughed at my theory when I said her father absolutely rigged that cow. It didn't matter how hard I pulled on her tits—nothing. When I came in an hour later, sweating my ass off with no more than an inch of milk in that stainless bucket, the smirk Walter tried to hide confirmed my suspicions.

Yeah, I loved my girl dearly, but a farmer I was not.

Walter sauntered in through the back door holding that same bucket filled to the rim. "Old Bess must not like you," he said, raising a brow.

Brae laughed as she sat beside me. "I guess not all females cave to your charms."

I placed my lips on her ear. "There's only one female's tits I'm interested in." While staring into her eyes, I slid my hand under the table and between her legs. Her eyes widened before cutting toward her father sitting one chair away and her mother serving the eggs and bacon I'd made.

"So, Jude. Have you given any thought to the wedding being here?" Ellen asked, passing me a loaded plate.

"Yes, ma'am. I'd love to have our wedding here in

October. But I insist on covering all costs, and hiring professionals to handle every aspect. All I'd like you to worry about is getting your daughter ready to walk down the aisle." Brae quirked up a brow, which I ignored.

"Well, isn't that generous of you? Although, I don't mind doing the cooking."

"I wouldn't have it. It would be my absolute pleasure."

"Honey, are you sure you don't want to talk about it?" Brae tilted her head to the side, and the expression on her face screamed, "Have you lost your mind?"

"No, darling. October is only five months away, and planning a wedding takes time. It wouldn't be fair to leave your mother hanging. Now, she can concentrate on herself."

Ellen grinned with a nod. "He is so sweet, Brae."

I gave my future mother-in-law my most dazzling smile. "Thank you, Ellen. I try."

Digging into my breakfast, I ignored the incredulous stare from my fiancée and the scowl from my future father-in-law. Nothing could ruin my mood. Before I knew it, we were at the door saying our goodbyes. And if her parents hadn't been watching, I would have sprinted my way back to the car.

☆☆☆

Tall buildings, sirens, and yellow cabs—just what the doctor ordered. Being back in our apartment felt like heaven on earth. Scratch that. Brae sliding into bed next to me completely naked did.

"Come here, soon-to-be Mrs. Soren." I tugged on Brae's arm to pull her into my chest.

"Sooner than I thought I'd be Mrs. Soren, you mean?"

She pulled my arm so it circled her chest. "What in the hell made you agree to the farm? The way you grumbled about the roosters made me think you didn't like it there."

"Sparky, those roosters were loud as fuck. Not to mention, those cocks got more action than I did." I burrowed my head in her hair.

Brae let out a laugh and her tits vibrated under my arm. "Really? More action, that's what you're going with?"

I shrugged, but she couldn't see me, so I turned her in my arms to face her. "Confession?" She nodded. "The Plaza is booked for the next two years and I'm not waiting that long for you to be legally mine."

Her face softened and her eyes sparkled in the moonlight. "You called The Plaza?"

"I did." I ran my knuckles down her face from her temple to her chin. "I love you, Brae, and I'd marry you tomorrow, but I know it's important to have our friends and family witnessing the most important day of our lives, so I'll wait five months, deal with a rooster as an alarm clock, hay in my shoes, and a cow that hates me, just to make you Mrs. Soren."

A tear escaped her eye, which I caught with my thumb. "Then the farm it is."

"That's my girl."

"I love you, Jude."

"I love you more, Sparky."

After a few sweet kisses and a few heated ones, Brae rolled and snuggled her ass against my stomach. It wasn't long before I heard my favorite sounds.

Purr . . . rumble . . . snort . . . whistle.

Purr . . . rumble . . . snort . . . whistle.

Purr . . . rumble . . . snort . . . whistle.

I smiled at the memory of her watching the evidence I had captured on my GoPro. Even as she stared at her image purring, rumbling, snorting, and whistling, she still claimed I doctored the tape before tossing it to the side.

Sweet apples were now my favorite fruit, getting bathroom time was a luxury, and listening to Brae arguing with my housekeeper had become a normal occurrence, but I wouldn't trade any of it for anything in the world.

With my lips on her ear, I whispered, "Thanks for picking me, Sparky."

Chapter 32

Jude

"FUCK ME."

"I would, but you said we were late to wherever it is you're taking me." Her reflection met my eyes as she smirked adorably while smoothing a hand over the black silk fabric of her dress. "It's okay?"

Okay? Was she kidding me?

The black sleeveless sheath dress I begged her to wear fit her like a fucking glove. It was the very same one she had on the night we met—the night she picked me to be her Mr. Right. The way it ended a few inches above her knees, showing off her gorgeous legs in those come-fuck-me heels was a perfect form of torture. From where I stood, I admired how the shiny fabric molded over her ass and the plunging backline showed just enough of her smooth skin. On her finger, the diamond that paled in comparison to her beauty. On her wrist, the white gold bracelet I bought for her in St. John. From head to toe, she was perfection.

Walking up behind her, I wrapped my arms around her body, resting my forearms under her breasts. I looked down to admire the way the fabric enhanced one of her best assets.

When our eyes met in the mirror, her smile was electric. "Well?"

"The only problem with this dress is I want to see the fabric shred between my hands as rip it off your body. I love this dress." She wiggled her ass against my slacks, and the effect on me was immediate. "Be careful, Sparky. You keep doing that, and we *will* be late."

"What exactly will we be late to?" One perfect brow raised in challenge, and when I shrugged, she turned in my arms. "Why won't you tell me?"

"Because it's a surprise." I loved surprising her, shocking her with weekend getaways or romantic nights at home sans clothing.

"That's not a good reason. Is it a show? Dinner? Oh, are we flying to Paris again? Or Rome this time?" Her voice hitched at her last question.

"What? No!" I placed a very sloppy kiss on her cheek. "I've created a monster. Let's go."

The pout on her face the entire time in the elevator and through the lobby didn't faze me in the least. The more I ignored her, the more she grumbled. Once outside our building, I pulled a black silk scarf out of my pocket.

"What's that for?"

"Humor me." Twisting her body, I tied the scarf around her eyes, laughing as her gripes got meaner and meaner.

"Jude Soren, I will not walk around with this blindfold on, or you can forget sex for a week."

"You don't scare me, Sparky. You're all talk, and you'd cave way before I would." That was a blatant lie. I smacked her ass and led her into the back of the cab.

It was only minutes later when we pulled up to our destination. After paying the fare, I led her out of the backseat to stand beside me on the sidewalk. The warm evening air felt cooler near the river. Without her sight, I watched her tilt her head, trying to decipher sounds and smells to help hint as to where I'd taken her.

"Careful, step up." Her sexy leg lifted until she felt solid footing beneath her. One by one, I instructed her on what to do with my arm firmly around her waist. The clanging of a bell and the squawking of a seagull caused her to twist her head toward my face.

"The river?" She halted for a moment, then when her heels hit the aluminum dock, she added, "A boat? You're taking me on a boat?"

"Quiet, Sparky. One more step." She followed my direction and waited for the next one. I led her to where we needed to be, and paused a few moments longer before I spoke. "Are you ready?" I whispered, allowing my lips to linger on the smooth curve of her ear. Goosebumps covered her exposed flesh despite the warm air.

"Yes," she said on a nod.

"Now, don't be mad at me."

"I'll try not to, but I can't promise."

I had no doubt she'd forgive me. I removed her blindfold and watched as she shook her hair loose while her eyes adjusted to our surroundings. Her gasp and the way she stared at all the eyes staring back with such awe written all over her face meant that I was forgiven.

The dozens of guests applauded and cheered, giving her a few minutes to survey the crowd. Scattered throughout the familiar faces were her parents, mine, my siblings, her friends, my friends, and even Shelly, Chip, and Barbi were in attendance. Although, upon hearing about our engagement, they tried to convince us to have our wedding televised while advertising *Ignite Your Spark*—which wasn't happening. Though, they were, of course, the real reason we were there on that luxury yacht celebrating our engagement.

"So much for listening," she said, throwing her arms around my neck. "Low-key is not in your vocabulary."

"Since when do I listen? You should know that by now. Surprise, Sparky." I kissed her long and hard, then pushed her toward those dying to embrace her. I watched with so much pride that I must have looked like a grinning fool. I'd do anything for that woman, and when she adamantly insisted we have a low-key party at José Ponchos for just our friends, I promptly ignored her and planned a proper celebration.

This party tonight was multi-purposed. Aside from celebrating the best thing to have happened to me, she'd be meeting my family. Because of her new job, we couldn't fly to Sweden as originally planned. And with the wedding only a few short months away, I, in essence, was killing two birds with one stone.

Once we greeted her parents, I took her hand and led her to the Swedes standing to the side, anxiously waiting to meet the woman who finally stole my heart.

"Pay attention, Sparky. I'd like to introduce you to my family." I waited until I had her undivided attention. "You'll meet my brother-in-laws, nieces, and nephews at the wedding. On short notice, only my parents and sisters were able to come to New York."

"Okay." Her hand clutched mine, and the closer we got to them, the harder she gripped.

When we came before my brood, her eyes widened. "Okay, ready? My mom, Janikke, my dad, Albin. I was named after Mom. My sisters after my dad." I pointed to my eldest sister, and rambled, "Adela, Agata, Akika." I glanced at her, and almost laughed at the look on her face. We all looked alike, and no doubt Sparky was noticing the family resemblance. "The youngest of the five are the twins, Alva and Auda. You know I'm the baby of the family. Everyone, this is Brae." I glanced back to her. "Got that?"

"No," she said, panicked. She plastered on a nervous smile and turned back to face them. Six women and one man all began babbling animatedly in broken English just as I said, "I told you to pay attention."

My family surrounded my fiancée like sharks surrounding a seal. I stepped back and left her to them while laughing my ass off. She threw me a dirty look, which I ignored as I walked away.

"That was mean, man," Luca said as I stepped up to the bar.

"She'll survive. Like ripping off a Band-Aid."

Kyle smirked as he leered at my siblings. "Damn, Jude. If you weren't related to them, I'd tap your sisters, all at once."

"This boat will be hitting the open waters in a few minutes. They'll never find your body, you cocksucker."

Music began, food was served, drinks were in abundance, and through it all, Brae survived. No doubt I'd get a scolding when we got home, but giving her a few orgasms would be sure to get me off the hook.

I took her into my arms. "Do you think you can stand a few more surprises?"

"Gee, I don't know. Will it matter if I can't?" Her

smile was radiant.

"Not in the least." I tucked an errant strand of hair behind her ear before reaching into my pocket. Her eyes followed my movement. "This is why you require a blindfold." The giggle that escaped made me laugh. "Happy engagement."

Her eyes widened like the full moon hovering above us as she studied the key between my fingers. "Is that . . . ?"

"The key to our place in St. John? Yes." Brae's eyes filled with tears as she threw her arms around my neck.

"I love you so much." I swiped away the happy tears rolling down her cheeks. "I can't believe you bought it. I didn't even think you liked it."

"That's where you're wrong, Sparky. It's the place where we had all our firsts. It's where I fell in love with you. How could I not like it?" Pulling her into my arms, we hugged until we needed to rejoin our guests.

Little did she know, I was just getting started. She had no idea what I had planned for the weekend. I arranged for our families to stay at The Plaza and we'd be squeezing all of Brae's favorite things into the next two days.

Matinee tickets to the best show on Broadway, dinner at her favorite restaurant, brunch on Sunday at The Palm Court, an afternoon of beauty for Brae to enjoy with our moms and my sisters. I'd be taking my father and father-in-law to a ball game. And at last, we'd all meet for dinner at our apartment to discuss wedding plans at the farm. Monday morning, everyone would be going back to their respective homes. Forty-eight hours of socializing was my expiration before I turned back into a horny bastard.

They were all just necessary steps to take toward the

one real thing I couldn't wait for. Yes, for obvious reasons, our wedding day. But it was that night, and more so the two weeks that followed, when we'd be back at our cottage in St. John, with no Internet, no phones, no Kyle to bother us—the very same cottage I bought for my bride-to-be.

That was the part I was counting the days toward.

When she'd finally be Mrs. Soren.

When we'd start populating the earth with my offspring.

When we'd begin our own social experiment and watch the spark we ignited develop into a roaring flame.

Our story wasn't even close to an end. It was only beginning.

Epilogue

Brae

"SINCE OUR MINISTER AGREED TO marry you in the
barn, I see hay bales set up in rows for our guests
to sit on during the ceremony. Of course, we'll have
white linen fabric over them to protect everyone's
Sunday outfits. How cute would that be? We'll set it up
under the big oak tree, which I can decorate with
twinkling Christmas lights." My mom sighed as she
brought her hand to cover her heart. "Brae, you
remember how beautiful it looks in October. I already
secured the church choir." Without warning, her face
scrunched before she said, "Oh dear, I hope it doesn't
rain. I'm not sure we'll be able to air out the barn in time
if it does."

Oh lord.

My mother continued to ramble as if someone
plugged a speaker up her ass. She hadn't stopped since
we arrived an hour ago. Jude looked like he was about to
pass out, and my father looked like he was about to
strangle her.

"They'll sing Ave Maria as you walk down the aisle.

So far, for the buffet, we have mac and cheese, my famous fried chicken, and Martha Winfield's award winning strawberry rhubarb pie. Oh, I think I have some left over in the fridge. Jude, you must taste it." She scampered out of the dining room before I could stop her.

"I need to milk a cow," my father said to no one in particular before leaving without a backward glance.

Jude leaned closer, and whispered, "What the fuck is a rhubarb?"

Ignoring him, I tried to hide my exasperation over this whole affair. On one side was my fiancé who wanted as close to The Plaza as he could achieve in bumblefuck New York, and on the other side was my mother who was painting a visual straight out of Green Acres.

"This is all your fault," I accused. "Can't we elope? Please?" I begged while rubbing my temples.

"It's too late for that now, Sparky. Stick to the plan, and tell her she needs to stop bothering you with all the details that aren't going to happen." He held my chin to turn my head. "That was the point of this impromptu visit. The quicker you shut her down, the quicker we can leave."

I sighed and nodded. "Okay. But you don't know my mother very well. Me telling her to stop planning is as effective as me telling the rooster to stop crowing."

My mother walked into the room with a heaping plate of pie. "Try it, Jude. It's absolutely scrumptious."

He looked to me for help. I snatched the fork, took a bite for myself, and then offered him one to appease his concerns.

"Yummy," he said around his mouthful.

"The best," my mom boasted.

Jude cleared his throat and pushed his thigh against mine. "So, Mom. We're here to tell you everything has been taken care of. Jude and I wanted this to be as easy as possible, and you don't have to worry about any of the details except your dress and hairdo."

No sooner were the words out of my mouth when there was a knock on the door. "I know who that is," she said in a singsong tone. Standing, she wiped her hands on her apron before another knock sounded. "Coming!"

"Oh my God. Kill me now," I begged when I heard a familiar voice greeting my mother.

"Who's that?"

"The mayor."

"The mayor?" Jude set his fork down. "The mayor is here?" He looked at me as if I had three heads—not two, three.

My mother escorted him into the living room, her arm looped through his. "Brae, you remember Mayor Hecht?"

"It's been a while, but yes, of course I do." I stood and shook his hand. "This is my fiancé, Jude."

The men shook hands. "This is such a thrill for me and the town. We all love a party." Mayor Hecht turned to my mom. "Ellen, remember the quilting festival?" My mom beamed, the mayor looked prideful, and Jude looked dumbfounded. "That was such a glorious day."

Jude leaned toward me, and whispered. "What the fuck is a quilting festival?"

I swatted his arm. "Shhh!"

"Sweetheart, the ladies guild has already started your family quilt." Her eyes misted over. "I can't wait for my grandbabies to be wrapped up in it."

Okay, I'd heard enough. "So, it was nice seeing you

again, Mayor." I quickly offered him my hand. "We need to get going."

Jude grabbed my hand with lightning speed. "Nice meeting you, Mr. Mayor." He couldn't wait to make the great escape, and I couldn't say I blamed him.

My dad walked into the dining room right as we were about to leave. "Bye, Dad." I kissed him on the cheek. "Bye, Mom." Jude and I power-walked toward the door.

"Wait. Brae, honey," my mom called from behind us. "The mayor has something exciting to tell you."

Jude grumbled with one hand on the doorknob. "We were so close." My head dropped and I had to force myself not to audibly sigh.

The mayor cleared his throat. "We'd like to offer you the VFW for your rehearsal dinner, and of course, I'd be honored to accompany you during the parade."

"Parade?" Jude looked at me as if I was the one who had suggested it.

"That's a very generous offer, but I think we'll skip that tradition." My mom gasped, I shrugged. Mom, please stop planning we've told you a million times we have everything covered for the entire weekend."

"But sweetie . . ." My mom prodded. "we really want to help."

"You are by just being my mom." That statement caused her to smile wide and hug me in acknowledgment.

Without hesitation, Jude said our final goodbyes as he pulled me out the door and shut it behind us.

"Holy fuck! What year is it in this town? A parade? Quilting festival?"

"It's not that bad," I said as we both slid into our rental car. After we were here the last time, Jude stated he'd never drive one of his cars there again. Apparently, mud on the tires wasn't something he cared for . . . and he called me OCD.

"Yes, it is that bad, but it only proves how much I love you that I'm putting up with this shit, Sparky." At his words, the rooster crowed. I let out a laugh as Jude mumbled, "Fucking cock."

Jude

FROM THE CORNER OF MY eye, I watched my two supposed best friends try to maintain their composure as I took a verbal beating from my soon to be father-in-law.

The list of his gripes went on and on, and it was hard for me to sympathize with any of them.

"Sixteen pallets of oak parquet flooring? Do you know what's happening to my lawn right now? It's dying, and I'll never be able to salvage it."

Lawn? He calls that burnt brownish patchy stuff a lawn? Regardless, I nodded to pacify him and offered a solution. "I understand, sir. But I couldn't have our guests ruining their shoes. I'll have new sod delivered in the spring."

He released a burst of air through his nostrils. "Two massive tents?"

"We needed one for the ceremony and one for the reception."

"So, when you said you'd marry in the barn, you really meant this frou-frou affair you invaded our home with?" he asked, pointing a stiff finger toward the classy set up I went out of my way to arrange.

I couldn't believe they took our promise literally. Yes,

we agreed to marry here on the farm, but not inside a fucking red barn where the stench of cows and chickens would make you want to vomit.

I wanted to say, *"But, sir, I couldn't have our guests sitting in stink all day and night."* Instead, I said, "I thought having all those people in the barn would upset the animals."

Kyle snorted, and quickly coughed to cover it up. Meanwhile, Luca turned a new shade of purple as he stifled the hysterics bubbling within him. At my glare, they uttered apologies and scampered out of the guest room we were sequestered in.

Mr. Daniels' eyes followed their hasty exit, but it was clear he wasn't done with me. When he began counting off all the other enhancements I arranged for our wedding day—flowers, photographers, band, caterers— I internally sighed. "It's a darn circus out there!"

Shit, all I wanted was to make Brae happy while making it easier on her parents. This man had a hard-on about my checkbook. I got it, he was a proud man who really never recovered from the humility he felt over almost losing his farm . . . but fuck, chill dude.

The only reason I stood taking this scolding was Brae. She begged, pleaded as recently as last night to elope. It was too late. But I did admit, after we secretly screwed one last time in the pickle pantry before her mom appeared to whisk her away at midnight, she had been right all along.

The door swung open and a boisterous, "Walter!" caused him to jump at the sound of his wife's voice. "You leave that poor man alone! Go put on your suit! The ceremony is starting in thirty minutes!"

"Crap," he muttered before walking out the door.

"I'm sorry, Jude. Ignore him. I think he's taking out the stress over losing his baby girl on you."

"I understand," I replied with a tight smile. *I didn't.*

She returned a smile of her own. "You look so very handsome. Brae sent me to see how you were."

"I'm great. I can't wait to marry your daughter."

"Well, it's just about that time." She walked farther into the room and handed me a note. "It's from Brae. I'll give you some privacy and see you in a few minutes."

"Thank you."

My thoughts immediately focused on my girl. I couldn't wait to see her, to make her legally mine, to escape all this chaos and hide for two weeks in our cottage, to keep her naked for fourteen days—my list was long.

I just had to get through this day.

All the stress of wedding planning dissipated at seeing her pretty script on the notecard.

Jude,

How did I get so lucky to find my spark?

Okay, stop rolling your eyes. I know we may have had a rough start, but I'd repeat every decision I made to get to this point. I love everything about you. I love every part of you. I'm so happy I picked you. I can't wait to get the hell out of here and finally start our lives as . . . Mr. and Mrs. Wrong.

xxx

Sparky

P.S. The earrings are stunning, thank you. I'm saving your present for later tonight.

Funny, I spent a small fortune on all the details my almost father-in-law was moaning about, yet now all I could do was stare at her. In hindsight, we could have been in the smelly barn with those damn animals stinking up the place and causing a racket—it wouldn't matter. We could have been in Vegas with a bad Elvis impersonator crooning his way through our ceremony—it wouldn't matter.

All I saw was my gorgeous Sparky walking toward me, looking more beautiful than anything I'd ever seen in my entire life.

The strapless lace dress she wore was perfection. It was the very same one she had picked out in St. John, the day my world fell apart. It was important for her to have that gown today, as she said it would be her one and only wedding dress. The way it skimmed over her perfect body in the sexiest of ways, with no visible lines, made me wonder what she had on under it.

She left her hair long and loose, just how I liked it. Her smile was electric, and the current zipped through the air separating us before jolting my frantically beating heart. The closer she got, the more it pounded in my chest.

I glanced at Kyle as he stood proudly beside me. He met my eye and winked. The bastard knew exactly what I was thinking. I owed a lot to that jackass. He knew it too, and I had no doubt he'd be sure to collect.

Miraculously, her father was smiling through his tears. He hugged Brae tightly before lifting her hand to place in mine. "Take care of my baby girl, Jude."

"With everything I am, sir." He clapped a firm hand on my shoulder and nodded. A genuine smile I had yet to see lit his face with joy. Remorse over calling him a few choice insults in Swedish washed over me.

Once we were standing side by side before the minister, our eyes connected and the world around us halted.

"Hi." The sweet sound of her voice made me smile wider than I had been.

"Hi, Sparky." When I leaned closer and put my lips on her ear, she tilted her head into my touch. "You look fucking spectacular, but I can't wait to rip that dress off and ravish you. Are you naked under there?"

Brae's eyes widened in shock before she curled her lips over her teeth. Kyle and Luca snickered, her friend Vanessa giggled, and the minister cleared his throat all at the same time. I guess I didn't whisper that as softly as I had intended. All I could do when I looked at the man was shrug. "Sorry."

He didn't look amused and raised a brow before asking, "Shall we begin?" We both nodded like scolded children while ignoring our obnoxious friends as they continued their immature heckling.

The ceremony felt like it dragged on and on—maybe because the man read practically every scripture from his bible. By the time he instructed us to face each other and exchange vows, I was seconds away from barking, *"Yeah, yeah, the lord loves us. Get on with it."*

"Brae Elizabeth, you may recite your vows to Jude."
Finally.

She glanced at the minister before pinning me with her stunning brown eyes.

"Jude, I can't believe we're standing here." She looked up at me, unshed tears filling her eyes. Taking my other hand in hers, she continued. "When we first met, never in my wildest imagination did I think we'd fall in love, but we did. I'll never forget our first kiss. I know I haven't told you this, but when you kissed me that first night on stage, my entire body came alive. You're everything I never wanted." I cocked a brow at her. "You know what I mean." She giggled, and I smirked at her. "I promise with all I am to love you for the rest our lives. Thank you for not wanting to be Mr. Right, or we might not be standing here."

Kyle cleared his throat and she glanced at him. I leaned down, and whispered, "Don't look at him. He's going to want our first born named Kyle."

Brae giggled, sniffed, and a few tears fell. "I love you more than I ever thought I could love someone. Thank you for putting up with my little quirks. Thank you for ignoring my OCD, thank you for asking me to marry you, and thank you for loving me." Her breath hitched, and I felt it in my chest. "For the rest of my life, I choose you."

I picked up her hands in mine and placed a soft kiss on them. Our eyes locked, and for a moment, I was lost in them.

The minister broke the silence. "Jude, you may now say your vows to Brae."

"Sparky, when we first met, I thought you were the most gorgeous woman I'd ever seen. Then, when I got to know you, I thought you were a crazy pain in the ass." She opened her mouth to say something, but I didn't let her get that far. "Let me finish." I winked, and she relaxed. "I've never met someone who took so much time to get ready for bed, who carried a bag of minor necessities with her at all times, whose idea of security was a steak knife under the mattress, who didn't care for maid service and was incapable of making toast." Brae rolled her lips between her teeth to stifle a laugh.

"I can't wait to spend every day of the rest of my life with you. Just knowing you'll be in my arms when I fall asleep and still in them when I wake up to your snoring makes me the happiest man alive." A few people started laughing, but Brae's cheeks turned a pretty shade of pink as she shook her head. "I can't wait to get started on having our six kids."

"Six?" Her eyes widened in shock.

"Six," I confirmed with a solid nod. "I never thought I'd want to share my life with someone, but my life is better with you in it." Brae's face blurred behind my tears. When she let a few of her own escape and roll down her cheeks, I did the same. "I promise to never make you feel unloved or unwanted. There will never be a day when I don't love you. When you're sad, I'll make you happy." Bringing my lips to her ears, I whispered, "I'm going to make you so happy when we leave here." She gasped and let out a small laugh. I cupped her face with the palms of my hands and wiped away her tears with my thumbs. "Brae, thank you for picking me, thank you for forgiving me, and most of all, thank you for sharing your heart. I promise never to break it. For the rest of my life, I choose you."

We exchanged rings, listened to yet another blessing, and waited for the minister to finally exclaim, "I now pronounce you Mr. and Mrs. Soren."

While applause and cheers erupted from our guests, I tilted her head and kissed her long and hard. Our lips sealed a union we had already adopted months ago. Despite all the kinks in the road that got us there, none of it mattered. In the long run, she found me, her Mr. Wrong turned Mr. Right . . . and I found the love of my life.

Thank you for reading our story.

Here's a tip: love trumps lust and logic.

Remember, something wonderful might just be waiting for you on the other side of that divider. You'll never know until you look.

Love and Sparks,

Jude & Brae

P.S. Stay tuned for Kyle's and Luca's tales in upcoming books.

The End

Acknowledgments

Finding Mr. Wrong is the first book we collaborated on and we had an absolute blast writing it. We laughed, cried, and swooned . . . and we can't wait to do it again.

We hope we don't forget anyone, and if we do, please know it wasn't intentional.

First, we'd like to thank the readers. We all love to read and talk about the books and characters we love, and we're so thankful for all of you.

To Jude Soren's Ladies, your enthusiasm and love for Finding Mr. Wrong thrilled us. We can't thank you enough for your support and being with us from the beginning. You truly are a wonderful group of women, and we are so thankful to know you.

To our beta readers, your feedback, comments, suggestions, and more importantly, your honesty, were incredibly helpful. Thank you from the bottom of our hearts.

Thank you to our very handsome cover model Kevin Luetolf, who captured our Jude so perfectly. To Nadia Von Scotti for providing that amazing shot we used for our cover, as well as the stunning photo that became a teaser.

Sommer Stein at Perfect Pear Creative Covers, your talents are unsurpassed. Thank you for creating the perfect cover for *Finding Mr. Wrong*.

The Next Step PR. Thank you for your support and for helping us spread the word.

To all the bloggers, thank you for all the time you spend supporting authors and reading our stories. You take time out of your personal lives, and we are very thankful.

Monica Black of Word Nerd Editing, thank you for helping prepare our book for release.

Virginia Tesi Carey, thank you for proofreading Finding Mr. Wrong. We appreciate you making the time for us. We love you!

Tami at Integrity Formatting, you're always a pleasure to work with. Thank you for making our words look pretty.

To the team at EverAfter Romance, we are so happy to be part of the EverAfter family. Thank you for all of your support.

To our families. Thank you for putting up with our long nights, take-out dinners and all the craziness that ensued while we wrote Finding Mr. Wrong. Without your love and support, we wouldn't have been able to write about the sexiest fucking man on the planet.

Last, but certainly not least, to our husbands—thank you for understanding that if we ever meet "Jude," we will be using our hall pass and will most likely need bail money.

About A.M. Madden & Joanne Schwehm

A.M. Madden

A.M. MADDEN is a USA Today bestselling author, as well as 2016 eLit Gold Medalist for Best Romance Ebook, and 2016 Ippy Award Silver Medalist for Best Romance Ebook.

A.M. is a wife, a mother, an avid reader of romance novels, and now an author.

"It's all about the HEA."

A.M. Madden is the author of the popular Back-Up Series, as well as several other contemporary romances. She is also a published author with Loveswept/Random House.

Her debut novel was Back-up, the first in The Back-Up Series. In Back-Up, A.M.'s main character Jack Lair caused readers to swoon. They call themselves #LairLovers, and have been faithful supporters to Jack, as well to the rest of his band, Devil's Lair.

A.M. truly believes that true love knows no bounds. In her books, she aspires to create fun, sexy, realistic romances that will stay with you after the last page has been turned. She strives to create characters that the reader can relate to and feel as if they know personally.

A self-proclaimed hopeless romantic, she loves getting lost in a good book. She also uses every free moment of her time writing, while spending quality time with her three handsome men. A.M. is a Gemini and an Italian Jersey girl, but despite her Zodiac sign, nationality, or home state, she is very easy going. She loves the beach, loves to laugh, and loves the idea of love.

A.M. Madden, Independent Romance Author.

Sign up for A.M. Madden's newsletter at www.ammadden.com to get up to date information on new releases, cover reveals, and exclusive excerpts.

Contact A.M.

Website www.ammadden.com

Facebook www.facebook.com/pages/AM-Madden-Author/584346794950765

Twitter @ammadden1

Instagram @ammadden1

Goodreads
www.goodreads.com/author/show/7203641.A_M_Madden

Email am.madden@aol.com

A.M.'s Mad Reader Group
www.facebook.com/groups/893157480742443/

Joanne Schwehm

JOANNE SCHWEHM is a mother and wife and loves spending time with her family. She's an avid sports watcher and enjoys the occasional round of golf.

Joanne loves to write and read romance. She believes everyone should have romance in their lives and hopes her books bring joy and happiness to readers who enjoy modern day fairy tales and breathless moments.

She is an independent romance author and has written several contemporary romance novels, including The Prescott Series, Ryker, A Heart's Forgiveness, The Critic and The Chance series which she has recently sold the screenplay right to and will be adapted into a movie.

Joanne looks forward to sharing more love stories in her future novels.

Contact Joanne
Website: www.joanneschwehmbooks.com
Facebook: www.facebook.com/joanneschwehm
FB Group Page:
www.facebook.com/groups/joanneschwehmsreaders/
Twitter: www.twitter.com/JSchwehmBooks
Pinterest: www.pinterest.com/nyy2fan/
Instagram: www.instagram.com/jschwehmbooks/
Spotify: www.open.spotify.com/user/1293937868
YouTube:
www.youtube.com/user/JoanneSchwehmBooks
Goodreads Reading Group:
www.goodreads.com/group/show/156533-joanne-schwehm-s-romantic-reading-friends
Newsletter: www.eepurl.com/cgUvSf

To the Reader

Thank you so much for purchasing and reading this ebook. Please support all Indie authors and leave a review at point of purchase as well as your favorite review forum. Indie authors depend on reviews and book recommendations to help potential readers decide to take the time to read their story. We would greatly appreciate it.

χοχο,

A.M. Madden & Joanne Schwehm

Join the Finding Mr. Wrong Reader group on Facebook.

www.facebook.com/groups/1317311534966197/

CPSIA information can be obtained
at www.ICGtesting.com
Printed in the USA
FFOW01n1019140217
32426FF